The Infinity Chronicles: Volume One

The Mortal God

E.F. Skarda

Copyright © 2020 E.F. Skarda
All rights reserved.

Book layout by ebooklaunch.com

Prologue

The rain started to fall just as the sun finished descending behind the mountains of Gallatia. Mac grunted and wiped the water from his camera's lens. It had been a three-hour hike through some of the most humid and sweltering jungle that he could remember, followed by several hours of waiting for the sun to go down as he fought off fist-sized mosquitos. By then he'd grown considerably miserable, and the last thing he wanted was to get drenched by this planet's relentless monsoon.

"You see anything yet, Mac?" Jay asked.

"Nothing yet," Mac said, the drops of rain jockeying for space with the flock of freckles on his cheeks. "He sure is taking his sweet time today. I was hoping we'd get out of here before this storm hit."

"He was probably waiting for it," Jay replied. He shook the water from his bushy blonde beard, then spat out a gnarled wad of tobacco. "He's hard enough to find in daylight. With the dark and rain, even we may not be able to see him."

Mac shrugged and peered back through the camera's telescopic lens. In the distance the woods fell away to a deep ravine about three hundred meters wide, and on the other side stood an immense Splinter complex. The rain had kicked up a light fog, obscuring much of the structure behind the high walls, but it was an impressive fortress nonetheless. Mac had never seen one so large, and certainly never in this sort of environment. It must have taken a lifetime to build, especially given the typically meager resources their enemies had.

He panned to the left and caught sight of Jackson sitting calmly on his perch about fifty meters forward of their position, his sniper's rifle extending from a branch of a giant Gallatian redwood more than a hundred meters above the forest floor. These trees were more than twice as tall as those that once existed on Earth, which made them ideal for camouflaging man-made structures among Gallatia's tumultuous terrain.

"Jacks looks bored," Mac said.

"What are you looking at him for?" Jay asked. "We need to be able to see Kyle once he gets in position."

"Just trying to get the zoom focused. I'll have to switch on the night vision. This haze is coming in fast."

Mac flipped a switch on his camera and the world suddenly lit up again. He peered over the outer walls of the complex, searching for the commander of their unit, Kyle Griffin. In truth, it was like looking for a ghost. Mac knew he'd only be seen if he wanted to be, and that's why he was the one shifting through the complex alone while they languished in the rain. Their reconnaissance mission relied on establishing a remote uplink with the Splinter intelligence interface, which meant that someone had to enter the compound to access their database. Kyle had taken the task as his own.

The security waiting for him inside the perimeter was substantial. There were three distinct tiers to the complex with several artillery cannons along each level. Each one was fully automated and enabled with both motion detectors and infrared scanners—advanced tech for the typically archaic Splinter forces, and a strong indication that they had come to the right place. Their marks wouldn't waste that kind of technology on just any installation. The intel they were looking for must be on site. The droves of guards wandering the grounds under the watch of three separate surveillance towers only added to that suspicion.

"There's a shitload of guys with guns walking around down there," Mac said. "I wish I knew how Kyle gets through security like that."

"He might be the only person alive that can do it," Jay said. "That's why he's in there and we're out here getting drenched."

Mac had almost forgotten about the rain, and the reminder made him scowl. It had turned into more of a mist in the last couple of minutes, but by then both of them had already been saturated by it. It made him wonder why these compounds were never built on the sand of a sunny beach.

But then, an anomaly suddenly caught his eye. The shadows seemed to flicker across one of the rooftops, though even with the night vision he couldn't make it out completely. His gaze frantically darted around the roof until he settled on the form of a man tucked against the edge of the building. He was tall and muscular, and clothed entirely in black.

"I've got him," Mac announced. "He's on the roof already. Check his comm to make sure it's working."

"Kyle, this is Jay. Do you read?"

"I've got you, Jay," Kyle's voice answered over the radio. "Do me a favor and get Mac on the line so he can tell me where I'm going."

"Can't get along without me, huh?" Mac asked, raising a hand to the comm in his ear.

"Your knowledge overwhelms me, Mac," Kyle replied. "Just tell me where I've got to be and I'll get there."

"Okay, there's a transmission tower about twenty meters to your left," Mac said. "All of their hardlines should be on the top floor."

"That's awfully close to one of those surveillance posts, Mac," Kyle said. "We'll need a back door."

"I can see a ventilation grate opposite the surveillance tower," Mac said. "Think you can squeeze your big ass through there?"

"I'll see what I can do," Kyle said. "You guys just make sure you're ready when I get the connection set up."

"We'll be ready."

Mac watched Kyle survey his path for a moment. Then he blinked, and by the time he reopened his eyes, Kyle had disappeared. Mac's gaze darted toward the tower, and he caught just a brief glimpse of their commander before he disappeared again into the vent.

† † †

Kyle touched down silently inside a cluttered mechanical room. For a man so large, he still moved like a whisper. The vent near the ceiling was narrow, less than a meter in either direction, and barely wide enough to squeeze his stout limbs through. His shoulders billowed like a thunderhead as he rose to his feet, the heat of the electronics swelling up from the floor beneath him. Rows upon rows of tangled wiring and stacked servers lined the room, creating a maze of cables and metal. It was very old tech, probably predating even the development of stellar fusion reactors, and likely scavenged by Splinter junkers from an abandoned Dominion outpost. It made everything appear unfamiliar and overly complicated to his eyes, even after having ventured into many such arenas in the past. This time, however, he was searching for evidence of possible embedded Splinter agents within the Dominion infrastructure, a task beset to him personally by the ruler of the Dominion; the Lord Gentry - Aeron. And when the Gentry ordered a mission be done, there was no second guessing.

"All right, I'm in," Kyle said. "What am I looking for?"

"This stuff is gonna be on a secure server," Mac said. "Look for something with an encryption filter, or that doesn't have an external port. They're not gonna risk any transmission of this data."

"Should have brought you in here with me, Mac," Kyle said, starting into the labyrinth. "This place is a mess."

"Just look for a heavy power source," Mac suggested. "It might even have a dedicated generator."

Kyle eyed the conduits overhead. There was a section nearly twice the size of the others that led to a unit against the back wall.

"I think we've got something here," he said. "No outgoing lines, heavy duty encryption device."

Kyle pulled a digital transmitter from his belt. He tapped it against the server, and a dozen cybernetic tentacles spewed out. They dug through the aluminum shell and into the components underneath. The outdated Splinter technology would be little match for devious piece of learning nanotech. It would infect the hardware like a parasite and sync it to Mac's console outside. Then the skinny redhead would do the rest.

"Should be transmitting now," Kyle said.

† † †

The system's mainframe flashed onto Mac's screen. There were several rudimentary firewalls built into the files, but they were little more than a speed bump.

"It'll take me a few minutes to get through this encryption," Mac said. "They've got a self-destruct safeguard on this data, but the nanotech has already deactivated it."

"Just get it done," Kyle said. "We're moving out in five minutes."

"Don't sweat it," Jay said. "It's smooth sailing from here."

Almost before the words faded, there was a sudden page through their radio. Jackson was trying to get their attention.

"Shit, maybe I spoke too soon," Jay said, activating Jackson's intercom. "What's going on, Jacks?"

"We may have some issues," Jackson said. "One hundred meters outside the east perimeter."

"What's he talking about?" Mac asked.

"Just copy the damn files," Jay said. "I'll check it out."

Jay looked through the lens of Mac's camera and scanned the forest. The haze hung like a veil above the thick canopy. He cursed, trying to find a line of sight between the trees. *There.* A half-dozen soldiers holding a position just to the east perimeter. The Royal Insignia of the Dominion was stitched onto their sleeves.

"It looks like another team," Jay said. "Those are our guys."

"What would another team be doing here?" Mac asked.

"I don't know," Jay said, "but they can't be hidden too well if Jackson can see them."

Jackson's voice came back over the radio. "Can you see who's in charge over there?"

Jay scanned through the soldiers until saw a familiar face among the crowd. "Oh shit, it's Tact General Donovan," Jay muttered. The stone-cut jaw and heavy brow were unmistakable. "I swear that asshole does this shit on purpose."

"What's going on out there, guys?" Kyle asked.

"Vaughn Donovan has another unit on site," Jay answered. "What should we do?"

"We're not gonna do anything," Kyle said. "Whatever they're up to, it has nothing to do with us. Let's just get our job done and get out of here."

Then the compound's alarm began to wail. Jay saw the Splinter soldiers swarming out of the courtyard building. Spotlights swiftly cut swaths of illumination across the dark jungle. Within seconds the artillery cannons would be searching for targets.

"Kyle, the whole place is going ape-shit down there," Jay said. "You've gotta get out."

"I don't think it's us," Jackson cut in. "I think they spotted Vaughn's group."

"Either way, they're gonna lock down the whole compound," Jay said. "Time to go, boss."

"Is Mac finished?" Kyle asked.

"I've got the files open," Mac answered. "You can pull the transmitter. I can finish without it."

Gunfire started to chatter, and an explosion lit up the trees on the east side of the complex. Through Mac's camera, Jay watched the other Dominion squadron scatter like a flock of birds. The turrets on the outer walls spun in their direction, and a barrage of shells tore through the canopy, sending up clouds of

splinters as they ripped through the redwoods' massive trunks. A squad of Splinter soldiers started passing through the perimeter and were closing quickly.

"Vaughn and his guys are in deep shit," Jay said. "They've got a unit in pursuit and are taking casualties. They're not going to make it."

"You and Mac get back to the ship right now," Kyle ordered. "Get to the emergency extraction site. Have Jacks circle around and give those men some cover. Maybe he can buy them some time."

"What about you?" Jay asked.

"I'm going to get them out of there."

† † †

The trees rushed by as Vaughn Donovan and his men hurtled through the woods. Branches snapped and bullets whistled by as they ran, spurring them like the scythe of the reaper. He could hear his soldiers yelling behind him, in front of him, and all around. It was bedlam, and they were suddenly caught right in the middle of it.

Vaughn saw his lieutenant suddenly drop as he ran alongside him. A burst of red blood popped into the hovering fog, announcing the bullet's exit wound like a flash of confetti. He fell into a tangle of leaves and moss with a thud. Vaughn glanced over his shoulder as it happened, even though he knew it would slow him down. The Splinter men were right on top of them, and it wouldn't take long for them to be overrun, not while running through this thicket.

But then, as if out of nowhere, several of their pursuers dropped as though they had been hit by a sniper. The shots came quickly and silently, seven of them total, and each one was precise and deadly. He had no idea where the cover had come from, and he didn't care. All that mattered was that the number of men chasing them had suddenly been cut in half.

He pivoted to break into a sprint, but a well-placed round punched through the flesh in the back of his thigh. Paralyzed by the shock, his leg collapsed as his weight came down on it, and he fell face-first into a puddle of muddy water.

Vaughn could feel his throat tighten as he rolled onto his back. His legs flailed wildly trying scurry away, but it was too late. The remaining Splinter soldiers were already on top of him, thrusting their weapons into his face.

He didn't waste any time hoping for mercy. Instead, he kicked hard with his uninjured leg, knocking the rifle from the first soldier's hands. He brought up his own sidearm swiftly, getting off one round before having it swatted from his grasp. The shot struck the first soldier in the throat, toppling him backward in another puff of crimson. Vaughn and the second soldier tumbled sideways as the Splinter man lunged for his weapon, A second soldier lunged for his handgun, and the two of the tumbled sideways through the mud, sending a flare of searing agony through the wound in Vaughn's thigh. He managed to roll on top and pull a blade from the side of his boot, then bury it into the soldier's side between two of his ribs.

The world flashed white as the butt of a rifle cracked against the back of his head. His face hit the ground again, but a kick to the ribs quickly somersaulted him onto his back. The canopy above him was blurred by both the blow and the rain, yet he could still see the remaining soldiers surrounding him, their sights trained squarely on his chest.

"Don't move!" a voice shouted. "You've got nowhere to go."

"Whatever you do … to me," Vaughn stammered, "you'll get ten times worse."

"I wouldn't be so sure," the soldier said, moving forward. "What are you doing here?"

Vaughn snarled but didn't answer. He lay with his back in the mud, awaiting the end.

"If you speak up, you just might live a little longer," the soldier said.

Still, Vaughn was silent. The muzzle of the man's rifle reached down and pressed against the skin of his forehead.

"Last chance."

Vaughn spit at the soldier's feet, inviting the killing blow. But it didn't come fast enough. The forest opened up behind the rebels, and a sudden sweeping blur rushed toward them. The first two soldiers were fortunate enough never to see Kyle come out of the trees. With a flash of his right foot, he dropped them both. The next man turned as the others fell, only to be greeted by the back of Kyle's heel crushing the right side of his face. By then, the rest of the squadron had spun toward him, opening fire in Kyle's direction. But Kyle was too quick. He sprung into the air over the shower of gunfire, coming down with the bottom of his boot in another soldier's chest. He whipped around again, catching the gun of the last soldier standing and ripping it from his grasp. His fist struck the man hard in the chest, throwing him backward as if hit by a cannon.

For just a moment, Kyle looked around to make sure his quarry was down. The whole thing happened in just a few seconds, and it was over definitively. He moved so quickly that the Splinter men seemed as though they were swimming in slow motion.

Finally, he looked over to Vaughn, taking a deep breath of the rain-soaked air. He glared at the wound on the general's leg and suddenly his ice-blue eyes burst into a fiery blaze. The wound seemed to catch fire in Kyle's Celestial gaze, and immediately Vaughn seized in pain. The iridescence chased away the darkness for a moment as the gash sewed itself back together, leaving no trace of the injury once the light had faded.

"Get up," Kyle ordered. "We've got to move before another squadron gets here."

Vaughn could only nod. His leg no longer crippled, he followed as Kyle's massive shoulders brushed past him. Moments later they had disappeared into the trees, the darkness and rain shrouding their escape.

CHAPTER 1

Earth was a good home for the human race. It was their first home. The planet where the species was born. Over billions of years it withstood innumerable disasters, everything from asteroid impacts to nuclear holocausts to manmade environmental calamities. In the end, however, it was not meant to last.

Some sixty millennia after the advent of modern man, Earth fell victim to a cosmic ripple, an astrological event that humans had no chance of predicting—or, most significantly, no chance of preventing. The event began with a massive extrasolar comet colliding with the planet Mercury along the inner ring of the solar system. The explosion was like nothing their system had ever seen, like a supernova outside the core of a star, and it was rumored to have blazed even brighter than the sun on Earth.

The event was thought to have triggered an extreme solar dissociation. The remnants of Mercury were torn from its orbit, and though they never struck Earth, its passing proximity was enough to throw the Earth's orbit into chaotic flux. Earth began to cool at a staggering rate. Storms of biblical magnitude were said to have blanketed the globe, blocking out the sun's saving light. By the time the clouds parted, it was too late. The world's oceans had frozen, and Earth had spiraled into a perpetual ice age.

Billions perished from famine and panic-induced violence. But humans were resourceful, conniving creatures. Those who survived spent the world's dying days trying to save their civilization by seeking refuge among the stars.

Their first efforts centered on the colonization of Titan, the largest moon of Saturn. It was chosen because of the presence of water, as well as atmospheric gases such as nitrogen and hydrogen, and the Earth-like weather phenomenon such as wind and rain. However, the moon was cold, and attempts at terraforming were wildly unsuccessful. The colony never became sustainable, and the rapidly diminishing food supply forced them to search elsewhere.

Though times were dark and the future uncertain, their way of life endured. New worlds were discovered. New frontiers were conquered. Ages of exploration saw humans go from a dying breed without a home to an expanding galactic civilization whose boundaries seemed limited only by their own ambition.

This was their history, more than just tales told by fathers to sons. Mankind had left Earth behind. It stood now as a globe of snow and ice drifting among the cosmos, desolate and lifeless, a relic that time had forgotten.

† † †

Age Five ...

Kyle felt like he was going to die. The skin on his face was getting hot. He could feel the heat wrapping over his scalp and into the back of his neck, like a spray of hot water was washing over his head. His vision started to sparkle, with little flares of light darting into his sight from every direction. It made him dizzy.

All he wanted to do was go home. To lie in his bed. To curl up under the blankets and let the whole word just float away. But he knew his parents would never let him. Not on Veneration Day, their day of worship. Nobody got out of going to church today.

The preacher standing behind the pulpit was droning on, as usual. The echo of his crier's voice thundered off the vaulted ceilings and Impersian marble floors. The church was at least fifty meters wide and a hundred meters long, all cold stone and glass and metal. But that cavernous chill didn't help Kyle's growing discomfort. Neither did the hard metal pew. At that moment the entire day seemed to be conspiring against him.

The preacher was now into the third hour of his sermon. He looked exhausted, with his tall forehead glistening with the shine of sweat, but he just wouldn't shut up. All these words, and every week it was pretty much the same thing. Kyle knew it all by heart. He had since the first time he heard it. But today was a bit more involved. It was a holiday in the Royal Church, which meant extra perks for everyone in attendance. Or at least that's what they made it out to be. But human sacrifice didn't have the same appeal to the congregation as it did to the clergy.

"Today we gather to give thanks and praise to our Lord Gentry, the all-mighty Aeron," the preacher said. He was an old man with baggy eyes and pale skin. The bulbous end of his nose jutted out from beneath a dark hood, and his drooped shoulders barely supported a flowing crimson robe. It was a very regal look, one that mimicked the Royal colors worn by the Gentry himself. "It was he who rescued the human race from certain doom some twenty-five hundred years ago. He found us, a scattered, wandering race living on a dozen worlds poorly suited to our survival. We had managed to escape the destruction of our home planet, but our leaders, the old Galactic Council, were unable to find a new world that could produce enough food and shelter to provide for our us. That was when the Gentry came as our salvation."

He found us, Kyle echoed inside his head. Of course he did. Out of nowhere, he found us. Very conveniently, he found us. The only sentient alien the human race had ever encountered. After some sixty-two hundred years of wandering the Milky Way, he just appeared. These sermons never explained how that happened. Kyle always wondered why. But he didn't expect to get an answer today either.

"The power the Lord Gentry showed us was … absolute," the preacher continued in a slow, methodical tone. "The majesty of the Celestial Spark was unlike anything our mortal eyes had ever seen. The power of God finally revealed to us."

Kyle remembered hearing a neighbor talk about the Gentry's power. They called it an "elemental telekinesis". Now, that was a fancy phrase for a five-year old, but Kyle's memory was always pretty good. In fact he remembered everything. Literally, he could recall every moment of his life in vivid detail. Everything he'd ever read, heard, seen, smelled, or felt. So when the neighbor said that this power allowed the Gentry to control matter with his mind, Kyle never forgot it. The source of that magnificent power was no secret either. It was an amulet, a red and platinum–colored stone embedded in the breastplate of his Royal armor. It blazed a luminescent white against the matte red of his chest-piece, and it permitted the Gentry to topple mountains with nothing but a thought. The church had a name for it: they called it the Eye of God. It was very dramatic, even for a kid that hadn't yet reached his sixth birthday.

Their neighbor was a physicist, a very scientific man, and he talked about it in such pragmatic terms. He spoke of the power in an evidence-based way, trying to explain not only how it might work, but also where the Eye might have come from. He suggested that it was a relic of an extinct alien civilization, or perhaps some kind of vessel to harness cosmic radiation. He couldn't prove either theory, of course, but apparently the church didn't appreciate him minimizing the Gentry's abilities as an acquired gift. He was their God, so he wasn't to be questioned. And the Dominion Garrison—the local extension of the vast Dominion Army—made certain that message was understood.

They came for the man in force. Dozens of Garrison troops marched through the streets from their Predator gunship. They dragged him from his home, in the middle of the day, ordering the others in the neighborhood out onto the streets to stand and watch as the Garrison Chief announced his crime from under the brow of his officer's helmet: blasphemy and heresy against the Royal Crown. They blew a hole in the side of his head right there on his front lawn, then left the body to rot in the sun.

It was the first time Kyle had seen a man die. It wouldn't be the last.

Sacrifices to the Gentry were common at the church. Men, women, even children at times were offered up in homage to their deity. There wasn't any discrimination, and there wasn't any quarter. A hundred million congregations across the habitable zone of the galaxy made those same sacrifices to the Gentry's grace. Once the preacher had chosen, all that was left was to bite your lip and stomach the heartache.

There were three such sacrifices during the worship calendar: one to commemorate the day the Gentry revealed himself to the human race, one to mark the establishment of the Royal Church, and one to celebrate the Gentry's victory over the Galactic Council—a day regarded as the birthday of the Dominion.

Today's service happened to mark the latter holiday. Veneration Day.

"It warms my old heart to see so many faces here to celebrate such an important day in our church," the preacher said. He was pandering to the congregation with that. Everyone here was forced to attend. "The event we commemorate today is perhaps the most important one in our history, not just as a society, but as a species. Veneration Day. The day the Gentry ousted the blasphemous Galactic Council, and the day that we found our true selves as a civilization."

Right, the Council. Their story was well known, even to someone as young as Kyle. After leaving Earth, humans colonized a dozen or so planets in hopes of reestablishing a home world. They struggled with it for centuries, getting by on synthetic food and recycled water. Eventually they came to the end. All their resources were being depleted at a steady rate, faster than they could replenish them. So they sent more explorations into the void, hoping against all odds that they would find what they were looking for. They found Aeron instead. The Gentry embraced them, and led the explorers to multiple lush, fertile worlds where they could produce everything they needed. Quite literally, it saved them all.

As a payment for his generosity, and as part of the bargain for the use of his worlds, the Representatives offered Aeron a position on the Council. From there, the Gentry's influence blossomed. His power - and mankind's tendency to worship powers greater than themselves - made him an obvious lightning rod for religious adoration. He was already their savior, but the people were quick to make him their God as well.

As the stories had it, the Council didn't care to see their authority dwindle.

"Unable to tolerate sharing their elected power, the wicked Council conspired to remove the Gentry from government affairs," the preacher continued. "They insisted that because he lacked humanity, he didn't understand how to lead us. So they sought to expel him from their ranks, to cast *him* out! Can you imagine? As though he wasn't good enough for their auspices. And this from men who couldn't even provide for the people who elected them!"

His voice went high and shrill. He obviously enjoyed this part. "They sent a team of their assassins to the Gentry's bedside, looking to kill the very being that saved them from a slow starvation amongst the stars. They never stood a chance. And like the cowards they were, the Council ran. They abandoned their appointed posts and disappeared into the depths of the galaxy. But they would be heard from again."

Kyle took a deep breath and exhaled slowly through pursed lips. The dizziness was getting worse. He would have cried, but the pastor didn't like being interrupted, and he hadn't yet chosen the lamb for today's sacrifice. Kyle didn't want to paint a target on their backs, even if it meant suffering in silence.

"In the end it was a woman, Calin Fustre, the wife of one of the vanished Councilmen, who set out to destroy the Dominion," the preacher boomed. "And this woman … she wasn't a soldier. She was a housewife. A homebody who preferred the comfort of her living room to anything outside her own doors. But they say she was galvanized by the disappearance of her husband. Embittered, she sought to injure the Dominion by whatever means available. And thus she founded the Splinter insurrection.

"Now some people say that Calin is just a myth. That she was just a figment of Splinter propaganda to show how bold and noble their cause was. I have always said we can give them that, because in the end it doesn't matter if she was real or not. None of their lies or misinformation earn them any sway here. We know our cause to be right. We know it to be just. Because we have God on our side."

Kyle stifled a cough. The effort hurt his chest. Suddenly the air was tearing at his lungs. He didn't know why; he just wanted it to stop. He leaned his head on his father's shoulder. It was thin and bony, not very comfortable against his cheek. Marcus Griffin had always been a gaunt, unimposing figure, but the last several weeks had been particularly difficult for him. He'd been sick, suffering through a bout of some kind of flu. *It's nothing*, his mother said. *Happens all the time. He'll be all right.* Kyle wasn't so sure. And now he wondered if he was catching the same thing.

He tried to focus on the sermon, hoping that it would distract him from the pain. But looking that far off in the distance hurt his eyes. Instead he settled on a family two rows in front of them. There were boys sitting to the right of their parents. Kyle recognized the middle child from their spiritual induction classes. He was probably a year or so older than Kyle, but shorter and not quite as wide in the shoulders. And he had a hard time keeping his thoughts to himself.

The boy turned to his older brother and whispered something that Kyle was able to make out: "The Splinter sounds pretty incredible to me."

There were gasps; Kyle wasn't the only one who had overheard. One of the Garrison officers stormed down the row, pushing parishioners aside. He was a wide-chested man with ceramic armored plates accentuating his broad shoulders. The boy's father shot up from his seat in protest and was met with a plated glove into his throat. He stumbled backward, and the officer yanked the boy from his seat like he was plucking a flower.

"What is this nonsense?" the preacher demanded, his voice now far more sinister.

The officer dragged the boy down the aisle and dropped him on the stairs in front of the pulpit. "This boy was speaking during your sermon," the guard said. "Apparently he has some respect for the Splinter that he just couldn't keep to himself."

"Is that right?" the preacher asked. "What did you say, boy?"

The boy just shook his head.

"Go on, child, tell him," the officer insisted. "Speak up!"

The boy cringed, too terrified to reply.

"Open your mouth, dammit!" the officer barked, smacking the child on the back of the head.

"I said … I said …" The boy's voice failed him.

The officer finally lost his patience. "You said the Splinter is '*incredible*,' did you not? Those were your words, isn't that right?"

"Is this true, boy?" the preacher asked.

"I didn't … I didn't mean …"

"There are no shades of grey here, child," the preacher said. "Did you say it?"

The boy nodded meekly.

The preacher shook his head, a scowl spreading across his face. "Well then, I suppose we've had our lamb chosen for us, haven't we?"

The boy's father screamed. He clambered out of the pew and stumbled down the main aisle like any panicked parent would. He didn't make it far. Two more Garrison troops quickly tackled him to the ground and landed a pair of blows with their electrified batons. The man's body twitched, then fell still. The guards dragged him to the base of the altar stairs, then snapped his head up toward his son by a fistful of his hair.

"You are this boy's father, I presume?" the preacher asked.

"Yes," the man replied.

"You object to his sacrifice, do you?" the preacher wondered.

The man nodded. "He's my son. I want him back."

"You realize the gravity of what your son has said?" the preached asked.

"He's just a boy," the man answered. "He doesn't know any better."

"He doesn't, does he?" the preacher hollered. "You claim him as your son, but then you insist he doesn't understand our customs. That reflects poorly on you as his father, doesn't it?"

"Sir, please, I beg you. Don't do this," the man wheezed. His voice was shaking painfully. His desperation was palpable. It made Kyle squirm. "Give him back to me. He can do better ..."

"No, no, no, you see that would create a much larger conundrum, wouldn't it? If I were to give your boy a reprieve, everyone would want one, isn't that right? No, this I believe provides us both a convenience and a teaching opportunity." He lifted his hands, addressing the congregation. "You see, it is your responsibility to ensure that your children are raised with the proper values in mind. We cannot forget this. That means not only learning the worth of faith in our Gentry Lord, but also the consequences of sympathizing with the enemy. They are a gangrenous disease in our otherwise fair galaxy. Empathizing with them carries with it the same cost as fighting for them. I trust we will all learn that lesson well today."

The preacher nodded, and the guard pulled the boy down onto his knees. One of the deacons stepped down from the altar and strapped an illuminated circular disc to the boy's chest, then bound his hands behind his back. The guard spun the child back toward the congregation. There were tears pouring down his face.

"Almighty Lord Aeron," the preacher began, "we, the imperfect people of your holy church, offer this sacrifice in honor of your liberation of us from the tyranny of the Galactic Council."

The boy's father let out a desperate wail, one that was met with another prod from a baton. This time the guard let the surge of electricity linger. The man seized under the shock, quivering uncontrollably. The guard finally released him, and saliva pooled next to his mouth as he lay flat on his stomach. His face was red with pain and heartache. His voice was charred dry. His mouth just gaped open, an empty plea dying at the top of his smoking throat.

"Lord Aeron, we accept that you are our one God, the savior of our damned souls and the one true path to righteousness. It is only through you that we find truth and salvation."

Kyle was struggling not to vomit. He knew this boy. They had played together. Joked together. Laughed together. And now he was going to die.

Kyle felt himself start to lift off his seat. His eyes were burning, and a sensation like bolts of lightning seemed to ripple down his arms. He felt like he was about to burst into flame.

Suddenly, Marcus grabbed his hand, and the scalding under his skin abruptly ceased. A fog deepened over his vision, and the cramp in his chest sharpened. The air started draining from his lungs, and by then he couldn't even muster the breath to ask for help.

"Lord, we ask that you accept this sacrifice in your name," the preacher continued. "For our lives are but a vessel for your everlasting glory. We offer you this unfulfilled life in thanks and gratitude for your never-ending beneficence. We pray that you will take this soul and purge it of the vile malady that afflicted it in life. So that in death, he may finally learn that you are Lord."

The preacher flipped a key on the pulpit, and the illuminated disc on the boy's chest glowed a searing white, spiraling open like a gateway into the heart of a star. The boy convulsed, his neck snapping back so hard it looked as though it would simply break. His mouth opened in a silent scream.

Skin blistered and smoked, and then the boy's chest caved in under the focused heat, like he'd been impaled by a drill made of pure light. His father wrenched against the guard's grasp, but by then his strength had left him. The hole in his son's chest had sucked him dry as well. The boy looked blankly toward the ceiling, unable to even find his father's eyes during his last moments.

And then, mercifully, it was over.

"Let us rejoice with the faithful!" the preacher exclaimed, lifting his face toward the vaulted roof. "Our sacrifice is good. It pleases our Lord like no other thing can." He looked back down on the congregation. "Go now and serve him proudly."

The Garrison soldiers removed the boy's body, dragging his father in his wake. Then the congregation slowly rose to their feet and began to file out. But Kyle remained in his seat. Even through the hazy veil that had fallen over him, Kyle was swallowed by heartbreak. It hit him like a sledge. He'd lost a friend, and that hurt. The anguish piled on to his already swimming head, making his mind summersault through his skull like it was rolling in the tide.

When he finally stood up, his vision abruptly went black and he collapsed into a heap between the pews.

† † †

Age Six ...

Kyle had never known who he was until that day in the Church. His parents had never told him where he'd come from, and he'd never thought to ask. Why would he? He was only five years old after all. But the incident on Veneration Day forced their hand. They had to tell him that he was a descendent of the Gentry.

He finally understood why people looked at his father so differently, with such astonishment. Everywhere they went people would point and stare. Strangers they'd never met would whisper his name or shout "*That's him!*" Marcus had always dismissed it, saying that they were mistaken or that they were thinking of someone else. But they weren't. They knew exactly who he was. That he was the son of Lord Aeron.

The attention wasn't exactly star-struck adoration either. Far from it. Most people saw him as a charlatan. Others as a traitor. All because he didn't sit next to his father in the Royal Palace. As if it were his choice.

Marcus had grown tired of explaining it. A lifetime of telling the tale would do that. His mother died while giving birth, poisoned by the same Celestial enchantment that had doomed so many mistresses and unborn babies before. The children were saturated with the power of the Spark, and in such a raw elemental form it was exceptionally toxic to human cells. The physicians looked at it as a type of radiation poisoning. In every documented case, it proved lethal. At least until Marcus was born.

He was a baffling case to the Dominion physicians. For centuries, the Spark had killed everything it touched. But somehow this one child survived. They had to know why. So they tested him. They prodded him. They pulled him apart and pieced him back together. After all of it, they concluded that he had a genetic mutation, a true evolutionary anomaly that allowed his cells to metabolize the raw energy of the Spark. They called it impossible. They called it a miracle. But there it was...the Spark. Like a brimming battery of ancient cosmic power just waiting for him to learn to unleash. And Kyle carried that same genetic gift.

At first the Gentry was smitten with his first born. He fawned over his every breath, and Marcus's fame captivated the galaxy. A true son of God, surely destined for great things. But he failed to live up to those expectations.

As he grew older it became readily apparent that the power of the Spark was not his to wield, that it was beyond his ability to control. And worse yet, his body's constant struggle to suppress the divine gift left him weak and frail. It ravaged him like an infection he could never cure.

Frustrated by Marcus's feebleness, the Gentry expelled him from the Royal Palace, exiling his son to live in a community of retired military officers on Churchwell, an obscure planet on the tail end of the galaxy's Norma Arm. There he was forced to watch those around him celebrate their long and successful careers as he lamented the life he was meant to have.

It was all a pill too bitter for Marcus to bear. He resolved to take his own life, only to have his courage fail him when the moment came.

And so it went for him: too frightened to take his own life and yet too ashamed to live it. It was an infuriating existence to be certain. Until the day he met Becca Foster.

Marcus stumbled upon her after a speeder crash just a couple of miles from his home. He often walked along a lonely path behind his homestead because he enjoyed the fresh air, the solitude, and the distraction it provided him from the recriminations festering in his mind. He smelled something odd, not quite gasoline and not quite smoke. Eventually he found the wrecked speeder, and its passenger lying injured nearby. Her leg was broken, and she had been left there alone for some time. Dirt smeared her cheeks, and her pants were in tatters. Marcus always said it was the most beautiful she ever looked. That always made Kyle blush.

She didn't have any family, except for her younger brother, who was a captain in the Dominion infantry at the time. He couldn't leave his post to care for her, so Marcus took on the task himself. And she was a welcome guest. Tall and thin, Becca was a rare beauty with hypnotic eyes and a tranquil demeanor. She gave him a lifeline back to the world, and he made her laugh. It was all either of them ever wanted.

Marcus always told his son that Becca saved him, and not the other way around. As a child, Kyle never fully understood what he meant, that she gave him a reason to keep living. Finally Marcus was freed from his self-loathing. The two of them were married in a quiet ceremony less than a year after they met.

Then Kyle came. He arrived joyously with all his potential and promise and hope. His life gave Marcus a glimmer of a real future. And a chance to be the father that he'd never had.

Except ... Marcus was always sick. Most days his body constantly ached, every nerve in his body somehow tuned only to pain. Every joint, every inch of skin throbbed and pulsed like it was all battered and bruised. But the flares were the worst. They knifed through him like shards of scalding metal. Some days he was incapable of lifting his head off his pillow. Others he thought it would be easier if he just died. Kyle could hear his screams echoing through the house.

That's what made mornings like this so sweet. Marcus was feeling well, or as well as his affliction would permit him to. And he was cooking breakfast.

Becca had left the house early for an offertory meeting at the church, an unpleasant chore that she had to attend to at least once a week. Kyle once asked her why she wasn't happy about going, and she reluctantly told him that she didn't much care for the meetings. Marcus shook his head, reminding her that the meetings were her duty, just like it was for all the other women in the congregation. She waited until Marcus turned away and then stuck her tongue out like she'd smelled something raunchy. It made Kyle laugh.

Marcus slid a plate of flapjacks in front of his son. They were piping hot and soaked in Serovian honey. It was Kyle's favorite. And he finally felt well enough to eat such a meal.

It had been nearly eight months since the incident on Veneration Day. His health had plunged alarmingly after that incident. His hair started falling out, he lost his hearing, and he started spitting up blood. He was certain that his life would end before his first kiss.

But it didn't. His episodes started declining. His symptoms subsided. He started holding down food. His hearing returned. The bleeding stopped.

Somehow, he would live.

He'd live to have mornings like this with his dad. Quiet time with just the two of them. Marcus was smiling. The flapjacks were sweet and fluffy. Life was good.

"How are those 'cakes, kiddo?" Marcus asked.

"Good," Kyle replied, his cheeks stuffed full of warm pastry.

Kyle spun his fork around in the syrup. He hummed a light tune to himself. Marcus leaned across the table and stole a forkful of pancake from Kyle's plate. He gobbled it down and gave his son a wry smile.

"Hey!" Kyle cried. "That's mine!"

Marcus swallowed and opened his eyes wide. "Whoops!" he exclaimed. "You want it back?"

Kyle snickered. "Gross."

Marcus smiled at his son, then took a sip of coffee. Kyle stuffed two big bites of food into his mouth and looked over at his mother's seat.

"Dad, why did Mom have to go to church?" Kyle asked. "She always looks so unhappy before she goes."

"Because she had to. It's her responsibility."

"What does that mean?" Kyle asked.

"Responsibility?" Marcus asked, considering the question. "It means it's something she's gotta do."

Kyle frowned. Responsibility was a difficult concept for a six-year-old, especially one who had spent most of the last year being sick and was never asked to do much of anything.

"So the church gives her responsibility?" he asked.

Marcus nodded. "Yeah, in this case," he said. "But she's got other responsibilities too. Like helping take care of you."

"How come the church gets to tell her what to do?"

"Because the church is very important, buddy. Besides that, it's a part of our family. Your grandfather is kind of a big deal in the church, remember? Wouldn't look very good if we didn't stay involved."

Kyle nodded, but still looked pensive. "Dad, why don't we ever see him? If he's my grandpa, why doesn't he ever talk to us?"

"He's just ..." Marcus stopped to consider his response. "He's very busy, pal. The galaxy relies on him to ... set the rules, and to enforce them. It's hard for him to find time for anything else."

"He doesn't like us, does he?" Kyle asked.

"It's not that, pal," Marcus said. "It's just ..."

Just then, Marcus' sat-comm rang. Kyle looked down at it with a scowl. Marcus looked down at the holographic display. It was a business call. An early morning business call, on a day that was supposed to be just for them. Kyle couldn't believe this was happening again.

"Sorry, buddy, I've gotta take this," Marcus said. He slid a small transmitter over his ear and turned away.

After Kyle was born, the Dominion Commerce Secretary had given Marcus a job as a director of trade for the small sector where they lived. It was an entry-level job, dealing mostly with imports and exports from various mining and agricultural sites. Kyle had once heard his mother describe it as a "pity position," something the Gentry could throw at his forgotten son to keep him occupied and out of the news. Marcus, of course, took it without a second thought. He'd do anything to appease his mighty father's whims. Or at least that's what his mother said when they were fighting about it.

"Yes, this is Marcus Griffin," his father said. "Good morning, Dennison, what can I do for you? No, I'm sorry, there's nothing else I can do, I've told you that already ..." Marcus briefly looked back at Kyle and pushed a tall glass of a thick bright orange sludge in front of him. "Finish up your shake, Kyle. You've still got two more of these to drink this morning."

Kyle nodded dully and pulled the sludge closer. He took a swig of it and gagged as the curdled chunks rolled down his throat. It always made him gag. Every day he had to drink three or four of these heinous things. He hated it, but they made him feel better. Ever since he had started taking them, his sickness started going away, so he just kept forcing them down.

Finally, Becca came in through the side door with an exhausted huff. She was dressed in a pantsuit and her hair was done up in an extravagant arrangement. It looked like she'd been arguing in court rather than working at a church. She threw her bag onto the floor and hung her jacket in the closet. Then she turned to Kyle and her weary expression brightened into a smile. Kyle put down the sludge and opened his arms for a hug.

"Hey, sweetie!" Becca exclaimed, throwing her arms around her son. "How's your morning been?"

"Good," Kyle answered. "Dad made flapjacks."

"They look pretty good," Becca said. "Did you save any for me?"

"No," Kyle joked. "They're all mine!"

"Hey! That's not fair."

Marcus pointed to the transmitter in his ear, and they hushed. "I understand your conundrum, Dennison, but you really don't have a choice here," Marcus continued. "This is the only supply of mineable stellar energy in your sector of the galaxy, and the Gentry charges a fee for extracting it. Or you can pay to have it shipped from a private deposit, but you'll have to pay the Dominion shipping taxes. There's really no options there. Either you pay us to mine it, or you pay us to ship it. You let me know what you decide." He listened for a moment to the cursing on the other end of the line, then said goodbye and disconnected the call.

Becca raised an eyebrow at her husband. "You're taking business calls today?"

"I had to," Marcus replied. "This excavating group on Rendiken keeps insisting that they should get a break on their mining fees because they used to privately own the land. It's been a disaster."

"They *used to* own the land?" Becca repeated.

"Couldn't afford the mineral rights tax," Marcus said. "So they defaulted. It belongs to the Gentry now."

Becca sighed. "Don't you ever think that those taxes are ... unmanageable? Seems like everyone defaults eventually. Does your father just want to own them all himself?"

"Well, most of these sites are on worlds he proctored previously. And no, he's not rigging the tax system, if that's what you're asking. One can make quite a nice living on these deposits if they're managed properly."

"Just seems like ever since you took this job, these are the only calls you take," Becca said. "People can't afford the taxes, so they're losing their land. It's going to cause a problem if it keeps happening to enough people."

"That's not our concern."

"Marcus, please," Becca moaned. "Isn't that what they said before the uprising on Eno? That whole agro-union had their farms seized, and they went into full revolt! Don't you want to avoid that sort of thing again?"

"I remember it," Marcus said. "How did their petty revolt work out for them?"

"Marcus, you know how I feel about that. I don't think those people deserved what the Gentry did to them—"

"All right, all right, that's enough! I don't want to argue about it again."

Becca nodded and passed him a small holofile encoder.

"What's this?" Marcus asked, pulling up the image on the drive.

The picture was of a large brick building. It was tall and sprawling, surrounded by leafy trees and many acres of grass. All the green made the red brick seem to burn in the image. The skies above the roof were blue and serene. It seemed so calm. So peaceful. Except at the bottom, where a drove of children were running through the courtyard.

Becca grinned and ran her hand through her son's hair. "It's time to send Kyle to school."

† † †

Age Seven …

Kyle's breath was hastening. Each one seemed sharper and shorter than the one before. His nostrils were flaring, he was sure of it. And the other kids were staring at him.

He'd barely touched the door. He just *touched* it. And the whole thing wilted like the hot wax of a burning candle. Everyone in the hallway stopped to look at him. He felt every eye boring into his back. They singed him like the molten slag the door had become. It felt like it was lighting the hair on his neck on fire.

The more he thought about it, the worse it got. He'd hyperventilate for certain. He'd pass out. Right here in front of the classroom. He'd never live it down. They'd all laugh at him. Then he'd never fit in.

Then the voices started. Voices that had no mouths or tongues. Voices that came right out of the ether. He heard them clearly from distant hallways and adjacent floors, from the next building over and from blocks away. It was like he could hear every whispered word without the sound ever escaping the speaker's lips. And every one of them seemed to say the same thing.

"Oh my god, what a weirdo …"

"I knew there was something wrong with that kid …"

"So creepy …"

"What a total freak …"

The words cut deep. He knew he was different. But all he wanted was to fit in. To be one of them. To be normal. This just proved he wasn't. And everyone was there to see it.

His hand was still hot. He looked down and saw a blue glow beneath the skin. Was he hallucinating? His eyes were playing tricks on him. And his ears were too? Oh man, he was losing it. He was actually going insane. Seven years old and he'd gone off the rails. Just like his dad.

The longer he stared at his hand the brighter the blue glowed. He held his breath, hoping it would fade, but instead it started to crackle like lightning. He panicked and stumbled backward, shaking his arm like it had caught on fire. The aura chased him across the hallway, and he screamed.

He tripped and fell on his back. A bolt of the lightning escaped his hand and gouged through the ceiling above him. A shower of mortar and steel cascaded down amid the thunder. There were three floors above them, and through the chasm he could see the clouds of the mid-afternoon sky.

His mouth went dry. His breathing stopped completely. No bodies came down with the rubble. No deathly screams followed the explosion. But that didn't matter. He could have killed someone. But by some providence he escaped such a disaster. The scrutiny, however, came down in spades.

The looks in the other kids' eyes were those of terror. Of horror. It was like a scene straight out of his nightmares.

The metal floors rang with the drumming of falling debris. Kyle jumped back to his feet and plastered his back against the lockers on the side of the hallway. His head darted from one side to the other, afraid that the rest of the ceiling would collapse on top of him.

The voices in his ears were deafening. Thousands of them. He couldn't turn it off. It was all he could hear. It was all he could see. Through the haze of airborne plaster and pulverized concrete, his eyes saw every panicked face, every tear and sob. They all wanted away from him. Away from the *freak.*

"Kyle?"

It was Ms. Getz, a mathematics instructor. She was leaning half-out out the door of her classroom. And she was scared too.

"Kyle, my god, are you all right?" she asked.

But she knew he wasn't.

At the other end of the hallway there was a clattering. Doors swinging open. Kyle saw soldiers, the military police. The Dominion Garrison. They were swarming inside.

And they had guns.

Kyle didn't want to explain what had happened. He wasn't sure he knew how. Instead he turned and ran toward the other end of the hallway. The floor felt like a trampoline under his feet. He started stumbling forward, moving so fast his head had a hard time keeping up. He caromed into a bay of lockers as he tried to pivot around a corner, caving in the metal like it had been hit by a wrecking ball. More dust came down from the ceiling as the girders shook from the impact. It was like he'd turned into an anvil but was suddenly moving like a gazelle.

He kept running. He heard boots on the metal tiles behind him. How he could hear them above the thumping of his heart or the panting of his breath, he didn't know. Then he suddenly realized that he *wasn't* breathing.

He had to get home. He *had* to. It was all he could think of. His only hope. His parents might know what was happening to him. Or better yet, how to make it stop.

He burst through another set of doors leading outside and ran right into the stomach of another Garrison soldier. The man fared about as well as the lockers. Together they tumbled down a set of steps into a pile at the bottom. Kyle felt the rough concrete rip the skin from his elbow, but he barely had a chance to feel the pain before another wash of blue light bolted down his arm and sealed the wound up like a wisp of smoke. He tried to scream but there was no air in his lungs. He couldn't understand how he was still alive. But he was. He scuttled to his feet, but the soldier grabbed him by the back of his shirt. He felt his shoes lift away from the ground.

The soldier looked confused as he stared at the panicked boy in his hand. "You're what this is all about, kid?" he asked. "What the hell kind of freak show are you?"

That word again. *Freak.* Kyle's face went hot. His teeth clenched. He started kicking frantically, but to no avail.

The doors swung open again, and the other soldiers streamed out. They'd take him away. He'd never see his parents again. Never find a place for himself in the galaxy. His whole life wasted.

"Hold him! Don't let him go!" one of the soldiers yelled.

"I've got him," the man holding Kyle replied. "Bit of a nutcase, this kid, eh?"

More insults. Kyle would remember every one of them. They boiled over in his head. His feet caught the ground, like he'd suddenly grown taller and heavier. Anchored, he thrust his hands into the officer's chest and sent him soaring backward like a leaf caught in the wind.

He'd done it now. He'd hit a Dominion soldier. And not just hit him, but *hurt* him. The man's head split open as it slammed against the concrete. It made Kyle suddenly start breathing again, if but to gasp.

"I'm sorry," Kyle muttered, but his voice was hollow. Not breathing would do that. So would pure panic. It made him realize he only had one thing left to do.

He ran home.

† † †

Age Eight ...

Kyle and his parents sat in their living room for hours after the incident, expecting the worst. Any moment now a brigade of the Dominion Army would march through the garden in their front yard and take him away. To throw him in the Palisade with felons of every description. His parents would live with the shame of raising a freak.

But no one came.

Days melted into weeks, then months. Still, no one came. But if anything, Kyle's anxiety only grew. He had stopped going to school for fear that they would look for him there. He refused to leave the house, too afraid that he would suddenly lose control again. That he would destroy something else. That he would hurt someone. Or *kill* someone. So he locked himself away in his room, cut himself off from the world as best he could. And for an eight-year-old, he did a very good job of it. Even his mother's pleas that he would be all right, that nothing was as bad as it seemed, were hollow. After all, the world had given him very little reason to believe that it *would* be all right. This latest incident at school simply confirmed what he already knew.

That he was better off alone.

But Becca's pleas were sincere. Of course they were; she was his mother, despite it all. She couldn't give up on her only child. She still remembered him as a happy boy, one who was invigorated by his physical gifts. He walked before he was seven months old. When he ran it was like a blink of light. His body healed as if by some supernatural charm. And he remembered every single moment of his life as if it had just happened. To her he wasn't a freak, he was a phenom.

To see her son like this made her desperate. She had seen this type of despair in their family before. It was all too familiar to her. Marcus had fallen into a similar depression just before they met, one that had almost driven him to suicide, and Becca was determined to protect her son from that torment. And she thought she had a chance.

Until that fateful knock finally came on their front door.

Kyle heard it from his room. In fact he had heard the man's footsteps on the soft grass in their front yard. He stood up and waited by the stairs as Becca went to answer the door. From where he watched he could see the man's sharp, freshly shaved jawline, his perfectly manicured hair, and his incisive, purposeful eyes. His suit was official, but it wasn't a Garrison uniform. The small pin on his lapel said it all: Intelligence Division.

He was a spy.

Kyle considered running. He could make it out the back window easily enough. How far could his legs take him before someone caught up? He knew he was fast—faster than anyone he'd ever met—but could he really outrun the Dominion's agents? And what would they do to his parents?

"Good evening, Mrs. Griffin," the man said, his voice low and heavy, like a bull grumbling out its nose. "My name is David Preston. I'd like to speak with you about your son."

"And who is David Preston?" Becca retorted.

"Right. I apologize, ma'am." Preston withdrew a card from his suit. "I'm a doctor with the Intelligence Division. We heard about the incident at the school, and I'd like to discuss it with you and your family."

Becca closed the door halfway and called up the stairs to Marcus. After a moment he lumbered down to the entrance. He tried to put on a strong façade, but it was a tough sell. Every step made him seem more sickly, downtrodden, and feeble. The Spark had flared on him this week as it did several times a year, sapping all his strength as his body struggled to fight it off. He was like a dying tree deprived of water.

The doctor smoothly overrode Marcus's objections, every word bringing him a step closer through the door. And a step closer to Kyle. He sounded like a poet, not a spy.

Kyle slunk back into his bedroom, again thinking about slipping out the back window and making a run for it. But before he could muster the resolve to do it, Becca came to the door and asked him to join them in the study.

Kyle walked downstairs and perched on an ottoman in the corner, feeling very small and very nervous. Becca pulled a chair over, sitting close enough to her son to brush her knee against his. Her hand rubbed his back like only a mother could, but it didn't soften Kyle's anxiety.

The doctor's eyes never left the frightened boy in the corner. He took the chair from under the desk and set it down just a foot or so away from Kyle. He calmly unbuttoned his suit jacket before sitting down, leaning forward with his knees wide. Kyle ducked his head, but the doctor's eyes kept boring into him. Kyle felt like his hair was going to catch on fire.

"You should know right off that we've been watching you for some time, Kyle," the doctor said. "Even before the incident at the school."

Kyle didn't dare look up.

"Is our son in trouble, Doctor?" Becca asked.

Preston smiled. "No, ma'am. Though I think the Garrison officer whose arm he broke and head he split open would object to that."

"If he's not in trouble, then why are you here?" Marcus asked from his seat on the couch.

"You should know that better than most, Marcus," the doctor replied. "The Gentry has asked us to keep an eye on your family. On your son in particular. We believe he has the Spark."

"No," Marcus said. "No, you're mistaken. What happened at the school was an accident. Nothing of the sort has happened since."

"I don't want to offend you," Preston said, "but you don't really think I'd believe that, do you? And it's not a matter of intuition, either. We've had bioenergetic sensors in this house for years now. We know all about his outbursts."

"You've *bugged* our house?" Marcus demanded.

Preston smiled. "Marcus, you are the Gentry's son. What kind of intelligence operation would we be if we didn't keep tabs on you?"

"Then you should know that he's getting better," Becca said. "He's learned to control it."

"No, he hasn't," Dr. Preston said. "Not when he's scared or when he's angry. Then it just bursts out of him like a sneeze.

But...," he wagged his finger in the air, as if what was to come was of utmost importance, "but if he comes with me... *then* he'll learn to control it."

"Comes with you?" Becca echoed, grabbing her son's hand. "You said he wasn't in trouble—"

"He's not in trouble," the doctor interrupted. "Do you think I care about one Garrison officer? Or the school for that matter? My job is to look after the Dominion as a whole. And I believe your son can help me do that."

"You want him ... to help you?" Marcus asked.

Preston cleared his throat and looked pensively at Kyle. Then he stood up and sauntered to the window, peeking casually through the curtains. Kyle wondered what, or who, he was looking at. How many agents were waiting outside? They were going to take him, one way or the other. It was just a matter of whether he went willingly. Or rather, whether his parents let him go willingly.

"What would he have to do?" Marcus asked.

"Marcus!" Becca exclaimed. "Don't tell me you're actually considering letting this happen?"

"Becca, if the Gentry wants this, I don't think we have a choice," Marcus said.

"Of course we have a choice," Becca insisted. "He's our son!"

Marcus shook his head. "Not if the Gentry wants him."

Kyle squeezed his mother's hand like it was all he had left to hold on to.

"Marcus!" she yelled, her voice going shrill. "Just because he wouldn't have you, doesn't mean it's okay for him to take Kyle!"

"Becca, please...," Marcus continued. "This isn't up to us..."

"I'm sorry," the Doctor interrupted, cutting through the percolating tension. "Of course you have a choice. I'm simply here to offer him a chance to come and join us. It's where he belongs."

"You can't just tell us that," Becca insisted, tears starting down her cheeks. "You can't just come here and try to take my child and tell me it's where he '*belongs*.'"

"Ma'am," he said, "you should know that we're offering him a placement in our most prestigious military training program. There are boys twice his age that would literally kill for this appointment."

"You're talking about the Fury," Becca said. "I don't want our son growing up with that mutant horde."

The Fury. If ever there was a terrifying, savage collection of grunts, they were it. Kyle knew the stories. Or he knew the stories that the other kids told on the playground, anyway. They were not tales to be told to boys.

His parents refused to speak of them. And for good reason. They were the Dominion Army's mutant infantry division, a legion of gruesome half-human beasts. They were, as the stories went, the result of failed deep-space explorations commissioned by Aeron to investigate the inner arms of the galaxy. There they were exposed to galactic tides of dark matter that caused brutish and horrifying mutations. It stripped their humanity clean, robbed them of every emotion except for raw, primal anger.

Aeron drew them together, gave them a purpose, first as his personal bodyguards and then as the hammer for his growing army. Eventually, he started sending prisoners from the Dominion Palisade into the toxic void to transform them into these ferocious creatures. With them on his side the Gentry had a never-ending supply of muscle to pad his growing influence in the galaxy. Until his influence became the only one that mattered.

Kyle had never seen a Fury mutant. He never wanted to. But he knew if he went with the doctor that he'd be put in front of one eventually. Suddenly, he couldn't hide his fear any more.

"Mom, I don't want to go," he muttered . "I don't want to go to the Fury. I'm scared ..."

"Honey, it'll be okay," his mother assured him. But she didn't look too certain herself.

"You wouldn't be going to the Fury" Preston said. "No member of Lord Aeron's family would be subjected to such a thing."

"How can we believe that?" Becca asked. "He's never wanted anything to do with this family."

The doctor raised his hands in a gesture of appeasement. "That was intentional. The Gentry didn't want the boy to have to deal with the same … disappointment that your husband had to live with."

"I'm still alive, you know," Marcus said. "And in the room, by the way. No need to talk about me in the past tense."

Preston sighed. "I apologize. I'm not used to recruiting cadets. Like I said, this is a highly sought-after appointment."

"He's just a boy," Becca protested.

"I understand that," Preston said. "He would be our youngest cadet by a considerable margin. But we know what his mental aptitude is. We know about his eidetic memory. About the conceptual recall. And physically … well, we all know what he's capable of there, don't we?"

"He's not ready," Becca insisted. "It's too soon. You can't ask him to do this."

"I know this is difficult. But I know that things haven't been easy for Kyle the way they are either." The doctor leveled his gaze at Kyle, its insight burning right through him. "Isn't that right, son? You feel like an outsider? Like an outcast? The other kids call you a *freak*?"

"Whoa!" Marcus snapped. "That's enough of that."

"Hold on just a moment, Marcus," the doctor replied, his eyes still plastered on Kyle. "I'm talking to Kyle now." Preston's gaze narrowed, like he was somehow peering into his soul. "Listen to me, son. This would be the best place for you. In my Infinity Program you can be among equals. It's a place where you can finally belong."

Becca leaned in between them, her usually soft face churned in a vindictive scowl. "Stop it!" she yelled. "Stop that right now. He's just a boy. Stop playing with his mind like that."

"Ma'am, I'm merely pointing out what the boy already knows," the Doctor replied. "This isn't his place in the galaxy. He's meant for more than this." He turned his gaze back to Kyle. "Son, you have to understand. You're strong. You're obviously gifted. You're a natural fit for us. All you have to do is say yes."

Kyle couldn't shake the doctor's eyes. They penetrated him like parasites knifing into his skin. He had never felt so violated. But even so, the doctor had a point. He did feel cast out. He did feel alone. There was no one here who made him feel wanted or comfortable. No one. Except for his parents.

"Well, son?" the doctor asked. "What do you say?"

"I ... " Kyle almost choked on his tongue trying to speak. It was like he was talking with a mouth full of newspaper. "I ... I want to stay with my parents."

Preston sighed with an obvious disgust. He slapped the armrests of his chair and stood up, then turned to Marcus. "Talk to your son. Perhaps it will mean something coming from you."

Marcus hesitated. The doctor didn't appreciate it.

"Or maybe you don't realize that this could be your last chance to make your own father proud?"

Marcus looked over at the doctor from beneath a furrowed brow. His eyes were heavy. Sweat was sweat beading on his temples. The flare of his powers was chewing him up. He didn't have the strength to fight both it and the lure of pleasing his father. After all these years, it was still what he wanted. And the look on his gaunt face seemed to scream that this was already out of his hands.

Finally he let out a long sigh of defeat. Kyle shriveled into the ottoman. He knew what was coming. The doctor was going to get his way after all.

"Kyle … buddy … I know you want to stay with your mom and me. But I don't think that's going to happen."

"Marcus!" Becca shouted.

"Becca, please," Marcus said. "Just let me finish."

Kyle shook his head so fast it made him dizzy. His father put a finger to his lips, but it didn't slow Kyle's racing pulse. He started to cry. He couldn't help it. It just started pouring out. What kind of soldier could he be? Aeron's champion wouldn't cry, would he? He wanted to crawl under the house and hide there forever.

"You can do this," Marcus said. "I believe in you. And I think that this might be the one place where you can go where you can be who you are."

"But Dad," Kyle sobbed. "I don't wanna go. I'm scared …"

His voice trailed off. He was ashamed to admit that he was frightened, but he was. What would they do to him there when they found out how scared he was?

He felt his power start to sizzle beneath his skin. His hands grew hot. His eyes seemed to swell. It was begging for him to let it go. And he almost did. Until his father brushed his flushed cheek.

"There's nothing for you to be afraid of, buddy," Marcus said. "You don't know it yet, but there is so much that you can be. You're so strong …" Marcus started sniffling as well. "I don't want you to end up like I did … like I was … before I found your mother."

Marcus looked up at Becca. She turned her head away.

"What do you say, bud?" Marcus asked. "Can you be brave for me?"

Kyle wiped his tears away with the back of his hands. He managed a nod.

Preston was grinning from ear to ear.

Becca stood up in a huff and stormed out. Marcus followed her into the hall, pleading for her to listen.

"Becca, wait!" he yelled, finally grabbing her arm. "Will you wait and just listen to me for a second?"

"How can you agree to this?" Becca shouted. "You know better than anyone how the Gentry is. If Kyle isn't what he wants, he'll just throw him aside—is that what you want for our son?"

Marcus sighed. "No. No, it isn't. But if my father wants him, he *will* get him. One way or another. You know that. At least this is on our terms."

"Our terms? What part of this is our terms?"

Marcus shook his head. "It's better than them coming in here and just taking him."

Becca let out one hopeless sob. "If he goes with them, he won't be the boy we raised any more. He'll belong to them."

CHAPTER 2

Age Ten ...

Kyle left his parents' home with very few friends. It was a sad fact, but nobody outside of his family would miss him. Not in the school. Not in his neighborhood. Nowhere. He knew that. That was the curse of an eidetic memory. Nothing escaped him. He carried every slight with him forever.

All that time, and he never had someone to share it with. And after two years in the Infinity Program, he still didn't. Almost two dozen young cadets had entered the Protocol during Kyle's first two years there, and not one of them lasted more than eight months. There were some older recruits who had been there since before Kyle's time, but they were mostly in their late teens and uninterested in befriending a child who had been brought there to usurp their position in the pecking order. The oldest of them, a seventeen-year-old named Vaughn Donovan, was especially sour on him. The reason was no secret. Vaughn was in line to become the unit's first commander, an appointment that was as rare as it was sought after. Kyle's arrival meant the naming of a commander was to be put on hold, and that didn't sit well with Vaughn and the older cadets.

Once again, Kyle was the outcast.

Most days he tried to avoid the others. He skulked around the halls of the training complex like a mouse, trying not to be seen. He found himself quite adept at it actually, shifting through the shadows and tiptoeing around prying eyes. Stealth tactics were part of his training, and with his physical gifts he became a savant at it. He could react faster than human eyes could see, and move swifter than their vision could adapt. All he ever was to them was a blur.

But there was one day when his shadowy theatrics caused him to stumble into an unfamiliar situation that changed his life.

The Infinity Program resided on a lush, forested world in the same sector as the Dominion capital planet of Dynasteria. The complex was carved out of the woods like a sculpture of metal and concrete amid the trees. It sprawled out next to a rock-filled ravine some twenty acres wide, and it housed some of the finest technology the Dominion engineers could muster. Anything that the instructors could desire to mold their recruits was at their disposal here. This was, like the doctor had said, a highly coveted appointment—even if life inside was like stepping into a meat grinder.

On that afternoon Kyle was walking back to his dormitory after a tactics meeting when he saw Vaughn and three other cadets coming toward him. Vaughn had a jaw chiseled out of brick, even at that age. He looked like a gargoyle with his low brow and sharp cheekbones, and his barely repressed rage throbbed in the vein running down the middle of his massive forehead. Not that it would be the first time he did so when Kyle was in his sights. If it weren't for Kyle's ability to heal, he'd probably still have the scars to prove it.

The routine had grown tiresome. Vaughn would try to assert his dominance and Kyle would try to convince him that he wasn't angling for anything. But Kyle's temper was thinning with each passing day. He was afraid of what he might do if he allowed himself to unleash that anger. He was afraid he might like it.

"Griffin!" Vaughn hollered, his voice already that of an old man. "You and I gotta have a talk."

Kyle didn't answer. He tucked his head and stepped into a deep doorway. Vaughn and his lackeys hurried to the entrance, but when they got there Kyle was nowhere to be seen.

"Get this door open," Vaughn ordered.

"It's got priority access locks," one of the cadets protested. "Only the instructors can open it."

"Then how the hell did he open it?" Vaughn demanded.

"I didn't hear it open."

"I didn't either."

"Well, it obviously opened, didn't it?" Vaughn grumbled. "Where the hell else could he have gone?"

He got nothing but blank stares. A sneer spread across his face and he stormed off, the other cadets following behind.

A moment passed and Kyle cautiously stepped out from behind another door across the hall. This was about as satisfying a result as he could have hoped for. Not only had he avoided a confrontation, he also left those bullies feeling cheated and irked. Raining his fists against their faces was the only thing he could think of that would be more cathartic.

He heard another set of footsteps coming down the corridor. Immediately he knew it wasn't Vaughn or any of the other recruits. The cadence was too light, too soft. It was a girl.

Kyle didn't know what to do. So he did what he was best at. He disappeared back behind the door, keeping it cracked just enough to watch her go skipping by.

Her hair was long, well into the middle of her back, and auburn brown. Her face was bright with luminescent eyes and smooth glowing skin. She couldn't have been more than Kyle's age, and she clearly still clung to the childish charms and folly that Kyle had long ago forgotten. She was humming to herself, a nymph-like tune with a high pitch. Her clothes were far too big for her, dangling off her arms and legs like curtains over a window, and her shoes were easily a half-dozen sizes too big. Kyle wondered where she had gotten them. *Perhaps they were her mother's,* he thought. But where would she have come from? And why was she here in the complex?

Then he noticed the ring on her right hand. It was bulky, made of an extremely valuable starmetal called dulcenite. Kyle had seen pictures of rings like this in a holofile maybe two years ago. It was an officer's ring.

Now he was intrigued. He had to know who this girl was, and where she had come from. So he slipped out the door and followed her.

The girl's dance took her all through the lower floor of the complex. She didn't seem concerned about any of the people she came across. People, machines, events...none of it seemed to break her trance. She just pranced in a carefree way Kyle had never seen before. He marveled at it. That kind of emotional freedom had always evaded him, perhaps even tortured him. Kyle wondered if she knew what she had, if she appreciated it. Because he would have happily given all his powers away in a heartbeat to spend a single day with that type of carefree whimsy. If only such a thing were possible.

Finally she skipped her way to the rear doors of the training complex, aimless as a feather on the wind. She sauntered outside into the courtyard on the east side of the building, trailing down toward the rock-filled gully some one hundred meters away. Kyle paused at the exit, watching from a distance for a moment. He knew he shouldn't go any farther. He had responsibilities after all. Training, classes, and meetings that he couldn't miss. If he skipped them, he'd surely face the Gauntlet, the Infinity Protocol's harshest punishment—a seemingly endless series of physical exhaustions designed to prove to the recruits just who was in control of their lives. Kyle had yet to endure it, but he knew of at least three recruits who had died as a result of its tortures. Would it really be worth it?

He shook his head in disgust. Then he walked outside.

The girl went out onto the rocks, humming that same tune all along her way. Kyle darted to a grove of trees toward the north end of the complex and leapt to one of the higher branches. From there he could see her bounding from rock to rock, giggling to herself with each jump. Apparently she was bold too. Kyle found himself holding his breath, waiting for her to fall.

Then she did. She slipped, losing her balance. The officer's ring slid off her delicate finger.

She yelped, but quickly stifled it. From his perch Kyle could hear the starmetal clang off the rocks as it tumbled down the ravine. The girl scampered after it in a panic, but it was a useless effort. It was gone.

For three hours Kyle sat and watched her search for the ring, but she never found it. She was crying with loud sobs of desperation. Kyle felt sorry for her. At first, he had resented this girl and the freedom she flaunted in a place where nothing was free, where the residents spent their every hour in a regimen that would make an android blanch. But now he saw it as naivety more than malice. And losing this ring had wiped that all away.

Finally she climbed out of the ravine, dried the tears from her otherwise brilliant eyes, and slowly shuffled back to the complex. Kyle leaned back against the trunk of the tree. He watched her walk, the glee now absent from her steps. He'd felt that same depression before, and it made him ache to see this girl feel the same.

He jumped down and stood at the edge of the ravine, peering down with his powerful eyes. Could they see what she couldn't? Perhaps. And maybe then he'd have a reason to talk to her. Maybe he could restore that look of innocence she had left on those rocks.

If only he could find it …

Fifteen minutes later he found himself walking through the halls again, dragging his heels. He would have to explain his absence to Dr. Preston whether he wanted to or not. The thought was frightening. It made his stomach churn enough that he actually started to feel nauseous, which was an entirely new sensation for his mutant body. He could only imagine how bad it would get when he saw the look on his mentor's face.

The thought had barely run across his mind when the doctor turned the corner in front of him. And just as Kyle had suspected, Dr. Preston's expression was grim.

And then he saw her again. The girl. She was standing by the doctor's side, holding his hand.

"Griffin, where have you been today?" Preston demanded. "You missed the entire afternoon."

"I'm sorry, sir," Kyle said.

"You didn't answer the question," Dr. Preston said. "Where were you?"

"I wasn't feeling well, sir."

"You weren't feeling well? And yet you weren't in your room. Or at the medical station."

Kyle cleared his throat. He kept his eyes down. Clearly lying wasn't his strongest attribute. And having this girl standing there watching him flounder wasn't making it any easier.

"Well?" the doctor pressed.

"I went outside, sir," Kyle continued. "I thought the fresh air would do me some good. I've never been sick before. I guess I didn't know what to do."

The doctor wasn't buying any of it. The look on his face screamed as much. But for whatever reason, he nodded. Kyle tried his best to hide his surprise.

"Very well," the doctor said finally. "Go back to your dormitory. I expect you to be ready for tomorrow."

As Kyle nodded, he couldn't help but sneak a look at the girl standing beside his mentor. Her tears had dried. Those eyes were clear. But he still didn't know who she was, or what she was doing here.

The glance didn't go unnoticed.

"Right," Dr. Preston said, gesturing toward the girl. "Kyle Griffin, this is my daughter, Angel Marie."

Daughter. Of course.

"My appointment here has reached tenure," the doctor continued, "so my family finally gets to join me. Say hello, dear."

Angel waved. "Hello," she said. "I hope you feel better."

"Thanks," Kyle mumbled, barely able to get his tongue out of the way of the words.

"Angel's just a few months older than you are," Dr. Preston said. "Perhaps the two of you can spend some time together. It might make things easier for you here."

Kyle nodded again, trying not to seem too anxious. "Yes, sir," he said. "That would be … that would be something."

Kyle saluted and stepped past them, heading for his room. The doctor had been kind to him. It seemed surreal. It seemed that this whole day was full of new sensations.

He got about three strides down the hall before the doctor called after him. This time his voice wasn't as forgiving.

"Make sure you get some rest, Griffin," he said. "You've got the Gauntlet tomorrow."

CHAPTER 3

Age Twelve ...

Kyle could taste blood in his mouth. His right eye was swollen shut. His jaw ached, as did his ribs. He was doubled over at the waist, hands on his knees. He'd taken some shots, that was for certain. But those weren't the pains he was focused on. His knuckles throbbed from the violence he had returned. They pulsated with each thunder of his heart.

It was a mutant heart, they told him. He had always wondered why he felt so different. Finally, the physicians at the Infinity complex told him why. After all the prodding and tests, he finally had his answer: he simply wasn't human.

It seemed so obvious, but he never wanted to believe it. In truth, it terrified him. He was raised as a boy, a human boy, and he wasn't certain what to do now that he knew he wasn't one. All his physical gifts—the strength, the speed, the agility, the superhuman senses—they all meant nothing now that he had lost sight of who he was.

The Infinity Protocol was happy to give him a new identity. They taught him to hone his gifts, to perfect his skills and focus them like he never had known was possible. They showed him how to harness his ever-present rage, to focus all the emotional energy that pervaded his youthful psyche and use it as the trigger for his burgeoning Celestial powers. And with that subtle guidance he became more powerful than he ever dreamed he could be.

But all that training had another purpose as well. It transformed him from a frightened child into a fearsome young soldier. Each and every day he heard the same chorus recited to him: that he was destined to be more than just a man; he was going to be a force of nature.

He spat out a wad of blood, but his mouth just filled up again. The gouge on the inside of his lower lip was pumping it out as fast as he could discard it. He could heal the wound if he wanted. His powers allowed him to mend nearly any injury at will. But Dr. Preston had forbidden him from using his Spark during this sparring exercise. He wanted his protégé to prove his mettle without it.

Up to this point Kyle had proven himself well. There were eleven other cadets teamed against him in the arena, all of whom were in their late teens or early twenties. Kyle had always been big for his age, but these were full-grown Infinity-trained soldiers. They were to be the jewel of the Dominion Army, more prized than even the Gentry's Fury divisions. But as Kyle looked them over, only two were still conscious. And they were barely standing.

Kyle rose back to his feet. His shoulders had grown wide, his back tapered, and his chest swollen. He didn't look like a twelve-year-old. He looked like a *god.* And currently he looked like a god uninterested in the rest of this exercise.

However, as he turned for the arena door, a booming voice roared out at him.

"Griffin!" Dr. Preston bellowed. "What are you doing? Your job isn't finished."

Kyle looked back at the squad he'd laid to waste. The two remaining cadets had huddled together to get their legs under them. One clearly had a broken arm, the other several shattered ribs. They were no threat to re-engage him. The fight was over.

"Sir, I've already won, sir," Kyle said. His voice hadn't caught up with his body yet, and still carried a prepubescent tone. "They're no threat to me now."

"Did you win?" Preston asked. "You must learn you will not be in the business of granting mercy or taking prisoners. *You* are an instrument of war. And our instruments finish their fights."

Kyle sighed. "The fight is over, sir," he said. "I don't think anything else is necessary."

"You're not here to think, Griffin. Now finish them. Or I will find someone who will."

"Sir, please—"

"Enough! I always knew your father to be a coward. I had assumed that trait had not passed down to you. Perhaps I assume too much …"

Kyle bit his lip. He felt the heat of anger wash over his chest. It was an undeniable sensation, one he'd felt a thousand times in his four years there. Kyle might be inhuman, but above all he was an emotional and nostalgic young man. He missed his home and his parents. And because of that everyone assumed he was submissive like his father. But in truth he was much more like his mother, strong-willed and quick-tempered. At times it made him quick to snap, and had often put him at odds with the demands of his mentor. But by then he didn't care. Not anymore. The Infinity Program had taken that yearning to please away from him. At times he wished he were more like Marcus so that he could leave this life behind. Forget it ever happened. Disappear.

But in the end he couldn't deny what he was born to be: a cold-hearted soldier.

He marched forward. The last two cadets panicked and stumbled over each other as Kyle came closer. They were afraid of the twelve-year-old. And for good reason.

The first cadet with the broken arm threw a helpless punch in his defense. Kyle ducked it, then snatched the cadet's other arm and twisted. The cadet screamed as his arm snapped.

Kyle leveled his right fist into the young cadet's jaw, and it splintered like an ice sculpture. The other turned to run, but he had no chance of escaping. Kyle was simply too fast. He leapt into the air, arching ten meters overhead, and came down in front of the frightened young man. Kyle stunned him with an elbow to the ear, then followed it with a pivoting roundhouse kick to the temple. It could have easily been fatal had Kyle not held back. Then the arena went silent.

Kyle took a deep breath, ashamed of the unnecessary violence. But mostly, he was ashamed of himself. These soldiers might never be the same after that punishment. But that didn't matter to the greater scheme of the Infinity Protocol and its design. They were happy to sacrifice these cadets' futures to test Kyle's willingness to follow their orders. And he had done it like one of their sheep. His mentor would be pleased. But his mother would not.

"Congratulations, Kyle," the doctor exclaimed. The first name. He was always so much more cordial when he got his way. "Another step in proving yourself."

Kyle couldn't hide his sneer. He didn't really want to. It only seemed to encourage the doctor.

"You're coming along nicely, son." Dr. Preston nodded toward the balcony on the other side of the arena. "And I'm not the only one who thinks so ..."

Kyle followed the doctor's gaze. Above them on the balcony was a dark doorway, dark like looking into a black hole. But Kyle's inhuman eyes cut through the black and saw the massive silhouette of an armored giant. He could see the flowing cape draped over its gargantuan shoulders, the scarlet and platinum adornments housing the Celestial amulet on its chest. He stared deeply at it, realizing just what he was looking at. It was Aeron himself.

A pair of red eyes flashed wide. The heavy crowned helmet nodded in approval.

Blue flame washed over Kyle's body. His wounds disappeared in the glow. He didn't acknowledge the nod. This was the authority who had taken him away from his parents, who had demanded all of these senseless sacrifices he endured since his childhood. And that just fueled his rage even further. Finally, he simply turned his back and walked away.

Chapter 4

Age Thirteen ...

Kyle awoke to a loud bang as his dorm door swung open. He was on his feet in the blink of any eye, a side effect of both years of military training and reflexes that bordered on precognition. His eyes focused immediately, even in the dark. There were five boys standing in the doorway, holding rucksacks.

Kyle looked over the short, skinny redhead standing in the forefront. His face was blanketed in freckles, and his arms and legs looked like pipe cleaners. The duffel over his shoulder seemed as though it would pancake him under its weight.

His eyes locked on Kyle, and they seemed to bulge out of his shallow cheeks.

"Holy shit," the boy said, his voice still as high as a child's. "Are we in the right room?"

"No, that's him," another boy said. He was slightly taller but much thicker with a sharp jaw and narrow eyes. He seemed to look at the whole room with suspicion, like everything he saw was somehow lying to him. "They said he'd be big."

"Yeah, but that ain't big," the redhead replied. "That's fucking *mutant* big right there."

Kyle felt a flush of anger fill his chest, and the skinny redhead must have seen the distaste creep across his face. He stumbled backward into the other boys to avoid Kyle's searing stare.

"Better watch what comes out of that mouth of yours," a third boy warned, stepping past the first two. "I don't think he likes that."

He walked casually past Kyle and threw his bag on one of the eight empty bunked cots lining the dorm. This one had longer hair, just over his ears, and the makings of a patchy adolescent beard poking out on his chin. His nose was more rounded, but it fit with the wide shoulders and thighs hiding under a loose-fitting set of clothes. He licked his lip, packing in a thick wad of tobacco root between his gums and teeth. Kyle could smell the tangy aroma with each breath the boy took.

Finally, he jutted out his hand in front of him. "I'm Jay," he said with a curt nod. "I'm a pilot."

Kyle took the offered hand reluctantly. It practically swallowed Jay's, but the boy didn't seem to care.

"This here is Jackson," Jay said, waving toward the young man with the cropped hair. "He's here for tactical school. Sniper training, right?" Jackson nodded dully. "Those two trolls hiding in the hallway are looking to get into spook training. Wouldn't tell me their names."

Kyle couldn't muster any interest. Jay kept talking anyway.

"They want to be spies," he said. "You know, '*if they told me, they'd probably have to kill me*' stuff, eh?"

Kyle was still stoic. Not much was funny to him anymore. He'd been in this place too long, seen too many harsh realities his parents never told him about. And besides, he'd been through these introductions before. These recruits never lasted. They all washed out eventually. He guessed six weeks, tops, before these kids tucked their tails and headed back home to whatever cushy lives their families had waiting for them.

He turned his attention back to the wise-ass redhead still lingering in the doorway.

"Right. And the mouth with freckles over there is Mac," Jay said, following Kyle's gaze. "He's here for the engineering program. And the astrodynamics program. And the ballistics program. And whatever other smart-ass programs the Dominion has here—right, Mac?"

Mac barely lifted an eyebrow. Jay went right back to Kyle.

"He's *supposed to be* a genius," Jay said. "Wouldn't know it by looking at him though."

Kyle scowled. He leered over at Mac. He'd grown such a disdain for those words. *Mutant, weirdo...freak.* He didn't have the patience to tolerate it from this little runt. Especially in the middle of the night. Besides, this kid would never make it through the program anyway. He looked like a stiff wind would blow him over. Kyle caught himself imagining what his fists might do to him.

Then he saw the numbers on the kid's arm. They were tattooed into the speckled skin on the back of his wrist, a barcode from the Social Service Division.

"Wait," Kyle said. "He's an orphan?"

Jay's face wrinkled as if the question was ridiculous. "Of course. We all are."

† † †

Age Fourteen ...

Kyle had never felt so stupid. He'd been staring at this damn circuit for nearly ten minutes without so much as a thought of how to disarm it. These trigger mechanisms were something he'd never seen before, and that had him befuddled. If he'd just seen a picture, read a snippet, heard a passing comment on its workings, he would remember it and this thing would make sense. Or at least maybe he'd have a place to start. As it was, he gaped at the components of this faux bomb like a dunce trying to decipher some extinct language.

He looked up at the clock. Less than seven minutes left in the exercise. He'd already wasted more than half of his allotted time and he'd literally done nothing. The red light over his station indicating that his trigger was still armed beamed down at him like a spotlight. The other cadets were all working dutifully, and there he was, the only one just sitting there. Frustrated, he considered putting his fist through the entire mechanism and taking the punishment that would come with such an outburst. But that would likely mean another trip to the Gauntlet, a torture he did not want to relive.

Then again, maybe it would be easier than disarming this damn thing.

Another moment later he heard a very faint "psst" come from across the room. It was so quiet that even his mutant ears barely made it out. His instinct was to ignore it—the cadets were strictly forbidden from speaking during this drill—but then he heard it again.

"Psst."

Kyle finally glanced to his left and caught the eyes of the skinny redhead. Mac let his gaze linger long enough for Kyle to know he was the one trying to get his attention, then quickly looked away. The light above Mac's station had turned green, with the completion time of 2:18 flashing underneath. So the little brat was mocking him. *Mutant*, Kyle heard in his mind, the boy mocking him on the night that they had met.

"Hey, big fella," Mac whispered. "Can you hear me? Clear your throat if you can hear me."

Kyle snarled. He didn't want to give that little shit the satisfaction of responding. Besides, what could he possibly want? Was he looking for Kyle to pummel him into paste? Taunting him in a moment of inadequacy was a sure way to tempt his fate.

"Oh, come on," Mac pushed. "I know those rabbit ears of yours can hear me. I want to help."

Kyle's anger turned to confusion.

"Your boy Vaughn is struggling too," Mac whispered. "It'll keep you a leg up on him..."

Kyle looked over at Vaughn's station. He was fiddling helplessly with his own device, looking about as frustrated as Kyle felt. It would be nice to see the look on his rival's face if he was able to complete this challenge and Vaughn wasn't. Perhaps even worth it enough to give this Mac kid a chance.

Kyle cleared his throat.

"Ha! I knew that would get you going," Mac exclaimed, but somehow still under his breath. "Nothing like a little competitive hate to grease the wheels."

Kyle shot a sharp glare over to Mac's station. Mac's eyes widened, and he quickly got back to business.

"You got a tough circuit there. I can see six different booby-traps from here, which means there's probably a dozen or more total. The easiest way for you to bypass is to block the current in the firing mechanism."

Kyle looked at the device and realized that he didn't even know where the power source was. All the cables and cords looked the same. He glanced over his shoulder again.

"Right," Mac whispered. "The power source is actually the two solenoids on the upper-left corner. They look a little like coasters."

Kyle saw them. They were small and a bit oblong, but he recognized what Mac was talking about. He grabbed his clippers and reached for the first cable coming off the discs.

Mac suddenly started coughing, a real loud obnoxious hacking cough that was almost too obvious in its purpose. Kyle stopped abruptly.

"Don't do that. That cord is the first booby-trap. The solenoids are electromagnetic. The impulse bounces between them, but it doesn't conduct down the fiber. It hops through the copper conductors, the little T-shaped rods running down the left side."

Kyle sighed and looked at the clock. Just two minutes left. The runt needed to hurry up.

"The two pointed poles at the bottom left are the actual firing mechanism," Mac continued. "If you disrupt the electricity between them with a piece of rubber, then throw the switch, it'll fault. The circuit will fail, and you're home free."

Kyle shook his head. He didn't have any rubber in his roll of tools. Just cutting items, a few sockets, and a voltmeter. Did that little shit just give him the runaround?

"C'mon, boss," Mac mumbled. "What do you got that's made of rubber?"

Nothing. He had nothing. The bastard was actively trying to sabotage him.

As Kyle pushed back his chair, his boot squeaked against the tiled floor. His anger washed away. He shook his head, feeling thoroughly idiotic. He grabbed the wire cutters and sliced a piece of the rubber sole off his boot. It slid nicely between the poles, and then he flipped the trigger.

The light flashed green.

Kyle looked at the clock. It clicked down to zero, and the lights dimmed. A voice came over the speakers and instructed them to exit. Vaughn's light was still red. Kyle smirked at the look of frustration on his face. But then…he *should* have failed as well.

By the time Kyle turned around, Mac was already on his way out the door. Kyle hurried after him. He had to find out why this kid had helped him. That was an awfully altruistic thing to do in a cutthroat place like this. It didn't make sense, and Kyle didn't like things that didn't make sense.

"Mac!" he hollered once out in the hall. "MacArthur, hold on. I want to talk to you."

Mac stopped and spun around. He wore a wide, close-mouthed grin, the type of look typically reserved for gloating. Kyle narrowed his eyes. What was this kid playing at?

"What was that all about?" Kyle asked.

"What do you mean?"

"*That,*" Kyle emphasized, pointing back into the testing amphitheater. "Why did you help me?"

"You think I need an ulterior motive?" Mac asked.

"Everyone here has one," Kyle said. "I just want to know what yours is."

Mac shrugged. "Maybe I was just getting bored waiting."

"Right," Kyle said, shaking his head. "Look, I get that you're smart. Obviously smarter than me. These tests are the only place where you can make up ground on the other cadets. So why give me an edge?"

"I thought maybe we could help each other."

"Help each other?" Kyle asked. "How?"

"Like you said, I'm outmatched on all the physical tasks," Mac said. "You're obviously not. I thought we could come to a mutually beneficial arrangement. You help me with the physical stuff, and I can teach you about the tech side."

Kyle rolled his eyes. "These devices won't fool me again. What makes you think I'll still need your help?"

"Kinda cocky, aren't ya?" the redhead snickered. "Look, I know about your eidetic memory. It's a helluva gift. But that's the whole point of this place. They've gotta give you something new every time. That's how they tease us, make us think we've got it all figured out and then drop a turkey in our laps. It's all part of their game. What are you gonna do the next time they give you something you've never seen?"

Kyle didn't have an answer. But then Dr. Preston walked up alongside them and rapped Kyle heartily on his shoulder. The two of them went silent immediately.

"Nicely done, Griffin," Dr. Preston said, a wide smile spread across his perfectly shaved jaw. "You solved our most trying trigger mechanism. How did you come up with the solution?"

Kyle shook his head. "Rubber blocks the conduction. I guess I just pulled it out of the air."

"I'm impressed. I hope you can keep that up." He glanced at Mac. "MacArthur—two minutes and eighteen seconds. That's a record for this test. Next time I'll have to give you a more difficult task."

"I welcome it, sir," Mac said.

Dr. Preston nodded at them both, then marched off. Kyle looked back at Mac, who was watching him with his eyebrows raised. Kyle sighed.

"All right, runt," he said. "You got yourself a deal."

† † †

Age Fifteen ...

Angel was tired. She barely slept at all last night. The horns started blaring incessantly in the early hours, apparently to wake the cadets for some deprivation training. But because her family lived in the officer's suites above the cadets' dorms, it left her as the one feeling deprived.

She never fared well without a good night's sleep. Not that she had much to accomplish on any given day. She spent about seven hours in home schooling with her mother, learning about Dominion history and math and some social sciences. It was basic and rudimentary, but it was what her mother knew. While her father was out teaching boys to be men, she was stuck watching holospheres about the early Dominion provinces. She grew tired of hearing about trade routes and commerce, and which planets produced what crops. What difference did it make? It was all controlled by the Dominion Trade Commission anyway.

After her schooling, she was allowed some free time, which she typically spent drawing. It was an antiquated hobby, but she enjoyed it. There was something about turning a blank page into a beautiful image that appealed to her. She could make anything she wanted with a sheet of clean paper and a pencil, which was a far cry from real life. In her reality everything was scripted, planned out down to the finest minute detail. She was told what time to eat, what time to sleep, when to shower, and when to use the restroom. Even the people she spent her day with were force fed to her. And they were never the people she wanted to be with.

At the moment she was getting breakfast in the mess hall with the Echo unit cadets. She despised Echo unit. It was comprised of all the older recruits who would push her to the back of the line. They'd snatch a plate of food right out from under her nose and tell her they needed it more. They were taking out their resentments against her father, she supposed.

There were days she thought of running to her father to tell him what his students had done and let him handle the punishment. But she feared the inevitable repercussions. After all, she knew these cadets were rare and gifted, and her father couldn't dismiss them for what amounted to childish mischief. And her father certainly would never leave this post, not to spare her some adolescent angst. This was his dream job, training these would-be soldiers.

Especially now that the Griffin boy was here. Her father was fascinated by him. He called Kyle the perfect soldier. And maybe he was, not that she cared. All that mattered was that she wasn't going anywhere, and those bullies would only intensify their torments if she turned them in to her father. Things were bad now. She didn't want to think about what they'd be like if she did that.

Instead, she chose to think about Kyle. That was a far more pleasant thought. He was easy to talk to. He had a nice smile. He laughed at her jokes and opened doors for her. In short, he made her feel welcome. He made her feel wanted. It was a feeling not even her father could give her as of late. Why couldn't she have breakfast with Alpha unit instead?

The mess hall was more crowded than usual. For a moment Angel thought it might mean better company, but she didn't see Kyle or the boys in his Alpha squad, and Vaughn and the Echo unit were still meandering near the entrance. Everyone looked tired and grumpy after their midnight maneuvers. Angel hoped perhaps she could sneak through the line and get to her seat before any of the cadets came looking for their meal. It would make her day infinitely better. In fact, she figured it would be the only way she would get her portion this morning. So she ducked her head and started through the line.

"You're here to cause trouble again, are you, Miss Preston?" one of the cooks said. He was a portly man with a round chin and protruding neck, and he seemed especially amiable for this hour. "You know I don't appreciate trouble in my line."

"Can you please just get me through?" she asked, her tone rushed. "I won't be any trouble once I have my food, I swear."

"I should make you wait till the end," the cook replied. "Those boys are bound to be a handful once they see you."

"Please, no!" Angel exclaimed, having to censor her own volume. "I won't have time. You know my father. He won't let me be late for my lessons."

"I *do* know your father. He hates it when we keep his recruits late. But he doesn't seem terribly concerned with *you*."

Angel's face fell. "Please, just give me whatever," she said. "I'll go eat it in the hallway if it will make you feel better."

The cook paused, but then he yielded to the look on her face. She was exhausted, she was hungry, and this whole situation had her very anxious.

"I have some food premade for the officers," he said. "I'll slip you a plate."

Angel let out a sigh, dropping her head backward in relief. "Thank you! Thank you! You're saving me, you really are."

The chef pulled a plate from a warmer behind him. It was loaded with Elysian eggs, crisp pork loin, and flapjacks. Angel swooned. She hadn't had such a meal in the three years since she'd arrived here. It made her salivate just looking at it.

She wanted to thank him again, but she was afraid she'd drool on the buffet in front of her. So she took the plate without another word. It was rude, she knew that, but she couldn't help it. Not with that food staring her in the face.

She spun around to find a place to sit, and ran right into the chest of Vaughn Donovan. The food went sprawling across his uniform. The tray clattered against the tiled floor. It was loud, and it was messy. Everyone's eyes spun toward them. Just what she didn't want.

"Dammit, Preston!" Vaughn snapped, wiping a glob of eggs off the front of his fatigues. "Watch where you're going."

"I'm … I'm sorry," Angel stuttered. "I … I … I didn't mean…"

"You didn't mean what?" Vaughn asked. "Go on, spit it out…"

Angel cringed. He looked even angrier than usual. She stepped in some of the eggs as she retreated, and stumbled backward into the railing in front of the buffet. Her foot caught Vaughn in the shin.

"What the fuck is your problem, Preston?" he demanded. "Too fucking clumsy to get a meal without throwing it all over someone?"

"No," she muttered. "I just—"

"You just what? You'd think your father would have taught you better than that."

Angel bit her lip. She straightened up, steadying her feet beneath her. She wished her father *would* teach her something. But he never did. Instead, he spent all his time teaching arrogant little pricks like this. A group of self-righteous bastards who only cared about themselves. She leveled her eyes at the much taller cadet. He represented everything she hated about this place, and it was time she said something about it.

"Do you have to pick on me just because you can't get the best of a kid seven years younger than you?" Angel demanded.

It drew a chorus of gasps from the gathered crowd.

Vaughn's eyes widened. "What did you say to me?"

"You heard me. You think you're some kind of tough guy, coming in here and pestering the teacher's kid, but Kyle's already more of a man than you'll ever be. And he's barely half your age."

Vaughn clenched his fists. But they remained at his sides. Teasing her was one thing. There was no proof of that torture. But if she went home with a bloody nose or black eye, that wasn't so simple. Maybe he wasn't as stupid as she thought.

"You're not worth the headache anyway," he said.

As Vaughn turned to walk away, his words echoed in Angel's ears. *Not worth it.* It hurt her worse than if he'd punched her. Every insecurity she had about her family, her father, her life came rushing up from a hole in her gut.

She snatched a glass of milk from the tray of one of Vaughn's crew and dumped it on the back of his neck. It dripped a white streak across the cadet's dark hair, trickling down his face and into the collar of his shirt. He whirled around, his lips immediately angled downward in a snarl. He shoved her down into the eggs and meat splattered on the floor. Her head hit the tile, and she felt her scalp split open and warm blood spread through her hair.

Her eyes went crossed for a moment. She could make out Vaughn towering over her, but her vision was blurry from the blow. Slowly her vision balanced out and she could see the rabid bloodlust on Vaughn's face. He looked like he was going to kill her.

Then MacArthur stepped in front of him.

"Whoa, whoa, whoa," Mac exclaimed. "I know you're always busy seeing red, buddy, but that's a chick right there. Maybe take it easy, eh?"

Vaughn was nearly twice Mac's size. Angel could see his shoulders and arms swollen beyond Mac's silhouette. He seemed like he could bite Mac's head right off.

"Get out of the way, MacArthur," Vaughn snarled.

"Look, I'd be annoyed if I got spunked on by a girl too," Mac joked, referring to the milk soaking Vaughn's shirt. "But at least it's not as salty as the last one you got in your mouth."

"You've got a big fucking mouth for a kid your size," Vaughn said, pointing a finger into Mac's face. "You sure you want to keep going down this road?"

"You realize she's the doctor's daughter, right?" Mac asked. "I just want to make sure you're as dumb as I think you are before you go through with this."

Vaughn pushed Mac aside like he was strand of tall grass. Then he looked back at Angel.

"You must really still be pissed that your parents left you, huh?" Mac called after him.

Vaughn spun back toward Mac. "What?" he rumbled.

"I remember you from the orphanage before my grandmother took me," Mac said. "Your parents, they left you, right?"

Vaughn looked around at the other cadets that had gathered. "You shut your mouth."

"Oh, come on," Mac said. "Half the kids here are orphans. Why do you think they bring us here? No visitors, no distractions. We're all theirs, and we're desperate."

"Don't lump me in with you, twerp," Vaughn said.

"Oh, I wouldn't lump you in with me," Mac said. "You're the worst kind of orphan. The kind that doesn't learn anything by the hard times. The kind that doesn't appreciate a good thing when it's offered to you. You still feel entitled even though your own parents didn't want you. To me that's just fucking sad."

Vaughn finally snapped. He drilled Mac three times in the teeth, then threw him to the floor at the feet of the other cadets. They all started roaring. Fights were nothing new. Rivalries were common among them. Nerves were constantly running thin, and anger often boiled over. That was part of the doctor's design, seeing who could make it through the nonsense and still become a good soldier. Vaughn was clearly failing that part of the protocol today.

"C'mon, runt!" Vaughn yelled. "Get up! Let's see you talk with your mouth swollen shut!"

"Be easier than doing it with that jizz in your mouth, sweetheart," Mac muttered, blood dripping down his bruised chin.

Vaughn reached down and grabbed Mac by the shirt. He reared back a fist, readying a massive haymaker. Mac looked over Vaughn's shoulder and smirked.

Kyle grabbed hold of Vaughn's cocked wrist.

"Let him go," Kyle said.

Vaughn pulled against Kyle's grip, but it was like a vice. As big as Vaughn was compared to Mac, Kyle was even bigger than Vaughn. His hand seemed to swallow Vaughn's arm.

"Stay out of it, Griffin," Vaughn said.

"Let him go, and it's over."

Vaughn was shaking with rage. There were people watching. Angel could tell that he didn't want to give in. But he didn't want to lose a fight to Kyle either. And Angel was pretty sure he'd lose.

In the end, Vaughn's pride must have gotten the best of him. He dropped Mac and threw a quick punch at Kyle's jaw. It hit nothing but Kyle's palm, stopping abruptly with a loud crack. The crowd broke into a chorus of awed squalls.

They stood locked there for a moment, trying to burn through each other with vitriolic stares. In Kyle's case it could have been a literal truth, but he restrained himself for the time being. The dense muscles in his forearms quivered, and Angel could hear the bones in Vaughn's hand start to crunch under Kyle's fingers. Vaughn was able to resist for a moment, but eventually he screamed and dropped to his knees.

Finally, Kyle released him. He pivoted and helped Angel back to her feet. He did so very gently, like he was lifting a piece of delicate china. She had no idea how he went from such primal brute force to such deft touch on a whim, but it was impressive. He looked her over, a concerned expression in his ice blue eyes.

"Are you all right?" he asked.

Angel patted the cut on the back of her head. "I think so," she said. "A little bloody."

Kyle looked at the wound. He tilted his head, then blinked, and suddenly she felt the gash on her head weave back together. It hurt at first, like the glow from his eyes was melting her flesh all down into a pool of primordial tissue, but she wanted him to do it anyway. It felt nice to be cared about for once, to be looked after. And it was him, which made it all the better.

Kyle nodded to her, then looked back at Mac propped up on the floor, elbows under his shoulders like he was watching a film. He reached his hand up for Kyle to pull him up.

"Give me a moment," Kyle said to Angel.

He walked past Vaughn, who was doubled over and nursing his injured arm. Vaughn cringed and stumbled away, pushing through the crowd like a wounded rat in search of his hole. Kyle didn't pay him any attention. Instead he pulled Mac off the floor and looked at the cut in his lip. It was deep, and his two front teeth were missing. Kyle's nose wrinkled.

"What?" Mac asked. "I wouldn't look like this if you'd have gotten here sooner."

"If I'd have known you were going to get in a fight, I would have hurried," Kyle replied.

His eyes flashed again and Mac's mouth healed, teeth and all.

"Shit!" Mac yelped. "Warn me the next time you're gonna do that!"

"Next time?" Kyle asked.

"Yeah, we had a deal, didn't we?"

"Oh, so you picked a fight because you knew I'd come save you?"

Mac sighed. "Is that what it looked like?"

Kyle shook his head. "No, actually. It looked like you stuck your neck out to help a good friend of mine. Guess I owe you one."

"Well, you did stop him from kicking my ass," Mac replied. "Maybe we call it even."

"Fair enough," Kyle replied.

The two of them shared a brief smile, then Kyle slapped Mac on the shoulder. They laughed it off, as boys are wont to do in such instances.

Angel huffed at the both of them. "Well, I'm glad you two are having fun." she said bitterly.

Kyle and Mac gave each other a brief glance.

"Actually, that was more fun than what we normally are doing," Kyle replied. "But you've gotta be a little more careful, Angel. Vaughn might be an asshole, but he's a dangerous one."

"More careful?" Angel asked, crossing her arms. "Are you kidding? He came after me!"

"I don't doubt that for a second," Kyle said. "I'm just saying, you need to watch out for yourself."

"All I wanted was to have my breakfast! What's so wrong about that?"

"Nothing, but—"

"You know, not everyone has things as easy as you do, Kyle," she interrupted. "We weren't all born *perfect* like you were."

"Perfect?" Kyle asked. "Look, I never said I was—"

"You don't have to," Angel snapped. "Everyone here thinks it. Makes the rest of us feel like crap." She shook her head. "Thanks for coming down off your pedestal to help me out."

She stormed off through the crowd, leaving Kyle and Mac there stunned in silence.

† † †

Age Fifteen ...

The new instructor was nearly twenty minutes late for the group's morning session. Kyle and the others sat in their desks staring into space, Jay was asleep, and so was Mac, who hadn't even bothered to hide it—he had passed out slouched in his chair with the back of his head resting on the desk behind him. His mouth was yawning open like a dead hog's, and occasionally a sharp snort escaped his throat to match. It made Kyle chuckle, another thing Mac was shockingly astute at.

Kyle jabbed Jackson in the back and flicked his head over at Mac. Jackson seemed unimpressed, as always, but Kyle had a smirk on his face that looked like trouble. He waved his hand at the cup of water sitting on Mac's desk, and the water streamed into the air as if gravity had forgotten it. Kyle's fingers flickered like he was composing a masterpiece on the piano. The water split smoothly into two floating rivers, one trickling over Jay and the other over Mac.

Finally, Jackson chuckled. Or he cleared his throat—Kyle couldn't tell the difference.

His hand waved open and the water splashed down on their dozing friends. Jay jumped right out of his seat like he'd been prodded with an electric baton, a trail of expletives following him. Mac sat up shaking his head, his arms lifted in the air like he was surrendering to some invisible enemy. Kyle erupted into a throaty laugh.

"Really?" Mac asked, water dripping off his freckled nose. "You're the class clown now?"

"Class hasn't started yet, Mac," Kyle replied, gesturing toward the vacant lectern at the head of the room. "Besides, if you're sleeping when they come in, you'll really be in for it."

"Couldn't have just tapped us on the shoulder, huh?" Jay asked.

He scratched at what had turned into a thick, scraggily beard.

"Figured you needed to wash that bush off," Kyle said. "How long's it been since you cleaned that thing?"

Jay shook his head. "You're not supposed to clean it. Keeps it from filling in right."

"Why do they even let you grow that thing?" Jackson wondered. His own trim grooming was very hallmark of the typical military man.

"They know they'd never catch me if they tried to make me get rid of it," Jay said.

Jackson rolled his eyes and went back to staring at the desk in front of him.

"Kyle, you realize this guy is already twenty minutes late?" Mac asked. "How much longer do we have to wait?"

"What else are we going to do, Mac?" Kyle replied.

"Oh, I can think of a thousand other things we could be doing," Mac exclaimed. "Hell, I've got a few things in my pants I could be giving some attention to ..."

Kyle quickly cut him off before that thought got any deeper. "I meant, what else can we do without getting strung up?" he interrupted. "I don't have any plans to get thrown back into the Gauntlet today."

"Is it that much worse than sitting around here like this?" Mac pondered, his head craned back toward the ceiling. "Feel like I'm going brain dead."

"If only," Jay muttered.

"C'mon, Kyle," Mac said. "You've been through it once. How bad was it? Worst day of your life bad?"

Kyle didn't know how to answer. He could see the whole day in front of him like it was still happening. Or rather, the whole two days. In all it took forty-nine hours for them to feel satisfied he had been punished enough. Physically, it was exhausting. But physically, Kyle could also shake that off in less than a day. So when he thought about whether it was the worse day of his life, the answer was a definitive no.

For him, the worst days of his life were the ones that were emotionally draining. The incident at the school. His first day in the program. The day that he was forced to leave his parents. Those were the hardest days he had ever experienced. It had been seven years. Seven years in the program. And he'd only seen his parents a dozen times since. That had been more difficult than enduring the Gauntlet.

"Kyle?" Mac persisted. "You with me?"

Kyle hadn't realized he had drifted off. Finally, Mac's question registered. "Not for me," he responded. "But believe me, it definitely would be for you."

"Oh, so we're gonna be nasty about it, huh?"

"Just trying to make a point. We don't want to get in trouble here."

The door to the classroom opened and a man walked inside carrying a stack of holofiles. He set them down on the lectern and wiped the bridge of his nose.

He was a stout man, heavy around the chest and shoulders, and thicker through the waist than his pants would have preferred. He had a dark beard that was just starting to grey, and eyes that looked tired. There were thick lines over his cheeks, like he hadn't slept in days. Kyle could sympathize. Sleep was a luxury he rarely enjoyed. Luckily, he didn't need much. But this guy, he looked like he'd been running himself ragged.

"Good morning," the man said finally in a hoarse, haggard voice. Then he looked at the clock and realized that the morning had already passed. Lord, this guy was a mess. "I am Major Adams. I'll be your new tactical operations instructor."

No apology for being late, Kyle thought. *This guy looks like a keeper.*

Adams wiped his forehead again. "Class is running a few minutes late. But I think that etiquette calls for some introductions." He pointed to Jay. "Why don't we start with you?"

Jay nodded, then stood up from his desk. "Yes, sir, my name is Jay Harrier. I joined the program as a pilot. I've been here just over two years now."

"Harrier ... Your father left you as a boy, correct? And your mother entered into a relationship with another man soon after, yes?" Adams thumbed through a brief dossier that must have been Jay's personnel folder. "A wealthy planetary developer. Seems like it would be a comfortable life. Why didn't you go with them?"

Jay cleared his throat. "I didn't want to leave my family's farm, sir. It was my home."

"And yet, eventually, the Dominion kicked you out for failing to pay their taxes," Adams said. "Why then come to work for them?"

"Either I did that, or they'd have thrown me in the Palisade," Jay answered. "When I got this offer from the doctor it seemed like a better option."

"Did it? You seem to have had a hard time fitting in. Ten demerits for fighting since you arrived. The most in the program."

Jay's face darkened. In most cases he was quite conscientious, almost reserved with his actions, but when pushed ... well, he seemed to become another animal entirely.

"I don't like to be pressed into corners," he said. "Whether that's by my mother, by the tax collectors, or even by you. It doesn't sit well with me."

"Very well." The major nodded, apparently satisfied with the response. He looked at Mac. "And you?"

Jay squatted back into his seat and Mac stood up, his face still glistening from his unexpected shower.

"My name is James McArthur, sir. But my grandmother always called me Mac, so that's what I prefer."

"I don't give a damn about what you prefer, McArthur," the major said. "Where are you from?"

Kyle could see Mac trying to hide a scowl—and doing a relatively poor job of it. But he managed to swallow whatever smart-ass comment that was brewing in his throat in favor of something more diplomatic.

"Tellura, sir," he replied.

Adams shook his head. "That's where your grandmother used to live, McArthur. At least until she died. What about your parents?"

Mac swallowed. "I don't like talking about my parents, sir. They left me when I was very young."

"I see that. Nine years in the Social Service Division before your grandmother came to get you. That's a long time." He paused, scanning through the holoscreen in front of him. "I see you have your father's aptitude for technology. That's a good thing for a cadet of your size."

"Sir, that's all I have in common with my father," Mac snapped. He was getting riled up, something that Kyle had never seen before. It made Kyle feel uncomfortable for him. "That's all I'd really like to say about them."

"Again, cadet, I don't really care—"

"Sir, can I ask what these questions are all about?" Kyle interrupted. "You have all this information there in your files. Is it necessary to recount all this out loud?"

"I'll get to you in a minute, cadet," the major said, waving Mac back into his seat. He glared at Kyle with eyes that were surprisingly penetrating. They looked intense, purposeful. Where had he seen that sort of look before …?

Before he could pinpoint the look, Adams shifted his gaze to Jackson, who stood up quickly at sharp attention.

"Jackson Hilton, sir," he said. "If you must know, my mother died when I was just a few months old, and my father raised me. He was Fleet officer up until he died about three years ago. That's when I came here."

The major nodded. "You see, that's how to introduce yourself. Have a seat, cadet."

Adams flipped open the last holofile. He looked at it briefly, then closed it without another word. The look on his face seemed like disinterest. It wasn't a reaction Kyle received often, and it had him curious.

"Sir?" Kyle said, standing from his chair. "You don't want to hear my story?"

"Quite the opposite, Griffin," Adams said. "I already know your story. As does everyone else. No need to recount it again here. Have a seat."

Kyle remained standing. "Sir, I don't understand. What point does all this serve?"

"I have my reasons. Now take your seat."

"Sir, I think these cadets deserve an explanation," Kyle insisted. "Those memories are difficult enough without having them thrown back in their faces."

The major dropped the holofiles on the table beside him. He leered at Kyle, running his tongue over the edges of his teeth like he was tasting blood.

"Fine," Adams said. "Sometimes I prefer to know how a cadet handles the worst moments of their life. It lets me know what kind of soldier they can be. Because being a soldier is all about dealing with loss and tragedy. That's inevitable. It's all about how they handle those trying moments. That's what I wanted to know."

Kyle sighed. "Then why not ask me?"

"Because your family is still alive," the major said. "You haven't lost anything yet."

Kyle fought back a growl. What did this fool know about loss? About what he'd gone through? Not a damn thing.

However, before he could talk himself into storming out, Jackson turned in his chair and shifted his eyes toward Kyle's seat. Mac and Jay did the same. Their point was pretty clear: don't take this down that road. They were right. The harassment wasn't worth him getting punished over.

Finally, Kyle relented and took his seat, albeit begrudgingly. The major quickly went back to the material at hand. Just like that, like nothing else had happened.

"Very well, then, we can get started," Adams said. "I understand that this is supposed to be a tactics class, but I also know that you've had plenty of that already." He wiped his forehead again. "So instead, today I'm going to show you some still frames of what happens in combat with the Splinter. I want you to understand that motivation is what drives us. There's a difference between fighting for a crown and fighting for a cause.

"I already know that you'll all be capable soldiers. You would be if we sent you out there today. But you can only be great if you believe in what you're fighting for. So pay attention, and maybe you'll get a feel for what real war is like. Any objections?"

There weren't any. Probably because the four of them thought that they'd seen these types of images before. And to an extent, they were right. But they were not prepared for what the major showed them that day. It was hard to believe that anyone could be.

The first image was a still-frame of a market on a commercial street. The front of the shop had erupted from the inside out, leaving a stream of debris that spewed across the street. But that wasn't the troubling part. A family had gotten caught in the path of the blast. There were pieces of those poor people spread across some two hundred square meters of asphalt.

"This was one of their food raids," Adams said, gesturing to the image. "They came in the rear doors and were caught by the man who runs the store. When the Garrison arrived, they ignited the heating elements, and this was the result. Twelve people died here, including those three children."

The next slide was a view of a large park, mostly grass with a picturesque lake in the distance. In between was a sandy beach littered with people, but that wasn't the obvious feature. Buried into the edge of the surf was a mid-sized Splinter transport, smoking from a pair of plasma blasts in its hull. It had hit like a meteor, and no one on the beach had survived.

"This was one of their scout ships caught after stealing medicine from a nearby pharmaceuticals manufacturer," Adams said. "One of our fleet ships was able to catch them, but this was the result. Sixty-five people dead."

He zoomed in on the edge of the crash site. Then again twice more to show the face of a young boy, probably no older than twelve, screaming in pain. His legs had been charred into blackened stumps all the way up to his waist. The blood trailing behind him was bright against the black dirt. It looked almost like it was glowing in the haze of smoke emanating from the crash.

"This boy was found on the scene," the Major continued. "The medics did what they could to save him."

Adams flipped to the next slide, which was a close-up of the boy's mangled limbs. They looked like ground meat with chunks of dirt clogging the open wounds. The picture captured just enough of his face to see the vacant expression of death clutching him. Jay gagged.

"Unfortunately he was beyond our help."

The third file was a video. It showed a building raging in an inferno. The screams coming from inside and around the structure made Kyle's mutant ears ring. The horror deepened when he realized that the building was a school, and the screams were those of children. Children being burned alive.

"This school was caught in a dogfight between some of our Predator starfighters and their Atlas wingships. The loss here was nearly two thousand. That's two thousand children. All dead."

Adams turned up the sound. The screams seemed to shake the walls.

This went on for an hour. Dozens of other atrocities flashed on the screen. More death. More destruction. It was like they wanted them to throw up all over the classroom. But for some reason, it all seemed odd to Kyle. Clearly, they wanted them to hate the Splinter. And that wasn't hard. The stories told of their unrepentant crime was known all through the Dominion. But this … this seemed like overkill.

"Sir, may I ask you something?" Kyle asked when it was over.

"You need more explanation than what I've just given?" Adams retorted.

"Yes, sir, I do. Can you show us the third slide again?"

"You want to see the video of the school again?" the major demanded, his bushy eyebrows lifting toward the ceiling.

"Kyle, c'mon, don't make us watch that again," Jay pleaded.

"I just need to see something," Kyle said. "It'll just take a second. If you would, sir?"

The major pursed his lips but honored the request. The video flashed back on the screen. The carnage was just as horrifying the second time. But Kyle watched it intently, waiting just until the camera panned out and a view of the grounds became visible.

"There!" Kyle hollered. "Sir, can you pause it there?"

The major stopped the scene as requested. "This is what you wanted to see?"

"Yes, sir. Those scorch marks … the ones surrounding the school. They're characteristic of therite plasma. It burns so hot that it turns the dirt to glass."

"What's your point, son?" the instructor asked.

"Sir, it's my understanding that therite plasma is only used in Dominion starfire missiles," Kyle said. "The Splinter doesn't have that type of weaponry."

The major shook his head. "What are you suggesting, Griffin?"

"I'm not sure I want to say, sir."

Adams crossed his arms, glaring at the young cadet in front of him. "Yes, you do."

Jackson turned and shook his head. What he was about to say could be treasonous. But Kyle wasn't afraid of that. He knew what he was worth to them. And he knew that something there wasn't right.

"The Splinter couldn't have done that," Kyle said. "That was done by one of our weapons."

A smirk flickered across the major's face. "This is exactly what the Splinter does, Griffin. They incite this chaos by living outside our laws. Do you really think that this school would have been hit by one of our weapons if they hadn't provoked us into battle there?"

"But why fight them there, sir? What did they do on that day that we had to fight them there?"

"I don't think you should be asking these questions, cadet." the Major said.

"It's just curious, sir," Kyle continued, ignoring the suggestion. "The Splinter doesn't chase supplies with their Atlas ships. They've only been documented as their advanced defense. So what were they doing with those ships out near a school in a crowded Dominion city?"

Adams sighed. If he had an answer, he wasn't sharing.

"The rest of you are dismissed," he said. "Griffin, you'll have to stay behind. There are some things we need to discuss."

Mac and the others filed out. They gave their friend some distressed looks, but Kyle didn't feel any concern. He gave them a firm nod, the edges of his mouth turning up ever so slightly. Jackson, ever the pundit, rolled his eyes at Kyle's indifference, but Kyle knew what he was doing.

At least he hoped he did.

Adams stepped in front of the desk at the head of the room. He leaned back against it, and crossed his arms again. Kyle could see the muscle still bulging on the man's forearms. He had clearly been an infantryman. What he had done to earn this appointment as an instructor here must have been impressive. But that wasn't what Kyle wanted to know about at the moment.

"This is a troubling line of questions—you understand that, don't you?" the major started.

"I know how it must sound. But you have to admit, they're legitimate."

"I don't have to admit anything. And you'd better be careful with your tone. I could already send you to the Palisade with what you've intimated here this morning."

"I know that," Kyle conceded. "And I would think most instructors would have sent me to the Gauntlet by now, at the least. But you haven't. And I think that's interesting."

"If you're questioning my resolve, cadet, I think you'd better reconsider."

"No, no, it's not your resolve I'm questioning. It's you in general."

The major paused, confused. "You'd best explain yourself, cadet."

"You said your name was Major Adams?" Kyle asked, like his memory needed refreshing.

The major's eyes narrowed. "That's correct."

Kyle smirked. "See, *that's* what's interesting to me. Because the pin tag just above your hip says 'Foster.'"

The major's eyes darted down to the tiny ID tag on the seam of his pants. It couldn't have been wider than the blade of a knife, but Kyle could still see it from across the room.

"See, Foster is a familiar name to me," Kyle continued. "It's my mother's maiden name. And she had a brother who was an infantryman …"

"And what? You think I'm somehow this missing uncle of yours?"

"I didn't say that," Kyle said. "Also didn't say he was missing."

The major didn't have a reply. That was all the confirmation that Kyle needed.

"Where the hell have you been?" Kyle asked.

The major sighed, but he didn't look disappointed. He looked proud.

"I was an infantryman, like you said," he answered. "I never had a choice about where I went. By the time I got into officer's training, you had already been sent here."

"What are you doing here?" Kyle asked.

"Your mother asked me to keep an eye on you." Foster's voice had lost some of the raspiness, like he'd cleared his throat of some obstruction. "It took me seven years to get appointed here. I'm just here to help you."

Kyle stood up from his desk. "I don't need your help."

"Oh yes, you do," Foster insisted. "And you know it. You miss your family. It drives you mad not seeing them, you're not hiding that. You need that connection here. I can give that to you."

"You're not my family," Kyle replied. "I've never even met you before."

Foster nodded. "That's fair. I wasn't there. I wish I could have been. It just wasn't something I could do. But I'm here now. I'm here now because your mother couldn't be."

Kyle marched toward the door, but Foster blocked the way.

"The only reason I'm not throwing you aside is because you're an officer and it might get me sent to the Palisade," Kyle said.

"Fine," Foster said. "Hate me all you want. But your mother wanted me here." He paused, letting that sink in to Kyle's thick, stubborn skull. "I'd think for her you'd give me a chance."

Kyle snarled impulsively and looked up at the ceiling. It wasn't often he'd acquiesce to anyone, but for his mother he'd do just about anything.

He nodded slowly and reluctantly. "For her," Kyle said. "What's your real name, by the way?"

"Bryan," the Major said. "My name is Bryan Foster."

† † †

Age Sixteen ...

Kyle could hear something creaking. At first he wasn't certain it was real, but it slowly became clearer, even over the crashing of waves against the side of the diving platform. The ocean winds were strong and blustery, whistling past the two tall surveillance towers, but in between those gusts he could still hear it. It was a metallic sound that he couldn't quite place, so he paused to listen.

That was when Mac suddenly shoved his diving helmet into Kyle's gut. Kyle looked down at his friend. He was climbing out of a submersible dangling over the edge of the platform some three hundred feet above the crashing waves. Kyle couldn't help but chuckle at how ridiculous Mac looked in his diving suit. He had actually sprouted quite a bit over the last year, so he wasn't as short as when they first met, but now he was even thinner. It was like he'd turned into a string of pasta that was stretched to the point of breaking. They couldn't even find a diving suit that fit him right. It was supposed to be form-fitting to cut down on resistance in the water, but with his pencil-thin arms it still hung off him like a robe. The whole thing had broken Kyle's concentration, but then again that seemed to be Mac's point.

"Hey, you forgot this," Mac said, gulping in air. The highly pressurized air in the deep was hard on human lungs. Something Kyle knew nothing about.

"Yeah, great, thanks," Kyle replied, glancing around again for the source of the noise. "Always forget about this useless thing."

Mac rolled his eyes and reached a hand up from the ladder. Kyle yanked him onto the platform like he was pulling a weed. Mac may have grown tall and lean, but he was still light as a wisp. It was a sharp, stark contrast from Kyle's swollen, brutish frame. It still shocked Kyle how Mac's enormous brain was able to squeeze into such a rail-thin body. What amazed him even more was how the stifling depths they just traversed in a metal can didn't somehow crush the redhead like a sheet of tinfoil. Kyle's body seemed built to bear it. But the others … well, there's a reason humans live on land.

"Must be nice not having to breathe," Mac said, water dripping off his red hair. "If only we were all so lucky."

"It's only nice when you're not forced wear this shit anyway," Kyle replied. "It's a distraction."

"Yeah, well, it seems a bit helpful for the rest of us," Mac said. He looked up at the other submersible, which was suspended by two high-tension wires just above the platform. "I don't envy Jay and Jackson having to go down now that those swells that are coming in. That shit would even make *you* sick."

Sick. Right. Once his body mastered the Spark, Kyle had never been sick, despite what he had told the doctor in the past. He'd done that to get close to Angel. And it had worked. Even though he had Mac, she was his best friend. So he thought the lies were worth it. After eight years in the program, with all the curriculum and protocols formulated to force him to become what they wanted, if that relationship was all he could claim as his own, then it made that friendship all the more valuable.

It started raining on the deck, a harsh spray that came slinging in sideways on the back of the wind. They were cold, and the water was thick and heavy, like pudding instead of liquid. Kyle squinted against the raindrops while Mac braced himself like they were going to blow him over.

The planet they had traveled to was covered in ocean, both deep and dark. It was called Aquariate, a giant ball of water floating through a dim star system in the middle of the Perseus Arm of the galaxy. Wind and rain were a constant here. It was one of those places that seemed too harsh for humans to withstand. But that's what made it the perfect place to train the Infinity recruits. After all, it was going to be their job to go where ordinary people couldn't.

Bryan Foster came clambering up the ladder behind them. His long hair was soaked and streaming down over his bearded cheeks.

"Gentlemen," he said in his ever-formal tone. "Get your gear and step inside, please. The next submersible is preparing for launch."

Kyle and Mac nodded. The rain was picking up, and splashing, slopping water layered over the waves and the wind. But Kyle could still swear he heard something creaking. He just couldn't figure out what.

"Fuck me, this is brutal," Mac said. "The major's got the right idea. Let's get out of this mess."

"I'm with you there," Kyle said. Bryan and the four technicians from their submersible were already scampering toward the tower doors. Kyle nodded Mac in that direction. "C'mon."

Mac stepped past him, and Kyle followed. He took only a few steps before he stopped again. The creaking was getting louder.

Mac turned back to him. "Hey! What are you doing?"

"Do you hear that?" Kyle asked.

"Hear what?" Mac hollered back.

"Something is creaking," Kyle replied, shutting his eyes and listening intently.

"Yeah, it's my fucking bones! C'mon, we're gonna get collared for standing out here!"

"Just give me a second. This doesn't sound right."

Mac shook his head. He didn't want to give their commanding officers an excuse to come down on them. But Kyle was being stubborn, following his own devices, as usual. Barely a moment later, a voice boomed over the speakers. It was Dr. Preston.

"Alpha team, get your asses off the deck! We can't launch Bravo team's submersible until you've cleared the platform."

Kyle looked up. Finally, he saw what he was looking for. The aft wire that was holding up the other submersible was fraying in the wind. The creaking was its desperate cry for relief. And that relief would come one way or another.

The cable snapped and the submersible swung downward, slamming its hull against the side of the deck. The whole structure shook, throwing Mac flat on his back. Kyle grabbed hold of his friend, but he never took his eyes off the swaying ship. It wriggled on the line like a hooked fish for a moment, until the second cable gave way as well. It plummeted downward, bursting into the water a hundred meters below.

Kyle rushed to the edge, his toes jutting over the precipice. He caught a glimpse of the ship as the sea swallowed it whole, sinking into the blackened depths. He could hear the voices of the men inside, each screaming for help as they spiraled deeper.

The hull had to have been damaged by the impact with the platform. They'd be taking on water. Once the pressure became too great, the whole thing would implode.

Kyle was breathing fast. He could still make out Jay and Jackson's cries even as the water grew deeper around them. Mac was stupefied as he stood next to him, chanting "Oh my god, oh my god" over and over. There was no denying it. Their friends were going to die.

"Griffin, MacArthur, get away from the edge!" Dr. Preston ordered. "Get inside now—double time it!"

Kyle looked up at the tower. His eyes were thin as reeds, his mouth clamped tight. He shook his head once, then leapt over the edge.

He went rigid as his feet hit the water, and his body knifed through the swells. He kicked his feet hard, propelling himself like a meteor through the frigid depths. He could see the submersible among the black backdrop. The thick water was slowing it, but somehow it couldn't slow him.

Huge orbs of air were escaping through a plate-sized split in the hull as he approached. It was like swimming through sludge, and it made his descent seem interminable. Finally he grabbed hold of the latch next to the door. Through the small porthole he saw his friends, neck deep in the invading water. Seeing him shocked them out of their panic, enough so that they could focus on his face outside the hatch. Two of the technicians floated limply, a cloud of red blood fanning out in the water around them.

Kyle pointed to his head, signaling them to put on their helmets. They nodded and did as he asked. He grabbed the door by the hinges, bracing his foot against the hull. With one heave the hatch burst loose, and the ship lurched suddenly downward. Jay and Jackson swam out, followed by the other two techs. Once they were clear, Kyle reached inside the vessel and grabbed the two unconscious men before starting upward.

When he broke the surface, Jay and Jackson had already found the ladder on one of the support columns. They helped the technicians out of the water and let them climb up first. In the light of the platform Kyle could see the wounds of the two men in his arms, and they were fatal. Both were dead already, their faces vacant and pale. It made Kyle's stomach ripple. It made him dizzy. For a moment he wasn't sure what to do. He just floated there with them, churning in the harsh sea.

Jackson called to him, asking him to bring them to the ladder. It wasn't much, but it broke his trance.

Once he was back on the platform, Garrison soldiers took the bodies. Mac led Jay and Jackson into the tower for examination. But Kyle just stood there, watching the soldiers drag the slain men toward the doors. In all honesty, Kyle half-expected them to just throw them overboard again. It would be cleaner that way. Less paperwork, he assumed. But they didn't do that. At least not while he was watching.

The rain was still coming down, though he didn't seem to notice it. He'd never held someone while they died before. He knew that someday he'd be sent in to combat, and he'd witness death. That he'd have to kill. But he wasn't expecting to see it today. It hit him harder than one of the waves.

Eventually, another Garrison soldier grabbed him by the shoulder. "Griffin, the doctor wants you front and center," he said.

Kyle nodded, but his feet didn't want to move.

"*Now*, cadet."

Kyle dragged his feet the whole way. He could feel what was coming. Bryan walked past him in the hall, barely managing a nod. He'd really stepped in something this time. And the look on Doctor Preston's face when he walked into the control room confirmed those suspicions. He was not pleased.

"Shut the door," Preston said immediately.

Kyle did as he was told. Then he stood at attention, stiff and tight.

Preston considered him for a moment. "What did I tell you, Griffin? What were the words that came out of my mouth while you were standing on the platform?"

"Sir, you told me to get inside," Kyle answered.

"Did you think that was a suggestion, son, or an order?"

"Sir, I believed it was an order," Kyle said. "But the others—"

"I'm not interested in your excuses, Griffin. They don't mean a damn thing to me. What I *am* interested in is knowing that you can follow a command when the command is given to you. Is that something you can do?"

Kyle nodded. "Yes, sir. Of course."

The doctor pursed his lips and shook his head. "I wish I could believe you," he said, stepping from behind a large desk. "But I don't. This has become a pattern with you, son. You seem to have it stuck in your head that you know better than me. You admit you knew that was a direct order, and yet you ignored it anyway. You know what the punishment is for that, correct?"

Kyle nodded again. The Gauntlet. He'd lived through it once before, but those sent in for insubordination hadn't always been so lucky. The designers tended to find ways to intensify the torture when it suited them, and if it didn't kill the recruit, it would certainly ensure that they couldn't continue in the program. That's what he stood to face right now.

"Do you think you deserve that punishment?" Dr. Preston asked.

"No, sir."

"Then perhaps you think you deserve special considerations because you have royal blood?"

Kyle shook his head. "No, sir. I don't want that."

"Then what is it, Griffin? Why is it that you think your actions are above our rules?"

Kyle was silent. He didn't have an answer. At least not one that the doctor would want to hear.

"*Answer me!*" Preston roared.

Kyle's eyes snapped wide open. The frustration was boiling into his throat. His teeth were clamped down tight. That familiar rage was building behind his eyes. He really didn't know if he could keep the composure he needed.

"Sir, those men would have died. My friends would have died if I didn't do something. Is that what you wanted me to let happen?"

"I wanted you to follow orders!" Preston thundered. "You've been here for seven years. You still don't seem to understand that's what this is all about. No one doubts your physical gifts. If I threw you into combat tomorrow, you wouldn't last a day because you haven't learned to listen."

Kyle swallowed hard. "Sir ..." he trailed off for a moment, debating whether to continue. Then he threw that caution aside. "Sir, I thought I was doing the right thing."

The doctor drew in a deep breath. He took three steps forward and leaned in close to his protégé, his lips peeling into a toothy snarl back before he spoke.

"You listen to me now, Griffin," he sneered. His voice was so sharp Kyle felt like it was going to burn his ears. "You are not a hero. You're a soldier. What you do, it's not noble. It's your duty. Either you do what you are told or you will be punished. Does that register with you?"

Kyle nodded.

"Good. Because if you continue to ignore my rules, to follow whatever whims you find appealing ... I don't care what blood runs in those mutant veins of yours. You will beg us for death before the end. Does that put us on the same wavelength?"

Kyle finally broke his rigid gaze, shifting his eyes toward the doctor. The heat of a burning sun blazed in them, aching to be released. Yearning to give in to that killing instinct that had lived beneath the surface for so long. But his will was still just strong enough. He bottled it up again to let it fester for another day.

"Will that be all, sir?" Kyle asked.

The doctor stepped back, perhaps seeing the cauldron brewing in Kyle's face. It may have been the first time Kyle realized he could kill someone. Physically, he always knew he was powerful enough. But emotionally ... well, today he finally felt ready to do it. Ready to take a life. He realized it wouldn't drown him in guilt. And he had Dr. Preston to thank for that.

"Get out of my sight," the doctor replied. "You're dismissed."

† † †

Age Seventeen ...

Kyle burst out of the arena, through the locked gates barricaded with thick iron bars. They shattered under his flaming blue fist. The two heavy portcullises tumbled against the far wall, dented and singed, before finally thumping down into a heap.

He stumbled out into the hall, drenched in sweat and shaking. He found nothing but frightened faces waiting for him, people with looks of sheer terror as his hands burned with bright blue light. Their fear was all too familiar.

He looked back into the arena and saw the dead mutant. Its bloody, beaten body lay on the metal floor. A steady stream of green blood oozed out from beneath it. The sight made Kyle's breath quicken. Suddenly his inhuman lungs couldn't work fast enough. He rifled in gulps of air so rapidly he started feeling dizzy. His hands started to cramp. There was tingling in his toes and he thought he might pass out.

He slumped against the wall next to the toppled gates, pressing his back into the cool metal to calm his nerves. It wasn't easy. Every time he blinked the fight flashed in front of his eyes. He could see the beast towering over him, easily reaching fifteen feet tall when it reared back on its haunches. It was covered in thick, razor-sharp fur, the hairs on its neck standing on end like the mane of a lion. It roared down at Kyle, the stench of its bitter, rotten breath washing over him. Kyle tightened his fists, a snarl curling over his face, and then he charged forward.

Kyle's eyes opened when he realized he was hyperventilating again. Instinctively he held his breath, looking around for anything to focus on. Immediately he knew it was a mistake. The hallway was full, and all eyes were on him. The stricken looks of shock and horror were all too familiar. He was the spectacle again. He was the *freak*.

He felt like a seven-year-old boy again, the boy who nearly destroyed his school with a power that he couldn't control. He looked down at his powerful hands, both awash with blue Celestial flame. He had to get out. He had to get out now.

He stumbled down the hall, his vision blurred. He felt his fists pounding into the beast's ribs, his heels pummeling into its abdomen, and his knee crunching against its chin. He could feel his teeth grinding in anger as he released those lethal blows. His wrath had finally poured out in a burst of his unmatched raw physicality. The dam burst on his reservoir of Celestial power, and he piled all of it into a skull-crushing hammer. The walls shook and the floor quaked. The mutant never stood a chance.

The beast's blood splattered up around his ears. The sound of the killing blow echoed inside his head. It made him feel like he would vomit.

Finally he stepped into a rut in the rock-filled ravine outside the east entrance to the compound. He fell onto his stomach, the sudden jolt shocking him out of his memory and back to reality. Tears dripped from his eyes. He tried begging for forgiveness, but the blood on his hands was too real. And there was no one to hear his pleas anyway.

But then a hand fell on his shoulder. It startled him, and he instinctively snatched the person's wrist so quickly he barely noticed himself move. His fingers squeezed tight, the peak of his rage still fresh in his mind. The bones creaked like the wood of a carrack in a storm, waiting for Kyle to crush them to powder. And he would have, until he saw who it was.

It was Bryan.

"Kyle … " Bryan said, his knees buckling beneath him. "Kyle, it's all right. It's all right. It's just me."

Kyle's breath finally slowed. Seeing his uncle focused his eyes, dragging the visions of his brutal fight with the mutant away from his vision. He started to notice the tears drying on his cheeks. He relaxed his grip and Bryan cautiously pulled his hand back, cradling it against his chest. He nodded at his nephew, and Kyle managed to return the gesture.

Kyle turned and sat down on the rocks, pulling his knees to his chest. He stared out over the ravine, feeling as though he'd lost yet another piece of himself in the arena today. Taking a life was a line he had previously avoided crossing. He was always afraid that once he took that step he would never look back. However, Preston had described the need for it very concisely—for what he was meant to be, he couldn't afford hesitation. This was meant to teach him that decisiveness. It was to be his final test. He supposed that he had passed.

"You did well, Kyle," Bryan said. "Exceptionally well, actually."

"Don't tell me that."

"Why? It's what you should hear. What you did in there today … it was unbelievable."

"I don't want to hear that," Kyle said. His eyes were locked straight forward.

"Kyle, listen to me," Bryan said. "You didn't do anything wrong. It was what you were asked to do. There's no shame in that."

"I killed that mutant," Kyle said, his expression blank. "That's what I'm ashamed of."

"It was just a Fury mutant. A mindless brute. You practically did it a favor."

"Doesn't matter what it was. It's dead because of me. I don't think I was ready for that."

"Yes, you are," Bryan said. "You're an incredible soldier, Kyle. The best I've ever seen. What you just did … killing a Fury foot soldier, with your bare hands, no less … no human has ever done that before."

Kyle's eyes wandered slowly over to his uncle. "That's because I'm not human."

"Oh, don't do that to yourself. You are what you are. And you have a gift, there's no doubting that. A gift that you could do amazing things with, if you choose to."

"But why?" Kyle demanded. "Why me? Why do I have this? Why didn't it kill me like all the others?" More streaks of tears were trickling down his cheeks.

Bryan shook his head, letting out a deep sigh. "I don't know, Kyle. I wish I did. I wish I could tell you. But I can't. All I know is that you can do things no one else can do. You could change the entire war with a wave of your hand if you wanted to. That's the gift you were given."

"I … I don't want it."

"I don't think you have much choice about that," Bryan said.

Kyle buried his head into his hands, and the tears came relentlessly. He couldn't stop them, and he wasn't sure he wanted to. At that moment he felt that his emotions were all he had left that made him human.

"Kyle, you have to understand what you mean to all these people here. They are counting on you to be everything you appear to be. Think of the friends you've made here. Do you think it matters to them where these powers of yours came from? Whether it was a brilliant genetic mistake or a touch from the hand of God himself, it makes no difference. It's only what you choose to do with it that matters."

Kyle pulled his face out of his palms. He looked over at his uncle. Bryan's face was sincere, a look he rarely saw from the others in command at the program. Everything they did was meant to deceive, to manipulate them into doing their bidding by playing on their insecurities. But thankfully his uncle was different. He seemed to want Kyle and his team to recognize their own worth and to fulfill it because it was what they wanted, not simply because it was their duty.

"A touch from the hand of *God*?" Kyle repeated. "I thought you believed that the Gentry was god?"

Bryan's his lips curled. "I … well, I believe he's powerful. That's what I believe."

Kyle wiped the salty trails from his cheeks. "Yeah," he said. "I don't believe it either."

† † †

Age Eighteen …

Kyle knew something was wrong as soon as the third team boarded the helio for evac. The barely concealed panic on their faces said it all. Except Vaughn. He looked the same as he always did.

The installation they had infiltrated was a known Splinter intelligence platform with several confirmed spies working out of its operating center. The Infinity Force had sent three teams into the compound, each with a different directive. Jackson led a group to disable their security manifold. Kyle took Mac and two other technicians to secure the intelligence server. And Vaughn's team was sent to run interference to allow the other teams to do their work. This was their first real mission, a live-fire, real-world exercise meant to prove their readiness to perform as a tactical unit—and it did not go according to plan.

Somewhere between their drop-off and the security systems going dark, Vaughn's team suddenly went hot. They opened fire in the courtyard, killing six Splinter troops and losing two of their own in the process. It was meant to be a stealth operation, with no engaging except as a last-ditch, life-or-death resort. Kyle was certain they hadn't tripped any surveillance equipment. He knew they hadn't been seen. Jackson guaranteed him as much. But somehow things went south anyway. Now there were men dead, and someone would have to pay the price for it.

Jay was with Vaughn when the fighting broke out, and all he could do was shake his head. Kyle shrugged at him, looking an elaboration, but Jay simply continued to shake his head. There was blood on his uniform. Bloody fingerprints on his collar. He'd held one of the two fallen Infinity men as he died. He'd probably taken one or more lives himself, and it had him out of sorts.

Vaughn climbed on board last, spiking his weapon into the cache at the back of the helio. Kyle quickly pointed him into his seat.

"What the hell happened?" Kyle demanded.

Vaughn was all sneer, but no answers. Kyle squatted down in front of him and repeated the question.

"Donovan, you gotta tell me what happened," Kyle insisted.

"We were compromised, that's what happened!" Vaughn shouted. "We did what we had to do to get out of there!"

"You gotta give me more than that," Kyle said. "I need to know exactly what went down."

Vaughn looked up at him with a snarl. "Go fuck yourself, Griffin," he grumbled. "You'll get my report at the hearing."

Kyle grunted. Vaughn was up to something, that much he was certain of. But he couldn't be sure what. And in all honesty, at that point all he cared about was getting the rest of the team back safely. With all of them on board he could finally do that.

"Fine, if that's how you want to play it," Kyle said, rising back to his feet. "I'll see you at the hearing." He turned to the helio pilot and spun a finger in a circle. "Let's go. RTB."

† † †

The next day …

The hearing was just over eighteen hours later, in a cramped room with two Dominion generals, Dr. Preston, and the deputy chief of intelligence standing at the front. Kyle and Vaughn stood in front of the panel, both as stern as they could be. Kyle had rarely ever put on a formal military uniform, mostly because he hated it. It was stiff and restrictive, like it was trying to put him in shackles. It was just another reason to despise Vaughn and this farce he was pedaling. And that's what Kyle believed this was: a farce. He believed that he would be vindicated quickly, and they could go on with their lives. If life was fair, that's how it would go.

Jackson, Jay, Mac and the rest of their infiltration unit were seated behind them, awaiting their turn to be questioned. Bryan was settled against the back wall as well, and Kyle was grateful for the presence of his uncle, who had actively in their corner ever since joining the program. He always said that he saw what they could become, and he pushed them toward that goal in a way that made them want to work for it.

However, it did strike Kyle as odd that he hadn't stepped forward here. They had never been in a debriefing with this many high-ranking officials before, and he'd thought his uncle would help to cushion that awkwardness. He didn't. And that made Kyle curious.

Vaughn had a pompous, nose-in-the-air look on his face. It made Kyle hot just looking at it. In a perfect world he could just take the three minutes it would require to wipe that smirk off his face, but in the real world he had to wait for the process to play out. He knew that Vaughn was likely to try something devious, especially with their graduation and commission just a few days away. If Vaughn wanted to make some move to be deemed commander, this was likely his last chance.

"You both know why we're here," Dr. Preston began. "We've gotten conflicting reports from the two of you about what happened yesterday."

Kyle tilted his head. "Conflicting reports? Sir, I wasn't aware of that."

"Well, your logs are exactly the same, up until when the Charlie team led by Cadet Donovan engaged hostiles at plus sixteen minutes. His report claims that your Alpha team triggered an alert, and they acted in turn to salvage their position. What do you have to say about that?"

Kyle looked over at Vaughn, whose gaze remained forward. So that was his play. Compromise the mission and try to lay it at his feet. He should have seen this coming.

"It's a lie, sir," Kyle insisted. "There was no such alert."

General Liang shook his head. "We have it right here on the surveillance log," he said. "At plus sixteen oh-four, a security alarm was tripped via motion sensor at the Alpha team's position. The gunfire started shortly after. How do you explain that, Griffin?"

Kyle shook his head, uncertain of how to respond. "Sir, I was assured by our surveillance team that no alarm had been tripped. Perhaps they can corroborate that."

The doctor leered over Kyle's shoulder toward Jackson, who stood from his seat.

"Sir, I can confirm that from our end," Jackson replied. "There was no alarm."

"If that were the case, Cadet, how do you explain the presence of it in your own operations log?" General Liang pressed. "I see it right here, plain as day."

Jackson's eyebrows went toward the ceiling. "Sir, I don't know what to say about that," he replied. "Unless someone has tampered with my report."

Dr. Preston grunted. The other officers looked equally displeased. Deputy Chief Vikander whispered something in the doctor's ear that even Kyle couldn't hear. It was muffled somehow by something he held in his hand, some kind of dampener. Kyle felt things turning on him and his friends. They didn't believe him, and why would they? The evidence in their hands told them what had happened, even if it wasn't the truth. That son of a bitch had them backed into a corner.

"Griffin, I expected more than this from you," Dr. Preston said.

"Sir, wait," Kyle said. "You think we made the mistake and tried to cover it up. But I am telling you that is not the case. Donovan is trying to dupe you into awarding him the commander's role. He's trying to frame us. I promise you, sir. I would not lie to you."

"Like you wouldn't lie to me about being sick seven years ago, Griffin?" the doctor asked. "Like you wouldn't lie to me about watching my daughter lose my officer's ring all those years ago? This reeks of you simply trying to save your own hide."

Kyle was stupefied. Preston had known all along. But of course he did. He was a spy after all. He was *the* spy. That's why he was in charge of this program. Because he knew these things. But Kyle was still telling the truth, and there had to be a way to prove it.

"Sir …" Kyle started, scouring his memory for answers. "Sir, Jay Harrier was with Charlie team when the gunfire broke out. Perhaps he can vouch for our statements."

Jay stood from his seat. "Sir, things happened very fast," he said. "I don't recall hearing the alarm before the first volley went off. Once the gunfire started, I'm afraid I can't tell you what happened when."

Kyle looked over his shoulder at his friend. Jay's face was painfully apologetic.

"I'm sorry, Kyle," he said. "I just don't remember."

Jay had spent a week in the psychiatric ward after the event. Killing those men, and losing two of theirs, had hit him hard. He refused to speak about it. Kyle could see the truth in his friend's face—Jay was just too traumatized to remember. But that didn't help his cause. So he went back to his own memory for the answer. He scoured it for something, anything else. Like flipping through a catalog, he saw it.

"Sir, you said that the alarm was plus sixteen into the mission, yes?" Kyle asked.

"That's correct," Dr. Preston confirmed.

"I can prove to you that the first gunshot went off before that," Kyle announced. "Would that convince you that it was not us that set off the alarm?"

"How can you possibly prove that?" Dr. Preston asked.

"Each one of the rounds we were issued was time-stamped. Check those logs—I guarantee that the stamp of the first round is before plus sixteen."

The officers on the panel were shaking their heads. They didn't seem to know what Kyle was talking about.

"Griffin, what in the hell are you talking about?" General Mirotic asked. "We haven't used that marker in decades."

"They're still in place, General," Kyle said. "I'm certain of it."

Vaughn suddenly was brought back to life. He leaned forward to voice his disapproval. "Sir, you can't really be listening to this nonsense, can you?" he protested.

"We're listening to anything that is relevant, Donovan," Dr. Preston said.

"How desperate must he be?" Vaughn continued. "Those markers don't exist anymore."

"They do exist," Kyle insisted. "They were noted in our pre-flight briefing. In the footnotes, slide ninety-two, two lines down. If you look at it, you'll see that it's there."

General Liang thumbed his way through the holographic interface, looking for slide ninety-two. Kyle could tell the moment that he saw it.

"You see?" Kyle asked. "Those markers are still in effect for training missions like this one. Those logs are still kept. Check the time. It will be before plus sixteen, I promise you."

Again the old men went through their docket, mumbling to each other for several moments. Kyle could feel Vaughn start to squirm next to him. His best-laid plans were starting to crumble in front of him, and there wasn't a damn thing he could do about it.

Finally, after a few painstaking moments, Deputy Chief Vikander lifted his head. "It appears that Cadet Griffin is correct," he said. "Plus fifteen the first round went off, from Vaughn Donovan's weapon."

Now Dr. Preston's face had turned a scarlet to match Vaughn's. "You tried to deceive this review board and falsely acquire a commissioned post, Donovan" he said, his voice low and ominous. "This is an egregious offense. I will have to confer with the deputy chief to decide your punishment, but you had best believe that it will be severe."

Vaughn suddenly broke into a fit, shouting like a man-possessed. "This is outrageous!" he rumbled. "These numbers don't prove anything! You're really going to let an outdated technology be the deciding factor here? What kind of discretion is that?"

"Cadet, watch your tone," Preston warned.

"Sir, you're letting him dictate the terms here!" Vaughn shrieked, breaking his stance and stepping toward them. "This is ludicrous! I've never seen such a blatant disregard for—"

"Cadet, I have given you fair warning to watch your tone!" Preston interrupted, the venom in his voice quieting the whole room. "You will shut your mouth now, or I will let Griffin shut it for you. That would seem fitting to me, given what you just tried to do to him."

Vaughn looked over his shoulder. Kyle didn't even try to hide his smirk. Finally, after a decade of harassment, that bastard was going to get what was coming to him.

A pair of Garrison troops stepped into the room and grabbed Vaughn by the arms. As they escorted him past Kyle, Vaughn suddenly lunged toward him, his face stopping just short of his own. Kyle barely blinked, which only seemed to further incense the older cadet.

"This isn't over," Vaughn snarled. "If I have to make it my mission in life to see you ground under my boot—I swear on my own life I will see it done. You hear me, you fucking *freak*? This is not the end!"

"Get him out of here," Preston said, and the soldiers pulled Vaughn away.

He went out screaming incoherent profanities. Kyle never heard those words sound so sweet. When he turned back to his superiors at the front of the room, there was a decidedly different air than at the start of the meeting.

"Gentlemen," Dr. Preston started. He was looking down, almost as if he were embarrassed. "I have to apologize for this. I should have seen this coming from him. It's been brewing since the day you arrived, Griffin. I hope ... well, I hope you won't let it spoil the satisfaction that your accomplishments here entitle you to."

Kyle shook his head. "No, sir."

"Very good," the doctor continued. "You're all dismissed. I will see you at commencement."

† † †

Three days later …

"So you have no idea where you're going to go?" Angel asked.

"Not yet," Kyle answered. "Our first orders will probably come tomorrow morning. Maybe tonight, depending on how urgent it might be."

Angel handed him a short glass full of a brownish liquid with two spheres of ice. It was Ambrosia whiskey, a bottle she had taken from her father just for tonight. Kyle had warned her not to, that the doctor would know that she had taken it, but she insisted. "You only graduate from the Infinity Protocol once," she had said. And she had a point. He just didn't want to be answering for it later.

"You're sure we're going to get away with this?" Kyle asked for what must have been the fifth time.

"Yes! My goodness, Kyle, chill out," she answered, rolling those glowing green eyes. "It's fine."

"Hey, you're his daughter, he's not going to kill you. Me on the other hand, I've got a whole career under his thumb."

Angel sat down on her bed across from him. He was squeezed uncomfortably into a seat beneath her window, fidgeting with his wide hips pressed into the narrow arms of the chair. Outside the glass the sun was starting to drop below the horizon, spraying a wash of pinks and oranges through the darkening sky. She stole his attention from it when she leaned forward, giving him a mischievous look like she had so many times before. It was both playful and devious, like she was playing both saint and devil all at the same time. Kyle was helpless against those charms, and she knew it. He wasn't even sure why he tried resisting any more.

"Look," she started. "If he knew that we were going to take it and he still left it there, then he must have wanted us to have it. It's the least he can do for you after all the torture he put you through over the last ten years."

She flicked her hair over her shoulder, revealing the low cut of her shirt. Kyle's eyes were quick, but the glint in her own eyes told him that she had noticed him look. He thought she would cover up, but she didn't. She just left the view there for him to drink in. Suddenly he felt himself using her own logic to his benefit. If she knew it was there and that he was looking, she must have wanted him to look.

Angel had changed a great deal since the day they first met, growing into a sensuous, desirable young woman. Her skin was tanned and supple, her lips soft and perpetually moist. He looked at her with the same longing as all the other cadets, and that made him feel good about himself, to know that he was capable of having such innately human desires. It was one of the things that he loved about her company: she never let him feel like he was any different.

"You're worse than Mac," Kyle said. "I'm surprised you never got me kicked out of here. At least not yet."

"Oh, come on, Kyle," Angel said. "This is our last night together before you fly off to who knows where. I want you to have some fun. You've earned it. I think we both have."

Those eyes weren't going to take no for an answer. So he sighed and raised his glass for her to clank with her own, and then they both turned them bottoms up.

Kyle whistled, though it felt like he might breathe fire instead. "Wow," he said. "That. Is. Strong."

"First time you ever had whiskey?" Angel asked, wiping a drop from her upper lip.

Kyle nodded.

Angel chuckled. "I don't know how you do it."

"How I do what?" Kyle asked.

"How you got through all this without letting loose a few times. Without blowing off some steam. Breaking some rules. Being a miscreant once in a while."

"Oh, I broke plenty of rules," Kyle said. "Just not this kind."

"You were more the valiant rebel, right?" Angel asked, standing up to pour them another glass. "Jumping up in class when something wasn't right, yeah?"

"Something like that. Or maybe saving someone's life when I was told not to."

Angel handed him back the glass with a perplexed look on her face. "Who would tell you not to do that?"

Kyle smelled the whiskey before answering. "Your dad, mostly."

"Why would he say that? That seems like a terrible thing."

"Look, it had nothing to do with your dad," Kyle said. "It didn't even have anything to do with the people that I saved. It had to do with me. They didn't want me risking *my* life. They thought I was too valuable to the Dominion or some stupid thing like that."

Kyle threw down the second glass of whiskey. It didn't burn this time.

Angel sat back down in front of him. "Well, maybe you are," she suggested.

Kyle shook his head. "I can't think that way."

"They obviously think that way."

"And they're welcome to. But I just want to be normal. To be human. If I start believing that I'm better than them, I feel like I'd lose whatever scrap humanity I have left."

Angel smiled and took his hand. She gave him a look that was both calming and seductive. Kyle wanted to pull her to him and kiss her, and he had some inkling that she wanted him to do that as well. He resolved to do it, just as soon as he built up the courage. Any second now. One, two, three ...

Just then, the door swung open and Mac, Jay, and Jackson burst into the room. They were each carrying their own bottle of whiskey, cackling like a herd of hyenas. Mac stumbled and almost fell right in between Kyle and Angel, catching himself at just the last moment.

Kyle dropped his head. Mac's lips contorted into an "Oh shit I'm sorry" shape.

"Hey guys," he said blankly with every ounce of awkwardness he could muster. "We're not, uh, interrupting something are we?"

"Not anymore, Mac, thanks," Kyle said, throwing gas on the fire.

"We can come back ..." Jay said.

Angel stood up and shook her head. "No, boys, it's fine," she said. "Have a seat. Pour us a couple drinks as well."

Jay did as he was told. Kyle stood up and took the glass from his friend.

"Looks like you're already a couple deep yourself," Jackson said, lifting the bottle that Angel had stolen from her father.

"We've had a few," Angel said. "Took some convincing to get Kyle going, though."

"Really?" Mac asked. "I thought you said you were all over this tonight?"

"I'm drinking it, aren't I?" Kyle asked.

"Yeah, but it doesn't count if we have to force you," Mac said. He hiccupped. "We're each planning on finishing a bottle each tonight."

"Well, then I suppose I should finish two," Kyle said.

His friends responded with a chorus of sarcastic ooos and ahhs.

"Well, well, well, boys. I do believe that is a challenge!" Mac exclaimed.

Kyle downed his drink, then handed the glass back to Jay for more. "It's not much of a challenge, really," he said. "After all, I am a mutant. Got to use it to my advantage when I can, right?"

Mac and the others laughed hysterically. They toasted and drank some more.

The night rolled on. In just a few hours they'd finally get their rewards for years of hard work. But then their celebration was interrupted by a sharp knock against the door.

Dr. Preston and Major Foster were waiting on the other side.

The boys tried hiding their bottles, but the doctor shook his head as if to tell them not to bother. He stepped inside and looked briefly at his daughter before focusing his gaze on Kyle.

"Enjoying ourselves, I see," Preston said. "Maybe just a bit much for this early hour, eh?"

"I'm sorry, sir," Kyle said. "I know that it's against regulations, but we felt like we'd earned the chance to have some fun."

The doctor nodded, a bit to Kyle's surprise. "That you have, son," he said. "That you have. But unfortunately not everything works out as we had hoped. I have orders for you boys."

Kyle handed his glass to Angel, straightening up. "Yes, sir."

"Before I pass them along, I think it's important for you all to know that Donovan has been removed from the program for conduct unbecoming. He's being reassigned to another unit."

Kyle scowled. "Reassigned? Not discharged? They're letting him stay in the service?"

"That was the news I received today, yes," the doctor answered.

"Sir, how is that possible?" Kyle demanded, trying his best to remain calm. "He falsified an official ops report. He lied to his commanding officer. He compromised a mission and cost two men their lives just to try and steal an officer's commission. Any one of those should be grounds for criminal charges—"

The doctor put up his hand. "I understand all that, son. And those were exactly my points when discussing this with Deputy Chief Vikander. But the decision came down from the Gentry himself. Apparently he says that he still has a need for him."

Kyle shook his head. The Doctor Preston put his hand on his protégé's shoulder.

"It shouldn't matter to you, Kyle," he said. "You've gotten what you wanted. Tonight you'll be commissioned as the Infinity Force commander. You'll be the first to ever hold the title. You should be proud of yourself, son."

Mac and the others hooted and hollered, slapping him on the back. Bryan showed a toothy grin. Maybe the first Kyle had ever seen him wear. But the Doctor calmed them all quickly.

"All right, all right, that's enough," he said. "It is an honor, and with it come some spoils." He handed a briefcase-sized box to the newly minted commander. "This is a gift from the Gentry. Congratulations."

Kyle took the case with a nod. It weighed almost nothing. At the urging of the others, he opened it and saw a cube of glimmering metal on the inside. Kyle had never seen anything like it.

"What is it?" he asked.

"This is the rarest starmetal in the galaxy, son," Bryan answered. "It's the strongest element we have ever catalogued. There's less than three pounds of it in existence. This represents all that we have."

"It's amazing," Kyle said. "What does he want me to do with it?"

"It was his hope that you'd forge yourself a weapon worthy of your new post," Preston replied. "It's my understanding that only your Spark is powerful enough to do so."

Kyle rubbed his chin, considering the possibilities. He had never done such a thing, but he was certain that with his powers so honed that he could accomplish the feat. The metal was so smooth, so pure, he could see how it might slide through anything. And that's how it hit him. *A blade.* A blade so sharp and powerful it could sustain him through even the longest of odds. He could see it so clearly—the perfect fuller contour, the gleaming hilt, the razor edge—like it was always something that he was destined to build. It made him smile.

Then the doctor pushed the case shut. "I'm pleased you like it, but this will unfortunately have to wait," he said. "You have a mission."

Kyle set the case down. "Yes, sir."

The doctor handed Kyle a small holodrive containing their orders, then he looked around at the half-hidden bottles of whiskey.

"Wait a few moments before you view it," Dr. Preston stated. "You have some time."

"If you don't mind my asking, sir, who will we be reporting to?" Kyle asked.

"Me," Bryan answered suddenly.

Kyle's head kinked to the side. "You, sir?"

Preston looked over at Kyle's uncle and nodded. "That's correct," he said. "The major here has been promoted as well. As of tonight he's now Lt. Colonel Foster. He'll be your primary contact. But your orders will continue to come from me."

Kyle nodded. What a fucking lightning bolt that was.

"Enjoy yourselves for the next few hours," Preston said. "But I wouldn't go overboard. You ship out directly after commencement."

Kyle nodded. "Understood, sir. We'll be ready."

And he was sure that they would be, just as soon as they had another drink.

Chapter 5

When Kyle looked back at his time in the service, it seemed that the years had just skipped past him. On the very day of their commencement, Kyle and his team left the Infinity Compound and went to war. That was fourteen years ago.

The fight with the Splinter became their purpose. They lived on the front lines. They cut their teeth in battle. They toiled. They worked. They bled. Whatever the cliché, they endured it. Though it was hardly a cliché to them. For years they watched fellow soldiers die. Countless good men gave their lives in the fight against the rebellion. They saw blood spilled. They lost friends. But in their vengeance the war began to turn.

Kyle was everything he was proclaimed to be. And the Splinter had no answer. He mowed through entire battalions with his bare hands. He infiltrated the strongest fortresses like a specter. He couldn't be seen, couldn't be overpowered, and if he did bleed, his Celestial powers healed the wound like sand filling in behind a rake.

The Infinity Force never encountered a mission they couldn't complete or an enemy they couldn't vanquish. They spearheaded more than a decade-long onslaught against the Splinter, and because of their influence the Dominion's enemies were reduced to the bitterest, most desperate dregs they had seen since Calin Fustre pulled them from the ashes of the old Galactic Council. For the first time the end of the war seemed mercifully within reach.

Until …

† † †

Present Day ...

The sound of the excavator crashing thundered through the typically serene palatial courtyard. Its tracks had sunken into a section of soft dirt, causing the heavy machine to topple into a deep sinkhole. Its task had been to bulldoze the pristine landscape surrounding the Palace to pave the way for a new defense armament, an automated system that Mac had designed to fortify the perimeter. By all estimations it was already an impenetrable fortress, resting at the apex of a mountainous crag knifing out of the surrounding metropolis. Beyond the walls it was surrounded by a thick grove of towering evergreen trees before sloping down to the galactic capital below. The structure itself was massive, stretching across nearly forty acres with spires reaching more than thirty stories into the sky. Its glimmer never faded, even at night, and it served as a constant reminder of Aeron's lording presence.

It was barely after midday when the construction had come to a screeching halt. The weather on Dynasteria rarely changed, but the day had seemed uncommonly hot amid the commotion. The project had been placed under Kyle's supervision on the Gentry's request, and he refused to be delayed by the situation. It was already a tedious chore and he wasn't about to be stuck doing it any longer than necessary. The workers had called for a hydraulic press to lift the machine, but Kyle knew that would slow their progress by nearly a day. Instead he climbed into the hole himself to remedy the problem.

"You sure you can lift that thing, sir?" a young cadet named Dan asked.

"We'll find out here in a minute, Danny," Kyle said. His voice was deep and firm. He spoke like a lion, calmly and confidently.

"We have ordered the hydraulics, if you'd rather wait, sir," the foreman said.

"I'd rather not waste time waiting," Kyle said. "Move everyone back and give me some room."

The gathering crowd stepped back as Kyle grasped the engine housing with his powerful hands. His arms and legs flexed with an explosion of his dense mutant muscle, causing an immediate lurching sound as the machine raised from the sinkhole. Kyle pushed it away from the soft dirt that wasn't strong enough to support it, and a tremor shook the courtyard as the treads again came down onto solid bedrock. His job done, Kyle rose out of the ditch, wiping a lump of dirt from his cropped blonde hair. He towered over the courtyard at nearly six and half feet tall, and his limbs were like sleeved boulders, rippling with layers of muscle even beneath his Dominion uniform. Most soldiers of his tenure wore a visage that had dulled with the desolation of war, but his deep blue eyes still glowed with the radiance of his inherited powers. His cheeks had grown taut and muscular, his lips straight and stern from those same years of service. All of his features had been chiseled by the life he had led, except for those eyes. They were still as bright as the day he left his parents' home.

Dan gave his commander a friendly pat on the shoulder. He stood almost at eye level with Kyle, and the two soldiers together looked like one mountain standing in the shadows of the crown peak of a towering mountain range. They had known each other for nearly twenty years, and Kyle had taken a protective interest in him like an older brother. Dan was Dr. Preston's son, and Angel's younger brother, and was currently the prized recruit of the Infinity Program. With just under a year left before he completed his training, the young lieutenant was to be the next in line to join their elite ranks.

Dan pulled off his helmet and wiped the sweat from his forehead. He had grown into something of a heartthrob over the last several years, with a sharp, symmetrical jaw and bright green eyes much like his father's. His looks garnered him more than his share of interest from the opposite sex, and for his part Dan reveled in the attention. Women were, to put it mildly, one of his more prominent vices.

"You gave yourself a pretty good scratch there, sir," Dan said.

Kyle followed Dan's eyes down to a long scrape across his left arm.

"Oh, thanks Danny."

Kyle put his hand over the scratch, and a pale blue glow rippled from beneath his skin. His nose wrinkled while his elemental powers seared the open nerve endings. It was a difficult sensation to describe, not unlike rubbing rock salt across burned flesh. Even for a man with skin as thick as Kyle's, it still felt as though the pain pierced right through him.

Finally the glow faded, and the wound disappeared.

"Doesn't that hurt, sir?" Dan asked.

"A little at first," Kyle said. "But if you hurt yourself enough, you get used to it."

"I'll try to remember that next time I get hurt."

"Well, don't plan on getting hurt on my watch. I think your father would kill me."

Dan laughed. "Are you kidding? I think he likes you better than me."

"Actually, it's your sister I'd be more afraid of."

"She's definitely scarier. But I think she likes you better than me too."

"What are you ladies gossiping about?" a voice called from behind.

Jackson was approaching from the doors to the south entrance with a digital holofile in his hand. At first glance the captain was not as imposing as Kyle or Dan, but he wielded a sniper's resolve behind his steely eyes and stubbled chin. In truth, his harsh outward persona made many people were uncomfortable, though his friends realized it was simply his way of grappling with the trials of being a soldier. As always, he carried his kinetic assault rifle with him, slung over his shoulder like a safety blanket. It was a non-projectile weapon, as most side arms were in the post-Earth era, and one with lethal accuracy in the proper hands. Its charge clips were rated up to a thousand shots, depending on the rate of fire, and rarely needed to be reloaded. Only the most skilled Dominion marksmen were issued such a weapon.

"Talking about how sexy you look with that unshaven chin," Kyle joked, looking down at the tablet in Jackson's hand. "Is that what I think it is?"

"Another mission," Jackson responded. "They're waiting for us inside."

"We'll have to catch up later, Danny," Kyle said. "Keep an eye on things here for me, will you?"

"Yes, sir. Not a problem."

Dan went back to the construction crew and Kyle paused to collect his gear, including the sheath holding his four-foot long enchanted war sword. Wide and serrated near the hilt, with two edges and a diamond-shaped tip, it was perhaps the only weapon in the galaxy beside the Eye that deserved to be called divine. It had taken him over two weeks to forge it from the metal gifted by the Gentry, and another three to bestow its Celestial charm. The whole thing drained him like he'd been sucked dry by some remorseless parasite, but in the end it was worth the toil. It had become exactly the companion he had envisioned all those years ago. Though it seemed an archaic weapon in such progressive times, Kyle was never without its company.

Most of the halls in the Palace had soaring, cavernous ceilings, their walls lined with sculpted testaments to the history of the Dominion and the life of its exalted leader. It was polished like a museum and adorned as one as well. Tourists came from around the galaxy in pilgrimage to this place like many religious disciples had in centuries past. However, the innards of the Palace were far more utilitarian. Kyle and Jackson entered through a narrow passageway along the foundation of the structure, one that was poorly lit and buzzing with a fluorescent din. It was one of a thousand such tunnels lurking beneath the building's gleaming, lustrous exterior.

"So I've heard Dan is handling the program well," Jackson said.

"As well as anyone can anyway," Kyle replied. "This time next year he'll be coming to these meetings with us."

"You think Vaughn and his goons will learn to stay out of our way by then?" Jackson asked. "Or will it just make him more bitter that Dan finished the program and he never did?"

"Well, it's not as though he wasn't good enough," Kyle said. "If he wasn't such an asshole he would have graduated from the program a long time before we did. We might have been working for him."

Jackson grimaced. "Ugh, could you imagine what that would've been like? Having to deal with that prick every day? It's bad enough they made him a field general."

They finally came to one of the briefing rooms amid a cluster of surveillance stations. They could hear several voices as they stood in the hall, which seemed strange because their missions rarely required extensive meetings. Kyle's keen hearing was able to make out Vaughn's voice inside, making him wonder what distinguished this from their typical meetings.

"All right, let's be civil in there," Kyle said, pausing at the door. "I heard Vaughn, and I really don't feel like arguing with him."

"I'll behave," Jackson assured him.

Kyle pushed open the door, and it quickly swung shut behind them. Immediately they could tell this was not going to be a simple briefing. There were a handful of officers scattered around the room, with Tact General Donovan standing on the other side of the circular table. He was in his officer's jacket, as was typical since he had received his appointment to command status just over a year ago. Since his exile from the Infinity

Program fourteen years ago, he had enjoyed a meteoric rise through the ranks, leaning on a promiscuous brutality as his signature in battle. By now he was in his late thirties and was showing more than a little grey around his temples, but he was still one of the more lethal men in Aeron's military.

The surprise was the presence of Dr. Preston standing across from Vaughn. Now in his mid-sixties, the added weight around midsection subtracted nothing from his formidable presence. When Dan had received his assignment to his father's command, Preston had taken the opportunity to retire from his position as chief psychologist. However, the retirement hadn't lasted long. He was convinced to take a position as deputy director of intelligence and was given a commission as a lieutenant general to oversee the battalions that enveloped both Vaughn and Kyle's units. He gestured to a pair of seats at the end of the table pragmatically.

"Have a seat, boys," he said.

Kyle and Jackson exchanged perplexed looks, but they complied anyway. Their mentor didn't look up at them as he pointed out their places, which made Kyle uneasy. He kept an eye on Vaughn, whose narrow eyes were eternally difficult to read, though Kyle swore he could see anxiety beneath his brow. This meeting was Vaughn's doing, he was sure of it.

"We were told you have a new mission for us, sir," Kyle said.

"We'll get to that in a moment," Vaughn interjected, setting his digital display on the table. "First we need to discuss our little encounter the other day."

Kyle and Jackson couldn't hide the confusion in their expressions. Kyle looked over at Dr. Preston, but the doctor's eyes remained fixed on his device. Vaughn's glare never changed, waiting for a response.

"I don't see what there is to discuss," Kyle said.

"Several men died, commander," Vaughn said. "We need to figure out what went wrong."

"We're looking for the facts," added Admiral Genoa, the commander of the fleet's forward warship squadron.

"The facts?" Kyle asked.

"That's right," Vaughn replied.

"Shouldn't everything be in the report, sir?" Jackson asked.

"That's where the problem lies," Dr. Preston said. "Your report and General Donovan's report don't add up. We need to know where the disconnect is."

Kyle blinked twice, a slight smile hiding his anger. He'd been to this meeting before, again due to Vaugh's influence. Now, fourteen years later, and he was the subject of the same damn witch hunt.

"I don't know what to tell you, sir," Kyle said. "We put what happened in our report."

"Commander, you state in your version that the Splinter surveillance was tipped off by the general's unit," noted Colonel Zhun, a beefy man with a red face and red hands. "His report insists that it was you and your men that made the mistake."

Jackson started to rise from his chair, but Kyle grabbed his friend's shoulder.

"Sir, I guarantee that we were not seen," Kyle said.

"Your unit was the only one to penetrate the perimeter," Colonel Zhun said. "There were numerous opportunities for you to be detected. With the amount of security they had on this installation, the four of you were far more likely to be noticed."

"Sir, there weren't four of us inside," Jackson said. "Kyle handled the incursion. The rest of us were just his cover."

"You went in alone?" one of the intelligence officers asked.

"Yes, sir," Kyle said. "With the amount of security they had, it was better for me to handle it myself."

"And you were still inside when the alarm went off?"

"Yes, sir. I was in the mechanical room."

"And after that is when you went off mission to assist Vaughn and his men?" the man asked.

"Yes, sir, after sending Lieutenants McArthur and Harrier to retrieve our ship," Kyle said. "I also had Captain Hilton give the general's men some cover so I would have the time I needed to get to them. Fortunately it didn't take me too long."

"And that was the end of it?" the colonel asked. "What else are we missing?"

"Sir, I don't know what else you were expecting," Kyle said, running thin on patience. "Maybe you're asking the wrong person."

"Just answer the question, Commander," Vaughn said, leaning forward on his fists.

Kyle paused for a second, trying to get over the impromptu interrogation. He knew that Vaughn was only doing this to cover the fact that his mission failed. The gall of it was almost more irritating than the accusation.

"You know, I don't see what the problem is here," Kyle fumed. "We got our job done."

"This is where you're missing the big picture, Commander," Vaughn said. "There were two missions that needed to be completed, and only one of them was."

"You can't possibly think that's our fault," Kyle replied.

"Men are dead, Kyle," Vaughn said. "Somebody has to be accountable."

"You're kidding, right?" Jackson exclaimed. "If it wasn't for Kyle, no one would have gotten out of there."

"I don't remember talking to you, *Captain*," Vaughn snarled, his face flushing red. "So stay out of it."

"Gentlemen, please—" Colonel Zhun started.

"This is exactly your problem, Commander," Vaughn snapped, ignoring the colonel's petition. "I didn't need you to intervene."

"That's not what it looked like when I found you," Kyle said. "But next time you're about to be shot I'll try to remember that you don't need my help."

"That was not your mission!" Vaughn yelled, thrusting himself up from his chair. "You had no right to get involved!"

Kyle shot up from his own chair, his frustration drowning out his better judgment. The table shuddered in front of him and the room seemed to darken as if Kyle's shoulders were suddenly blotting out the lights.

"Don't give me that jurisdiction bullshit, General," Kyle seethed. "You can't hide behind your orders. You fucked up, and they caught you. We had separate missions—that's fine, I'm happy to stay out of your way. But when your mistakes put my men in danger, I have every right to get involved to make sure nothing happens to them. And you're damn lucky that I did, because those guys would have killed you. So I'm telling you right now: *get off my back*."

"Commander, you're speaking to a general," Dr. Preston interjected. "Try to maintain your discipline."

"I'm sorry, sir, but with all due respect, I have operational command of my missions," Kyle said. "We were not made aware of the general's presence on site, so we can't be expected to account for them. When we saw his men in trouble, I made the decision to go after them. They'd be dead if it wasn't for our help."

"You have no proof that it was our unit that set off their alarms," Vaughn snarled.

"Oh, I see, they saw one of us and decided to come after you instead," Kyle said. "Why don't you just admit that you fucked this one up?"

"You had better watch your mouth, Commander—"

"Or what?" Kyle asked, throwing his arms out to his sides. "I'm not one of your lapdogs, General. Your intimidations don't work on me."

"That is enough!" Dr. Preston roared.

The room was abruptly filled with an embarrassed quiet. The tension seemed so heavy it was weighing everyone down. The color faded from Vaughn's cheeks, replaced by a sweeping paleness. Kyle huffed like an angry bull, his fists half-clenched.

"It's clear that we're not going to get anywhere with this," Dr. Preston said. "Men died on this mission, and you two are more concerned about measuring dicks. I'm tired of looking at both of you. Colonel, give the commander his assignment."

"Yes, Director," Colonel Zhun replied, sliding a holofile across the table. "Thanks to the information you obtained for us, we've found a new subject that's scheduled for clean-out."

Kyle sighed as he took the file. Assassinations were dirty chores that he and his men despised. They were rarely asked to perform such tasks unless the Gentry wanted to send a message.

"Who's the target?" Kyle asked.

"Colonel Bryan Foster," he replied. "He's the commanding officer at a port in sector—"

"Whoa, hold on a second," Kyle interrupted. "Bryan Foster? You want us to *kill* Bryan Foster?"

"You've heard of him?" Colonel Zhun asked.

Kyle looked across the table at Preston, whose eyes had returned to his tablet.

"He's my uncle," Kyle responded.

"Your uncle has been playing both sides of the war," Vaughn said, his confidence suddenly returning. "He's been feeding information to the Splinter."

Kyle paused, shaking his head, but Vaughn's expression was steadfast. This was not the joke he had hoped it was.

"What is this, some sort of test?" Kyle asked finally. "We don't agree on a report and suddenly you're asking me to kill my own uncle?" His eyes focused on the doctor again, but his mentor still refused to look up.

Vaughn grinned. "I'm not asking you to do anything. These orders came straight from the Gentry. He wants you to deal with this personally."

Kyle leaned toward Dr. Preston, his expression begging for help. The doctor begrudgingly looked up at his old pupil. All he did was shrug.

"This is a legitimate mission," Preston said. "He was named in the intel you just recovered for us on Gallatia. We don't have a choice. The Gentry wants this done, and he wants to make a statement by having *you* do it."

"I don't … I don't believe that he did this," Kyle said.

"It's plain as day, son," Dr. Preston said. "I wish we were wrong."

Kyle grunted, realizing that Vaughn had him trapped. It was a capital crime to disobey the Gentry's orders, and the punishment would be far worse than he cared to imagine. Finally, he nodded reluctantly.

"All right," he said. "We'll take care of it, sir."

"Be sure that you do," Vaughn said, "because you know what happens when a soldier defies the Gentry."

"Don't worry about me, General," Kyle said, opening the door. "My jobs always get done."

Kyle strode out the door before Vaughn could reply. His head was swimming and he hoped that the quiet in the hall would clear his thoughts. But he was barely a few steps down the corridor before he was stopped again.

"Commander, hold it right there."

The voice belonged to Dr. Preston, and there was a decidedly displeased tone to the order. Kyle halted in his tracks, his broad shoulders clogging the entire hallway. He turned back to his mentor without a word, afraid if he opened his mouth he'd say something he would regret.

"What the hell happened in there?" Preston asked.

"I'm sorry, sir," Kyle said. "I let my frustration get the best of me."

"That is a major damned understatement. You threatened a superior officer. You give him every excuse to come after you like this."

"I understand, sir. It won't happen again."

"Son, you and I both know that's not true," Preston replied. "You have got to get a handle on this thing. Stop letting him get to you."

"Yes, sir," Kyle said, avoiding his mentor's eyes.

"I'm serious, Commander," Dr. Preston continued. "You have got to learn to control that temper, because it's going to get you into trouble. You didn't even salute the other officers when you left the room. They could suspend your command just for that."

"Pardon me, sir, but maybe that would be best," Kyle said. "Then they would have to do their own dirty work for once."

"Kyle ... son, I need you to listen to me now," Preston said, choosing his words carefully. "I want you to know that I did everything I could for your uncle, but he's just in too deep. We give you these assignments because we know you can get them done. I wish things could be different, but the Gentry has spoken."

Kyle paused, a solemn look crossing his face. "Will that be all, sir?" he said finally.

"That's all, Commander," Preston said. "You men look out for yourselves. I want to see you back safe by tonight."

Kyle nodded and gave the doctor the salute he was looking for before turning and storming down the corridor.

"Kyle," Jackson said as he hurried to catch up, "what are we doing?"

"We're going to find Bryan," Kyle confirmed.

"You sure you want to do this?" Jackson asked. "I could take the others and handle it."

"No, it's my uncle, and it's my job. If he's done what they say, then he'll have to answer to me for it."

"*Answer*? Why does that sound like we're giving him a chance to explain?"

"Just contact Jay and Mac," Kyle said, dodging the inquiry. "Tell them to meet us at the observatory station in the Emporia sector. We'll brief them there."

Jackson grabbed his commander's arm, pulling him to a stop.

"Kyle," he said, searching his friend's face for answers. "Are you all right?"

"I'm fine, Jackson," Kyle said, his voice less than convincing. "Make the call."

CHAPTER 6

The bay doors at the Emporia Observation Station hissed open as Kyle and Jackson's transport approached. The ship's electromagnetic thrusters blared as the doors closed behind it and the vacuum of space was sealed off. This was truly a barren sector of space near the inner boundary of the galactic habitable zone. Relative to the vast empty distances that characterized the outer arms of the galaxy, the stars were tightly packed here, and few planets offered magnetic fields robust enough to shield humans from the heavy radiation in the sector.

Emporia Observation Station orbited the planet it was named for, the lone terrestrial planet in a system of gas giants. It had a strong atmosphere capable of supporting life thanks to centuries of volcanic activity, though they had been rendered dormant by the Dominion's geothermal drilling. What was left was a lush forest amidst heaving rocky mountains. It was a rugged and often impassible terrain, but it was stable enough to support a military outpost. That was where they would find Bryan.

The observatory was a man-made, non-military installation tethered to Emporia by an artificial gravitational field, which prevented the station from being pulled away by the neighboring gas giants. The complex was constructed for the sole purpose of monitoring comets, asteroids, rogue black holes and planets, as well as potential gamma-ray bursts—always an unnerving threat in this crowded space. It was manned mostly by astronomers and astrophysicists, with only a small military liaison on site. Kyle knew he could talk more freely there.

As Kyle and Jackson came down the ramp from their transport a tall, thin master sergeant waited for them. His free hand shot up and saluted as the two approached. The smooth skin along his knuckles and trimmed nails indicated that he had never seen battle. Kyle briefly wondered if his world had changed at all since this morning.

"Commander Griffin, we weren't expecting you today, sir," he said.

"It's a bit of an impromptu visit, Master Sergeant," Kyle said. "Did you receive our clearance?"

"Yes sir," the man said. "We're at your disposal."

"We're expecting two others," Kyle said.

"Yes sir, they have already arrived," he replied. "They are waiting for you upstairs in the cafeteria. Should I call to Emporia to request more troops?"

"No, that's not necessary," Kyle said. "We'll be headed there shortly. We just need a few minutes before we're on our way."

"May I ask what this is about, sir?" the man inquired. "We don't typically have military personnel stop here."

"You're gonna need a hefty raise to get that question answered, Sergeant," Kyle answered, shaking his head. "Just go on with your day. We'll be out of your hair in short order."

Kyle stepped past him without another word. They followed a staircase up to the mezzanine level and found Jay and Mac waiting in the cafeteria, sharing a sandwich and cold drink. Jay was sitting on top of one of the tables next to his pilot's gear, his hair pulled back from his eyes. His typically unkempt beard had gotten especially unruly since the mission on Gallatia, and it had become good at catching bits of food when he ate. He was very thick around the legs and shoulders from years of working on his parent's farm, and the stretch in his uniform made that build obvious. Not much of his appearance would make someone think that he was possibly the best fighter pilot in the Dominion fleet.

Mac was on the other side of the room, fiddling with the automated coverings to the large bay windows overlooking the expanse between the observatory and Emporia. It was rare that he ever found a piece of machinery that he wouldn't tinker with, even if one hand was occupied by his sandwich.

"Hey boys, it's about time," Jay said after swilling down a gulp of water. "You wanna let us in on why we're way out in the middle of nowhere today? I thought we'd have at least a few days off after that last mission."

"Yeah, Kyle, what's the deal?" Mac asked. "I was all primed for three days of drinking and sleeping."

"Easy fellas," Jackson cautioned. "Now's not really the best time for jokes."

"I think you've told me that every day since I met you," Mac said. "Haven't you ever heard that old Earth adage, 'the boy who cried wulp?'"

"It's wolf, Mac," Jay said.

"What?" Mac asked, perplexed.

"The saying," Jay repeated. "It's 'the boy who cried *wolf*,' not 'wulp.'"

"Are you sure?" Mac asked.

"Positive."

"Nah, that just doesn't sound right," Mac insisted. "I think you made that word up."

"Would you two stop it?" Jackson said. "We need you to pay attention."

"You're extra bitter salty today," Mac said. "I need to get a vote on this. Kyle, what do you think?"

Kyle reached up and pulled the video cable from the surveillance camera over the door. "We've got more important things to talk about, Mac."

Mac went quiet immediately, his bright-eyed expression suddenly dampening. Jay wiped the bits of food from his beard and stepped down from the table. Jackson shut the two doors to the cafeteria, locking in the somber mood.

"We got a new assignment from the palace today, direct from the Gentry himself," Kyle said. "I'm not sure what to do about it."

"Well, what is it?" Mac asked. "More recon? Another incursion?"

"No, we've got a high-level target set for clean out," Kyle said. "We're supposed to be on our way right now."

"A hit?" Jay asked. "Is it a Dominion target?"

"It is a Dominion target," Kyle said. "Military. It's Bryan Foster."

Mac shook his head, trying to make the words make sense, but he couldn't. "What? You're fucking with us, right?" He looked at his friend's face.

"I wish I were, Mac," Kyle said gravely.

"That's insane. We can't do that."

"I know, Mac," Kyle said. "If you keep thinking like that for about another hour, you might end up where I am right now."

"Wait a minute," Jay said. "I don't understand. What the hell could he have done to make the Gentry want him dead?"

"They've got some intel that he's been providing classified information to the Splinter," Kyle said.

"That's bullshit," Mac interjected. "How reliable is their intel?"

"It comes straight from the files we just hacked from that base on Gallatia a few days ago," Kyle said. "We gave them the information."

"Oh shit …" Mac moaned.

"Jackson and I went over the data on our way here, and it seems airtight," Kyle added. "Like it or not, this is the way it is."

"So what are we gonna do?" Jay asked. "We're here. Are we really gonna go do this thing?"

"What else can we do?" Jackson asked.

"Why can't we just ask to be reassigned?" Mac suggested. "Get someone else out here to handle this?"

"The Gentry wants Kyle to handle this himself," Jackson said. "He wants people to see what happens if they cross him."

"So they're punishing Bryan *and* Kyle?" Mac asked. "Where's the justice in that?"

"Mac, we don't have any options here," Jay said. "Either we do this or we're the ones that go under the knife."

"I can't be a part of this," Mac said. "We've known Bryan since we were teenagers. There's gotta be a mistake somewhere. Tell 'em, Kyle."

"This is why I need you all here," Kyle said. "I need to hear both sides."

"What sides?" Mac asked. "This is your uncle. A guy we've known half our lives. A guy we've gone to war with. Are we really talking about just going down there and shooting him?"

"We're talking about doing our job," Jay said. "Following our orders."

"We're not fucking robots," Mac replied. "Just because the guy upstairs says it doesn't make it right."

"Actually, that's exactly what it means," Jackson said. "What the Gentry says, goes. If we refuse it's not something they'll tickle us for. They will kill us."

"And what about Bryan?" Mac demanded. "We don't care about his side?"

"Mac, when the hell have we ever cared about a mark's side of the story?" Jay asked.

"When the mark also happens to be an old commanding officer of ours, and a part of Kyle's family!" Mac yelled.

As they argued Kyle sat quietly. Listening and thinking, a thousand options flashing in front of his mind every second. None of them presented a reasonable option. Everything he could think of either left his uncle exposed, or left *them* exposed. Babysitting a construction site was starting to seem more appealing all the time.

"Kyle …" Jackson said, his voice now hushed. "We can debate this all day, but eventually you're the one that's gonna have to make the call."

Kyle took a deep breath and sighed. Then he looked up suddenly. *Fuck it,* he thought. If he couldn't win, might as well go with his gut.

"I know Lord Aeron wants this done," he said. "He wants us to go in there, get him alone and take him out, no questions asked. Well, I can tell you right now I'm not going to do that."

"Yes! Thank you!" Mac exclaimed.

"Kyle, we're toeing a pretty fine line here just talking about this," Jackson said. "If we don't get this done, it's full-blown treason. You know what that means."

"Just let Jackson and I handle it," Jay said. "We'll write up the report. No one will know the difference."

"I appreciate your concern, boys," Kyle said, "but this isn't open for debate."

"Kyle, hold on a second—" Jay started.

"The decision has been made," Kyle he paused before continuing less harshly. "Look, I'm not saying we won't do the job. If it turns out he's playing both sides like they say, then he deserves what's coming. But first I'm going to find out what he's been doing and why. I won't let this happen until I understand."

"Kyle … I think you're making a mistake," Jackson said.

"If you disagree with me, now's the time to leave," Kyle said, pointing to the door.

"I'm with you, Kyle," Mac said.

"What do you expect to accomplish with this?" Jackson asked. "Do you think you're gonna get over there, and he'll tell you some story that clears everything up? You're not gonna get to shake hands and go on with life this time."

"And I can't go on with life without knowing why he did this," Kyle said. "Or *if* he did this. Now either you're in or you're out. Make up your minds."

Jay sighed, shaking his head. "If you feel that strong about it, I'll go along."

Jackson threw up his hands with a frustrated grunt. The others watched him roll his eyes, giving him that moment to vent.

"What's it gonna be, Captain?" Kyle asked.

"Fuck, this is not how I pictured today going," Jackson said. "You sure this is gonna be worth it?"

"No," Kyle answered. "But it's better than never knowing."

"All right, goddam it," Jackson said after a brief pause. "If you've gotta know, let's get it fucking over with."

† † †

Barely ten minutes later their glistening starship, the *Gemini*, dropped into the thick Emporia atmosphere. It looked more like a pitchfork knifing through the skies than a typical Dominion starfighter, with four sweeping aerofoils arcing forward and away from the ship's hull to form a pair of bladelike wings next to the ship's cabin. Mac and Jay had designed it years ago, right down to the substantial artillery payload and electromagnetic thrusters. It was notably larger than other assault vessels in the fleet, but it was also far faster because of Mac's alterations to the hyperdrive algorithms. It was a prized warship to be certain, both aggressive and stealthy, and one that had served them well during their service.

The installation came into view as the *Gemini* descended from the clouds. It was a cumbersome complex, half-built into the side of a rising peak and half-supported by colossal pedestals reaching into the chasm below. The port was scarcely manned, requiring only essential operating personnel. It had been built years ago to house an overseeing military presence for the observatory nearby, but it also served as a launching point for exploratory missions and as a refueling stop for passing Dominion transports. Bryan had served as the commanding officer here for several years after his last tour of active duty. It was an uneventful assignment for a man who had served most of his tenure as a battle-hardened commander and Infinity Program instructor, but he always insisted it was what he wanted.

"We've got a visual on the port," Jay said.

"Start hailing 'em," Kyle ordered.

"Emporia tower, this is Starship *Gemini*, clearance code 057613," Jay called. "Requesting direction to an open bay. Over."

"We read you, *Gemini*," a voice called over the intercom. "Clearance code verified. Please proceed to Dock 17. An emissary will be waiting. Over."

"They're sending someone to meet us?" Mac asked. "What's with that?"

"You think they know why we're coming?" Jackson asked.

"I don't know," Kyle said. "If he does, we can't be certain if any of his men are involved with him. We'd best put up the front shields."

"I'm not reading any weapons tracking," Jay said. "We're clear all the way in."

"Make sure you've got a full charge in your sidearms anyway," Kyle said. "If they have anything laid out for us, we're gonna be ready."

The *Gemini* locked in to their prescribed gate, the grip of the jetway shaking the ship's hull. For some reason it felt foreboding, like they suddenly were trapped in something they wouldn't be able to escape. Kyle had never felt the sensation before, and he wasn't sure how to shake it. Or if he even should.

Kyle pulled his handgun from the holster on his hip. He checked the charge and reset the safety, then slid it back into the familiar position along his waist. The others did the same, with Jackson taking an extra moment to fine-tune the scope on his kinetic rifle.

"Maybe now would be a good time to test these out," Mac said, holding up a sleek metal cylinder that looked like a long wristband.

"What the hell is that?" Jay asked.

"It's an assault gauntlet," Mac answered. "New design. Not as obvious as us walking in with our cocks swinging from our holsters."

"*'Assault gauntlet?'*" Jay asked. "Sounds like an oxymoron."

"Yeah, it's like the term *daring pilot*," Mac countered. "Sounds like something somebody made up."

Jay just rolled his eyes, but didn't press the matter. Mac shrugged, holding up the device for debate.

"Where'd you get them?" Jackson asked, looking it over curiously.

"I built them," Mac responded. "What do you think I do all day when we're not on a mission?"

"What do they do?" Jackson asked.

"Glad you asked, they've got—"

"Put those away," Kyle barked. "They're not ready."

"They'll work," Mac insisted.

"That's the last thing I'm worried about," Kyle said. "But we're not using untested tech today. This is too important. Now get your shit. We're going in."

Nobody dared argue. The team quickly gathered their things and then walked through the waiting airlock.

The ramp leading into the complex was empty, and their entrance into the cavernous engineering terminal seemed to go unnoticed. There were dozens of soldiers milling about their daily tasks, but none seemed concerned with their guests' arrival.

The garage smelled of hot metal and ammonia, one of the few chemicals that could safely clean electromagnetic engines. The screech of hydraulic lifts and buzz of welding torches made for a steady clamor, one that Kyle hoped would shroud their presence.

Finally, a fair-skinned corporal approached, his stride not quite a trot but obviously hurried. He was well under six feet tall with a thin neck and sloped shoulders, and the smooth complexion on his face accentuated his youth. He stopped in front of Kyle and the others and gave them a rigid salute.

"Commander Griffin," he said in a tenor's pitch, "it's a pleasure to meet you, sir. I'm here to welcome you to Emporia."

"Thank you, Corporal," Kyle said, his mature frame dwarfing the young soldier. "We're here to see Colonel Foster."

"Yes, sir," the corporal said. "The colonel has been expecting you. Follow me, please."

Kyle shot a glance toward Jackson. They would not have been surprised to be met with Bryan's absence, or even with some aggression, but to have him expecting an unannounced visit put Kyle back on guard. Without a word of response, Jackson wrapped his arm through the strap on his rifle and slid a tentative grip around the handle.

The corporal led them into an elevator on the far end of the garage and pressed the button for the fourth floor. Kyle felt his nerves tighten as the elevator rose. He glanced at the corporal standing next to him, wondering if he knew what was waiting at the end of this ride. The calm in his eyes seemed to say no, but by that point Kyle had given up trying to figure out what to expect. Nothing about this was predictable, and that made him anxious. Before he could dwell on the thought, the lift stopped and the doors slid open.

They exited into a large conference room full of people. At first glance Kyle thought they were walking into an ambush, but he quickly realized none of the crowd was armed. They had interrupted some kind of meeting, and all eyes turned toward them as they entered.

Bryan was sitting at the head of the room, mulling over a set of schematics. He looked up when he heard the elevator open, and grinned as he saw Kyle and the others walk in. He quickly abandoned his work and came around the table to greet his former pupils, the wide smile on his face in stark contrast to his typical matter-of-fact demeanor. His beard had grown thick and streaked with gray since the last time the four had seen him, and his hair had lengthened over the back of his neck. He was heavier around the midsection and walked with a more noticeable limp from an old knee injury. It all made him look notably older, especially around the eyes. The creases were deeper, and there was a heaviness to them Kyle had never seen before. He wondered if his uncle was sleeping at all.

"Gentlemen," Bryan said, his rasping voice almost painful to hear. "It's good to see you."

"It's nice to see you too," Kyle replied, shaking his uncle's hand. "How have things been?"

"Well, you know how it is," Bryan said. "Nothing exciting ever happens around here. I'm interested to hear about your recent adventures."

"I wouldn't even know where to start," Kyle said.

"I've heard they've been keeping you busy," Bryan said. "In fact I was just thinking about how long it would take for them to send you here. Honestly, I thought it would be sooner."

"You know why we're here?" Kyle asked.

"Yes, I do."

"And you're still here?"

Bryan nodded. "I am."

"Do you think we should talk some place a little more … private?" Kyle asked.

"We can go up to my office," Bryan said calmly. "It's this way."

Bryan politely excused himself from the meeting. Kyle looked around at the faces of the people in the room, but they showed little concern over their intrusion. It made him wonder whether any of them were involved with what Bryan had been doing. *If* he'd actually been doing what he'd been accused of. Damn, even he was already condemning his uncle.

Bryan took them up a small staircase on the side of the room. Kyle tried his best to shake the emotion from his mind with each step. He struggled to cope with the idea that Bryan may never leave this office, and that he would have to be the one to pull the trigger. And to make matters even stranger, Bryan seemed unconcerned by that scenario as well.

As the door opened Kyle made sure that Bryan went in first, then closed and locked the door behind them.

"You seem uncomfortable, Kyle," Bryan said, pouring a glass of water. "Does this not agree with you?"

"What do you think?" Kyle said. "It's not every day we have to make these kinds of visits."

"You know, I was starting to wonder if I'd even see you coming. Part of me thought you'd just be a ghost in the building."

"No, I had to hear it come from you," Kyle said. "Why did you do this? Why are you helping them?"

"I'm not helping them, Kyle. *I'm one of them*," Bryan said. "I always have been."

Kyle shook his head. "What does that even mean? You and I have fought together against these people dozens of times. Now you're telling me you've always been one of them? Do you have any loyalties to anything at all?"

"I know it's hard to understand," Bryan said. "I wish it wasn't so complicated. Let me show you something."

"What makes you think I'm interested in anything you have to say after what you just told me?" Kyle asked, indignant.

"Because if you weren't, then you would have killed me already," Bryan said, pulling a small encoder from his pocket.

He handed the thumb-sized encoder to his nephew. The crest of the Dominion Archives stood out on the front.

"What is this supposed to be?" Kyle asked.

"This is a DNA-coded file from the archives," Bryan replied. "It requires an alpha-level clearance to open it. Not even I have that kind of access." He nodded at the encoder. "But you do."

"What's supposed to be on it?" Mac asked.

"Do you know who Calin Fustre was?" Bryan asked.

"Of course," Jay said. "She was the woman who supposedly started the Splinter."

"She's a myth," Kyle said. "There's no record of her actually existing."

"Actually, there is," Bryan said. "And you're holding it right now. Open it up."

Kyle wanted to disagree, but now he was curious. His uncle nodded at the device again, his expression insistent. Kyle debated for a moment, trying to deduce what good might come of knowing what these files held. It was a useless effort. Whatever he held in his hand likely would determine if Bryan lived or died. He felt that he at least owed his uncle the time it would take to view it. He sighed and put his thumb over a small stripe on the device. A holographic screen appeared in front of him. The image was of a birth certificate, and the name at the top of the page read: CALIN ELIZABETH FUSTRE.

Kyle's eyes narrowed. He scrolled through the labyrinth of information, hundreds of pages in all. There were medical records, addresses, marriage forms, all under the heading of the Galactic Council. Finally he came to what appeared to be a family tree near the end of the file. The genealogy began with Calin and her husband and stretched down over multiple generations, coming to a stop almost a century before the present day.

"How did you get this?" Kyle asked.

"We have a man with access to the archives," Bryan said. "It took a long time for him to get this to us."

"So what is this supposed to prove?" Kyle asked. "That Calin Fustre existed eight hundred years ago? What does that have to do with anything?"

"This isn't so much about Calin," Bryan said. "It's about the Council. It's about what happened to them."

"We know what happened to them," Jackson interjected. "They tried to supplant the Gentry. They bit off more than they could chew."

"That's what the history scrolls tell you," Bryan said. "That's what the church tells you. But it's not what happened. What you have there tells the real story. The one that the Gentry doesn't want the public to know."

"Kyle, we shouldn't be listening to this," Jackson said.

Kyle paused, staring down at the encoder. Jackson was right; he shouldn't be listening to this. It was mutiny. Worse yet, it was heresy. But he couldn't help it. He had to know.

"Then how is your history different?" Kyle asked finally.

Bryan smiled. "Our history is the truth. The Council didn't run from the Gentry. They didn't disappear into the inner arms. They didn't leave their families behind to save their own lives. They were executed, by order of Lord Aeron."

"Executed?"

"Is it really that hard to believe? What is it that they told you about how he came to be 'the Lord' we all know him to be?"

"They don't have to tell us anything," Jay said. "It's who he is. He's the reason we're all here."

Bryan nodded. "Right. And you're his favorite ambassador, aren't you? An orphan he had thrown out on the street because you couldn't pay his taxes. Happened to dozens of families on your home planet, Jay. And those who did pay had their properties seized anyway. We've talked about this in the past. I know you remember it. But he's still the type you want to stand up for, is he?"

Jay choked on his own tongue. He had no response to that. Bryan turned back to his nephew.

"I know you want to hear what I have to say, Kyle," Bryan said again. "You wouldn't have allowed this meeting if you didn't."

Kyle gnashed his teeth. His uncle was wrong; he had no desire to hear what Bryan had to say anymore. He'd made a mistake. He should have let the others handle this. Now he'd heard too much. His curiosity was stronger than he was. He had to hear it, even if he didn't want to.

"You've got five minutes," Kyle grumbled. "And I better be impressed."

"I don't need you to be impressed. I just need you to be convinced."

Bryan took the encoder from his nephew and flashed an image of a large industrial mining colony on the screen. The image was grainy, obviously old. There were graders in the distance; spires of conveyors and crushers littered a quarry some two miles wide. The only things more numerous than the machines were the people. There were workers scattered throughout the quarry like ants on a hill. It was a busy place.

"This is Datura," Bryan said. "A mining colony in Sector 2671. Looks like a blue-collar place, right? A lot of hard-working men who do their jobs, go home to their families, then do it all over again. What the hell could they have to do with this, right?"

Bryan flipped to the next slide. It was like he'd open a window into Armageddon. The spires had toppled. The graders had burst into flame. And the bodies … the bodies were everywhere. It was a massacre.

"This is what the Gentry had done to them," Bryan continued. He zoomed in on a corner of the image, revealing a Fury transport in the distance. "There was an industrial accident here. And that's all it was, an accident. But the workers went on strike afterward, saying that the incident could have been prevented if they had gotten some safety equipment they had requested years before. One thing led to another, and a riot broke out. Some of the Garrison men were killed in the incident."

He cut to another photo of a pile of bodies. And they weren't just men, but women and even children. The Fury's rage showed no bounds. Kyle knew its reach all too well.

"The Gentry was a part of the Council at the time, but he bypassed them and sent the Fury to Datura against their judgment," Bryan said. "They didn't discriminate, as you well know."

Bryan thumbed through a half-dozen other pictures of the devastation. Kyle tried his best to be stoic, but Mac had to turn away. For a man who had seen so much war, the images on that drive were still too much.

"Make your point, Bryan," Kyle insisted. "What do these pictures have to do with Calin Fustre?"

"I'll tell you," Bryan replied. "After the incident on Datura the Council came out in strong opposition to the Gentry's decision. They tried to remove him from government affairs, but by then the people had taken the Gentry as a god. As *the God.* And they thought that if he was angered, that any of them could end up like the people in these pictures.

"Aeron was furious at the Council for their stance, and he knew the influence he had with the congregations. He had the Council members rounded up and brought to him. And that's when he had them all killed." Bryan paused, then pulled up another photo of a young man probably no older than Kyle. He had the same blonde hair and blue eyes. "This is Ackley Watson Fustre. He was once the captain of the guard for the Galactic Peacekeepers. He also happened to be Calin Fustre's husband.

"Before he was brought before the Gentry to die, he was able to get word to his wife—to his pregnant wife—that she had to escape with their unborn son. So she did what she had to do. She gathered as many of the Council's families as she could, and she took them out into the depths of our Galaxy. And … well, you know the legends from there."

The images were striking. They were piercing. Kyle had seen enough. But apparently his captain had not.

"Oh, give me a fucking break," Jackson snapped. "Kyle, this is bullshit propaganda."

Bryan shot him a hagridden glance, those creases along his eyes deepening. "I always knew you were the skeptical type, Captain. Never thought you were totally closed-minded."

"I'm sorry, you're asking us to believe that some long-forgotten congress was the reason why the Splinter became an enemy of the state," Jackson huffed. "If that were the case, then why the hell have we never heard this before?"

"Do you really think that the Gentry would leave that knowledge out there knowing how it could sway public opinion? He's not an idiot, Captain."

Jackson turned to Kyle. "You can't really be listening to this. How do we know these files are even real?"

"Those are encrypted Dominion files," Bryan said. "Kyle, you know those encoders cannot be duplicated."

Kyle sighed, thumbing through the files as the others debated. He came across a timeline of the first human encounters with the being calling himself Aeron. According to those dates, the Gentry didn't enter the record books until several thousand years after the twilight of Earth. And the details of the apprehension and execution of the Council members were damning. Assuming, of course, that they were real.

He closed the files abruptly, then passed the device to Mac. "Pull this thing apart and see if you can verify its authenticity. We need to know if this information is legit."

"You got it," Mac said, starting to work.

"You're putting a lot of faith in the stories of a woman who may only be a myth," Kyle said, turning back to his uncle.

"I've got it on good authority that she did exist," Bryan said.

"I don't need to argue about this," Kyle replied. "Whether this woman was real or not doesn't mean anything to me."

"It should. Because you're one of her descendants."

Kyle was caught breathless, which was difficult to do to a man who didn't need to breathe. He didn't know what to say, instead just standing and staring with a vacant expression. Everyone's eyes fell on him, but still he couldn't respond. The claim was outrageous, he thought. How could he have descended from this woman?

"Bullshit," Kyle said finally. "There's nothing here that proves that."

"You're right," Bryan said, "but that genealogy ends almost 100 years ago. The Splinter went through a lot of trouble to make sure the Dominion lost track of her family."

"Kyle, this is ridiculous," Jackson said.

"I'll handle it, Jacks," Kyle snapped, not taking his eyes off of his uncle. "My father is the Gentry's son. There's no chance they were able to get to Aeron."

"I never said it was your father," Bryan replied.

Kyle's face went white. "You … You're saying …"

"It's your mother, Kyle," Bryan confirmed. "*Our* family. We've been a part of this since the very beginning."

"Don't you do that. Don't you drag her into this. This is your mess."

"Drag her?" Bryan asked. "Kyle, she wouldn't be held back by anybody, least of all me."

"Kyle, you can't seriously be listening to this," Jay said.

"You've got less than thirty seconds to explain yourself," Kyle warned. "After that you're not gonna like what you see."

"It's a simple story," Bryan started. "Your mother and I were born to a Splinter family. For years we had been trying to infiltrate the Dominion system, but your mother was the one who finally found a way. It was your father. After he was sent away by the Gentry, she sought him out. She knew that if she could get involved with him, we'd have a pipeline into the royal family. But honestly, things didn't evolve the way we expected. We never dreamed that the outcome of all of this would be you."

"You have no proof," Kyle said. "As far as I'm concerned, you're making this up to save your own ass."

"You don't have to believe me," Bryan said. "You can ask your mother."

Bryan hit a button on his display, and a video screen lit up behind his desk. The image was of a middle-aged woman, thin and beautiful.

"Mom ...?"

"Hi, honey," Becca said, an easy smile crossing her face.

"Mom," Kyle said. "What is going on? Tell me that none of this is true."

"I'm sorry, honey. But I'm afraid it is."

"Why ... why didn't you tell me?"

"Kyle, you were so young when they took you. You weren't ready. You would have been in so much danger."

"So you left me to be ambushed with it twenty years later?" Kyle asked, his voice wavering. "Was this all part of the plan?"

"Kyle, we always knew you were so special," Becca said, her eyes swelling. "Even when you were young and sick. But we weren't the only ones that saw it. They swept you away from us so fast ... we had no choice but to let you go."

"So this...all of this is true?" Kyle asked.

Becca nodded. "Yes, it's true. Every word of it."

Kyle's hands were beginning to glow. "You knew what the Gentry did, and you let me fight for him?" he demanded. "How could you do that? I have *killed* for him!"

"I'm so sorry, honey," Becca said. "I never wanted to hurt you."

"And Dad?" Kyle asked, his eyes burning. "Did you just use him too?"

"God, Kyle, your father is a good man." Tears were cascading down her cheeks. "He and I—"

The screen abruptly went to static. Kyle looked at his uncle, who seemed equally surprised.

"We lost the signal," Bryan said.

"Doesn't matter," Kyle said. "I've seen enough."

"Kyle, I'm sorry," Bryan said. "I know this is awful. I wish it didn't have to be this way, but the Splinter is dying. At this point we don't stand a chance against the Dominion. We had to find a way to tip the scales in our favor."

"Bryan, you realize that we were sent here to kill you, right?" Kyle asked.

"I know what's at stake here," Bryan said, "but the risk is worth it. Here are your options: Believe what I'm telling you and accept the fact that your life will never be the same. Or you can ignore the information in those files, do the job you were sent here to do, and try to go back to the life you have now. Either way, you're the one that has to make the choice."

Kyle felt his face go hot. The world suddenly felt suffocating. He wanted to lash out and satisfy a primal urge for blood and punishment. The soldier in him yearned for it.

His eyes locked on Bryan, and he strode toward him. His feet shook the floor, his stare hot enough to burn a hole in cement. He towered over his uncle, his massive shoulders eclipsing Bryan's face.

"I should kill you just for putting me in this position," Kyle roared.

The words were barely his own. Anger, confusion, and betrayal somersaulted through his head, and the tumbling made him dizzy. He felt cornered and surrounded, and his first reaction was to push back.

Bryan's eyes dropped, but he didn't recoil. Kyle snarled through clenched teeth, but he didn't strike. The pause grew longer, and his stare softened. Finally, he turned away.

"Damn you," Kyle said. "Why did you do this to me?"

"Kyle, I swear this isn't about you," Bryan said. "It's about what's best for our cause. We can feel the war slipping away from us, and we're circling the drain even faster with you on their side."

"What do you expect me to do?"

"The same thing you always do," Bryan said. "Save the day."

Kyle rolled his eyes and walked to the window. He ran his hand down his face, a thousand thoughts tumbling through his mind at once. His hands settled on his hips, and in spite of his stare, he saw nothing of the world outside. His life had seemed so simple this morning.

"Kyle…," Mac interrupted. "These files are legit. There are Dominion markers all over the components. They might even be the originals."

"How the hell did we get here?" Kyle sighed. His uncle was right. Despite his doubts, he couldn't ignore what he had heard. They could never go back to the way things were.

His eyes refocused as he stared out at the woods. He caught a glimpse of something among the trees across the ravine, a glimmer of light peeking from between the leaves. At first he thought it was a trick of the forest or a glint of sunlight off a pool of water. But then he saw it: the fleck of light moved, disappearing behind one tree and reemerging behind another. It suddenly had a very human element to it.

Kyle's heart sank. He turned back to the room, the look of concern clear on his face.

"We may have company," he said, trying to remain still.

"Company?" Jay demanded. "What do you mean '*company*?'"

"Calm down," Kyle said. "Jacks, get a look, tell me what you see. Eleven o'clock, about four hundred meters out, just below the ridge."

Jackson slid to the edge of the window and scanned the forest through the scope on his rifle. The foliage was a thick cover, but he could see what had Kyle worried. The light was a reflection off the glass lens on another Dominion rifle.

"Shit," Jackson muttered. "Kyle, we've got two—scratch that, three—Dominion troops looking this way."

"Vaughn sent someone to follow us?" Mac asked.

"Oh shit, we're screwed," Jay said.

"What do we do?" Mac asked. "They obviously know that Bryan's not dead."

"I've got a good shot," Jackson said. "I can drop all three of them right now."

"No," Kyle ordered. "We've gotta find out what they've sent back to Vaughn. Jay, you and Mac stay here with Bryan. Jackson and I will handle them."

"Kyle—" Bryan began. "I don't…I don't know what to say…"

"Not now, Bryan," Kyle said. "You just start thinking about where we can go if this goes sour."

† † †

The Dominion scouts were still holding their position as Kyle and Jackson approached. The chest-high underbrush was thicker than they had thought, making it difficult to remain silent. Jackson circled toward their right flank to block any escape to the north and to keep them in front of Kyle.

Kyle came out of the brush like a wave, his sidearm drawn. The first soldier spun to raise his rifle, but Kyle caught the barrel in his left hand, then landed his right boot against the man's chest. He tumbled back into the trees as the others scurried to their feet, but before they could aim their weapons, Jackson leapt out behind them.

"Drop your weapons!" Jackson shouted, his gun thrust forward.

The soldiers whipped around, their guns darting from Kyle to Jackson. Kyle waved his hand and the rifles ripped out of their grasps with a surge of his telekinetic power. They stumbled over each other trying to get away and ended up in a heap on the forest floor.

"Don't be stupid," Kyle said. "Get up."

The first soldier gasped as he was lifted to his feet by his comrades. Kyle's foot had hit like an anvil, but he had held back just enough not to crush his heart. They slowly raised their hands in surrender as Kyle and Jackson surrounded them.

"Where the hell did you come from?" one of the soldiers asked.

"Funny, I was gonna ask you the same thing," Kyle said. "What are you doing here?"

"I think you already know that," the soldier responded.

Kyle sneered. "What have you told them?"

"Enough."

Kyle fired a shot through the first soldier's thigh, dropping him back to ground. The other two started to scatter, until Jackson herded them back together. Kyle stepped forward, his sidearm aimed at the man's forehead.

"You've got one minute to live," Kyle warned. "I suggest you fill it with an explanation."

"How did you think this would go?" the soldier demanded. "You ignore a royal mandate and let that traitor live? General Donovan said you'd be a risk, and it sure looks like he was right."

"So what happens now?" Kyle asked.

"Now you pay the price," the soldier said, swallowing hard.

"Is that a threat?" Kyle seethed, taking two thundering steps forward.

"What did you expect?" he said, slinking backward. "You're not above this. The general knows what it would mean to come after you, so that's not what he's going to do. No, he wants to hit you in a place you can't fight back. So he's going to go after your family instead."

Kyle dropped his gun and snatched the man off the ground with one hand. The soldier's feet dangled like he was hanging from a noose. Kyle swung him around as though he was made of feathers and slammed his back against the trunk of one of the sequoias.

"You've got one chance to tell me what they've done with my family," Kyle snarled. "Speak up, or I swear to god these will be your last breaths."

"Fuck you, traitor," the man choked. "I'll be happy when they burn you and your family to ashes."

Kyle's elbow shot up and spiked into the man's side. The man's ribs collapsed with a nauseating crunch and blood erupted out of his mouth. His eyes rolled toward the back of his head as the shock hit him with a numbing dizziness. Kyle pulled him closer, staring into his suddenly bloodshot eyes as if he was trying to look right through him.

"Do you feel that?" Kyle asked. "That pressure in your chest? That's your lung collapsing, and in another five seconds it'll be full of blood. Now either you tell me what they've done with my family or you're going to die a very slow death drowning in your own bodily fluids. It's up to you."

"It's … too late," the soldier gasped, choking on the blood in his throat. "The Gentry … already gave the order. They'll be dead … before you can get to them."

Kyle pressed his free hand into the soldier's broken ribs, causing him to writhe like a hooked fish. Then Kyle's powers poured through his fingers and into the man's body, illuminating the grass with a fluorescent blue glow. The telekinetic wave morphed the wounded lung back together like he was molding clay, but stopped at mending only the life-threatening injuries, leaving the broken ribs as a parting gift. Then he turned and tossed the soldier at the others as if he was flipping them a coin.

The image of his mother cutting to static looped over and over in Kyle's head. At the time it hadn't seemed significant, but now … was the Dominion already there? For the first time in his life, Kyle felt like he couldn't move fast enough.

"Jackson, get on the radio and tell the boys to come pick us up," Kyle ordered. "Have Bryan send someone to pick up this garbage, and then get him off-planet."

"What are we gonna do?" Jackson asked.

"We're going after my parents," Kyle said. "We're going to Littenderon."

CHAPTER 7

The *Gemini* dropped into Littenderon's atmosphere less than an hour later, but by then the billowing smoke could be seen from miles away. Kyle could make out the column of black smoke even before they entered his home planet's orbit, and he immediately assumed the worst. His heart slipped into his throat as they approached, and the terror rising in his chest to replace it felt like it was searing him from the inside out.

The fire had swept across the landscape unrelentingly, consuming more than a dozen homes in a five-mile radius. His parent's home was at the bottom of a wide river basin, but even the nearby water had barely given the blaze pause. It had roared up the valley walls like a volcano, leaving nothing but a singed streak across the face of the terrain. The black cloud became suffocating as the ship moved closer, stifling their vision and confirming their darkest fears: Aeron's men had arrived before them.

"Oh my God," Mac muttered.

"Kyle—" Jay started.

"I see it," Kyle said, his voice shaking. "Just get us down there."

Kyle's gaze never changed as he spoke. He simply could not pry his eyes away. Jay swallowed hard and dropped the stick, arcing the ship down into the haze.

"I'm reading zero Dominion tracks," Jackson announced. "We're clear all the way in."

The *Gemini* darted through the rising plume, then settled on the charred landscape. As they opened the hatch, the pungent stench of scorched flesh assaulted their senses. It was a nauseating cocktail of ash and sulfurous fumes, one that they had unfortunately experienced before. The grass evaporated into a rising wash of dust as their boots left the ramp of the ship. It hung in the air as if gravity had disappeared, and yet the four of them felt weighted down like they were each wearing an anvil.

Finally they dragged their feet through the burnt rubbish that was once Marcus and Becca's front yard. The house had collapsed on itself, leaving a gaping hole for the column of smoke to escape through. They swept the area with their weapons aimed forward, but seeing nothing they turned back to the front door. The smell had become even more intense, forcing Mac and Jackson to cover their noses. Kyle's eyes burned from the swirling ash as he stepped onto the front porch. He pried the door open, snapping the heavy bolt that had been anchored to the frame to lock them shut, and a thick swath of smoke surged out.

"Kyle," Mac said, grasping his friend's shoulder, "maybe you should let us go first."

"This is my family, Mac," Kyle said, his face now stained with salty streaks. "I have to see for myself."

Kyle slowly passed through the doorway, each step causing the weakened floor to creak under his feet. The others followed, their weapons still at the ready. The fire had completely ravaged the interior, burning hot enough to scorch the paint off the walls. The residual heat alone was so intense that Kyle could still feel it singeing the hair on his neck.

They scattered across the first floor of the house, systematically checking each room for Kyle's parents, their hope dwindling with each empty room. Kyle caught himself hoping that they wouldn't find anything, that he could hold on to some hope that they were still alive. But then he made it to the door leading to his old bedroom, the one at the end of the hall. His parents never closed it, insisting that by leaving it open he would remain a part of their home. Today, however, the door was closed and bolted shut. Kyle pushed against it, but the surface was scalding hot. He put his fist through the door, splintering it into a thousand tiny shards. A sickening rush of fumes forced him back.

The door gaped open, and it was a passage into his worst nightmare. From the hall he could see two thin, delicate feet dangling from the ceiling. Kyle's gun dropped to the floor, throwing a puff of soot into the air. He walked inside with his eyes now streaming tears, and there he saw his mother, hanging by the neck in the burnt remains of his own bedroom. He fell to his knees in the ash.

"Oh my God," Jackson wheezed.

Mac knelt down next to Kyle. He placed a hand on his friend's quivering shoulder, swallowing hard in an attempt to regain his ability to speak.

"Kyle...," he said finally. "Kyle, I'm so sorry."

Kyle was breathing ferociously through his mouth, as if he was trying to keep himself from exploding. His face had turned a deep red, and his eyes were swollen from the constant stream of tears.

"This is my fault," he sobbed. "How could I have been so stupid?"

"Kyle, please don't blame yourself for this," Mac said. "You couldn't have known—"

"I should have been here," Kyle sobbed. "I could have helped them ..."

"If we had been here, they would've killed us too," Mac said. "Then this - all of this - would have been for nothing."

"She didn't deserve this, Mac," Kyle snapped.

"No one deserves this," Mac agreed. "Especially not your mother. But I swear to you, we are going to find whoever did this. We're gonna find them, and we're gonna rip them to shreds."

Kyle turned to his lieutenant, his glare suddenly crackling with a fury he had never felt. It had been two years since the last time he had set foot in this house. Two years since the last time he had held his mother's hand. And now he would never have the chance to do that again. And it was because of him. Because of him … and because of … *Vaughn.*

Kyle felt his head swelling like it was going to burst. He had never experienced such an onslaught of emotion. Grief, sorrow, heartache, despair, fear—they all flooded his mind like he was drowning in it. He had to escape it, or he wasn't sure what he would do. So he latched on to whatever other emotion he could find. Rage was it. And Vaughn gave him a target. He turned to Mac and nodded finally, the lure of retribution helping him to swallow that indelible sadness. The trembling in his shoulders slowly subsided, and he squeezed the last of the tears out of his eyes.

"We'll get her down for you," Jay said.

"No," Kyle said. "No, I want to take care of her."

As Kyle stood up, he heard a creak on the floor behind him. Jackson and Jay swung their guns toward the door as the noise slowly came closer. The footsteps stopped just before the other end of the hallway, and a bloody hand appeared around the edge of the blackened wall. Then Kyle heard the aching of a very familiar voice.

"Son …"

Kyle ran toward his father as Marcus collapsed into a heap in the doorway. He landed face down on the ashen floor, his right arm buried beneath his body and his white shirt stained a horrifying red.

"Dad!" Kyle yelled, rolling his father onto his back. "Dad!"

"Kyle …" Marcus coughed, "your mother …"

"Shh, Dad, don't talk," Kyle said. "Let me see where you're hurt. Let me see it."

Kyle rolled his father over and lifted up his tattered shirt. There was a massive gash just below his ribcage that had nearly split him in two. The heavy blood loss had caused Marcus's skin to turn a ghostly white beneath the soot, and the way his side had collapsed made Kyle realize that most of his ribs had been crushed. After just a few seconds, a pool of blood had already gathered beneath him, turning the light gray dust into a thick black paste. Marcus's eyes started to twitch violently, then slowly rolled toward the back of his head.

"Oh God, Dad," Kyle sobbed, his voice shaking. "It'll be all right, just hang on. Please, just hang on …"

† † †

Less than an hour later, Kyle stood in the front lawn, looking down at the makeshift tombstone he had crafted for his mother. The more he thought about it, the more he started to believe that the small wooden cross he had fashioned wasn't enough to mark her grave, though he realized he had few options. He didn't know what the cross stood for, if anything—it wasn't part of the Gentry's religion, but he remembered seeing it in photos of some older settlements. Back then it had meant something, something of worth to those the deceased had left behind. It might have been an Earth tradition long since abandoned, but in his grief it was all he could think of. And he'd be damned if he marked his mother's grave with any of the Royal Religion's adornments.

It had only taken him a few moments to bury her once he had resuscitated Marcus and brought him back to the *Gemini* for treatment. The work had distracted him long enough for his tears to dry up, though he could still feel the salt on his cheeks. He looked down at his right hand, at his mother's simple sterling wedding band that he had found amid the rubble in his bedroom. It was stained with soot and oxidized from the heat, leaving it with a swirl of tarnish. He spun it through his fingers, debating whether he should leave it with her. In the end, he couldn't part with it. After all, it was all he had left of her now. He slid it into his pocket and looked up at the darkening sky. It was overcast from the rising smoke, though a stiff wind had swept much of the ash off the valley floor. The breeze rattled the cross, and Kyle shook his head, wishing that his last words to his mother hadn't been in anger.

Jay walked slowly across the yard, dragging his feet as he came closer to his friend. Their time was short, and this place was not safe for them.

"Kyle?" Jay started timidly. "I'm sorry to bother you, but...but we need to get moving."

"How's my dad doing?" Kyle asked, his eyes never leaving the grave. "Is he going to be all right?"

"I think so," Jay replied. "We gave him some fluids and set him up with an IV. He's not out of the woods yet, but I think he's going to make it."

"Thank goodness," Kyle sighed. "He came so close."

"Yeah, it's a good thing we got to him when we did," Jay said. "Without your powers to heal that wound, it probably would have been a different story. He was really lucky."

Kyle sighed. "Jay...I need to ask you ... Do you ... do you still think I should have done things differently? Would she still be alive if we had just done our job?"

Kyle's gaze finally strayed from his mother's grave, his weary eyes refocusing on his friend. Jay took a deep breath.

"Kyle, I don't...I don't know," Jay said. "I was afraid of what would happen. But knowing what we do now, I don't think I could go back to the way things were."

"I just can't stop thinking that she's dead because of me."

"You had to make a tough choice. But if your mom was really one of them, then she knew the risk she was taking by telling you. You're not the one who got her involved, and you're damn sure not the one who killed her. You didn't do this."

"Maybe not, but we've done enough," Kyle said. "When I think of all the things we've done, how many of them we've killed … I'm not going to let Aeron get away with this."

"We're with you," Jay affirmed. "No matter what, we're with you."

Kyle nodded. "Give me a minute. I'll meet you back at the ship."

Jay flashed a brief smile beneath his beard and walked away, leaving Kyle to say his final goodbye. Kyle watched him go for a moment, then turned back to the wobbling cross. He steadied it with one hand and scooped up a handful of dirt with the other. The grains felt heavy in his hand, almost as if they carried with them the gravity of his loss. He let them fall through his fingers, the wind sweeping them across the grave. He took a deep breath, and really felt the air touch his lungs for the first time.

"Goodbye, Mom."

Kyle stood there only long enough for his words to fade, knowing that if he allowed himself more time he wouldn't be able to leave. He walked away with his eyes down, trying to swallow his pain and lock it away inside himself as best he could. His father and friends were the ones who needed him now. At least there was still something he could do to help them.

He lifted his head again as he approached the *Gemini.* Jay and the others had left their gear lying outside the ship, and it was strewn about haphazardly. They were nowhere to be found.

Kyle's eyes narrowed as he looked around, quickly noticing several sets of foreign footprints embedded in the ash-covered ground. By the time he pulled his gun from its holster, it was already too late. Dominion soldiers swarmed in from all directions, closing like a pack of wolves encircling their prey. Just as Kyle was about to open fire, he saw his friends being dragged down the boarding ramp of the *Gemini*, their hands tied behind them and automatic weapons pressed against the backs of their heads.

Kyle cursed under his breath and slowly lowered his weapon. He looked around again, counting the number of soldiers surrounding him. It was more than forty in all, including several drooling Fury beasts. He had seen worse odds, but he wasn't willing to risk his friends' lives to take action now. He tossed his handgun to the ground and placed his hands behind his head.

Finally, he saw what he had been waiting for: General Donovan walking down the ramp of the *Gemini*, clapping his hands with a devious smile across his face. Kyle's fists tightened impulsively, aching for the opportunity to knock that smile through the back of Vaughn's head. He counted the number of strides it would take for him to get there and turn that bastard inside out. He guessed twelve seconds total.

Dammit, too long.

A soldier nervously crept up behind him, then pulled Kyle's sword from the sheath on his back. A second soldier softly asked him to drop his hands, and then shackled his wrists with a pair of heavy carboranium cuffs. Kyle felt a drain go through his body, like something had suddenly sucked him dry. He'd felt the effects before. The cuffs must have been treated with serosa chloride, an extremely rare mineral that had properties capable of suppressing the Celestial Spark. It was a closely guarded fact, but Vaughn was one of Aeron's more trusted generals. Kyle did his best to hide the sudden impotence. He just couldn't give that piece of shit the satisfaction.

"I was wondering when you were going to show your face," Kyle snarled.

"Well, I had to make sure you weren't going to cause a scene," Vaughn said, still showing that stupid grin. "I would hate to have to kill your friends just to teach you a lesson."

"Like you did with my mother?"

"You can't blame that on me. I wasn't the one who decided to ignore my orders."

"No, you were the one who hanged and burned her while she was still alive."

"Please," Vaughn said. "Don't try to peg her as innocent in all this. We heard your conversations. We know that she was working with the Splinter. How did you think this was going to end?"

"Are you really just going to ignore what the Gentry did?" Kyle asked. "All those lives he took just for political power?"

"I know about the Council, Kyle," Vaughn announced. "I've known about it for years. The Gentry has trusted me to protect his secret. Even if that means disposing of you."

Kyle dropped his eyes, shaking his head. "I should have known," he said. "It doesn't matter who dies, as long as the Gentry gets what he wants."

"Do you want me to cry for some forgotten bureaucracy? They were men who thought they could question a god. The Gentry only did what the galaxy needed. If a few people had to die for that, so be it."

"Fuck, that's so typical. Everything at face value, right, General? Have you ever had a thought for yourself?"

"Have you?" Vaughn asked. "One sob story from your mother and suddenly you're a revolutionary?"

"No, I'm just not an idiot," Kyle said. "Or a coward. Just because Aeron speaks doesn't mean he's right."

"Shit, would you listen to yourself? Why does everything you do have to be so noble?" Vaughn sneered condescendingly. Every twitch of his face made Kyle want to peel his skin back. "I warned you what would happen if you disobeyed the Gentry. But you wouldn't listen. And now we're stuck in this predicament. Believe it or not, the Gentry considered giving you a second chance if you were willing to handle your uncle and your mother. But I knew that anger of yours would get the best of you, and you'd turn on us. You're far too sentimental for a mutant."

"Why not just kill me then? And leave my family and friends out of this?"

"I can't do that, Kyle," Vaughn said. "You dragged them into this. And we've got to make an example out of all of you. Your men here, Dr. Preston and his family. All of them."

"You leave them out of this," Kyle said. "They had nothing to do with it."

"It's too late for that," Vaughn said, his face spreading that infuriating smile again. "I'm especially excited to spend some time with the doctor's daughter before she goes. I've always had a thing for her."

"If you touch her, you son of a bitch, I swear on my mother's grave I will fucking kill you."

"Is that so? Barely dead a few hours and you're already swearing on her grave. And here I thought you were sentimental," Vaughn quipped, turning away. "Won't matter though. You'll be dead long before I'm finished with that sweetness. I'll tell her you said goodbye."

Kyle could feel his blood boiling as he watched the general tell his lieutenant where to take them. His wrists strained against the shackles to the point where blood began to drip from his skin. The alloy was too strong even for his mutant strength to break, and even if he did, there's no guarantee that he could reach Vaughn before the platoon swarmed him. He would be no good to anyone dead.

A group of four soldiers forced Jackson and the others toward Kyle's parents' house. A pair of transports looped over the ridge above the valley, the hum of the thrusters drowning out Vaughn's voice as he barked orders to his troops. Kyle felt a gun muzzle jab into his back, and he reluctantly started toward the house. He tried to see how many men loaded into the transports, but each time he received a sharp rap from the gun in return.

Mac tripped over the front steps and went down into a heap. He was pulled back to his feet by a pair of soldiers and thrown through the front door.

"I'm sorry, Kyle," Jackson said as they approached. "There were too many of them. We couldn't..."

The captain was abruptly cut off by a sharp blow to the stomach. Kyle turned, but suddenly felt the butt of the lieutenant's rifle crack against the side of his jaw. The strike made his ears ring, but it didn't knock him down. The barrel of the rifle immediately appeared in front of his face, again goading him through the door.

"Shut your fucking mouths!" a lieutenant screamed. "Damned traitors, I don't want to hear another word. Now get moving."

Two soldiers yanked Jackson back to his feet and dragged him inside. One of the two transports whirled overhead, distracting their captors long enough for Kyle to count eight troops and one Fury foot-soldier still milling around the grounds. The other transport was running, waiting for the others to finish their chore. A hand grabbed the back of Kyle's shirt and pulled him into the house, the stench of the fire still permeating the walls.

"Get down on your knees," the lieutenant ordered, gesturing with his rifle. When the four of them hesitated, the lieutenant kicked Kyle on the side of the knee, then crunched the rifle against the back of his head. Kyle's knees buckled and fell to the floorboards, the room suddenly spinning beneath him. The lieutenant pulled his pistol and aimed it down at Kyle's temple.

"You wouldn't be doing this," Kyle slurred, "if you knew the things that we know."

"We don't give a damn about what you know," the lieutenant snapped.

"Then you better kill me now. Before I turn that gun around and point it at *your* head."

"I wasn't planning on waiting," the lieutenant replied, pressing the barrel against Kyle's head.

Just then, the ceiling creaked, and several streams of charred dust trickled down through the rafters. The four soldiers immediately stopped and looked up, watching the trail of falling ash move across the room. Even with his ears ringing and the rustle of the engines outside, Kyle could hear footsteps shuffling across the floor above.

"Sir?"

"I hear it," the lieutenant said. "You two go check it out."

Two soldiers started up the remains of the front staircase. Jackson gave Kyle a curious glance, but Kyle could only shrug. The floor above them was weak from the flames, bending and moaning with each cautious step. After a moment the footsteps stopped and the gunfire began. It was a jarring sound, enough to even startle Kyle in his haze. The lieutenant flinched at the outburst, but then quickly froze as the thump of two bodies hit the floor.

"Shaw? Turner?" he called.

There was no reply. A trickle of blood came down through a crack in the ceiling.

The lieutenant took a few steps toward the stairs, then contorted as gunfire erupted again, a single round blowing out his chest like a bursting balloon. A second shot dropped the final soldier as he sprinted for the front door. The commotion had shaken some of the cobwebs out of Kyle's head, but he still stared with dizzied eyes at the two fallen troops. Then they heard the footsteps again, this time moving quickly toward the stairs.

"Commander?"

It was Dan Preston. He was carrying two rifles over his left shoulder, and Kyle's sword over his right. His face lacked its typical exuberance, and he had a purpose to his step.

"Holy shit, kid!" Mac exclaimed. "Where the hell did you come from?"

"My father asked me to keep an eye on you," Dan replied.

Dan unlocked their shackles, and they scooped up the scattered firearms. Kyle felt a rush of strength swell through his veins, his Celestial power quickly returning after the serosa chloride was pulled away from his skin. His eyes finally cleared, and he regained his balance.

"Well, you picked a fucking great time to jump in," Jay said.

"Everybody's keeping tabs on us today, huh?" Jackson said.

"Hopefully not," Dan said. "There's still a handful of stragglers out front. I managed to get a couple on the outskirts, but not all of them."

"Anything helps, Danny," Kyle said. "What do we got out there?" he asked Mac, who had crept to one of the shattered windows and was peering over the sill.

"I count nine targets, one mutant. He's a big one, wearing some kind of armor."

"Is the *Gemini* still operational?" Jay asked.

"It's still there," Mac said. "Looks like it'll run."

"They've got another transport too," Jackson said. "Out the front door at ten o'clock."

"You got anything you can shoot with, Jackson?" Kyle asked.

"It's not great," Jackson replied, "but I can hit some guys with it."

"Go upstairs and start picking them off," Kyle said. "The rest of you give me some cover while I deal with that mutant."

Kyle marched out the front door, his sidearm in his left hand and war sword in his right. One of the soldiers shouted, pointing toward him as he strode boldly into the yard. Several shots rang out from the second-floor windows behind him, and three of the troopers immediately hit the ground. Kyle fired two shots to his left and dropped another pair before leveling the weapon toward the mammoth mutant in front of him. It was a hulking creature with long arms that ended in large, knotty hands like two spiked flails. It snarled at him like a wild dog, but Kyle never broke stride. He fired half a dozen shots from the pistol, but the rounds simply clanged off the beast's ceramic armor.

The creature roared and reared back with one of its fists. As it slammed into the ground like a wrecking ball, Kyle was already past it, whirling his sword overhead. The enchanted blade sliced through both armor and flesh, neither posing any resistance to the mystical blade. The mutant hurled down its other fist, but Kyle deflected it aside with the broad side of his sword, then plunged the blade upward into the beast's throat. The flesh punctured with a sound not unlike a rock hitting a puddle of mud. Its eyes went dark and it crumbled to the ground with a thump.

Kyle pressed his boot against the mutant's jaw and yanked his weapon from its neck. A gout of thick, murky blood followed his sword out like a stream. It was a putrid green, just a shade darker than rodent dung, and equally as fetid.

The others had finished cleaning up the scraps by the time he turned back to them. They pilfered whatever munitions they could salvage from the bodies, and Jay and Dan were sweeping the *Gemini* for any stowaways or booby traps.

Kyle checked his wrist. Nearly eleven minutes had passed since Vaughn departed. He figured it would take him over an hour to reach Angel's home, even by warp drive. They were horribly behind.

"Boys, on me," Kyle hollered. "Quickly, quickly. I want you four on the *Gemini.* Danny, if you've got a direct line to your father, now's the time to use it. Tell him to get your family off-planet. Find a rally point, something obscure, and you take them to rendezvous with Colonel Foster."

"How do we find him?" Dan asked.

"We've got a trace on his transport," Mac said. "We'll find him."

"Wait a minute," Dan said. "This is … we're going to a Splinter camp? How do we even know they'll take us?"

"They need us," Kyle said. "They'll take us in."

"They need *you,*" Jackson said. "Where the hell are you gonna be?"

"I'm going to get Angel," Kyle said.

"Whoa, wait! Alone?" Jay exclaimed. "Are you out of your mind? They're probably already there."

"I don't have time to argue about this," Kyle said, his internal clock ticking in his ear. "If I don't go get her, she's dead."

"Commander, let me come with you," Dan said. "I can help."

"I need you to help your parents," Kyle said. "They're in a much more occupied sector. If things go wrong, these three will need you more than I will."

"Sir, she's my sister—"

"I know, Danny," Kyle said. "I won't let anything happen to her."

The young lieutenant nodded reluctantly, then followed the others into the *Gemini* as Kyle sprinted toward the remaining Dominion transport. Another four minutes had passed. Damn, too slow. Why did he feel like he was suddenly moving in molasses? As the Dominion transport lifted off and pulled away from Littenderon's atmosphere, he found himself begging it to find another gear. He set the coordinates of the hyperdrive to drop him into orbit above Angel's home, and crossed his fingers that she could stay alive long enough for him to get there.

CHAPTER 8

Dan Preston had no idea what he was doing. Literally. His mind just couldn't comprehend what had just happened at Kyle's family home. In fact, he could barely figure out how he got to this point, much less decipher what he should be doing next. His father had told him that Kyle and his men might be in trouble, that they had a delicate assignment and things could easily turn complicated. He told him that this was recon only, to not get involved under any circumstances, because it would only make things worse. Dan had thought it strange, but he didn't ask questions. He just did as his father asked.

He just never expected to see what he saw.

And now he was neck deep in some sort of galactic mutiny. Or maybe it was a conspiracy. Shit, he didn't even know the right word to describe it. All he knew was he had just killed four Dominion soldiers and thrown himself right in the middle of it all. His father had been pretty specific about not doing that too. But he couldn't let those men die. Kyle was his idol, and they had all been so good to him as he went through the program— helping him, mentoring him, reassuring him that he had what it took to be one of them. So he did what he knew Kyle would do for him. He just wished that he wouldn't have to explain all that to his father ...

The *Gemini* dropped out of hyperspace above the planetoid Quanteru. Its thrusters burned into the atmosphere as the craft descended toward the manufacturing paddocks below. Quanteru was a civilian industrial colony within the inner sectors of the Dominion system, just a momentary warp jump from the capital itself, but it was the closest rallying point for Dr. Preston and his family, as well as the handful of others they felt may be in danger because of their association.

They had chosen a decommissioned assembly platform for their rendezvous. Doctor Preston had been adamant that he would not meet them without an explanation of what had transpired, but Jackson had insisted that it wasn't safe to discuss over the communication link.

It was the middle of the night on this slice of Quanteru, though the lights of the machine-riddled landscape produced a perpetual twilight. In the distance they could see the silhouettes of the factory stacks, and winding away from the central manufacturing plant was an intricate web of utility pipes and conduits. Above them the sky was grayed with the heat of the machines, as if the whole planet had taken part in the blue-collar efforts that were the trade here.

Jackson ordered the *Gemini* fully cloaked and shielded as it swept over the pumping stacks, making it invisible to any surveillance nearby. The installation may have been non-military, but they were concerned that a Dominion platoon might have followed the Prestons to this planet in order to track them down.

"We've got a visual on the platform," Jay announced. "I'm reading fourteen heat signatures on site. Looks like everyone is there."

"Mac, how's our perimeter?" Jackson asked.

"Right now I've got no military tracks," Mac responded. "We're clear."

"All right, set it down," Jackson said. "Keep the cloaks up and the engines running. We're out of here in a heartbeat if we get any surprises."

"We'll have to drop the shields to set down," Mac said. "Can't get anyone on board with those up."

"Fine, do it," Jackson said. "Mac, you and Jay stay here and keep an eye on the scanners. Danny, suit up. You and I are down the ramp."

The ship wheeled over the platform on top of the abandoned factory, throwing up a swirl of wind among the gathered group of refugees. Dan followed Jackson into the boarding area below the bridge. He could feel the inertia shift as the *Gemini* set down on the roof, the sudden thud rocking his weight forward as he checked the charge on his rifle. He tapped the earpiece for their communicator and heard the echo that confirmed it was active.

Jackson tapped him on the shoulder and gave him a thumbs-up. Dan nodded and hit the hatch release. The airlock cracked open and they felt the rush of air from the thrusters flashing past them. Dan watched Jackson ready his rifle and then followed him down the ramp and onto the roof. He dropped to a knee about thirty feet from the ramp, surveying the surrounding stacks through the scope on his weapon.

Jackson hurried toward the waiting group of people. They were huddled along the edge of the roof near the scaffolding leading down to the service floors below. Many of them looked confused and frightened. These were their neighbors, classmates, and family friends. Other than two former Infinity Protocol trainees, these people were not soldiers. They had been pulled away from uneventful lives, lives where a difficult day involved missed deadlines or long lines at the market. Hopefully they counted themselves more fortunate than the other loved ones they'd been forced to leave behind.

"Dr. Preston, we're glad you made it, sir," Jackson said with a brief salute.

"Spare me the pleasantries, Captain," the doctor snapped. "What are we doing on this rock?"

"I'm sorry, sir," Jackson started, "I'm not at liberty to discuss here. We'll brief you en route."

"I am not getting on that ship until you tell me why we had to abandon everything to meet you here."

"Sir, we really don't have time to talk about this now." Jackson glanced over his shoulder, checking the horizons. It didn't go unnoticed by the veteran officer.

"It's not the Splinter that's after us, is it?" Preston asked. "Where is Commander Griffin?"

"Sir, we need to get off this roof."

"Where *is* he, Captain?" Preston's tone demanded a response this time.

"He's gone to get your daughter, sir," Jackson answered. "He'll meet us at our destination."

"What the hell have you boys done? You've pulled my son and daughter into this?"

"Sir, I must insist that we get everyone on board before we discuss this further," Jackson said, waving Dan over. "We're leaving in three minutes, with or without you."

Preston gave Jackson a harsh look, one the veteran soldier had probably seen hundreds of times before. It usually extracted the answers the doctor wanted, but today Jackson didn't have the leeway to crumble under his gaze.

"Sir...Dad...we've got to go now," Dan insisted finally. "It's not safe here."

Suddenly there was a garbled voice sputtering over their communicator, the words barely discernible despite coming from the ship just a few feet away. Jackson and Dan's hands immediately darted to their ears, trying to clear the message. Finally, they caught Mac's voice on the other end.

"Do you copy?" Mac called. "We ... multiple ... craft coming our way. Multiple military ... signals. They're closing fast. Do you read me?"

"That's it, we're going now," Jackson ordered, directing the group toward the *Gemini.* "We read you, Mac. We'll be saddled up in twenty seconds."

"Copy, we're plotting our course now," Mac said.

Dan looked up abruptly, having heard a faint clink off in the distance. He caught a glimpse of a silhouette darting across the adjacent platform. Then there was another. And another. Before he knew it, over a dozen marks filed onto the roof, and he realized their time was already up.

"Captain, on your six!" Dan yelled. He raised his rifle and took aim. The sudden bursts of light illuminated the stacks as he dropped three members of the incursion group with his first salvo. Jackson started pulling Preston and his wife toward the *Gemini* as Dan laid down suppressive fire. The men across from them slowed, then fired a return volley.

Mac's voice sounded in Dan's earpiece: "Turrets are coming online."

A moment later a roar from the *Gemini*'s cannons announced a wave of high-ordinance plasma fire, ceasing the enemy barrage as they dropped or clamored for cover. Dan hurried back toward the *Gemini*, and a second barrage of gunfire erupted from the opposite side, sending him sprawling to the ground. Several shots struck the hull of the *Gemini*, scattering shards of the cloaking panels across the platform. The cloaks flickered with the impacts, sending splinters of metal across the invisible frame like hovering spider webs.

"Dan, we're still taking fire!" Mac's voice trumpeted. "Get on board now!"

"Dammit, there's another hostile group to the south!" Dan yelled, scurrying toward the ramp.

"We've got tracks everywhere!" Mac shouted. "We can't raise the shields until we're in the air. You've gotta get on board now!"

Dan cocked the explosive launcher on his rifle and fired a charge toward the south platform. Lit in an eerie green by the shower of weaponized plasma, he scrambled up the ramp and hit the lever to close the hatch.

"I'm in, let's hit it!" he hollered.

Instantly the ship lifted into the air. The hull echoed with more gunfire, each shot drumming like they were inside a hollow tin can. There was a sudden lurch in the takeoff, and a loud explosion that followed it. The emergency lights began flashing across the cabin.

"Danny, get up here!" Jackson shouted. "We've lost the cloaks. You've gotta take the munitions while Mac sets the hyperdrive!"

Dan hurried up the ladder into the bridge, leaving the group of civilians to buckle up in the passenger bay down below. Another blast knocked him off his feet. The alarms were blaring now, a steady wail as he regained his footing and took the seat in front of the artillery console.

"Do we have the shields up?" he asked.

"They took a few hits," Jay answered. "They're at sixty-three percent."

"Jay, get us out of the atmosphere so we can hit hyperspace," Jackson ordered. "Dan, light 'em up down there."

The targeting systems flashed like a strobe light against Dan's face. There were targets in every direction. He guided the armaments to their marks and unleashed a battery of missiles. The stack platforms and towers ignited in an orange fury, flooding the sky with fire and smoke.

Jay leaned on the throttle, and the *Gemini* arced upward. There was a perceptible drag on the left flank as though the thrusters had been damaged. Dan went through a weapons check, noting a malfunction in the port missile hydraulics. The primary artillery systems all seemed intact. The pull on the left eased as the ship approached the top of the stratosphere and gravity relented.

"Jay, how are we looking?" Jackson asked.

"Port thrusters took a hit. They're below thirty percent," Jay responded. "We'll be all right as long as we don't lose any more."

"Weapons are in good shape," Dan said. "One bank of missiles is offline, but we've got plenty left."

"Mac, what about the hyperdrive?" Jackson said.

"It's good," Mac replied. "We'll be set to go once we clear the gravitational field."

The calm was cut short as their proximity alarms began wailing through the cabin. The lights dimmed as the radar went into overdrive. Something was closing fast.

"We've got multiple bogeys incoming," Mac announced. "Coming up fast from the south horizon."

"Their radar is all over us without the cloaks," Jay said. "They're gonna get a lock."

The intermittent beeps quickly became a full-blown siren. Several tracks appeared on the screen in front of them.

"They've got missile lock!" Jay said.

"I've got inbound ordinance!" Mac hollered. "Seven—make that eight—rockets on us. Impact in ten seconds."

"Jay, evasive maneuvers," Jackson ordered. "Jettison the water tanks."

There were several rhythmic booms as the heavy water tanks detached from the ship's hull. Jay took control of the stick, pulling the ship sharply to the right. The whole structure shivered as it darted away with the wounded engine, and a loud explosion echoed behind them.

"We lost three!" Mac yelled. "Still have five on us."

"I can't shake these rockets with that engine out," Jay said. "Hang on, this is gonna be rough."

Jay threw down the stick, and the *Gemini* plummeted back toward the Quanteru surface. The torque slammed them back into their seats, the weight of the g-forces feeling like an anvil on their chests. The ship slammed into the atmosphere like a falling stone, sending a tremor through the cabin and each of its passengers. The sky in front of them burned against their struggling shields, lighting up the bridge as though they had flown into a star.

"Jay, we're gonna be incinerated!" Jackson shouted. "Pull it back!"

"Just another second," Jay said.

The missiles tore into the atmosphere behind them, but the heat of reentry was too much for their thinner shells. They burst against the thickening air just meters from the Gemini's tail, thrashing them into a spin as they dropped. Jay hit their retro-thrusters and pulled hard on the controls, throwing them forward against their harnesses. The ship rolled drastically to the right but leveled off among the clouds. The target lock finally went silent.

"Holy shit, please don't do that again," Dan muttered.

"Nice work, Jay," Mac said. "But we've still got those bogeys tracking us."

"Can you get us clear of the atmosphere to hit the hyperdrive?" Jackson asked.

"We'll never outrun them with the port engine sputtering," Jay said. "But I could maneuver through them if we can blaze a path."

"Danny, put everything into the forward cannons," Jackson said.

"I hope you don't get queasy," Jay said. "Cuz we're gonna be turning and burning."

"Just do it," Dan said. "Get us out of here."

The *Gemini* sliced through the cloud cover and into lower orbit. The sky went black as the atmosphere was left behind, but among the expanse there was the glint of Dominion Predators coming toward them. First four, then nine, then fourteen total. These were high-payload combat vessels and the *Gemini* was damaged. The hyperdrive was their only chance.

"Here we go," Jackson said. "Danny, cut it loose!"

The forward cannons churned like an angry volcano, spewing out a hundred rounds with each burst. The first Dominion fighter punctured as the rain of munitions tore through it, but in space there was no explosion. It caved in on itself before shattering into a mist of debris.

Quickly, the other ships returned fire. The *Gemini* dipped and dove through the wave of enemy shots, spinning effortlessly around their assault. Two more Dominion craft imploded as they knifed through the swarm, scattering their formation as they plunged past them. Jay hit their reserve propulsion boosters as they cleared the squadron, and with a heavy jerk they rocketed away from their pursuers.

"Switch all fire to the aft cannons!" Jackson yelled. "Get ready for the jump to hyperspace."

The forward guns went silent and the rear cannons picked up the rhythm. Another star-fighter was gashed with the barrage and veered into its nearest ally. They both capitulated, forcing the others to split like a river around a rock to evade the wreckage. With that small window, the *Gemini* pulled away, cruising toward deep space.

"All right, we're clear," Mac said. "Activating the hyperdrive."

The ship stretched out beneath them. Dan felt the familiar pressure of the warp effect pull him thin like a piece of spaghetti, and then yank them into hyperspace. Dan gagged as the sickening feeling swept over him, his mouth filling with spit as he struggled to keep from heaving the contents of his gut all over the cabin.

After ten wrenching minutes, the hyperdrive deactivated and they dropped out of warp. The ship pitched to the right with the damaged engine waning and the momentum of the warp jump throwing them forward. There was a chorus of groans from the passenger bay below, but there was enough discord on the bridge to go around already. The view in front of them was desolate, and there were no terrestrial bodies within range of their instruments.

"Mac, where are we?" Jackson asked.

"Sector 2759," Mac said. "A long way from anything with Aeron's name on it."

"What are we doing here?" Jackson asked, wiping some sweat from his forehead. "We don't have time for a bunch of detours."

"I couldn't get a lock on our tracer," Mac said. "They might have been jamming our signals, so I got us to a place where we can get a clean look. Plus, if they tracked our trajectory, they could have followed us right to the colonel's location."

"Could they track us here?" Jay asked.

"Sure, at least in this direction," Mac said. "But we're out in the middle of nowhere. They'll be looking for a planetary system along this course, and we're not in one."

"How long do we have?" Jackson asked.

"It'll take me a few minutes to track Bryan's location, and another few to set our course. I think we can be gone in ten."

"Jay, see what you can do about that engine from here," Jackson ordered. "Dan, go check on the passengers."

Dan unlatched his harness and staggered to his feet, the rumbling in his stomach barely subsiding. He lowered himself down to the passenger compartment below and was met with a number of anxious stares. His mother had her head buried in his father's shoulder, and she was sobbing openly. He resisted the urge to go over to them, his own emotions not quite in check at that point.

"Everyone all right?" he asked. "Is anyone hurt?"

There were no answers, just several aghast looks. His father's glare burned into him, but he said nothing.

"We're setting our next course," Dan said. "We'll be out of here soon. Just hang tight."

He climbed back up to the bridge, where Jay was chest deep in an access console on the left side of the room, trying to pull whatever extra power he could out of the damaged engine. Jackson was at the ship's controls, yelling back and forth with Jay about the electromagnetic output. Mac was frantically pacing back and forth between their hyperdrive controls and the tracking systems. The frenzied pace was in stark contrast to the stunned silence below.

"Dammit!" Jay said, pulling his head from the panel. "I can't fix this from here. We're gonna be flying on one wing."

"I'll factor the drag into our course heading," Mac said. "But it'll take me a few more minutes."

"Just get it right and get us out of here," Jackson said. "Everyone okay downstairs, Danny?"

"They're a little shell-shocked right now," Dan said, "but no injuries."

"And you're damn lucky there weren't."

Dr. Preston was halfway up the ladder behind Dan, and the tone of his voice was less than pleased, to say the least. He climbed up into the bridge and closed the hatch to the passenger bay behind him. The bustle of the cabin came to a screeching halt as their mentor entered. Their attention quickly turned to him.

"You have some major explaining to do," Preston seethed. "What in the hell did you do to bring this down on us?"

"Forgive me, sir, but none of us are too excited about this either," Jackson said. "We didn't wake up this morning with this in mind."

"Don't get smart with me, Captain," Preston said. "What the hell happened?"

"Sir, honestly, I don't even know where to start," Jackson said.

"It was Colonel Foster, wasn't it? Kyle let him live, didn't he?" the doctor accused. "I *knew* he would do something stupid like this. Doesn't he realize he can't save him this time?"

"It's not as simple as that, sir," Mac interjected. "Kyle's mother was involved also."

"His mother?" the doctor asked. "You're certain about that?"

"Yes, sir, she told us herself," Jay said. "She was on a video feed when we arrived on Emporia. Apparently the Fosters have been in league with the Splinter for a long time. They were one of the pioneering families of the resistance."

"Kyle's mother?" Preston gasped. "That skinny woman that used to send him care packages? *She* was a Splinter spy?"

"Yes, sir," Jackson said. "We were just as surprised as you are."

"Then she's the one you should be concerned about. If that intelligence gets back to the Gentry, she's as good as dead."

The four of them paused. Then Jackson shook his head. "She already is, sir."

Preston's eyes went wide. "*What*? How?"

"We were followed by some of General Donovan's men. They had surveillance on the meeting with the colonel."

"The meeting that never should have happened."

"Sir, Kyle wasn't willing to end his uncle's life without an explanation," Jackson said. "And now his mother is dead."

"And his father is back in the med-bay," Mac added. "He's barely hanging on."

Preston sighed. "How the hell did they get to the Royal family?"

"Sir, that I don't know," Jackson said. "Right now my concern is with the safety of the people on this ship."

"And what's the plan for that?" Preston asked. "Where do we go that's safe?"

"We're going to take refuge with Colonel Foster," Jackson answered.

The doctor let out something halfway between a laugh and shriek. "Well that's fantastic! After all this, you want to take us right into the lion's den. How do you expect that to work out?"

"Sir, we have reason to believe that the Splinter have a legitimate cause for their dissension," Jackson said. "And Kyle feels we can be safe there."

"Dammit, Captain, please to do not tell me you've bought into whatever bullshit the colonel has fed you."

"Honestly, General, I haven't bought into anything yet," Jackson said. "But we don't have any other choice. We will never make it out here in deep space with no supplies and a damaged ship. We can't go back to the Dominion, whether we agree with it or not."

"How do we know that the Splinter troops won't kill us themselves?" Dr. Preston asked.

"We don't," Jay answered bluntly. "But that's where Kyle is going. And if we're gonna get stuck on the wrong side of the Gentry, I wanna be where Kyle is."

Mac and Dan nodded. Jackson shrugged, but didn't dissent.

"Shit, this just gets better and better," the doctor said. "Are you at least going to let me in on what they told you that was so damn convincing?"

"Yes, sir, we will," Jackson said. "But right now we have got to find some shelter."

"The course is set, Jacks," Mac said. "We're good to go."

"Then let's get moving," Jackson said. "I'll fill you in on the way."

Jackson started in on the details of the Galactic Council and their demise at the hands of the Gentry. Dan was wide-eyed as the tale was told, as much from shock as disbelief. His father, however, was far more skeptical of the account, even with the evidence outlined in the stolen Dominion files to persuade him. Dan assumed a lifetime of following Dominion protocols would do that. But to him the proof seemed legitimate. Perhaps it was just wishful thinking, that they needed the stories to be true in order to justify where they were going. Either way, by then their course had already been set. There was no turning back.

With a final command from Jackson, the ship pivoted toward their destination, the hyperdrive roared to life, and in an instant they disappeared.

CHAPTER 9

Dusk had already set in on Angel's home planet of Vadara, with the first of the system's twin suns having fallen beneath the horizon. The twilight here was a strange experience, occurring at two different times as each of the sister stars nestled in for their slumber. The Vadarian terrain flourished in the abundance of light and rich soil, and the picturesque landscape made for a very well-to-do population. In fact this was an exclusively residential planet, with no industry to speak of and only a small military magistrate. The many industrious entrepreneurs in the sector hungered to exploit the planet's vast mineral supplies and arable land, but no amount of zealous enterprising ever had a chance of competing with established money.

After she left her home at the Infinity Compound, Angel followed her father into government service by performing corporate relations, but after several years she made a small fortune after transitioning to industrial finance. The job afforded her a chance to work at home, and she splurged on a sprawling estate along the banks of the Calacatta, one of Vadara's larger rivers. There was a range of rolling foothills just outside her front door, and they dropped down into a sparkling river valley in the rear. The river widened to nearly a mile across beyond her backyard, and one of the planet's largest trading posts resided on the far bank. Here she had everything she needed to live a comfortable life—everything except family and friends.

At the moment she was standing in her kitchen with a coworker named Nicole, trading stories over a cup of Elysian tea. Angel had bribed Nicole for a visit by promising a gourmet meal—one that had promptly turned into a disaster. The poultry tasted like sawdust, and the mashed potatoes had been whipped into a consistency that more closely resembled glue than food. Angel was thoroughly embarrassed, but Nicole had endured the amateur dinner admirably and the two had managed to enjoy a few laughs anyway.

Angel brushed back a wisp of her auburn brown hair as she took a sip from her cup. She had a sterling complexion with a soft caramel tan, and her green eyes were perpetually bright. She wore a tight black shirt with a low-cut collar that showed off her figure—way over the top for dinner with a colleague, but she rarely got the chance to dress for special occasions, and she was going to take advantage of the opportunity. She was a beautiful young woman, and every now and then she just needed to feel beautiful.

"Are you going to be coming in to the office any time soon?" Nicole asked.

"In a few weeks," Angel said, setting down her teacup. "I've got to be there for the Perkins contract signing."

"I can't believe you managed to close that deal," Nicole said. "I'm starting to wonder what other types of favors you're offering during your pitch …"

"Oh my goodness, stop it!" Angel gasped. "I haven't done that sort of thing since I left my government job."

"You're terrible."

"You started it." Angel looked back at the barely touched dinner on the table. "I'm sorry again about the food."

"Oh please, it's fine," Nicole said. "I've had a good time anyway. And I really love your house."

"Thank you. Sometimes I think it's a bit much for just me."

"Maybe, but what a view," Nicole said, walking to the back windows that overlooked the river. She looked down for a moment and picked up a picture frame from an occasional table. "Who is this?"

Angel came over and took the picture from Nicole. She looked at it for a second as though she needed to examine it. The image was probably ten years old, judging from her dated haircut. She was standing between two men, one an older gentleman and the other a towering hulk with a blinding smile.

"Oh, that's my dad."

"Your dad? You're kidding, right?" Nicole pointed at the other man. "Who's the other guy?"

Angel blushed. "A friend of mine. His name is Kyle."

"Oh my lord." Nicole took the picture back and ogled it. "Do you keep copies of this next to your bed?"

"Come on…"

"Seriously, how do you know this guy?"

"It's not like that. He used to work with my dad," Angel said, gently pulling the photo from Nicole's unwilling hand and placing it back on the table.

Nicole picked up the picture again. "This guy worked with your dad? Is he in the military or something?"

"Yeah, you might say that," Angel said.

"How long have you known him?"

"Probably … twenty-five years," Angel said. "My brother's joining his company next year."

"Do you get to see him very often?"

"Um … not as much as I'd like."

"So he's not gonna be coming over later?" Nicole laughed. "I'd be happy to hang out a while longer …"

"No, he doesn't make it out here very often," Angel said.

"Can I keep this picture?"

"He's not *that* good looking, Nicole."

Nicole shrugged. "If you say so."

"Can I get you some more tea?" Angel asked, trying her best to change the subject. "I've got some overcooked desert you can try."

"Thanks, but I should probably be going," Nicole said, finally replacing the picture. "I need to go across the river and pick up a few things from the market before it closes."

"Oh, okay. I'm glad you could make it."

"Thanks. We'll have to do this again."

"You can come by any time," Angel said, trying not to appear too eager.

Nicole waved as she walked out. Angel sighed and looked around at the cluttered kitchen. Despite the mess it felt empty and hollow. She started loading some dishes in her sink, but stopped after just a few moments. She looked around at all her plush furnishings and expensive artwork, then down at the cooling meal. *All this trouble just for a little company*, she thought.

She decided that the cleaning could wait. All of a sudden, the quiet of the huge empty house felt a tad overwhelming. She walked out the broad sliding glass doors onto her back balcony, hoping that the crisp river air would do her some good. Nicole's hovering skiff went speeding across the water, leaving a gentle wake on the surface of the river. Angel looked up at the sunset as her guest drifted out of sight. The second sun had touched the horizon, signaling the end of another day.

She turned and curled up on her favorite sofa just outside the kitchen door. A deep sigh escaped her lips as she picked up a worn-down charcoal pencil and a large bound book of paper that had become the latest in her ever-growing collection of sketchbooks. She opened it and turned to her last work, a heavily shaded rendition of a starfire flower that she didn't especially care for. Her eyebrows wrinkled in disgust, then she started carefully guiding her pencil across the paper.

She looked up again as a light breeze rustled the paper beneath her hands. The wind picked up quickly and blew her hair back from her face. Outside, several large, dark shadows went sweeping across the water. At first she dismissed them as a flock of the giant therahawks that migrated through this area every year. However, the rippling tide suddenly pushed back from the shore, and then she heard the thrum of starship engines quickly rising to a roar.

"What…?"

The pencil slipped out of her hand. Then the book slid off her lap. She stood up and walked to the railing, unsure of what she would see. There were three Dominion transports descending around her home, and two more ships already on the ground on either side. Soldiers were flooding out into her yard, swarming toward her house like angry hornets. The pounding of their boots and the clatter of their weapons immediately turned her curiosity into panic. She stumbled backward, tripping over the fallen sketchbook and landing on her hip. She let out a yelp as she hit the floor, but managed to stifle it with her hand over her mouth. Downstairs, her back door gave way with a crash. She could hear them rushing inside, their heavy boots thudding against the ground as they spread through her home.

Her legs froze. The walls felt like they were caving in. And yet she couldn't move.

The crash of a window breaking snapped her out of her haze. She grabbed a knife from the kitchen counter and sprinted up the stairs to the third floor. She skidded to a halt as she heard footsteps on the tile roof above her. Out of options, she turned and ran back to the kitchen, then hurried down the stairwell behind the pantry that led into the storage room beneath the house. The thick wooden door creaked as it opened and closed, and she clenched her teeth, hoping it wouldn't give her away.

The stairs seemed to echo with each step, and she couldn't steady herself enough to keep them quiet. She stumbled down to the floor and ran into the wall at the foot of the stairs. The basement was dark and cluttered. Her grip on the knife was making her hand sweat. The soldiers were calling for her now, demanding that she show herself and go with them quietly. Each shout gnawed at her back like the claws of a rodent. It made her skin crawl under her taut black shirt. She covered her ears and forced herself to focus, hoping to find something, anything that could help her.

Then she saw something on the far side of the room. It was a window, small and rectangular, but it was a way out. She could see a thin beam of faint light streaking in through the glass, the allure of its freedom beckoning her closer. In between lay a maze of old belongings—dated clothing and furniture, and countless boxes of useless junk that could only get her killed if she knocked one over.

She inched forward, sweating furiously and cursing each lost moment. But after several painstaking steps, she finally reached the sill. It was horribly small, hardly bigger than a pillow, but her thin waist could easily fit through it. However, before she rose up to look for a path to escape, she saw a cluster of soldiers on the grass outside. They were fanning through the trees as they sloped up the hillside. There were so many—how could she make it past them?

Angel whirled around as she heard footsteps hurrying down the basement stairwell. She quickly buried herself behind a pile of boxes and pulled an old blanket over her head.

The boots stepped off the wooden stairs and onto the concrete floor. Angel saw the lights come on through the fabric, which was followed by a pop as the fuse immediately shorted out. The burst made her flinch, and she kicked one of the boxes next to her. It rattled as some long-forgotten knick-knacks clattered against each other. The sound seemed deafening.

The thump of boots started into the room, drumming in her direction. She clenched her eyes shut as tight as she could, afraid that the intruder might somehow be able to hear her heart pounding against her chest. The soldier threw a box aside, its contents crashing across the concrete floor. She squeezed the knife as though she was trying to crush it, even as the soldier put a hand on the boxes behind her. A scream began to rise in her throat, and for a moment she thought her pounding heart had stopped beating.

Another box was knocked over, and then she heard the sharp yet wet sound of metal stabbing into flesh. There was a muffled gurgling, followed by the wretched noise of a man quietly choking on his own blood. Angel gasped uncontrollably as she heard a body hit the floor, her stomach having suddenly turned itself upside down. She covered her mouth to silence herself, afraid that the next sound she made would be her last. But then, she heard something she did not expect.

"Angel?"

The voice was familiar, immediately releasing the swelling tension that had frozen her arms and legs. She pulled the blanket away from her eyes, and there he was. Kyle was staring back at her.

He tried with obvious effort to give her a reassuring smile. Angel jumped to her feet and threw her arms around his neck, instantly feeling safer in his arms. She struggled hopelessly against a stream of tears, clutching him tight to keep herself from crying hysterically.

"Are you all right?" Kyle muttered, placing his strong hand on the back of her head.

"Kyle, I'm … I'm so scared. I … I don't know where they came from. They just dropped out of the sky and … and broke into the house. I didn't know what to do …"

"Okay, okay, it's okay," Kyle whispered. He stooped down to her eye level and looked right at her. "I'm not gonna let them hurt you. We're going to get out of here, all right?"

"How … how did you know …?"

"We don't have time for that now," Kyle said, his voice dropping another octave. "I'll have to explain later. Right now I need you to tell me exactly how many transports you saw."

"I don't know," Angel said, her breathing growing steady. "Maybe five or six."

"Okay, good," Kyle said. "This is what we're going to do..."

He let his voice trail off. He looked sharply at the stairs, his eyes narrowing as he peered over.

"Get down," he said.

"What?"

"Someone's coming. We have to get out of sight." Kyle handed Angel the blanket and motioned for her to duck behind the boxes again. He quietly pulled the dead soldier behind an old armoire, then crouched down as the sound of footsteps once again began to fill the basement.

"Thompson?" a voice called. "You down there, mate?"

The footsteps stopped at the bottom of the stairs. The soldier called out for his missing comrade, but got only silence for an answer. He tried the light several times, then grumbled a curse as he started across the basement.

"Thompson, c'mon, man," he said. "We gotta go sweep the grounds. This chick ain't here."

Underneath the blanket, Angel could see nothing in the darkness. Several horrible moments of anticipation slowly passed. Then, like before, there was the awful sound of stabbed flesh, a short struggle against death, and the thud of a body hitting the concrete.

Angel lifted the blanket and saw the vast silhouette of her friend. He reached out his hand to help her to her feet. She wondered for a moment if there was blood on it, but eventually she took hold of it anyway.

"Come on," Kyle said. "We've got to get out of here before they send more men looking for these two."

"I can't do this," Angel gasped. "Kyle, I can't do this."

"Yes, you can. You have to. Just trust me and follow my lead."

Angel took a deep breath. "Okay. Okay."

"All right," Kyle said. "We've gotta get some distance between us and the house. I'm gonna have a look around." He turned and pried the window open. His muscular frame barely squeezed through the window's meager dimensions, though he managed it with hardly a sound. A moment later he reached back in and lifted Angel out of the basement in one smooth motion, then shut the window behind them. A small patch of bushes at the edge of the carefully manicured grass helped them blend into the darkening landscape. He paused only for a split second, and then motioned for Angel to follow him.

The air was cooling quickly now that the second sun had dropped below the horizon, though with the clatter of the soldiers tearing through her house in an increasingly frenzied search, the night was hardly peaceful. There were two transports between the house and the riverbank, and Dominion soldiers were everywhere. How would they ever—

Before Angel could finish the thought, Kyle swiftly pulled her across the yard and into the trees. Her vision blurred as Kyle carried her across the grass at his superhuman speed. He paused behind a pile of firewood, and Angel's senses finally caught up with her.

Kyle eyed the transport by the water. Its engines were still idling, and there was a group of soldiers standing nearby. There were others deeper into the woods, their boots cracking twigs and leaves as they searched for their prey. Kyle glanced toward the other transport near the front of the house, and pulled his sidearm from the holster on his hip.

"Wait here," he said. "I won't be gone long."

He shuffled off even before she could answer. Angel lost sight of him as he swept through the trees, moving like a phantom through the descending dark. She managed to catch a brief glimpse of him near the other starship at the front of the property. He pried open a panel on one of the engine casings, and ripped out a cluster of hoses. She could see a steady stream of fluid leaking into the landscape before Kyle disappeared back into the shadows.

At the same time she heard a commotion coming from the house. There was an officer shrieking curses at a gathering crowd on her back patio. With a start she realized that Kyle was standing beside her, peering intently over the woodpile toward the scene on the balcony. He seemed to recognize the shrill voice. His face wrinkled into a snarl.

"Vaughn …"

He started to lunge forward, suddenly seeming oblivious to everything else. Angel clutched his forearm, suddenly snapping him out of his building rage. She didn't dare speak, but her eyes begged him not to leave her. Kyle sighed and turned his attention back to the leaking starship across the grounds. He pulled his sidearm again.

"Hang on," he whispered. "This is going to be loud."

One shot rattled from his gun. The round struck the second starship, and suddenly the engine erupted into flames. The explosion sent the Dominion soldiers into a frenzy, rushing in a blind panic toward the smoldering vessel. After a moment the flames reached the oxygen tanks and the whole ship detonated like a grenade, hurling chunks of metal and scalding debris through the trees. Nearly a dozen soldiers were felled by the shock of the blast and the scattering shrapnel.

"To the ship by the water," Kyle whispered. "Go!"

Angel jumped at Kyle's order, stumbling over her own feet for the first few steps. The ground seemed to spin beneath her like a treadmill track, her legs moving like she was running in a dream. She never looked back, being spurred on by the sound of Kyle's weapon rattling off several shots toward the house. She skidded into the ship's hull and pounded on the access panel for the boarding hatch. Several shots punctured the frame around her, and she dove inside to escape the barrage. She risked a look back into the chaos and saw Kyle backing toward the ship, picking off oncoming troops with surgical precision. Then he turned to run toward her.

A shot struck him in the back of his left shoulder, spraying blood across the side of the ship. It spun him completely around, but he kept his footing. Troops were swarming down the slope now, and the gunfire was incessant. Angel screamed for him, but her cries were drowned out by the teeming assault. Kyle fired a few more shots, but the numbers were too many. Out of options, Kyle quickly summoned his Celestial powers, his right arm engulfed in an enchanted blue blaze. He threw his fist into the grass at his feet, and suddenly the ground buckled and heaved in a swelling avalanche toward the house. The soldiers were buffeted mercilessly as the world wrenched beneath them and the concrete foundation beneath the house gave way with a boom.

Kyle didn't even wait for the dust to settle before climbing on board. His entire left side was streaked with blood, and his arm dangled limply by his side. The hatch closed swiftly behind him, leaving the devastated homestead in his wake. His arm flushed with a Celestial glow, and the gruesome wound coalesced itself, bone and all. Angel could barely speak as he walked past her to the cockpit. She'd seen his parlor tricks and telekinetic wizardry before, but what she had just witnessed defied any logic she could muster. It was unbelievable. And he made it look so easy. Had he always been so transcendent?

The starship lifted off the ground, and then blasted toward the expanse. Angel gripped the arms of her seat like they were all that was keeping her from floating away into the eternal blackness. The lump of fear in her throat still felt like it was going to strangle her even as they sailed away from the tattered remains of her home.

Kyle was silent as the ship sailed into the void. He seemed so far away, as if his mind had somehow left body. The quiet felt awkward and uncomfortable to Angel, especially in the presence of her best friend, and she didn't know how to break it. Something was clearly very wrong, and the fact that Kyle hadn't spoken was telling. As though the brigade of Dominion soldiers kicking down her door wasn't enough of a clue.

After a moment, Kyle reached under his seat, and with an audible snap pulled out a hunk of wiring with a Dominion tracking unit attached. He tossed it aside and set the coordinates for the hyperdrive. That was the last straw. Angel couldn't wait any longer. She had to know what had just happened.

"Kyle, what is going on?" she asked. "Where are we going?"

"I'm sorry, Angel," he said blankly. His eyes reluctantly met hers. "We have to go away. We've got to go away and never come back."

Angel had no response. The ache in her expression was answer enough. Her entire life was on that planet, and now she had to simply leave it behind. She turned away from him and looked out into the sea of stars. The ship rumbled as the hyperdrive activated, her whole world suddenly became nothing but a memory.

CHAPTER 10

The *Gemini* lurched out of hyperspace like a lame duck, listing away from its lone functioning engine as though drunk from the travel. The trip had taken nearly an hour even at warp, taking them far into the reaches of the Perseus spiral near the edge of the habitable zone. This sector was known for the harvesting of rare fuels and minerals on lonely planets and asteroids populated only by excavating companies and mining operations. In fact it was rumored the starmetal Kyle had forged into his war sword was found here, matter bound by the strong interaction force that was somehow extracted from a neutron star.

Whether or not that rumor was true, this was a dangerous region to flee to. The resources exploited here were vital to the Dominion Army, which had a hand in every one of those endeavors. But as the *Gemini* came out of hyperspace their instruments showed no colonies or population clusters. There were no vessels within range. No artificial radio signals. No heat signatures. Nothing.

They were inexorably alone.

And yet, their tracers said otherwise. The signal from their beacon on the transport carrying Bryan and his crew was here somewhere. They just had to find it.

There was a haze of sorts surrounding the ship as it exited hyperspace. It seemed like smoke for a moment, but that would mean fire and oxygen, which was impossible in the vacuum of space. As the *Gemini* glided forward, they heard a faint rattling along the hull, like grains of rice hitting glass. The haze was a dust ring in orbit around a massive planet up ahead.

The mood on the bridge was decidedly somber. Dr. Preston had retired back to the passenger bay to be with his wife, but the cloud of his cynicism had remained. Without Kyle present and with the ship failing, they had very little to be confident about as they ventured into an unpredictable situation. Dan and Jackson were standing at the front of the bridge, marveling at the sheer size of the world in front of them.

"Mac, these coordinates show that this is the Aranow system," Jay announced.

"That's right," Mac answered. "This is where our tracer is."

"Fuck, Mac, when were you going to tell us that?" Jackson demanded.

"I'm telling you now."

"Mac, you know how close that puts us to Xenon," Jackson said. "We've got no cloaks, damaged shields, and a ship on one good leg. How are we supposed to navigate this?"

Now they knew why there were no signs of civilization here. Xenon was a bestial world covered in hellish volcanoes and searing lava rock. Its atmosphere was mostly carbon dioxide with clouds of sulfuric acid and temperatures in excess of 900 degrees Kelvin. Yet somehow evolution had managed to spawn one of the most fearsome and savage creatures in the known galaxy: the Infernals. These beasts were gargantuan supraterrestrial animals capable of deep space flight on reptilian-like wings in their never-ending search for food. Very few images of them existed in the Dominion, as they tended to destroy everything in their path. But they were certainly savage creatures, blunt and gray, with a jagged mane of black quills and a mouthful of serrated teeth. Their hides were thick and leathery, and plated in scales as thick as battle armor. They were rumored to spew some kind of thermogenic discharge from their double-hinged jowls, though no one had seen them do so. And that was in addition to their rippling frames and razor-like talons. Nothing had ever survived an encounter with one of their kind. As a result, the Aranow system was a desolate expanse, abandoned eons ago in respect of their hunting grounds.

"You told me to get us to where Bryan is," Mac said. "This is where our instruments say he went."

"Jay, how far out are we?" Jackson asked. "I don't want to be out in the open like this any longer than we have to."

"Coordinates are for one of Aranow's moons," Jay said. "We'll breach the atmosphere in about seven minutes."

"Mac, what's the environment like down there?" Jackson asked.

"Pretty clean," Mac said. "Nitrogen and oxygen. A little high in argon content, but it's breathable. Terrain is rocky. A lot of canyons and mountains, but stable. Temperature is moderate. Magnetic field is no joke but the moon's not aligned with any of the bands."

"Well, take us in," Jackson said. "Jay, get the shields up. Danny, have the forward cannons online."

The *Gemini* sailed into the moon's stratosphere, and the tremor from the damaged engine made its presence known. The massive profile of Aranow consumed the moon's horizon in front of them. With a diameter of more than twenty-five thousand kilometers and a mass that pushed the uppermost limit of what a terrestrial planet could contain, the radiation from its core heated the surface an ominous red. This moon's surface was gray and bleak, with nothing but rocky crags and empty valleys as far as their eyes could see. The glow from Aranow gave them about three miles of visibility in any direction at this point in its revolution, so they had to rely heavily on their instruments. There was also a sharp wind in the skies, rattling the wounded starship with each gust.

"Damn, this wind is awful," Dan said, clutching the arm of his seat. "Any chance we level this out?"

"We're in some kind of jet stream," Jay said. "This is gonna be rough with one engine."

"I'm picking up some subterranean water," Mac said. "This place may have supported life at one point."

"Probably until the Infernals wiped it out," Jackson said. "Where are we on locating this signal?"

"We're getting some interference," Mac announced. "The transmission isn't stable."

"Atmospheric?" Jackson asked.

"No, it's strange," Mac said. "Seems artificial, but it's nothing like what we use. Gotta be really old tech."

Suddenly, their radar lit up as the proximity alarms were tripped again. Mac threw up his hands in frustration. Jackson's eyes darted toward the instruments, but he didn't even recognize what he was looking at. Whatever was coming was like nothing he'd ever seen before.

"Whoa, we've got some tracks incoming," Mac said. "Heavy profiles, high heat signatures."

"Ordnance?" Jackson asked.

"I don't think so," Mac said. "They're moving too slow. They look like aircraft."

"What the hell kind of ships have heat signatures like that?" Jackson asked.

"We're about to find out," Jay said. "They're coming up on our wing right now."

The roar of the approaching ships' engines was deafening, even through the walls of the *Gemini.* Jackson moved to the front of the bridge to see what they were dealing with. The vessels rose up next to them on either flank. They had fixed wings and a singular cockpit. The engines descended from the wings and emitted a flame behind them. They appeared clumsy and cumbersome against the headwind, but still managed to keep up with the *Gemini* in its current state. The alloy was obviously heavy and worn, and had no cloaking or shield panels. The word

"Raptor" was emblazoned on the sides. Jackson couldn't help but wonder how old these things were.

"What are you seeing, Jay?" the captain asked.

"Those things are ancient," Jay said. "They're using combustion thrusters and pitch maneuvering systems. We used to have a plane with a similar engine on my parents' farm, but it never worked. I've never seen ships like this actually flying."

"Should I target the cannons?" Dan asked.

"No, they're not in attack formation," Jackson said.

"They're in position to escort us somewhere," Jay added. "Plus, those hulls aren't air-locked. We could go sub-orbital and they wouldn't be able to follow us."

"Jacks, they're hailing us," Mac interrupted.

"Why can't we hear it?" Jackson asked.

"It's on a really strange frequency," Mac responded. "I'll try and patch it through."

There was a crackle of static as the transistor signal came through their intercom. The muffled voice behind the noise was demonstrative in its tone, repeating the same mantra.

"Dominion starcraft," the voice echoed. There was a ringing behind the voice, like two microphones that were too close together. "You have entered Splinter-controlled airspace. Acknowledge this transmission or be fired upon. This is your final warning."

"This is the starship *Gemini*," Jackson announced. "We acknowledge your transmission."

"*Gemini*, you will adjust your heading to two-two-seven and follow our escort to a predetermined landing area."

"Splinter aircraft, we are here to contact Bryan Foster," Jackson said. "We have reason to believe he is at your location. Request that he be present at the landing zone."

"Adjust your heading," the voice repeated. "We have artillery tracking you. You will be shot down if you do not comply."

Jackson muted the intercom. "Mac, are we tracking any radar signals?"

"Not that I can tell," Mac said. "But who knows with the ancient equipment they're using?"

"We're not in any condition to evade enemy fire," Jay said.

"Shit," Jackson said, looking around the cabin. He reengaged the intercom. "Splinter aircraft, we are adjusting our heading to two-two-seven. We'll follow your lead."

The three ships banked to the left and followed a gaping canyon down the rocky landscape. Another resounding vibration shot through the cabin as the *Gemini* veered against the drag from the damaged thruster. They dipped below the surface into the ravine. The meager light from the neighboring halo went black, and the hull spotlights flashed on. The canyon walls were steep and cavernous, stretching nearly three miles apart and what must have been nearly a mile deep. After a few moments they saw a glimmer in the darkness, one that grew brighter as they drew near.

"What is that?" Dan asked, squinting out the forward windows.

"I don't know," Jackson said. "Mac, what are we looking at?"

"It's huge," Mac muttered. "It's like … it's like a city."

Finally, they came over the edge of the sprawling Splinter colony. It spread out for miles in either direction, the dim kindling of the city lights pushing back against the blanketing dark. A fortified barricade surrounded a military installation that was nestled up against the canyon walls with several towers and artillery banks poised within the grounds. Beyond the perimeter was an apparent civilian borough. There were several billowing plumes of exhaust from what appeared to be old fossil fuel generators scattered throughout the streets. The buildings were stacked one on top of another like an old erector set, with barely enough room between them for the hordes of people to walk. The four of them never knew there could be so many people.

"My god, look at this place," Jay muttered.

"This is unbelievable," Mac gushed. "It's like a museum of old-world tech. They're using gas lines and wind turbines. They've even got a uranium reactor! That thing is actually radioactive. I can't believe this stuff still exists—"

"Mac, take it easy," Jackson said. "This whole thing isn't making me very comfortable."

"Hang on a second," Jay interrupted. "They're not taking us to the airfield inside that installation. We're on a course toward the other side of the colony."

"Can you get a make on what's out there?" Jackson asked.

"Not much," Jay answered.

The captain suddenly had a very ominous feeling. "Danny, get down to the armory and get us some weapons."

"Yeah, will do."

Dan climbed back down through the passenger bay and returned a few moments later with a handful of rifles and some body armor. Jackson took one of the guns and groaned. He had lost his sniper rifle during the incident on Littenderon, and this model was a poor substitute. Regardless, he needed to have a weapon in his hand, so he checked the charge on the clip and pulled on the body armor.

"Here we go," Jay said. "We're coming in."

The *Gemini* looped over a small landing pad, and they got a directive from their escorts to set the ship down. There was a huge swath of dust thrown up as the ship settled onto the ground, and a bank of glaring spotlights flooded the bridge. Jay flipped a switch on the controls and a motorized screen closed over the cabin windows. The wash of light was blinding, and the last thing they wanted was to be at a visual deficit while the Splinter troops could see them. Through Mac's outboard cameras they could make out several groups of soldiers surrounding the ship, fanning out in an offensive formation.

"Those men are armed," Mac announced. "Doesn't look like a warm welcome."

"How many?" Jackson asked.

"It's hard to say," Mac answered. "Our instruments go on heat, and those lights are fucking up the image."

"I'm not getting a good vibe here, Jacks," Jay said.

"I'm not either, but we're committed now," Jackson said. "If they're hostile, there's no way we're making it off the ground."

"What do you want to do?" Dan asked.

Jackson rubbed his jaw. "I'm gonna go outside."

"Outside?" Jay asked. "Like, out there, outside?"

"That's what I said," Jackson answered.

"Well, that seems like a terrible idea," Jay said.

"I've got to talk to them," Jackson insisted. "If Bryan is here, if I can speak with him, then maybe we have a chance."

"That's your plan?" Jay asked. "You're gonna walk out into that hornets' nest and just ask if Bryan is home?"

"Yeah."

"Captain, no offense but that seems like a very bad idea," Dan said.

"No shit it's a bad idea," Jay chimed in. "Jacks, you can't do that."

"Well, we can't just sit here," Jackson said. "If any of you have a better idea, I'm all ears."

Silence was all he got. Not that he expected any revelations.

"All right then," Jackson said. "Keep the other passengers inside. If something happens to me, fire off a couple of missiles and do your best to get the fuck out of here."

Jackson handed his rifle to Dan, and those two made their way to the rear boarding ramp. Dr. Preston hollered at them as they walked by, but the captain waved him off with a curt "not now." Apparently the blunt answer didn't sit well with their old mentor, who chased them all the way into the exit bay.

"What is going on?" Preston demanded. "I thought they were going to be expecting us?"

"We're seeing some aggressive posturing," Jackson replied. "I'm gonna go find out what's going on."

"You're going out there?" Preston asked. "Unarmed?"

"If I show them that we're not a threat, then maybe this can still work."

"Son, you're gonna get yourself killed out there."

"Sir, this is what Kyle would do."

Preston scoffed. "That might be the case. But Kyle can wave his hands and wipe out an entire platoon if he wants to. You're not going to have that luxury."

"Sir, I— have to do something,"

"I can't let you do this, Captain," Dr. Preston said. "Now I am ordering you to stand down. We'll come up with another option."

"With all due respect, sir, with Kyle gone I have tactical command of this unit," Jackson said. "This is my call. You can read me the riot act later."

After a long moment the doctor acquiesced, retreating to the cover of the passenger bay as Dan and Jackson walked toward the boarding ramp. There was a loud rumbling from outside. Jackson took a deep breath in through his nose.

"You sure you want to do this, Captain?" Dan asked. "I could handle it..."

"It's my responsibility," Jackson said.

"Do you want me to cover you?"

"No. And tell the others to stand down also."

"You're sure?"

"We don't stand a chance in a fight right now," Jackson said. "Our priority is keeping these people alive."

Dan's eyes creased. "I'm sorry, sir, but how are we supposed to do that?"

"Just do what you can," Jackson said. "Kyle will come for us. Then everything will be all right."

"Yes, sir. I hope you're right."

"Hit the door," Jackson ordered with a nod of his head. "Then get back upstairs."

Dan triggered the hatch and the seal released, dropping the ramp in a whir of mechanics. Light flooded the bay, making Jackson wince. He could hear the clatter of weapons outside, the shuffle of feet hiding behind the blinding glow. *This idea just kept getting better*, he thought. All he had wanted when the day started was to get to bed early and get a good night's sleep. As he started out into the yard, he wondered how things could have gone so wrong.

He raised his hands overhead when his feet touched the ground. A pair of propellered aircraft hovered overhead, each with a bank of cannons pointed in his direction. The spotlights were mounted on a half-dozen ground vehicles, as were additional artillery systems. It seemed a bit much, unless they were expecting Kyle after all.

Finally, he heard a voice shout out: "Down on your knees! On your knees!"

Jackson nodded and slowly lowered himself down to his knees. Splinter soldiers rushed out of the surroundings, crowding around him and the ramp to the *Gemini*. The ramp started back up, but a shell was fired out of the platoon. It hit the hull next to the hatch, and a burst of electricity ground the hydraulics to a halt. A dozen soldiers climbed on board, weapons in hand.

Jackson turned, but was stopped by more shouting.

"Don't move!" the voice shouted. "Get your hands on your head! Hands on your head!"

The man shouting was stalking straight toward him. He had a rifle thrust forward, its muzzle staring down at his chest. Jackson nodded demonstratively and placed his hands on top of his head. The soldier stopped about three paces away and lowered the weapon just enough for Jackson to see his face. He recognized him.

"There are civilians on board," Jackson said. "You have our surrender."

"How many?" the soldier demanded. "How many people on board?"

"Eighteen," Jackson said. "Only seven military. They've been told to stand down."

"Why are you here?"

"We followed Bryan Foster to this location," Jackson said. "He can tell you why we're here."

The familiar soldier lowered his weapon and took the final three steps forward. Jackson could see the dark stubble on his jaw, the sharp nose, and the heavy brow beneath his helmet. But what made him unmistakable was the scar on the left side of his neck, the one that Kyle had given him almost four years ago. Jackson knew him as Major Adam Brady, one of the few Splinter battle commanders that they had never been able to eliminate.

Suddenly, there was a ruckus behind them. The others were being brought off the ship.

"Bryan Foster?" the major asked.

"That's right."

Brady glanced toward the ship, then back at Jackson.

"Never heard of him," he said.

Jackson felt a crack on the forehead from the butt end of the rifle. His chin thudded against the ground. The world started to swirl in front of him, and suddenly the flood of light went black.

† † †

Jackson was jarred awake by a tremor beneath him. He felt himself slide across a metal surface on his back. It took him a moment to realize that he was lying in the cargo bed of one of the Splinter vehicles. There was no roof above him, and his muddied vision could just make out the dim glow of Aranow at the top of the canyon walls. He tried to roll onto his side, but his arms were bound behind him and the rocking of the transport kept him off balance.

He slid into a pair of boots, and saw that it was one of their old neighbors. He craned his neck and counted eight others, including Dr. Preston and his wife, seated along the edges of the truck. Dan and the rest of their team were nowhere to be found.

The vehicle hit a bump and Jackson was jolted like a sack of grain. They must have been traveling in an ancient terrain transport instead of the more common hover-engine convoy. The buildings outside were made of brick and mortar and steel. They looked on the verge of collapse even as some stood just a few feet away from each other. There was a definite smell of rot and mildew that made Jackson wish he was still unconscious.

Finally the transport came to a stop and the tailgate dropped open. A handful of ragged soldiers hurried the others out of the bed. Jackson was grabbed by the collar of his shirt and thrown onto the ground. There were a few inches of standing water that splashed across his face, and a hard, uneven pavement underneath.

Jackson struggled back to his knees and saw that they were within the courtyard of the military installation. The walls were some thirty feet high with a primitive razor wire along the top. There were a half-dozen or so rocket launchers mounted along the perimeter, and several more on the rooftops of the campus buildings. Jackson felt like he had traveled back in time. It was an imposing fortress, if dilapidated, but truly several hundred years out of date.

There was another vehicle parked nearby, and he wondered if the rest of his unit was inside. As he watched waiting for its doors to open, a soldier smacked him in the back with the butt of his rifle. Jackson reluctantly rose to his feet and staggered toward the building in front of him. It looked like a prison, with bars on the windows and reinforced doors. Their unit had raided dozens of Splinter strongholds, but Jackson had never seen anything like this. Hell, he'd never even heard of anything like this. They'd built a damned castle at the bottom of a canyon in one of the most dangerous sectors in the galaxy. They had always been crafty bastards, but this was a new level of guile.

He must have slowed thinking about it, because he took another blow to the back that dropped him back to his knees.

"Move your feet," the striking soldier ordered.

Jackson stumbled as he tried to regain his footing. Suddenly he caught himself wondering why he was still alive. What did they have in store for him?

A large overhead door ratcheted upward, its gears creaking and groaning as the heavy portcullis lifted. Inside was a long, tall corridor stretching into the depths of the complex. Dr. Preston and the rest of their passengers were walking in front of him, surrounded by men with guns. Major Brady was standing next to the entry, supervising the march like a foreman on an assembly line. It gave Jackson a strong sense of foreboding, like they were being herded into a slaughter.

He darted away from the line, panicking the troops around him. Their weapons spun in his direction, but there were no shots fired. Not yet anyway. Brady pulled a sidearm as Jackson rushed to him, the handgun the only thing keeping Jackson at arm's length.

"Where are you taking us?" Jackson demanded. "Where is Colonel Foster?"

"Get back in line!" Brady shouted.

"Tell me where you're taking us."

"Get back in line or you go inside without a head."

"Go ahead and shoot then."

Brady snarled and pressed the gun against Jackson's bruised forehead, but then he paused. All stares were on him, but his resolve seemed shaken. His eyes shifted to the side without his head moving, seeing the sudden audience. Jackson decided he was nervous.

Brady pulled the gun back and struck Jackson on the bridge of his nose. He felt the bone fracture, causing his eyes to well up as he dropped back to his knees. Then there was another thud against the back of his head, and again his body went limp.

† † †

Jackson came through another cloud, this time with a pain like a railroad spike had gone through his temple. His head felt as though it would split open if he so much as coughed. He tried to take a deep breath, but his nose was plugged with dried blood, and he could feel the pressure swelling behind his eyes. He shifted his weight, suddenly realizing that he was shackled to a chair.

There was a shadow in front of him. He blinked several times to clear his eyes before being able to make out Major Brady standing at the edge of the room. He was leaning against the wall with his arms crossed, staring at his captive with tireless attention. He was tall and broad in the indoor light, with thick legs and a wide chest. By now he had to be in his early forties, and there was a noticeable discomfort in his posture from years of hard military service. Despite that wear he was still an imposing figure, even through the fog in Jackson's vision.

"Bit of a headache?" Brady asked.

"Why don't you unchain me and I'll show you," Jackson said.

"Not sure that would work out for you. You look a little woozy. Probably best if you keep sitting down."

"What have you done with the others?"

"Oh, them," Brady said. "They're being … taken care of."

"There were civilians who had surrendered," Jackson said. "If you've harmed them…" He stopped, silenced by the drumming in his head.

"You need to calm yourself," Brady said. "This is not helping you."

"Where is Colonel Foster?"

"You keep asking me that," Brady said. "I'm not sure why you think that matters."

"What do you want with me?"

"I want you to tell me why you're here."

"I told you," Jackson sighed. "Colonel Foster—"

Brady snapped and grabbed Jackson by the shirt, pulling him forward: "Shut your mouth about Foster. You and your friends have been a holy terror for us for over a decade. Why should I have faith that you're not here to harm us now?"

"You don't know?" Jackson gasped, Brady having yanked him forward against his restraints. "Kyle's mother … the colonel's sister … they killed her. They killed her because they found out she was one of you."

Brady's head tilted subtly to the side. "Dead?"

"That's right," Jackson said. "Hanged and burned in her own house."

Brady released his hold on Jackson's shirt. He turned and cracked the door open, muttering something imperceptible to whomever was outside. Then he closed the door again, seemingly at a sudden loss for words.

"Looks like your big scheme to get Kyle on your side didn't work out according to plan," Jackson said. "Or was it always it always going to cost Becca her life?"

"I warned you to shut your mouth," Brady growled. "Do it now or I'll shut it for you."

"You're a big man," Jackson continued. "Beating up a guy who is chained to a chair."

"You're testing my patience," Brady said. "The only reason you're alive right now is that Foster wanted you alive."

"So you do know who he is."

Brady scowled. "He's the Star Marshal, our commanding officer."

"And he's the one who told you to manhandle civilians and batter my brain to a paste?"

"We can't afford to take chances." Brady's eyes grew dark.

"Right, and here I thought you were just harboring a grudge from some of our previous meetings."

"Well…I can't say I didn't enjoy this. You've killed a lot of good men. It's too bad your commander wasn't here."

"That is too bad," Jackson said. "I haven't seen him kick your ass in a while."

Brady's eyes narrowed, but he was quickly distracted by the door swinging open. Bryan walked inside with an armed escort, dressed in Splinter fatigues adorned with his officer's markings. It was bewildering for Jackson to see him like this, so ensconced in his rebel persona. Brady snapped to attention.

"Well, look who finally decided to make an appearance," Jackson snarked.

"I'm sorry, Captain," Bryan said, his expression plainly distraught. "I didn't want to have to do this. But I'm sure you can appreciate our need to protect ourselves."

"Your girlfriend here was just explaining it to me," Jackson said.

Brady cleared his throat. "Sir, your sister … he's saying that—"

"I know what happened, Major, thank you," Bryan said. "We received word about an hour ago. Just after the *Gemini* landed."

Jackson could see Bryan was hurting from the news, but the pounding behind his eyes sapped all his sympathy. "Are you satisfied, *Marshal*?"

"I'm not sure that I care for your tone, Captain."

"I'm not sure that I give a shit," Jackson said. "You brought this down on yourself. And Becca's the one that paid the price."

"You don't get it, do you, Captain?" Bryan asked with a noticeable tremor in his voice. "No one feels worse about what happened to my sister than I do. *Nobody*. And I have to live with the consequences. But she knew the risks of this operation. She thought it was worth it."

"You're just lucky that Kyle wasn't with us," Jackson said.

"Right, I'm glad you brought that up," Bryan said, his mind suddenly back on business. "Where is the commander?"

"I don't know."

Bryan sighed. "Captain, when we put this plan in motion, we did so trying to get Kyle here. We need his help. You, however ... well, we would settle for you just not being on their side. How that happens isn't important to me."

"You won't hurt us," Jackson said. "How do you think he'll respond if he finds out we came here and *then* something happened to us?"

"I suppose you're right," Bryan said, sounding somewhat facetious. "Maybe it is just an empty threat. Then again, if we disposed of you and your ship, how would he know you ever made it here? I could tell him whatever I want."

The door opened again and another soldier walked in. He whispered something to Major Brady, who nodded.

"Sir, we have another Dominion ship inbound," Brady when the soldier had left the room. "The contact is claiming to be Kyle Griffin."

Bryan glanced at the major, then looked back to Jackson.

"You were saying, Marshal?" Jackson said. "He'll have a track on the *Gemini*. He knows we're here."

"Sir, what do you want us to do?" Brady asked.

"Escort him in," Bryan said. "Take two platoons out to meet him."

"I don't think you want to do that," Jackson said.

"Is that right?" Bryan said, sounding bored.

"You really have no idea what you've started, do you? His mother is dead. His father is holding on by a thread. You've torn him away from everything he's ever known. He could tear that whole platoon apart if he wanted to. Maybe you ought to consider being a little more diplomatic this time."

"If he's going to be hostile, we have to be prepared for that," Bryan said.

"Send me out to talk to him," Jackson suggested.

"Right," Brady said. "Why should we let you go?"

"Do you really think he's going to listen to any of you after what you've done?" Jackson inquired.

Bryan paused. The captain's words seemed to sink in thoroughly. They couldn't stop Kyle, and Jackson knew they didn't really want to. If they went out there in force, Kyle would tear the entire colony down, and he may not stop there. All of their commander's emotion would pour out in the form of pure, unadulterated wrath. It was Jackson's worst nightmare.

"All right then, Captain. I'll have the major here escort you out to meet him."

Bryan nodded at Brady, who released Jackson's shackles. Jackson slowly stood up from the chair, still uncertain of his balance. He looked over at Brady for a second, then approached Bryan. He glared at his old instructor for a brief moment, and then dropped him with a punch to the jaw. Bryan hit the ground like a sack, his lower lip split wide open from the blow. Brady pulled his sidearm, but Bryan quickly halted him.

"Brady!" Bryan yelled from the floor. "Let it go."

Brady reluctantly holstered his weapon, but the cross stare remained.

"That's right, that's a good boy," Jackson said.

"You son of a…"

Bryan cut off Brady before he could counter. "Stop it, both of you." He said, climbing back to his feet and wiping the blood from his mouth. "Do you feel better now, Captain?"

"I feel less like killing you," Jackson replied. "Does that count?"

Bryan sighed. "Fine, fair enough. Major, would you please escort our guest out to the landing pad?"

"I'll expect the rest of our group released as well," Jackson said.

"They'll be released once we know the situation is under control," Bryan said. "Go speak with your commander. Keep him calm, and we'll have the others waiting."

Brady led Jackson out of the room and to the installation's airfield. As the door opened gusts of wind announced the arrival of the Dominion transport. The air had gotten considerably colder as Aranow had moved past the crests of the canyon, leaving only the incandescent lights from the base and the city to illuminate the endless darkness.

The ship set down with a jerk, a trail of smoke following it to the ground. There were several gashes in the side of the hull leaking various fumes. Jackson wondered how the transport even made it through deep space to find them.

He started toward the ship, but Brady grabbed his arm abruptly.

"Keep it brief and get him inside," Brady said. "We've got eyes on you."

Brady flicked his eyes upward. Jackson followed his glance and saw several riflemen spreading across the rooftops. He looked back at Brady briefly, then walked out onto the tarmac.

The transport's engines calmed to a dull hum as he approached, and finally the hatch on the side of the ship hissed open. Jackson stopped a few yards short of the entry and waited. He saw the blood spattered across the hull and immediately he feared the worst. What would Kyle do if that was Angel's blood?

Kyle appeared in the doorway. His shoulders nearly touched the frame on either side, and he had to duck to step down onto the tarmac. He never looked at his captain until he was right in front of him, instead scanning the surroundings with his powerful eyes. His hand brushed the hilt of his sidearm on his hip before Jackson cautioned him.

"Careful, they've got about a dozen guns on us right now," Jackson said.

"I see them," Kyle replied. How he could do that through the dark, Jackson would never understand. "What happened to you?"

"We didn't have the warmest of welcomes," Jackson responded, gingerly touching the bridge of his nose. "Adam Brady did this."

"*He's* here?"

"He's fairly chummy with your uncle, actually."

"And how does he look right now?"

"I haven't hit him yet," Jackson said. "I did punch your uncle though."

"He probably deserved it," Kyle said, looking toward the rooftops again. "Are they serious with this?"

"I think it's posturing," Jackson answered. "I think they want us to feel lucky that they took us in. But they're definitely nervous."

Jackson looked down at the streaks of blood along Kyle's side and arm. He saw the singed fibers and gaping hole in his sleeve from the gunshot that had struck him on Vadara. Kyle had obviously healed the wound already. Jackson would give up a finger to be able to use that talent on his head right now.

"Looks like you ran into some trouble," Jackson said. "Are you all right?"

"I'll survive."

"And Angel?"

"She's okay," Kyle said. "She's on board."

Jackson let out a sigh. "Thank God."

"Yeah, she's pretty shaken up. But I think she'll be ..."

Kyle trailed off when the door to the installation swung open again. It creaked loudly, even over the drone of the engines, and then Bryan walked out onto the airfield. Brady was trailing behind his superior, covered in full battle garb. Jackson wanted to caution his friend again, but Kyle stepped past him before he had a chance. There was a purpose to Kyle's stride, one that Jackson had rarely seen. He wondered how this could possibly end without fireworks.

† † †

Kyle immediately noticed the swollen lower lip that his friend had given Bryan as he approached. The Splinter uniform Bryan was wearing looked all wrong. Everything about it seemed like a walking oxymoron. Kyle couldn't help but ask himself who this man really was.

"Commander, welcome to the Aranow system," Bryan said. His tone was much more cordial than it had been with Jackson.

"Wish I could say I was glad to be here," Kyle said.

"You look like you might want to hit me too."

"The thought had crossed my mind."

"Well, your Captain already took care of that for you."

"And you think I should consider that enough?" Kyle asked.

Brady shifted his finger onto the trigger of his assault rifle, feeling the tensions rise. Kyle took notice and leered over Bryan's shoulder at his old adversary.

"Put a leash on your dog," Kyle demanded. "I'm not in the mood to deal with his act."

Brady adjusted the rifle in his hands, but his trigger finger never moved. Bryan hesitated as though he was considering the options. Kyle's eyes blinked with a Celestial light and the weapon suddenly crumpled in Brady's hand like a piece of paper. Brady let out a startled shriek as he pulled his hands away. It sparked a rustling on the rooftop.

"Kyle!" Bryan hollered. "What are you doing?"

"Tell them to stand down," Kyle ordered.

"Kyle, this type of aggression isn't—" Bryan started.

The sidearm on Brady's hip burst into tiny fragments. Brady stood awkwardly, afraid of what Kyle's powers would reach for next. Bryan spun back and forth between the major and his nephew, his expression aghast.

"Kyle ...!"

"Tell them to stand down," Kyle repeated. "*Now*!"

Bryan paused just long enough to take a breath, then turned to Brady and nodded. Brady signaled the men on the roof, and they withdrew their aim. They filed out to leave the men on the tarmac to their meeting.

"Major, would you give us a moment please?" Bryan asked.

Brady gathered himself and walked back toward the building.

"Goddammit, Kyle, are you out of your mind?" Bryan asked. "These men here are not like the soldiers that you know. They've got itchy trigger fingers and are just looking for an excuse to drop a high-ranking Dominion officer. You were one hothead short of getting shot."

"I've already been shot once today," Kyle said. "You think I care about more gunfire right now?"

"That's not the point," Bryan said. "If you're going to be a part of this, they have to trust you. How are they supposed to do that if they see you assaulting the major and disrespecting their commanding officer?"

"Oh, get off your high horse, Bryan," Kyle said, his booming voice echoing off the canyon. "How do you expect us to trust you when all we've seen are guns pointed in our faces? You let that dirty shit Brady beat Jackson's face in after you practically dragged us out here, for fuck's sake!"

"We have to protect ourselves. We welcome you in like a Trojan horse and you could wipe us out. We can't let up our guard without being absolutely certain first."

"And you think this bullshit is calming me down?" Kyle said. "You used my mother as bait!"

Bryan was caught breathless. He wasn't prepared for this.

"Kyle, listen to me. We didn't know … we didn't know about your mother, about what they had done to her." Bryan paused to gather his composure. "But I never should have left her. She's dead today because of me."

Kyle grimaced and looked away. The image of his dead mother was still far too hot in his mind. He wanted nothing to do with any platitudes, regardless of who they came from. He knew they wouldn't bring her back.

"I know you don't want to hear this, especially from me," Bryan continued. "But we have a chance to make sure that she didn't die for nothing. With you here fighting for us, it will not be the same war."

"Let's get something straight right now," Kyle said. "I didn't come here to fight for you. I came here to fight *against* them. Unfortunately it doesn't look like I can do one without the other."

"I'm sorry you feel that way," Bryan said. "I really am. I wish there was something I could do to make you—"

Bryan stopped abruptly when he noticed some movement at the door of the Dominion transport. Kyle saw his gaze drift away and spun around. Angel was standing in the door to the transport, a blanket wrapped around her shoulders.

"Kyle, is everything all right?" she asked.

"Everything's fine. We're safe here."

Kyle helped her down from the hatch, but she pulled away from him as he tried to put his arm around her shoulders. Kyle sighed and nodded to Jackson as they walked across the tarmac, and the captain gave her a warm embrace before escorting her into the building. Kyle stopped in front of his uncle, his gaze still following Angel as she walked away.

"You want to do something for me?" Kyle asked. "Take her to see her family. Give them a bed and something warm to eat. And then maybe you and I can talk."

"That's a fair deal," Bryan said. "I'll set it up."

Kyle sighed and walked off without a word, but Bryan called out to him after just a few steps.

"Kyle?" he said, waiting for his nephew to look back.

Kyle paused, but barely turned. His typically superhuman eyes looked shockingly tired.

"You *are* safe here."

Kyle sighed again. "I know."

CHAPTER 11

Kyle threw a handful of water onto his face and let it drip into the sink. The water was cold and gave him a brisk eye-opening, something he sorely needed. He looked into the mirror and saw a few tired lines beneath his eyes, a sight that he was not typically accustomed to. It had been nearly eight hours since their arrival on the Aranow moon, and while the others had retired to their new quarters to get some sleep, he had come to the hospital wing to check on his father. Sleep would be a difficult task, but that was fine with him. He was afraid of what might haunt him in his dreams anyway.

He dried his face and walked back into the dreary hospital room. It was still very dark outside, and there were only a few dimly glowing lights on in the ward. Apparently there was only a seven- to eight-hour window during the moon's daily revolution when any natural light made its way into the depths of the canyon. They relied mostly on the glow from Aranow's fiery core, but even that cast only a reddish gloom on the colony.

There was a light above his father's bed that buzzed incessantly. Kyle had decided that the filaments were probably loose. Once he'd solved that mystery, it was a struggle to find something else to think about.

The hospital was less than impressive, with dirty floors and rickety old equipment. The floors creaked constantly, and the cold from the night air seemed to leak in through every window. There was also a whiff of mildew in the air, which made Kyle wonder how anyone left this place better than they came in.

He took his seat next to his father's bed. The chair was far too short for him and his knees rose up above his waist. Marcus still seemed very pale beneath the dull lights. A web of tubes and hoses encircled his body, another sight that Kyle had never seen. But this *was* a far more primitive place than he was used to.

Marcus had been unconscious since they arrived, which Kyle had assumed was due to the loss of blood. His powers were not able to reproduce the volume of fluid loss and this hospital was drastically under-equipped to handle such injuries. They had no plasma generators or stem cell capacity like Dominion physicians had at their disposal. It seemed that Splinter personnel with such wounds were doomed to embrace their end.

It had been a lonely night to that point, but finally the glass door slid open and a young woman dressed in scrubs walked in. She was short and muscular, with a thin waist and a delicate neck. Her blonde hair was pulled back in a ponytail, revealing her high cheekbones and smooth creamy skin. She never even looked over at Kyle as she pulled the chart from the foot of the bed, intent on her work.

"Hello?" Kyle said.

The woman jumped. "Oh my god!" she shrieked, finally looking his way. "You scared me."

"I'm sorry," Kyle said. "I didn't mean to frighten you."

"No, it's okay. I just wasn't expecting anyone."

"I suppose this place is pretty quiet at night," Kyle said.

"Um, yeah … I guess it is," she said.

Her gaze was now fixed on him. The corners of her mouth tilted upward with her stare. He stood up from the chair and stepped to the side of the bed, his powerful shoulders spreading like wings as he moved closer. Her eyes were a bright blue even in the dim hospital lights, and her lips a deep pink against her light skin. After a moment she looked away, down at Kyle's father.

"How's he doing?" Kyle asked.

"He's, um, better than I would have thought, given the blood loss," she said.

"So is that encouraging?" Kyle asked.

"I think so," she replied. "But to be honest, I've never seen someone survive an injury like this. Whatever was done to heal him, it...it really saved his life."

She looked up again and this time her eyes truly struck him. He suddenly felt off balance and uncomfortable.

"Are you one of the nurses?" he asked.

She let out a brief irritated laugh. "No, actually I'm the doctor."

"No kidding?" Kyle said, and her blue eyes narrowed. "I'm Kyle. This is my father."

"I know who you are, Commander," she said. "I think everyone here knows who you are."

"Right. I suppose I should keep to my room from now on."

"Oh, I ... I'm so sorry," she said. "That was rude of me."

"It's okay," Kyle said. "After so many years, it would be strange for them not to hate me."

"Well, if it's any consolation, I've always really wanted to meet you."

"You're joking. Why?"

Her cheeks flushed red. "Well, I...I mean, as a doctor, I've always thought it would be interesting to meet someone that can heal a person just by looking at them."

"Oh, I see," Kyle said, fighting a grin. "Professional curiosity."

"Yeah," she said, flashing a full smile. It hit Kyle like a burst of sunlight.

"What's your name?" Kyle asked.

"I'm Ellie. Ellie Decker."

The glass door slid open and Dan poked his head into the room. Ellie hugged the chart to her chest, seeming a bit embarrassed.

"Sorry to interrupt, sir," Dan said, his voice almost a whisper, "but Bryan and Brady are asking for us upstairs."

Kyle nodded and glanced back at Ellie. "It was nice to meet you, Dr. Decker."

"You can call me Ellie," she said quickly.

"Ellie," Kyle repeated. "Thank you for everything that you've done for my father."

She gave a closed-mouth grin and nodded as Kyle followed Dan into the hallway. Kyle shut the door behind them, even as Dan leered over his shoulder at the doctor. She watched them for a moment before turning back to Marcus' chart. Dan looked at his commander with a raised eyebrow as they shuffled down the corridor.

"Sir, what was that all about?" Dan asked.

"She's the doctor," Kyle replied.

"Excuse me, sir, but can I have permission to speak freely?"

"Danny, I'm gonna tell you this one time. You don't have to be formal with me."

"Is that permission, then?"

"Dammit, Dan, just tell me what's on your mind."

"That woman back there?" Dan said. "She's seriously into you."

"Danny, come on…"

"I'm serious, sir…Kyle, I mean Kyle," Dan stammered. "What did you say to her?"

"Nothing," Kyle answered. "She really is just taking care of my father."

"Not from my angle," Dan said. "And she's a knockout too. Tell me you didn't notice."

"That's not the first thing on my mind right now," Kyle said.

"I know, but damn. I might have to hurt myself so I can get to know her a little better."

"You're gonna make me regret letting you talk freely, aren't you?" Kyle stopped in the hall and looked around with a confused expression. "Where the hell are we going?"

Dan dropped the inquisition and pointed just down the hall. "It's this room right ahead."

Dan pulled open the door and they walked into a large office. There was a whole wall of windows on the opposite side of the room overlooking the installation's yard and the colony beyond, its chaotic streets given a false serenity by the distance of the view. Bryan was sitting behind a large wooden desk that was cluttered with stacks of paper instead of holoscreens. Brady was standing just to the side of the desk, and Kyle noted that this time he was unarmed.

Jackson and the others were already sitting off to the left and seemed relatively relaxed. Jackson had the makings of a black eye, even though Kyle had healed the broken nose. Mac yawned like a slumbering hippo and leaned back in his chair, the meeting obviously coming too early for him. He almost hit Jay in the face with his arm as he stretched, and Jay swatted away his hand with a grunt.

Kyle had expected Dr. Preston to be present, but he was nowhere to be found. He had yet to speak to his mentor since his arrival, and it was a conversation that he was dreading. He knew there would be questions that he just didn't have the answers to.

"Good morning, Commander," Bryan said.

"Is this what qualifies as morning around here?" Kyle asked.

"Technically, yes," Bryan answered. "We're on a thirty-hour day here even though we only get about eight hours of natural light. But the artificial daylights should be engaging within the next half hour."

"This is a helluva operation you've got here," Mac interjected, suddenly seeming more awake. "I've never seen so many technological relics. I mean, you've got an actual functioning nuclear reactor."

"We have to get by on scavenged parts and weapons," Bryan said. "We don't have the capabilities to manufacture our own components so we make do with what we can find."

"How safe is that thing?" Jay asked. "I thought they were all decommissioned because they were prone to blowing up."

"That was for the ones on board active starships," Bryan said. "The reactors were poorly contained and could be affected by stellar radiation. Ours is buried beneath the canyon walls and has a magnetic deflector to shield it from any residual cosmic radiation."

"Similar to the electrostatic repulsion we use on the *Gemini*?" Mac asked.

"If you say so, Mac," Bryan replied. "At any rate, most of our power is geothermal and hydrostatic. The reactor only powers our emergency systems and some of the armaments. We keep its output relatively low to avoid detection."

"I guess you're awake now, Mac," Kyle said. "Seems a little early for a science lesson."

"Did you get any sleep, Commander?" Bryan asked. "You look a little tired."

"I'll be fine," Kyle said, sidestepping the question. "Was there something in particular you wanted to see us about?"

"I just felt that we should talk," Bryan replied. "I know things didn't exactly start out on a good note."

"Gee, I wonder why that might be," Jackson said.

He glared over at the major. Bryan put up his hand as if to ask for calm.

"We've already apologized for those circumstances, Captain," Bryan said. "I'm hoping we'll be able to put that behind us."

"Right," Jackson said, scowling at Brady. "If I were you, I'd want us to forget about that too."

Brady grinned. "How's your eye this morning, Captain?"

"Major…" Bryan warned.

"I'm sorry, Marshal," Brady said, but he didn't look sorry at all.

"Commander, I hope you and your men understand our situation here," Bryan said. "We're in this together, whether we like it or not."

"I think we all get that we're stuck with each other," Kyle said. "So I guess we'll have to learn to live with it."

"We have to stop this constant bickering," Bryan continued. "We have a real chance to change the war now. But we can't do that if we are always at each other's throats."

Kyle grunted. "I know what you're trying to do, Marshal. But let's not pretend we're all going to shake hands and be friends. We've been at each other's throats for years. That's not going to change anytime soon. But it's like you said, you need our help, and we have nowhere else to go. So let's just leave it at that."

"Fine," Bryan said, shrugging. "What's that old Earth-saying? 'An enemy of my enemy is my friend?'"

"No, that's where you're wrong. We are *not* friends," Kyle growled. "I don't even know who you are anymore. The only reason I'm trusting you now is because my mother did."

Bryan grinned, an odd response. But what did he care? He was getting his way. "That's enough for me," he said.

Bryan stood up from the desk and walked around to his nephew. "We'll send out an all-points. I'll write you a commission as a commander, and our men will be at your disposal."

Kyle nodded.

"You'll be reporting to me," Bryan continued, glancing over at the major, "and *only* me."

"How many men do you have?" Kyle asked.

"At this installation, just over sixteen thousand. There's about another two thousand as a part of this cell at a handful of other locations."

"Eighteen thousand. That's it?" Dan asked.

"Wait a minute," Mac interrupted. "You said *'this cell.'* What does that mean?"

"Sir, this is privileged information," Brady cautioned.

"It's all right, Major," Bryan said. "They need to know."

"What are you talking about?" Kyle asked.

"The infrastructure of the Splinter is divided into individual cells. Separate locations, separate commanding officers, separate agendas. We don't even know where the other groups are stationed. It prevents any one man from compromising our entire cause."

"How many cells are there?" Kyle asked.

"Currently, there are twenty-one," Bryan answered.

"And each cell has about the same personnel?" Jackson asked.

"I really can't tell you that," Bryan said. "That I just don't know."

"Doesn't seem to matter," Kyle said. "It sounds like those additional men won't be available to us?"

"No, they're not," Bryan said.

"So eighteen thousand," Jay repeated. "That's not much. The Fury alone has four times as many."

"We know that this war isn't going to be won by lining up and fighting man for man," Brady said. "We don't have the numbers or the firepower for that."

Kyle sighed and stepped toward the window. "How many people in the colony?"

"About two million residents," Brady said.

"Where did they all come from?"

"Most of them are descended from the original members of the Splinter, the people who escaped with Calin Fustre," Bryan said. "Some are Dominion defectors, whether for political reasons or because they couldn't pay their taxes. They come from all over."

"That's a lot of people to feed and protect," Jackson muttered.

"Would you rather us turn them away?" Bryan asked.

"Maybe," Jackson replied. "I'm just thinking of the resources that go into a population that size."

"They produce most of our food, maintain the power grid, mine for materials," Bryan said. "They're not just dead weight."

"Forget the numbers, they're not important," Kyle said. "We need to focus on our military assets and how we use them."

"What are you thinking?" Bryan asked.

"From my perspective, everything you have done over the last few years has been either defensive or reactive," Kyle said. "You need supplies, you make a raid. You get attacked, you try to escape. I can't remember the last time the Splinter made an offensive strike."

"Have you not been listening?" Brady asked. "We don't have the resources to mount an offensive against a Dominion installation. We risk too many losses by engaging them like that."

"Then how do you ever expect to be anything other than a group of refugees hiding in a canyon?" Kyle asked. "They will find you here eventually, you realize that, I'm sure. What will you do then?"

"Spoken like someone who's been here for about ten minutes," Brady sneered. "What makes you think you know better?"

"I know that you can't keep going on like this," Kyle said. "And isn't that why you brought us here in the first place? To change things?"

"What did you have in mind, Commander?" Bryan asked, intrigued.

"We attack them, the same way they attack you."

"And how do you expect us to do that?" Brady asked.

"How confident are you in your men's combat skills?"

"They're competent," Brady responded.

"Competent?" Kyle repeated. "That's how you want to describe it?"

"Well, what do you want me to say? We're dramatically outmanned and outgunned in every engagement. It's kinda tough to judge their skills when we're being overrun. I would have thought a *mutant* like you would understand that."

Kyle bared his teeth. "Overrun, is that it? I think you mean running away with your tail between your legs."

Brady's fists went tight. Kyle saw it and did the same, inviting the fight that he was aching for. He yearned to finally unleash all of that brimming savagery. He was tired of hiding it. Tired of acting like a civilized man, because he wasn't one. He was a mutant, like the major said. An instrument of war. Isn't that what they all thought of him? They all just wanted to use him as a means to an end. To pull the trigger on his infinite payload. To set him off.

Well, maybe he would set himself off first.

That's when Dan stepped in front of him, and Kyle quickly pulled back. The young lieutenant mouthed something, imperceptible to the others, but Kyle's ears could still hear it: "Don't, please. We have nowhere else to go."

Kyle took a deep breath. He glared over Dan's shoulder at Brady, who was getting a similar speech from the Marshal. The major grunted and ducked his head, then turned toward the windows.

Bryan spun back toward his nephew. "I can't have this, Kyle. I can't have the two of you looking to kill each other every time you're in the same room. You've both lost good men to each other, but we have to put that behind us."

Kyle refused to answer. He just stared straight ahead, avoiding his uncle's eyes.

"Commander?"

Kyle grunted. "He watches what comes out of his mouth, and I won't put my fist through it."

Bryan turned back to Brady. The major squeezed his eyes shut, then nodded reluctantly.

"Well, that's just beautiful," Bryan said. "Finally, an accord. Can we get back to strategy now?"

"We were talking about the combat readiness of your men," Mac said.

"Right," Bryan said. "If you want an honest assessment, they don't have the tactical skills to mount the kind of missions that you're used to. Most of them have never been involved in an incursion. I'm just not certain they'll be able to give you the support you'll need."

"They can if we train them properly," Kyle said.

"You want to train them?" Bryan asked. "How are we supposed to do that? More importantly, *who* is going to do that?"

"Dr. Preston," Kyle answered. "He's the best there is."

"That's true," Mac said. "If anyone can do it, it's him."

"Did anyone talk with the doctor?" Kyle asked. "I thought he would be here."

"Yeah, I spoke with him," Jackson said. "But he flat-out refused to come with me. He wants nothing to do with this."

"He's not happy, boss," Jay said.

"Well, who can blame him?" Mac asked. "This is pretty much exactly what he told us not to do."

"Maybe Dan and I should go talk to him," Kyle said. "See if we can change his mind."

"That's fine," Bryan said. "The major and I have some other things to attend to before the light hits the canyon. We'll talk later."

"Kyle, the *Gemini* needs some attention," Jay said. "It's got a damaged engine, cloaking system, and lord knows what else."

"We can get you set up in the engineering bay," Bryan said. "But I doubt we have the materials you'll need to make the repairs."

"Jay, take Jackson and Mac down to engineering and run a diagnostic," Kyle ordered. "Find out exactly what we need."

"We'll do the best we can," Jay said.

Everyone filed out, but Mac apparently had more to discuss.

"Kyle, would you mind if I spoke to you alone for a moment?" he said.

"You want to talk now?" Kyle responded.

"Yeah, it's important."

Kyle sighed: "Danny, why don't you head on down. I'll catch up with you in a few minutes."

The others went about their business. Mac waited until they were out of earshot before saying anything.

"What's on your mind, Mac?" Kyle asked.

"Kyle, I just had ask you, before we go down this road…is this really what you want to do?" Mac asked. "And I mean, do you *really* want to do this? Because we're gonna put a lot of people in a lot of danger if we start attacking the Dominion."

"Mac, I know why you're asking me this …"

"Then you can give me an answer," Mac said. "Is this all about revenge?"

"You're damn right it is," Kyle growled.

He was gritting his teeth so hard it hurt. Mac's eyes went wide, as if even he was surprised by the venom coming from his commander's mouth. But Kyle couldn't help it. Not after what they had done.

"When they took my mother they crossed a line that shouldn't have been crossed," Kyle continued. "I am going to *burn* them to the ground for that—"

"Goddammit, Kyle, these people think that you're here to help them. Not to sacrifice them to serve your vengeance. I'm asking you—I'm begging you—don't do this for selfish reasons."

"I can't just sit here and do nothing—"

"That's not what I said," Mac interrupted. "I want to piss on them as much as you do. But let's be sure we do this right."

"I can't listen to this now."

"Well, you'd better listen," Mac said, emboldened. "We need these people, maybe more than they need us. If you try and run these people into a buzz saw just to get at Vaughn … I won't be a part of it."

"Mac, knock it off."

"I'm serious, Kyle," Mac insisted. "If we are going to drag their troops into combat with the Dominion army - or worse yet, the Fury - then they are going to have to trust us. They can't do that if we run off head-hunting at the first opportunity."

"You're not going to let this go, are you?"

"You think I should?"

Kyle groaned and ran his hand through his hair. His friend was right, and he knew it. He just wanted blood, and at this point he wasn't sure if it even mattered whose it was. It made him suddenly frightened of his own lust for retribution.

"No...I suppose you're right," Kyle admitted finally. "I just ... Every time I close my eyes, all I can see is her ..."

Kyle shuddered. Mac squeezed his commander's shoulder.

"Try and save that image for when we find Vaughn," he said.

After a moment the corner of Kyle's mouth curled into a grin. "Right. I'll do that. Thanks, Mac."

"You can thank me by letting me watch you take that fucker apart."

† † †

Dan knocked on the door to his parents' quarters, and his mother meekly cracked the door. She held it ajar just enough for him to see one of her frightened eyes. Dan couldn't blame her. Staying in this place was like sleeping in the lions' den. Every knock on the door had to feel like someone was hunting them.

Kathryn Preston was a quiet woman, but she had never been as meek as at that moment. Even after seeing Dan, she still hesitated to open the door for several moments. Dan tried his best to give her a reassuring smile, but he knew she could see right through him. It was obviously tough for him to sell them on tranquility when he wasn't certain of it himself. Finally, the doctor brushed his wife aside and pulled the door open. He gave his son a stern look, then waved him inside. He checked each end of the hallway before closing the door to the dingy room.

"I came to your room looking for you earlier," Preston said. "Where were you?"

"I was in the meeting with Bryan and the major," Dan said. "I thought you were supposed to be there."

"Dan, you need to listen to me now. It's not safe here."

"Dad, don't do this again."

"There's nothing *but* this, son," Dr. Preston continued. "We have to get out of here."

"Dad, we've been over this already—"

"Then we'll go over it again," the doctor insisted. "We have to get out of here. These people are our enemies. They will use us for any information they can get, and then they'll kill us."

"I don't think so," Dan said. "I really think they need us. We didn't just walk in here looking for help—they came to us."

"That's exactly how these intelligence scams work! They come to you as a friend and make you think that you're important to their cause. Then when they've got nothing left to take, they put you out of your misery."

"Do you have any idea how paranoid you sound right now?" Dan asked.

"Son, I've seen this a thousand times. I've *done* this a thousand times. It's no different."

"It *is* different," Dan persisted. "Look at where we are. We'd be dead already if these people hadn't taken us in."

"Dan, you have to trust me," the Doctor said. "We cannot stay here."

"Dan, please, just listen to your father," his mother added.

"Where would we even go?" Dan asked. "We can't go back home."

"Actually, I think we can," Preston said. "I can speak with the Director of Intelligence. I can work out a deal for us."

"A deal?" Dan asked. "What are you talking about?"

"I think if we tell them where this camp is, they'll give us our lives back."

"Are you kidding?" Dan demanded. "You want to give them up?"

"It's the only way we get our lives back, son."

"And this deal, is it for all of us?"

"It will be for our family. I think that's all I can do."

Dan shook his head. "I can't do that."

"I'm not going to argue with you about this!" the doctor shouted.

"You can't ask me to do that to the others!" Dan exclaimed. "After all this time, you just want to leave them here to die?"

"Do I want to do this? No!" the Doctor yelled. His voice was getting more and more frustrated. "But I didn't get us into this. And this is the only way that I can protect my family."

"I can't leave them here, Dad."

"Dammit, Dan, will you listen to me just once? I know it's hard to argue with the commander's strength, but believe me, eventually they will find another warrior that is even more powerful than he is. They always do." His eyes were stone cold, like there was more than just conjecture behind his warning.

"I'm sorry," Dan said. "But I won't be a part of this."

"Son, please, just listen for a minute…"

Dan cut him off. "No, now I think it's *your* turn to listen. You didn't see what they did to Kyle's parents. But I did. There was no mercy there. It was cold-blooded. Becca didn't deserve that."

Preston sighed. "If she was working with the Splinter, then maybe she did—"

"Is that what you believe?"

The voice came from outside the door. It was familiar, and froze the room in an instant. Dan opened the door to reveal Kyle, who was standing in the hallway with a scowl so deep that it practically swallowed his face.

† † †

"Kyle, I—"

"Lieutenant, Mrs. Preston, would you mind giving us a moment?" Kyle interrupted.

Dan nodded and led his mother out into the hall. Kyle waited for the door to close behind him, then turned a grim stare back to his mentor. The doctor was a shade paler as he looked at his protégé.

"Kyle, I hope you don't think that I mean…"

"What *did* you mean?" Kyle grumbled. "Because it sure sounded like you think my mother got what she deserved."

"Kyle, I was just thinking from the Dominion's perspective," Preston pleaded. "Obviously if they found out that she was in league with the Splinter, they were going to come after her."

"I'm not interested in their perspective," Kyle said. "What do *you* think?"

"Commander, please don't make me answer that."

"That's all I need to hear," Kyle said, turning to the door.

"Kyle—son—this doesn't change the respect that I have for you."

"Respect?" Kyle spat. "And Jackson and the others? Rats have more loyalty than you."

"I'm just trying to do what's best for my family."

"Well, let me give you a little advice," Kyle continued. "If they were willing to turn on me that quickly, they'll be happy to do the same to you. You might think you're helping your family, but they'll be in even more danger if you go back."

"You really want to believe in this thing now, don't you?" Preston asked. "You want to believe that the Gentry is evil and that you did the right thing. That way you don't have to take responsibility."

"My mother believed it. And they killed her for it. I'm not sure what other proof I need."

"And what if she was wrong? What then?"

"Honestly, sir, I would rather die on her word than live on theirs," Kyle said. He turned for the door again, but the doctor called back to him one more time.

"Commander, wait," he said. "This isn't why you came down here. What did you want?"

"I came to ask for your help. But I'm not sure I want it anymore."

The doctor's eyes creased. "Help with what?"

"Why?" Kyle asked. "You're interested now?"

"I'm curious," Preston said. "Or are you too angry to tell me now?"

Kyle scratched at his jaw, debating with himself. "We need someone to train the Splinter soldiers on incursion tactics."

"Incursion?"

"You heard me right," Kyle confirmed.

"You're going to take these men and attempt an assault on a Dominion installation?"

"Not if we don't have a way to train them."

Someone started pounding on the door. It was Jackson, who was clearly out of breath.

"Kyle! There's been an attack!"

"Where?"

"One of their outposts, here on the moon," Jackson said.

"Dominion?" Dan asked.

"They don't know," Jackson said, still panting. "They just got a distress call from the men there and then lost contact."

"How quickly can we get there?" Kyle asked.

"Jay and Mac are prepping a transport now," Jackson said. "Brady's getting a unit together too. I think we can be on site in fifteen minutes."

"All right," Kyle said, turning to his young lieutenant. "You ready to get your hands dirty?"

Dan paused and looked at his father, who just shook his head. Dan sighed and glanced back at Kyle. “Yes, sir,” he said. “Let’s do it.”

CHAPTER 12

"Commander, we're approaching the outpost," Major Brady said.

Kyle stepped next to the major and peered out the old, hazy window of the Splinter transport. He could barely make out the tattered structure among the ribbons of smoke. The small installation was hidden within a heaving ridge of rocks, though at this point it looked more like a scrapyard that had been hit by a tornado.

"I don't see any hostiles," Kyle said. "What do we have on the instruments?"

"Nothing," the pilot replied. "Motion sensors are silent. The heat signatures are all screwed up by the fire, but we're not reading anything alive down there."

"Is it possible that they've moved on already?" Brady asked.

"We'd still be picking up something," Kyle said. "It doesn't make any sense."

"How's that?" Brady prodded.

"They should be waiting here," Kyle said. "It's the perfect place for an ambush."

"What's the function of this place?" Jackson asked.

"It's a hydrogenerator site," Brady said. "There's a shallowing of the underground river here."

"How many people on site?" Kyle asked.

"Twenty-seven," Brady said.

"Set down on top of the ridge," Kyle said. "Let's keep the high ground."

The pilot looked back at the major.

"Set it down on the ridge," Brady said.

The old ship trembled as the combustion thrusters pivoted to lower them to the ground. There was a loud clunk and thud as the landing gear touched down. Kyle looked down at the Splinter combat suit he was wearing. It was nearly two sizes too small, feeling tight against his hulking arms and chest, but mainly it just felt alien to him. It felt like it should be singeing his skin after all those years toiling under the insignia of the Dominion. But it didn't burn, which almost made him feel like he could belong here. Like they might actually accept him. Wouldn't that be something?

Kyle shook away the thought as the engines cut off. He turned back into the passenger bay and looked over the fifteen men waiting in front of him. Jackson and the rest of his team looked calm and comfortable in the face of their task, despite their unfamiliar uniforms. Even Dan seemed to have control of his nerves other than an anxiously bouncing right knee. The Splinter men, however, were racked with obvious concern, gripping their weapons and chewing on their cheeks.

Kyle pulled on a helmet and checked the charge on his rifle. They were able to find a handful of extra Dominion-issue weapons in the armory of the *Gemini*. If there were Garrison soldiers waiting for them here, they would need every advantage they could get.

"Major, this is your show," Kyle said. "But if I were you, I'd send ten men to set up a perimeter, including Captain Hilton and Lieutenant Harrier, and have them pick off anything that isn't familiar. The rest of us go in to look for survivors."

"All right, gentlemen, you heard the man," Brady said. "Captain, take those men and get the perimeter established, two hundred meters out. Safeties off. Drop anything that might be hostile."

The rear hatch hissed open and the cold surface air rushed in. Brady looked over to Kyle from beneath the visor on his helmet. Kyle could tell that the major was nervous, his pulse pounding against the long scar on his neck. He put up a good front though, with a stern scowl and even breath.

"You want to lead us out, Commander?" he asked.

Typical, Kyle thought. Talks a big game, but when the chips are down, he asks his old nemesis to go first. Still, it was better for him to go. If there was an ambush, it was likely meant for him anyway.

Kyle nodded and stepped off the ramp. The ground was a hard rock that crunched beneath his boots. It would be difficult to keep quiet, though the howling wind would help. He settled the butt of his rifle into the crease of his right shoulder and started down the ridge toward the installation.

There were shards of metal scattered everywhere. He glided past them in his effortless style, but when he reached the bottom and looked back, the others had fallen well behind. *So this is how it will be*, he thought. He saw Jackson sprint out across the crest of the valley and then disappear into a good nest. Jay did the same in the other direction. Their swiftness disparaged the lumbering march of the Splinter men, their plodding echoing across the rocks.

Dan was the first to come up behind Kyle, with Brady several steps behind. The large doors had been blown inward, which meant that this hadn't been done by an artillery strike. Whoever had done this forced their way inside.

Kyle flanked the opening and waited impatiently for the others. There was a smell emanating from the entry, a sulfurous mixture of heat and scalded flesh. But there was something else, something he couldn't place. It had a swampy musk to it, like sewage rotting in a well. However, their instruments showed no chemical or biological toxins, so he set it aside for the time being.

Kyle reached down and picked up a small copper cylinder from the ground. It smelled of gun powder and heat. Brady had said that this outpost was armed mostly with old projectile weapons, and sure enough there were empty shells littered all around. But there were no traces of blood. Had they hit nothing?

Kyle turned into the entrance and headed inside. The emergency lights flickered on and off, doing little to show him what was ahead. He saw a handful of rifle lights flash on behind him, their streams darting from wall to wall and floor to ceiling. The installation seemed larger than it looked from the outside, drowning their lights in its cavernous size. At the end of the first corridor was a staircase leading down, seemingly into the depths beneath the valley. The bullet casings continued down the metal risers, and portions of the iron railings were either crushed or ripped from their footings. A haze hung beneath the ceiling, scattering the light across the dust in the air. All Kyle could hear was the rush of the river from deep below.

"Commander?" Brady whispered, concerned with Kyle's pause.

"What's down the stairs?" Kyle whispered back.

"The hydraulic turbines," Brady said.

"There are more shell casings on that landing," Kyle muttered. "If there are any survivors, they're gonna be down there."

"Then we head down," Brady said. "I'm going to leave a pair of men here to watch these other access points. Can you spare your lieutenant?"

Kyle nodded, then waved them down the stairs. The metal risers clunked under their boots. The rotting swamp smell lessened as they descended, but the smell of seared skin gradually got stronger. The metal of the installation ended about halfway down, giving way to the moist bedrock underneath. It was at least twenty degrees hotter than on the surface, and the floor felt like the top of a stove under the soles of his boots. At the bottom they found a pair of scorched corpses melted to the floor, still clinging to the weapons that couldn't save them.

"Fuck me," Brady groaned, covering his mouth and nose.

Kyle looked back at him and caught a glimpse of three deep claw marks gauged into the stone wall.

"I don't think the Dominion did this," Kyle said facetiously.

"Son of a bitch...," Brady grumbled. "Infernals."

"So that's why we couldn't get any readings," Mac said.

"It doesn't look like they made it down this hall," Kyle said. "The burn marks stop right here."

"We've gotta make this fast," Brady said. "We can't be caught in here if they come back."

"Mac, head back up to the main level," Kyle said. "Radio out to Jackson and the others. Tell them to keep an eye on the skies."

"Yeah," Mac said. "Work fast."

Kyle started down the tunnel, his weapon at the ready. The corridor was dark and musty, with the smell of water vapor replacing the vulgar stink of the previous areas. The sound of cascading water was rapidly increasing, and the floor grew slick. The hall veered to the left, and finally they saw a faint glow in front of them. They hurried forward, their feet splashing through the steadily deepening water on the ground.

The hall opened into an underground cave, dimly lit by the remaining emergency lights. The roar of the water came to a crest as a heavy waterfall poured out of the cave walls, dumping into the clumsy hydraulic turbines. A heavy mist permeated the air, but the fresh smell was a welcome relief after the pungent stench on the floors above. Kyle's eyes darted all over the cavern, but there was not a soul to be found, until Brady hollered out from the side of the room.

"Commander, over here!" he yelled. "The engineering room!"

Kyle rushed around the machinery to a small armored door tucked into a crevice among the rocks. The thick metal beams above the door had buckled some, probably under the combined stress of the rushing water and the onslaught by the Infernal. Either way, it seemed jammed even as Brady strained against it. He stopped and pounded against the metal, shouting for anyone inside.

"Can anyone hear me? We're here to get you out!"

There were no voices, but there was a return thud against the inside of the door. Brady turned to Kyle.

"Tell them to step back," Kyle said.

Brady leaned into the door. "Get back, we're coming through! Knock twice if you understand!"

There were two muffled thumps, and Brady stepped aside. Kyle reared back and hit the door with a thunderous kick, denting the metal like a battering ram. With his second blow the door swung open on its hinges with a reverberating clang. Several chunks of rock crumbled down from the overhang. Inside there was a huddled group of eight survivors cowering in the dark. Brady hurried in and started leading them out, but several staggered backward when they saw Kyle's towering figure.

"No, no, he's fine. He's with me," Brady insisted, pushing them back out the crumbling door. "We've gotta go now."

"Are there any other survivors?" Kyle asked.

"We don't know," a heavyset man said. "We grabbed who we could. The others must still be upstairs."

Something rumbled above them and lines of dust trickled down from the ceiling. The whole group went immediately silent.

Kyle broke the stalemate first. "Jackson, do you copy?"

"Kyle, I read," Jackson said. "You've gotta get topside now. An Infernal just set down in the valley."

"Do you have a shot?" Kyle asked.

"I don't think we're gonna take this thing down with the weapons we've got," Jackson said.

"Keep a bead on it," Kyle said. "I'm on the way."

Kyle glanced over at Brady. "Give me a minute, and then start heading up," he said. "We'll see if we can give you a path to the transport."

Brady barely had time to nod before Kyle disappeared down the dark corridor. There were several loud booms as he sprinted, rattling the pipes and mechanics lining the ceiling overhead. He came screaming into the light at the base of the staircase as Jackson started back over radio.

"It's moving toward the entrance!" he yelled. "I'm opening fire!"

The muffled sound of gunfire trickled down from the entrance above, followed by the blistering roar of the vicious beast. Kyle had never heard anything like it, a crackling and piercing bellow like an angry demon. Mac was several steps up the stairs as they began to shake.

"Kyle, what do we do?" he demanded.

"Brady's got survivors coming out," Kyle said as he ran past. "Help him get them clear of the structure!"

When Kyle reached the top of the stairs, he saw Dan and the other soldier firing their weapons toward the entrance. He saw the sparks of several shots rain out of their weapons, and then watched them duck back into the cover of the entryway. Dan dove from the right to the left of the door as a wave of fire flooded inside. The metal frame around the doorway liquefied in the torrent, and the header over the gate slumped downward. As he helped the other soldier to his feet, a huge shadow crossed in front of the entry, and the Infernal's fearsome face cut through the rising smoke. Its pointed snout and sharp angled eyes gave way to a long, sloped forehead. Behind it was a thick mane of daggerlike quills, each one jagged enough to skewer a man like a spear. Its gargantuan shoulders jammed into the high arch of the doorway, causing the rafters to shake like a tent in the wind. Rows of dagger-like teeth snapped at their heels as it writhed to get through. The Splinter soldiers stumbled and fell, and Dan stopped to pull him back up. The Infernal's jaws opened, and Kyle saw a spark kindle from deep in its throat.

Kyle felt a surge through his chest, and he thrust his hands forward, spewing his Celestial energy in a torrent. It hit the beast just below the chin and threw it backward as though it had been hit by a train. There was a loud boom as it crashed into the rocks outside, followed by the creature's injured whimpers.

"Find another way out!" Kyle ordered. "I'll cover your backs."

As Mac led, Dan, Brady and the others away from the entrance, Kyle let out a ragged breath and then ran out the door. The smoke was still rising from the building, but Kyle was more distracted by the swath of sulfur in the air. The Infernal had gouged a trough in the rock before crashing into the base of the craggy incline. It writhed and growled, trying to roll off its back, kicking slabs of rock in every direction. Kyle fired a handful of shots from his rifle, but they simply ricocheted harmlessly off its armored hide as it regained its footing and spread its membranous wings.

The beast craned its neck toward him, grumbling at the annoyance of the attack. In the open air the Infernal seemed smaller, just over thirty feet from head to tail. Its shale-colored armor blended into the gray landscape, and its talons crunched into the stone with each step. Its mouth yawned open and roared as Kyle fired off another volley from his rifle. The monster winced as the shots caromed off its cheek and forehead, rearing back onto its haunches like an angry bear. It lunged forward and retched out a stream of red napalm.

Kyle leapt aside as the fire scalded the valley floor. He rolled across the hard stone, feeling the boiling heat of the Infernal's breath beating down behind him. There was a constant clatter of gunfire now, pelleting the beast from all directions. The Infernal reared back again, its tail thrashing side to side. Kyle fired an explosive charge from the launcher on his rife, and it burst against its exposed chest. It was blown backward again, this time crashing down onto the remains of the installation's entry. The sagging roof crumpled like cardboard under its weight.

Kyle tried to signal Jackson on the top of the ridge, but the beast had already managed to clamber back to its feet. It shrugged to its left and heaved a huge slab of the metal frame over the incline and onto the top of the ridge. A pair of the Splinter men disappeared beneath the rubble as they tried to flee.

The Infernal's attention drifted back to Kyle, who was distracted by the peril of the men from his vantage point at the bottom of the basin. The beast released another wave of fire, and Kyle was forced to throw up his hands and conjure a Celestial shield at the last moment. The fire slammed against his spell like a tidal wave, seeming to swallow him whole as he strained to keep it at bay. Finally the searing heat relented and the cool moon air swept over him again.

There were beads of sweat seeping down his temples, and his arms felt weary and heavy. The Infernal paused as if stunned that its adversary had withstood its onslaught. It poised itself to strike, baring its fangs.

Kyle reached a telekinetic hand down beneath the surface, down beyond the clay and bedrock, delving through layer upon layer of heavy rock with his mind's eye. With a grunt he heaved a rush of water from the underground river up through the crust, engulfing the beast in a cooling geyser from below. Then he threw his other hand forward with a burst of freezing air. The water petrified around the crouching monster, encasing it in a cocoon of solid ice.

The valley went eerily calm as the gunshots fell silent and everyone stared in amazement. Kyle dropped to a knee, exhausted. It had been some time since he'd been forced to summon such raw, elemental power, and even then he couldn't remember ever performing such a godly feat. It felt like the effort had drained something vital from his body.

The blast of arctic air had left a light flurry of snowflakes hanging over the basin, and the cold gave him goosebumps on the back of his neck. His daze was broken by a cacophony of voices on his communicator, none making any sense as they spoke over each other. He shook off the remaining wooziness and rose to his feet, then tried to make sense of the noise.

"All right, all right, everyone calm down," he said. "Sound off, what's your status?"

"I'm clear," Jay called. "I've got six others here on the west ridge. We're good."

"This is Brady. I'm with lieutenants Preston and McArthur. We have the survivors with us at the west entrance. Everyone is alive and accounted for."

"Any other survivors?" Kyle asked.

"Negative," Brady reported. "The dragon clearly made it through this wing. It's pretty grisly in here."

"Kyle, this is Jackson," a third voice said. "You'd better get up here. We've got a couple of men trapped by debris on the east ridge."

"I'm on my way," Kyle confirmed, starting up the hillside. "Everyone else start loading up on the transport. We need to be moving soon."

"How long will that ice hold the Infernal?" Brady asked.

"I don't know," Kyle said. He reached the top of the ridge and saw the men pinned by the large metal slab from the entryway. "But I'm certain we don't want to be here to find out. We'll get some artillery from the *Gemini* to vaporize it once we get out of here."

Both trapped soldiers were still alive, one held down by his right leg, and the other pinned shoulder-deep into a shallow groove in the hillside. The first soldier's pelvis and femur were clearly broken, his thigh turned at nearly a 45-degree angle. There was blood seeping into the fabric of his pants, and he looked pale in the face. The second man seemed alert and relatively uninjured.

The slab must have been twenty-five feet long and nearly two feet thick of solid metal. It had to weigh more than two tons if it was an ounce. Regardless, Kyle wedged his hands beneath the debris, and with a powerful push of his legs the slab lifted enough for Jackson to pull the two men clear. Kyle let it back down with a clang, blowing a ring of dust off the ground as it landed.

By the time he turned back to the man with the broken femur, the blood had saturated his entire right pant leg. He'd likely severed the femoral artery. Kyle would need to heal it immediately or he would bleed out. Kyle bent down and placed a hand on the leg near the break. The man's pulse had already started to weaken. There was a sudden flash of blue light as his energy reached through his skin and fused the bone and tissue back together. The soldier had already drifted off into unconsciousness, but his body still trembled as Kyle's powers did their work. The flow of blood ceased, the bone was made whole.

Kyle rose back to his feet. "Get him back to the transport. He's gonna need medical attention."

Jackson and another Splinter trooper lifted the wounded man onto a collapsible stretcher and started across the ridge toward the ship. Kyle took a deep breath. The air was still soaked with sulfur and ash from the Infernal's seething flames. It felt hot and rough trickling down his throat and into his chest. For a man who didn't need to breathe, Kyle still found himself wishing for some fresh air.

Or a moment of rest would do, he thought.

As he started toward the transport, he heard a faint crackling sound coming from the valley floor. At first it seemed like a trick of the wind, but then it became more pronounced. Then he heard the panicked screams of the other men.

"Commander!" It was Brady's stricken voice over the intercom. "The Infernal is breaking loose!"

Kyle spun back toward the basin in time to see the beast's head burst out of its frozen shackles. There were a handful of rifle bursts from the direction of the transport, with those shots bouncing off the Infernal's impervious skin. More ice crumbled free with each heave of its body. It spewed fire into the air, struggling to aim its venom toward the group of humans scurrying across the ridge. Kyle saw Jackson and his companion scrambling over the uneven terrain with the injured soldier, then glanced over at Dan and Brady hurrying the survivors from the west entrance to their ship. They would never make it before the Infernal broke free.

"Everyone hold your fire!" Kyle yelled. "Get back to the transport. I'll draw its attention."

Kyle didn't even wait for a reply. He started bounding around the valley ridge toward the east side of the complex, away from the others. He fired several small bursts from his rifle that dotted the side of the beast's head. It writhed in his direction several times until its tail broke free, slinging it back and forth like a huge medieval flail. Finally, the ice shattered and the Infernal shook the remaining chunks from its back. Kyle squeezed the trigger again, and the creature obliged his taunt, turning its back on the others and crawling after him alone.

"Kyle! Are you nuts?" Mac shouted over the comm. "What are you doing?"

Kyle didn't answer. He unstrapped his rifle and tossed it aside, then reached behind his head and pulled his sword from its sheath. The Infernal stalked toward the ridge, its fearsome jaws dripping a steaming drool from between its jagged teeth. Kyle held steady as the monster's deep growl echoed off the rocks around him. The Infernal paused cautiously at the base of the rise, seeming to realize that Kyle was not some helpless prey to be trifled with. Its talons scraped against the stony ground, and its wings folded close to its sides. Then it lunged forward with its jaws wide open, salivating in anticipation of tasting flesh. Kyle took one step and dove headfirst at the oncoming beast, driving the blade of his war sword through the scaly armor on its throat and into the soft skin underneath. The wound crackled and burned as the sword split it open, and the Infernal's roar seemed to lose its thunder.

Kyle hit the ground first, sliding unscathed across the rocks. The Infernal slammed into the crest of the ridge with a crash. It pulled itself back to its feet, swinging drunkenly around in an attempt to locate its prey. The gash in its neck gushed thick yellowish blood like a fountain, each drop hissing as the hot fluid hit the cool rocks. Finally it toppled over, choking painfully on its last breath.

The seeping blood trickled down to Kyle's feet as he wiped the blade of his sword. He placed it back in its sheath, gathered his rifle, and made his way back toward the transport. This time there was no cheering or shouts from the others, only a stunned silence, at least until Jay broke the hush.

"Is it dead?" he asked.

"Yeah," Kyle said, glancing back at the Infernal's corpse, "I'm pretty sure it's dead."

"Holy shit," Jay gasped. "Are you okay?"

"I'm good, Jay," Kyle replied. "Is anybody else hurt?"

"I don't think so ..."

Jay trailed off as Brady and the others from inside the compound came trotting up to the transport. Mac didn't allow the survivors to linger and see the carnage outside, instead herding them immediately into the waiting vessel. Brady stopped to take a look, and he seemed less impressed. He marched over to Kyle with a stern glare hardening his face.

"Are you out of your mind, Commander? What were you thinking?"

"I'm not sure how you expect me to answer that," Kyle said.

"You could have gotten yourself killed!" Brady hollered, his voice escalating. "You *should* have gotten yourself killed."

"Easy, keep your voice down," Kyle said. "What did you want me to do? Let it tear us apart?"

"I've never seen anything so reckless and dangerous," Brady insisted.

"Well, I appreciate your concern, Major," Kyle said with an obvious sarcastic overtone. "You're welcome, by the way."

"Dammit, Commander—"

"Hey!" Jackson interrupted. "Can we do this later? We've got injured men that we need to get back to the colony."

Kyle nodded, embarrassed. "Of course."

"We need to tie things up around here," Brady said. "The corpse of that thing could attract more of them."

"You go ahead with the transport," Kyle replied. "I'll keep a few men here and clean up."

Brady nodded. "We'll talk more when you return."

"Can't wait," Kyle snipped.

The transport lifted off and disappeared in the direction of the colony. Kyle kept seven soldiers, including Mac, who was eager to study the Infernal's body and take samples before they disposed of it.

Kyle shrugged and loosened his neck. He felt an unfamiliar ache across his shoulder blades, a tension his godlike body had never suffered. The effort he'd expelled in dispatching the massive beast was gargantuan, and the power he had summoned was something he hadn't known he could muster. It had him both curious and concerned. Was he just unleashing some of the pent-up anger he'd been harboring from his mother's death? Or was it something else entirely? The fatigue wasn't helping clear his thoughts, and he decided to ignore it and go on with the task at hand. After all, his attention was more paramount elsewhere, and he was certain malaise would resolve shortly. It always had before.

CHAPTER 13

Vaughn Donovan grimaced and cursed as the biogenerator meticulously stitched together a gaping bone-deep laceration on the outside of his right thigh. He had been sitting with his leg inside the device for nearly three hours after the incident on Vadara, and the process was just now about finished. The worst of it had been much earlier, when it pulled out a jagged five-inch piece of shrapnel from beneath the severed muscle. He had nearly blacked out at that point, but caught himself when some of the matrix fluid splashed into his groin. The machine itself was quite a wonder, inspired by the same mechanism that Kyle's powers used to heal wounds. It produced an acceleration of the regenerative process by flooding the damaged tissue with undifferentiated stem cells, and then used a biochemical welding process to fuse the new flesh with the old. It was a luxury that few men had access to, even among executive officers of the Dominion Army. However, Vaughn had become quite familiar with its torture over his long career, as much as he wished he hadn't at that particular moment.

Kyle's powers were much swifter and more thorough in their healing abilities, though also far more painful. During his life Vaughn had endured the sting of both, but in the end he preferred the machine. Despite its grueling hours, at least it meant he owed nothing to the commander.

Finally the machine shut off and he pulled his leg out of the gelatinous soup that filled the biogenerator chamber. He was still seeing stars from the caustic burn of the treatment as he stepped off the plinth, but considering that he just had a house dropped on top of him, he felt pretty damn good. He tested his weight on the leg, and after an initial twinge he gave a satisfied grunt. He dried his skin haphazardly and pulled on a new pair of pants. The agonizing time in the biogenerator had distracted him from the frustration of Commander Griffin's escape on Vadara, but now that came rushing back to him. The reports from the units in pursuit all offered the same conclusion: Kyle had eluded them without a trace.

The doors to the medical bay slid open as Vaughn finished getting dressed, and a dark-skinned captain marched in. The insignia on his uniform designated him as a pilot, but the officer's uniform meant that he was the ship's chief aerospace aviator. Typically, battlecruiser vessels such as this one did not carry an official of Vaughn's rank, but it was the nearest hyperspace-ready ship after Kyle had destroyed their other transports outside of Angel's home. As such, it would have to make do. The captain maintained a strict stare beneath his cap, though the general mostly ignored his presence. He stopped just a few feet from Vaughn, and saluted dutifully.

"General Donovan, sir, I apologize for the interruption," he said.

"What is it, Captain?" Vaughn grumbled. "I have things to do."

"Sir, I just wanted to make you aware that we are approaching the capital," he said. "We will drop out of hyperspace momentarily."

"The capital? We were to be headed to Fury headquarters. Who gave you permission to change our course?"

"I'm sorry, sir, but the orders come from the palace. Lord Aeron wishes to speak with you."

Vaughn sighed, his lips clenched in front of his teeth. "Very well. Fetch me an officer's jacket. I would be better dressed when I meet him."

The captain did as he was told, though the only remaining officer's coat on board was at least a full size too big for him. He irritably tugged on the sleeves, but they slid right back over the palms of his hands.

The ship dropped out of hyperspace with only a slight shiver as Vaughn walked into the wide shuttle bay at the rear of the vessel. He climbed into one of the personal descent pods, and it jettisoned from the cruiser with a burst. For a moment Vaughn could see the size of the vessel from the outside—nearly a dozen city blocks in length—before the pod spun to drop into Dynasteria's atmosphere. It darted past one of the many orbiting defense stations on its descent, the massive floating complex of radar systems and munitions dwarfing the one-man craft.

The galactic capital was not just a city on the galaxy's most extravagant planet. No, here the city *was* the planet, stretching across every square inch of the surface, and even towering hundreds of stories above ground in glistening, shimmering skyscrapers. Entire worlds, and indeed entire star systems, had been mined dry to construct this utopian metropolis, and in all it had taken generations to build. This was where the Gentry lorded over his domain, with his own lustrous palace and all its decadent adornments as its crown jewel.

It was early morning as the pod descended toward the palace grounds, but the din of the busy metropolis was audible even as the ship nestled onto the tarmac within the courtyard. A pair of armed guards waited outside the hatch as Vaughn stepped out. The general rolled his eyes as he saw them.

"General Donovan," the man on the left started. "We are here to escort you to the Gentry's chambers."

"I don't need an armed guard," Vaughn snapped.

"The Lord Gentry commands it, General. You will follow us."

Vaughn swallowed a jagged lump of his own pride and submitted to the escort. This was one of the few places in the known galaxy where his command was not the sovereign rule, and despite his distaste for being docile, it was clear that the Gentry was not pleased. More specifically, he was not pleased with *him.*

They passed through the soaring entry corridors with their shimmering walls and elegant stone floors before coming to the gargantuan carboranium doors that led to the galactic throne room. Two guards in sleek, mechanized electro-combat suits pulled the gates open and motioned him inside.

The throne room was at the center of the huge palatial complex, and rose like a spire over the rest of the grounds. It opened to a balcony on one side that overlooked the north slope of the region with a view that stretched for many miles in almost any direction. The floor was inlayed with platinum and ruby-colored precious metals, all etched into ornate patterns of his choosing. Light flooded in from between mammoth ivory pillars that supported a crystalline ceiling arching overhead. The early morning sunshine sparkled like raindrops between the ceiling and floors, dancing in front of the general's eyes as if he'd floated directly into the facets of a diamond. It was blinding at first, and in stark contrast to the Gentry's reclusive nature. It always seemed as though he would be brooding in the perpetual dark, but in truth he loved the light. He surrounded himself with it. Bathed himself in it. No one really understood why.

Perhaps that's simply what gods did.

Vaughn's boots echoed across the twinkling floors as he walked through the cavernous room. The throne was directly in front of him, cast in a muted gold with spiraling millwork along the edges and a massive capstone that mirrored the Gentry's own crown and helmet. The whole thing was placed at the top of a dozen stairs like a pyramid, resting in front of the opening to the balcony beyond. However, as the general stopped in front of the pedestal, the throne stood vacant.

His eyes darted around for a moment, uncertain of how to comport himself in an empty throne room. At least until he heard the low thunder of Aeron's voice from behind the pyramid.

"**General,**" the voice grumbled. It was a slow, deliberate tone, both visceral and raw, like the depths of a volcano had suddenly spawned a tongue.

The floor rumbled as Aeron stepped from behind the throne platform. The dawning sun was rising in the east, giving a rare glimpse of the spectacle that was the Gentry in the growing light. He had thick, maroon armored plates covered his shoulders and hips. A long silken cape draped from his shoulders, and a matte black garb covered the rest of his colossal body. His face was shrouded by the crown and helmet that extended down below his jawline, and even in the morning light only his luminous red eyes were visible beneath the cowl. And of course, as always there was the glowing amulet—the Eye—anchored within his breastplate.

The Gentry took several steps up the stairs as Vaughn genuflected to one knee. "You wished to see me, My Lord?"

"**You've been busy today, General,**" the Gentry growled.

"I'm sorry, sire," Vaughn said, his head still bowed, "I'm not sure I understand."

"**Then let me enlighten you**," Aeron said, taking a seat on his throne. "**Your task was to draw out any rebel agents who may have infiltrated our infrastructure. *Not* to drive away our most capable men.**"

"My Lord, we knew that this may happen," Vaughn explained. "As soon as we learned of Colonel Foster's involvement, we knew that the commander may be a risk. That is why we chose to send him to Emporia, because he would be able to draw out more intel from the colonel than we ever could."

"**You assured me, General, that should the situation turn this way, that Griffin could be handled.**"

"I understand, sire, but we could not have predicted that his mother would be involved as well. Initially we simply feared that he would refuse to carry out the assassination order on the colonel, but once his mother became a part of the equation, we had no choice but to eliminate all of them. They would simply be too much of a risk within our ranks."

"Then why, General, is Griffin not *dead*?"

"My Lord, we set the trap as we planned, at his parents' doorstep. It all worked as we expected. But they had help ... from Dr. Preston's son."

"And now the doctor has gone missing as well."

"They all have, My Lord," Vaughn said. "Everyone we could link them to. They are gone without a trace."

"And the colonel?"

"Also gone, my Lord."

"And you still have learned nothing of the Splinter infiltration of our forces?"

"Sire, I believe we were able to prevent Commander Griffin from becoming one of those agents," Vaughn pleaded. "And we were able to weed out both the colonel and his sister—"

"**Enough!**" the Gentry thundered, his deep baritone suddenly finding a sharp octave. "**You have done nothing that they weren't prepared for. You have killed a housewife with no military status, and you have gifted them our most powerful soldier! So, explain to me again, exactly what it is that you have accomplished today?**"

"My Lord, I think we have suitable replacements for the commander with our projects in the Sol system. I believe between those prospects and your efforts to create charmed Vicars—"

"**You've made progress, then?**" Aeron asked. "**With our research in the Sol system?**"

"Well ... no, sir," Vaughn confessed. "We still have the same problems. The embryos never survive. But it's just a matter of time for us to find the right sequencing, and then I think we'll get our army of super-sol—"

Aeron let out a rumble from within his throat, and his red eyes raised several watts. "**I am not interested in what you think, General, only what you do. And today you have only weakened my army, and strengthened theirs.**"

Vaughn's shoulders slumped, the Gentry's snarl weighing him down.

"**Do not assume that your knowledge of my past will protect you, General.**"

Vaughn swallowed hard. "Yes, sire."

"**This is your task now,**" Aeron said. "**You will hunt them down and destroy them, whatever it takes, whatever the cost. It will be the sole purpose of your existence. Do you understand?**"

"It will be done, My Lord."

"**Kyle Griffin will not be the end of me.**"

Vaughn was taken aback, and his eyes drifted up toward the Gentry atop his perch. He quickly realized his mistake and dropped his chin toward the floor again, but oddly the Gentry seemed distracted. If Vaughn didn't know better, he could have sworn that it was doubt lurking behind the mask.

"**Go.**"

Vaughn gathered himself and dragged his wounded dignity out of the throne room. He had never been on the receiving end of the Gentry's ire, and there would be worse to come if he did not succeed at his new charge.

Ever since his days as a battle-hardened major, he had been in the business of making Aeron's past disappear. Labor disputes, tax evasions, mistresses—he made them all go away. It had become his specialty. But Kyle Griffin was a different animal. He was possibly the most powerful, most dangerous man in the galaxy … if you could even legitimately call him a man. Now his own life depended on his ability to find and defeat an enemy who had never lost a fight.

Vaughn had never been able to reconcile how easy things were for Kyle. The golden-boy treatment lavished on the commander drove him into a rage every time he thought about it.

However …

He now had been given carte blanche to throw the entire arsenal at him. Whatever he needed to achieve the victory he had always desired over his most bitter competitor was now within his reach. The more the thought cascaded through his head, the more he started to relish the opportunity.

He made his way into the military catacombs beneath the palace, his mind swimming with the steps ahead. He knew that if he waited the commander would come to them, that his fury at the death of his mother would drive him to revenge. He just needed a way to put that to his advantage.

Before he made it into the command center he was met by a dark-skinned captain with a long bushy beard and tank-sized legs. Terrance Jones had twice been court-martialed for the use of brutal force against civilians, and was on his way out of the Dominion Army before General Donovan pulled him off the scrap heap. Now he was Vaughn's right-hand man, and if that were possible, perhaps an even more feared black ops soldier than his mentor. Jones handed the general a small encoder as he approached.

"Are you all right, General?" Jones asked.

"Fine," Vaughn replied tersely.

Jones cleared his throat. "The Gentry is angry?"

"Have you ever known him to be otherwise?" Vaughn asked.

Jones shook his head but didn't speak. Vaughn shrugged, considering the thought.

"The Gentry has been a fool," Vaughn said finally. "For years he's allowed the Splinter to fester under our feet, thinking that their presence allows him a target at which he can point his armies. It gave him something for the people to fear more than they feared him. Amazing when people are focused on war, they don't tend to notice things like taxes and annexes. But now things have gotten out of hand. Now they have a weapon that could truly threaten the throne."

"You think Commander Griffin would actually fight for them?"

Vaughn huffed. "I have no doubt. We took away one of the few things that made him feel human. He'll do everything in his power to burn the Dominion down."

"So where do we start?" Jones asked.

"Have our men finished on Emporia?" Vaughn asked.

"They're still going through some things now, sir," Jones said in his raspy voice.

"What have they found so far?"

"Unfortunately, not much. They torched most of the files, and what is left seems useless."

"Goddammit," Vaughn fumed. "They had less than an hour. They *had* to have left something behind."

"Well, sir, the best I can find is on the encoder there."

Vaughn swiped the thumb piece and a hologram flashed in front of him. "What are we looking at?"

"These are the shipping manifests for the Emporia station," Jones said, pointing to a highlighted line in the center of the page. "From the transcripts of the conversation with Commander Griffin, we know that they received information from the Archives. This is a delivery to the station from the Archives barely two weeks ago."

"Does it say what was shipped?"

"No, but when we cross-referenced it with the outgoing shipments at the Archives, there was no corresponding number. When we looked into it further, there was an outgoing shipment that was slated to have thirteen items, but managed to leave with fourteen."

"Does it say who approved the shipment?" Vaughn asked.

"No, but when we checked the employment roster for the day, there was only one officer on duty with permissions to authorize shipments. A Lieutenant Colonel Jonathan Ashford."

"So he could be the mole in the Archives."

"That's my thought, sir," Jones said.

Vaughn closed the hologram and handed the encoder back to his captain. "Gather a unit. We're going to pay this Ashford a visit."

Chapter 14

The colony's artificial daylights had already cycled back on for their second stint of the day by the time Kyle and his group made it back from the outpost. It had taken far longer than he had anticipated for them to secure the location and take care of the Infernal's body. Mac had done some field tests for protein consistency and tissue toxicity levels, and it turned out that the soft flesh beneath the beast's armored scales was quite edible. It was impossible to turn down nearly six tons of fresh meat, especially considering their reportedly sparse rations. So they spent most of the day trying to salvage as much of it as they could.

Kyle sat on the edge of an open-cabined helio as they circled toward the tarmac within the walls of the compound. His Splinter combat suit was streaked with the drying yellow blood of the monster that he just filleted with his enchanted blade. He thought it odd that such a savage creature would have such delicate meat, or at least that it didn't stink to high heaven. Seeing as he was literally coated in it, he felt grateful for that little bit of luck.

As they neared the compound, he saw a crowd had assembled at the gates, and they erupted in cheers as the helio swooped overhead. Kyle glanced back over his shoulder at Mac, who was leaning toward the opening. The lieutenant pumped his fist at the gathering, which drew a raised eyebrow from his commander.

"Might as well enjoy it," Mac said with a shrug.

Kyle couldn't help but chuckle. He looked back at the crowd and held his rifle over his head. There was a roar from the people below that echoed until the helio dropped below the walls of the complex. Jay and Dan had gathered several duffels worth of components from the damaged hydrogenerator in hopes that they could be used elsewhere. Dan nearly took off Mac's head as he threw a pair of them over his shoulder. Mac chortled and fell back into his seat, but at this point the mood was too good to be broken.

Jackson was waiting for them as they stepped off the transport. He covered his eyes as the wind of the propellers flushed across the ground.

"Took you long enough," Jackson shouted over the drone of the engines.

"I wasn't expecting to have to play butcher today," Kyle said. "Any word on the wounded?"

"Mostly just bumps and bruises," Jackson replied. "The guy with the leg fracture is getting some transfusions. They actually had his blood type. Looks like we got off pretty lucky."

"What's the deal with the party going on outside?" Kyle asked.

"I guess word got out about what happened," Jackson answered. "They've been out there chanting your name for the last two hours."

"I suppose we should be flattered."

There was another loud fluttering as a second transport came over the walls carrying the beast's carcass. Kyle could hear the masses outside cheering as it descended, struggling under the heavy load of its cargo. He stopped and motioned toward the waiting ship.

"Go keep an eye on that transport," Kyle said to Jackson. "I don't want to hear about any issues later."

Jackson nodded and ran off. The tarmac was swarming with troops rushing to see the fallen creature. Several refrigeration units pulled out of the open hangar in front of them as the ship's motors disengaged.

"You think there's gonna be a riot or something, Kyle?" Mac asked.

"Feels like a riot already, Mac," Kyle said. "I've never seen anything like this."

Another crowd of men rushed out of the hangar and surrounded Kyle and the others. If it weren't for the shouts of celebration, Kyle would have sworn they were being attacked. The Splinter soldiers patted his shoulders and jumped around like kids on a holiday.

"You are the fucking man!"

"Thank God you were here!"

"Un-frickin'-believable!"

The exclamations of praise just kept raining down. They had to stop just a few paces into the hangar because the crowd had gotten so large. The applause rattled off the high hangar walls and beat down around them. Behind him, Kyle heard Mac hollering along with the cheers.

"Woo! That's right, you ain't seen nothing yet!"

Kyle looked back at his friend again, and Mac just shrugged. He was clearly enjoying this, though Kyle was embarrassed by the attention. He'd spent his entire adult life trying to avoid the spotlight. He rarely remembered anyone being present after they returned from a mission, let alone coming back to a full-blown mob. The whole thing felt surreal.

Finally the cheering died out and people began to return to their work. Bryan wended through the thinning crowd with a wry grin beneath his speckled beard. Kyle snorted, trying to hide a smile of his own. He looked back at the rest of his crew and saw smirks all around. It was a decidedly different feeling than one day ago.

"Well, Commander," Bryan said, "you certainly know how to make your presence felt."

"Wouldn't have been my first choice of excuses," Kyle replied.

"Mine either," Bryan chuckled. "But this time you really outdid yourself. Not only did you save twenty lives, but you also managed to bring home enough food to feed the entire colony for a week. Unbelievable."

"You shoulda seen him tear that thing down, Bryan," Mac said, still caught up in the enthusiasm. "Even we've never seen him do anything like that."

"Too old for that now, Lieutenant," Bryan said. "But I'm damn glad we've got somebody that can handle it." He lifted his chin, playing to the crowd. "Love seeing somebody that can kick some ass, eh boys?"

The crowd roared again. Kyle felt a dozen hands slap his back. Dan threw an arm around his neck and shook his shoulders with the other hand. Kyle briefly raised one hand and nodded in appreciation, but his head wasn't in the celebration. He stepped forward and put a hand on Bryan's shoulder, leaning in to whisper among the shouts.

"I need a word," he said.

Bryan nodded. He gestured toward the rear of the hangar where a door led back in to the compound. Kyle spun back and waved at the crowd so as not to appear ungrateful, then followed Bryan away from the raucous soldiers. Mac, Jay, and Dan shook a few hands, then trotted after their commander.

Brady was waiting by the door. He had shed his combat suit in favor of a set of fatigues, and his expression was ever the same. He pulled the door open for them, and Bryan walked inside. Kyle stopped for a moment to speak with his men.

"I need you guys to gather up our gear," he said. "All of our equipment stays with us. Then get some rest. We've gotta start working on the *Gemini* in the morning."

Kyle handed Mac his rifle and stepped through the door. Brady and Bryan were waiting in the empty hallway, standing in the flickering fluorescent light. Kyle took a moment to pull off his sword's scabbard and leaned the weapon against the wall, then unbuttoned the stained combat suit and took off the shirt. The Infernal's blood had soaked through in some places to mark the white shirt underneath, though the shirt itself already looked like it was stretched to its limits by his chest and arms. He dropped it next to the sword and turned back to Bryan and Brady.

"Bryan, what's going on here?" he asked finally. "Why is there a damn party going on outside the gates?"

"Apparently there was a leak about the encounter with the Infernal," Bryan said.

"Is that how things work around here? Details of military operations are leaked to the civilian sector?"

"Kyle, they just wanted to show their appreciation."

"I don't have a problem with them," Kyle said. "I like the fact that they're willing to support their cause. My concern is security."

"I can guarantee that nothing sensitive will ever leak," Bryan said.

"You're that certain?"

"Yes, I am," Bryan confirmed.

"How can you be so sure?" Kyle demanded.

"Because I'm the one that leaked it."

Kyle ran a hand down his face. "Please tell me you had a good reason for that."

"I think I do," Bryan said. "I need these people to love you. I need them to trust that you can pull them out of this canyon and give them their lives back. They have to believe, like I do, that we can genuinely change the war with you here. If they know that you're willing to go toe-to-toe with one of those monsters for them, they'll be willing to follow you to edge of the galaxy."

"Holy shit, you're really pulling all the strings here, aren't you? Did you arrange to have that Infernal dropped on the outpost too?"

"Fuck, Kyle, try and give me a little credit," Bryan scoffed. "I saw the Infernal as an opportunity, so I took it. The men here, the people in the colony, they needed that."

"And what about the dozen people who died today?" Kyle asked. "Do they just get forgotten in all this?"

Bryan's face went blank. The question seemed to hit him in a sensitive place.

"Kyle, I want you to know something," Bryan said, his tone growing more stern. "We *never* forget our dead here. Never. We know these people. We've spent most of our lives with them. And we don't forget about them just because it's convenient."

Kyle had no response this time. He just waited for Bryan to finish.

"But in the end, regardless of what happened out there today, we need these people to trust you," he continued. "And now they do."

"All right, I get it," Kyle said. "I'm going to get some rest."

Bryan smiled. "I suppose you've earned it."

"Do me a favor and make sure the *Gemini* is in the mechanical bay tomorrow morning," Kyle said as he lifted up his sword and placed the strap over his shoulder. "We need to start on it bright and early."

Bryan nodded and Kyle turned down the hall. He heard the door close behind him, but then oddly noticed a few footsteps still in the corridor.

"Commander," Brady called after him. "Griffin, wait one minute."

Kyle stopped with a sigh, not bothering to turn around. Brady jogged up alongside him. He was taller than Kyle had remembered from the battlefields, maybe just a couple of inches shorter than he was. There was some stubble covering the scar on his neck, but it was still very noticeable. Kyle remembered that day well, and even had a gunshot scar on the back of his shoulder that the major had given him to prove it. Seemed like a lifetime ago now.

"I need to speak with you," he said.

"Do we have to do this now, Major? Let me get some sleep and then we'll fight some more, I promise."

"Will you just shut up for a moment and let me say something? This isn't easy for me."

"All right," Kyle said. "If you have to, go ahead."

"I just wanted to ... to *thank* you for what you did for my men today," Brady said, struggling through the words. "I swear I won't doubt you again."

Kyle caught his mouth hanging open. "You're welcome, Major," he said finally.

There was an uncomfortable silence. Kyle knew that neither one of them had much experience with burying the hatchet, unless it was into someone else's skull.

"Listen, I really have no idea where I'm going," Kyle said, breaking the hush. "Think you can point me in the direction of my room?"

"Yeah, you're gonna want to go down to the end of the hall," Brady said. "The refugee quarters are on the third floor, east wing."

Kyle nodded. He walked away confused, but oddly satisfied. Maybe this whole thing had a chance of working after all.

† † †

Several hours later it was stretching into the late evening on the moon. These hours had been playing havoc with Kyle since they arrived, especially since the natural light disappeared nearly six hours before the "day" was over. He had spent the entire first night here looking in on his father, and the events at the outpost had sapped him dry. Despite the rumors and conjecture, it was a great effort for him to summon his Celestial powers, and the fatigue made it all the more difficult. He needed this rest more than he'd let on.

The room he was given was small. There was only a rickety metal bed frame with an uneven mattress in one corner, and a leaky faucet with a small circular mirror in another. A stream of light from the artificial daylights leaked in through the one window despite the drawn shade, highlighting the chipped green paint on the walls. For the first couple of hours he just lay on the creaky bed, his feet hanging off the edge, and stared at the water-stained ceiling. There was a musky odor that kept him awake for a while, like the inside of a broken refrigerator. Once he did finally drift off it was a restless and fitful sleep, and he got maybe an hour's worth of true rest over that time. When the knocks on the door came, he wasn't certain if they were real or another tumultuous dream.

He sat up in bed abruptly. The thin sheets were wet from perspiration. He rubbed his eyes and looked at the clock, but the time here was just jargon to him. The daylights were still on, so he decided it was sometime in the late evening. He stumbled out of bed, the tile floor cold against his bare feet. He had stripped down to a pair of baggy pants and had discarded his shirt. In his haste he lumbered over to the door without putting it back on.

He pulled open the door, expecting to see one of his friends, or perhaps Bryan or Brady. So he was surprised when it was Ellie. He squinted against the harsh light from the hall as Ellie's eyes wandered down to his carved torso. She quickly looked away, then smiled awkwardly, her cheeks flushing red.

"Dr. Decker," Kyle said, shaking off his surprise. "Ellie, I wasn't expecting … what can I do for you?"

"I am so sorry, Commander," she said. "I didn't realize you'd be sleeping …"

"No, it's all right. Please, call me Kyle."

"Kyle…I…I really didn't mean to wake you. I could come back."

"Please, it's okay, it's okay," Kyle said. "Is there some news about my dad?"

"Oh, no, nothing new," Ellie said. "That's not why I came."

Kyle raised his eyebrows, waiting for her to continue. He tried to conjure a smile without seeming forced. She smiled back and brushed her blonde hair back from her face.

"I just wanted to let you know that the soldier you healed today, the man with the broken leg—we were able to discharge him after a couple of transfusions. He's going to be okay."

"That's good," Kyle said. "You came all the way up here just to tell me that?"

"Well, actually, I wanted to ask you … I mean, I'm so interested in how you're able to heal people. I was hoping you'd be willing to tell me about it sometime, maybe over a drink?"

Standing there without a shirt, Kyle suddenly felt very self-conscious. It felt an awful lot like she was asking him out. His discomfort deepened when he heard footsteps down the hall and saw that they were Angel's. She was looking at them with an unreadable yet intent expression.

"Uh, I'm sorry, Ellie," he said. "I'll come by the hospital some time and we can talk then. Okay?"

"Um … sure. Okay," Ellie said somberly. "Thanks." She ducked her head and walked down the hall past Angel. Kyle felt a pit in his stomach as she left. He didn't mean to seem so blunt, but he didn't want Angel to get the impression that something was happening there. He'd hoped to do that without hurting Ellie's feelings, but he'd clearly done a terrible job.

Angel walked closer, leering over her shoulder at the young doctor as she scurried away. "I wasn't interrupting something, was I?"

"No, no," Kyle said. "Ellie is my father's doctor."

"Ellie?"

"Yeah, Dr. Decker," Kyle said, clearing his throat. "She was just giving me an update on another patient."

"That's not what it sounded like," Angel said.

Kyle felt awkward. Worse yet, he knew that Angel could sense it. Why in the hell was he suddenly fumbling around like a clod?

"Did you want to come inside?" he asked.

Angel nodded. "Sure." She stepped into the dreary room and Kyle quickly pulled on a shirt. She was wearing borrowed clothes, a tight white turtleneck sweater and gray pants that hugged her tempting curves. Her hair was down and wavy, a relaxed look he rarely saw on her. Even in the grime of the room, she looked stunning. Kyle had to break his own stare to go over and pull open the shades to the lone window, letting in the full glare of the artificial daylights. Angel stood in front of the disheveled bed, the sheets still damp from his sweaty, anxious sleep. Kyle knew it looked awfully incriminating.

"Listen, Angel, I'm sorry that I haven't been by to see you yet," he said, trying to break one sore subject with another. "Things have just been really hard with being here, and with my dad still not out of the woods..."

"No, I get it," Angel said. "How is your dad?"

"Ellie says he's doing marginally better," Kyle said, "but he's still in a coma."

"Will he be okay?"

"She thinks so," Kyle said. "But she can't be certain."

Angel paused for a moment. "I'm so sorry about your mother. She was such an amazing woman."

"Yeah," Kyle said, looking out the window. "She just..." He cleared his throat, forcing the images from his bedroom out of his mind. "She just wasn't who I thought she was."

"Dan told me about ... all of that," Angel said. "But I'm sure that doesn't make it any easier. She was still your mother."

Kyle swallowed hard. The sting was still a little too close, the images still too clear in his memory. As though that would ever change. "Yeah, um, do you think we can talk about something else?"

"Well, what do you want to talk about?" she asked.

"I don't know, anything else," he said, shaking his head.

"I'm not sure what to say," she started. "I feel like we haven't actually spoken in a long time."

"I guess a lot has changed," Kyle said.

Angel nodded. "Well, what's this I hear about you killing an Infernal with your bare hands?"

"You heard about that too?"

"Of course I heard about it, the people here won't stop talking about it," Angel said. "You could have gotten yourself killed, you know."

"I know," Kyle replied. "But if I didn't do anything, a whole lot of people *would* have been killed. I didn't think I had a choice."

Angel's eyes were welling up. She wiped a few drops away with her right thumb.

"Kyle, you can't let anything happen to yourself," she stuttered. "What would we do here if you were gone?"

"Angel, nothing is going to happen to me," he insisted.

Angel chortled, another tear running down her cheek. "That's easy for you to *say*. The people here think you're invincible. But you can bleed just like anyone else."

"Where is this coming from all of a sudden?" Kyle asked. "You've never been this worried about what I do before."

"Yes, I have," Angel said. Tears were welling up in her eyes. "I just never see you anymore. I never see *anyone* anymore. It's all just so right in front of me."

"Angel, I don't know what you want me to say," Kyle said. "I'm sorry I haven't been there as much. I wish that I could make more time, but I can't."

"Well, you certainly seem to have plenty of time to make new girlfriends," Angel grumbled, wiping her eyes with the heel of her hand.

"What is that supposed to mean?"

"Did you sleep with that girl?"

The curtness of the question caught Kyle off guard. "Did I *what*?"

"Just answer the question."

"Angel, please don't do this."

"You can't even answer me, can you?" Angel asked. "God, that's so typical."

"What's the matter with you?" Kyle asked, suddenly frustrated. "Why are you being like this?"

Angel choked down a hard breath and shook her head. She bit her upper lip, the soft skin of her forehead creased in angst.

"I just can't do this," she moaned. "I get so lonely all the time, and now you're here and I still never see you."

"Angel, I—"

"Don't, don't. Just don't." She wiped her eyes again. "I'm sorry, I shouldn't have come here. I just wanted to see you. I won't bother you anymore."

She hurried out of the room, her arms crossed tight in front of her. Kyle was staggered like his feet were encased in concrete, a task that innumerable enemies had wished they could accomplish. By the time he made it into the hall, she was already several doors down. He called after her, but she didn't even turn to look at him. He threw up his hands in disbelief, unsure of how things had gone so sour. All he could do was watch her walk away.

† † †

Angel was in such a hurry to get away from Kyle's room that she had gotten herself lost. Her quarters were on the fourth level of the compound, but she felt like she had made a wrong turn somewhere. Or the elevator had taken her down instead of up. Something, she wasn't sure. She was so distracted replaying the fight with Kyle in her head that she couldn't even remember which way she had come from.

By the time she stumbled onto the mess hall twenty minutes later she was kicking herself for the whole encounter. Was she being unreasonable? Why couldn't he just answer the question? If he would have just admitted to sleeping with that doctor, she wouldn't have gotten so upset. Right? It's not like they'd ever had a relationship or anything.

She stopped and leaned back against the wall outside the cafeteria. There were still a couple dozen people inside having a late dinner, and for once she didn't want to be around anyone. The thought occurred to her that Kyle hadn't admitted anything because he hadn't done anything, and she blew up at him anyway. No wonder he never came to see her.

A handful of soldiers walked out of the mess hall. Angel tried to compose herself, embarrassed by how she must've looked. One of the men paused and looked in her direction. She remembered him from the tarmac when she and Kyle had first arrived. He was the tall officer who was with Kyle's uncle. Brady, she thought.

He waved the rest of his group on and walked in her direction. She tried to straighten her rumpled hair as he came closer. He had a rugged allure to him, more gruff and raw than Kyle, but still handsome. His eyes were bright despite his obvious fatigue. They drew her in, and reluctantly she let it happen.

"Are you all right, ma'am?" he asked. There was a deep husk in his voice, but the tone was genuine.

"Yes, I'm sorry," she said. "I must look like a total mess."

"I wouldn't say that. You look upset."

"No, I'm fine, really. It's just been a tough week."

"You're Commander Griffin's friend, is that right?"

"I'm Angel," she said, trying to beam a smile. "Angel Preston."

"Adam Brady," he responded, shaking her hand. "That's quite a smile you have. I definitely prefer it to the scowl you had a minute ago."

"That's nice of you to say. Thank you."

"So, can I help you find something?" Brady asked. "You seem a little lost."

"Is it that obvious?"

"Most people usually go into the mess hall—they don't hang out outside."

Angel sighed. "Honestly, I don't even remember how I got here. I was trying to get to my room."

"What level are you on?"

"Four, I think."

Brady smirked. "Wow, you are lost. You're on the second floor now. Do you know where the elevators are?"

"I know there *are* some," Angel said with a shrug.

"Well, let me show you a shortcut. "There's one just around the corner."

Angel followed him down the hallway. She found herself walking slowly at his side, and very close. The brush of his arm against hers seemed very comfortable, almost scintillating. She looked up at him curiously.

"How long have you been here?" she asked.

"Oh, I was born here," he said. "My family was one of the first involved in the split from the Dominion."

"Really?"

"Yeah, my ancestors were on the Galactic Council. Do you know anything about it?"

"I just learned about it a few days ago," Angel said. "Our education back home was a little different."

"I can imagine," Brady said. They came around a corner and he summoned the elevator with a button near the door. "I suppose you left a good home behind when you came here."

"I guess so," Angel muttered. "It still seems kinda surreal. It hasn't sunk in that I'll never get to go back."

"Well, I'm very sorry that you had to give up so much," Brady said. "I know it can't be easy."

"It can't be any harder than living here," Angel said. "Always hiding, never knowing what the next day will be like, where your food is gonna come from."

The elevator dinged and the door slid open. This was a very old mechanism, complete with steel cables and pulleys instead of the compressor systems that were common in the Dominion civilization. Angel had never seen anything like it.

Brady smiled as the doors closed. "We do better than you think."

"Oh yeah? So what do you do around these parts for fun?"

"'*Fun*?" he repeated, pretending to be confused. "Is that some sort of Dominion slang?"

"Oh, stop it," Angel said, giving him a light nudge. "You know what fun is."

"I suppose I do, but honestly I don't have much in the way of free time."

The elevator creaked to a stop and the doors opened. Brady let her off first and then pointed her down the hall to the dormitory rooms. She waited for him to accompany her, and he obliged.

"There's gotta be something you do for yourself," Angel pressed.

"No, not for a long time now," he replied somberly.

"Then what did you used to do?" Angel asked. "Maybe you could try it again someday."

"Well, when I was younger I used to draw quite a bit. I was pretty good at it, I suppose. But I haven't done that for years."

"Get out of here!" Angel exclaimed, giving him another playful shove. "That's one of my favorite things to do."

"You're kidding?"

"No, I'm not," she gushed. "It's how I spend all of my spare time."

"Well, how about that?" Brady said. "Who would've thought that we'd have something in common?"

"So can I ask you something?" Angel asked as they turned another corner.

"Sure."

"Do you hate everyone in the Dominion?"

Brady raised his eyebrows. "Do I hate them? No, I don't hate the people. I feel sorry for them."

"Sorry?"

"Yeah, I just… I can't imagine living my life without knowing what I know. I believe in this cause. And I get the chance to fight for it. Most people in the Dominion will never get the chance to believe in something like this. I don't think I could live like that."

Angel stopped and looked at him. She had always thought of the Splinter as savages, but this man seemed deep and genuinely emotional. He was not at all what she had expected.

"So, um, which room is yours?" Brady asked, breaking the silence.

"Oh!" she gasped, looking around the hall. "Actually, I think it was a couple doors back that way."

Brady smiled and stepped aside, and they walked to her door. Angel didn't open it right away. She wasn't ready to say goodnight just yet.

"Well, thanks for your help," she said. "I probably would have wandered around this place all night without you."

"It was my pleasure," he replied. "Maybe we could talk again some time."

"Yeah, I would like that," Angel said, flashing her smile again.

"So tell me," Brady started, inching a bit closer. "The commander … are you two … involved?"

"Kyle? No, no, definitely not," she said, the words just flooding out. "We've just known each other a really long time."

"I see. Well, I hope we can do this again. Maybe I could show you around the colony some time."

"Definitely." Angel said, a little bounce in her legs.

"Good night," Brady said and started to walk away.

Angel took a deep breath as though she was going to call him back, but after a moment she let the breath go quietly. Instead she just returned the courtesy.

"Good night."

The major turned back and waved. She gave him a sultry look, one that would ravish any man caught in its glare. It happened without a thought, but she didn't regret it. A moment later she opened the door and went inside.

Chapter 15

Jonathan Ashford had always felt like he lived on an island. And not some sunny, breezy paradise with aquamarine seas. No, his had always been a lonely, desolate, shipwrecked kind of exile, the type that drives the wrong kind of man into madness. Such was the life of a Splinter spy.

The last several days, however, had been especially uncomfortable. He had received an urgent communiqué from Bryan Foster requesting copies of a highly classified set of files from within the secure servers. And these were not just "eyes only" files—these were DNA coded, above-top-secret records that maybe a hundred people in the galaxy would have clearance for.

Sure thing, Marshal, I'll get right on that.

Up until about a month ago he would not have even had access to such files, but he had just been promoted to a senior intel analyst, a commission that gave him full reign of the Archives vault. And he was not fooling himself; there was little chance that the timing of Foster's request was a coincidence. After nearly thirty-three years as an undercover agent within the Dominion Information Technologies Division, this was something that the Splinter had been thirsting after for a very long time.

As promised, he had delivered the intel, but ever since then he had been on edge. After all, his typical week was fairly mundane. The Archives Depository was in a sector adjacent to the Dynasteria system, but very rarely did anything occur there. He was only allowed two days per month away from the facility, and even then he rarely strayed more than a few hours from the complex. Most days he went to work and did his job like any other analyst, and only occasionally would he hand-deliver a report on Dominion intelligence missions to an unnamed Splinter contact. By all accounts he felt very safe, very secure, even as a lamb amongst the wolves. But not anymore.

His shift started in about ten minutes, and he was being bludgeoned with a wrenching hangover, so he walked very purposely down the corridors, trying not to reveal any changes to his routine. The walls were framed with an electrostatic mesh to prevent the transmission of any signals in or out of the complex. He tried to tell himself that this wasn't the first time that he'd been asked to retrieve information for the Splinter, not by a long shot, but something about this operation felt different. He had tried to drink away his anxiety the night before, but all that had brought him was a searing headache and uneasy stomach. He wondered for a moment how the other infiltration agents would react to his anxiousness.

He stopped outside the door to the technician's booth and glanced briefly at the security camera perched in the corner to his left. He saw a distorted reflection of himself in the wall panels beneath the camera and grumbled at his thickening waistline. When he was first recruited into the Splinter's Infiltration Unit as a twenty-three-year-old staff sergeant, he had been quite fit. But the thirty-plus years of working a desk could be counted in the flab around his waist like the rings of a widening tree. His chin had doubled, and his creased eyes and silver hair seemed to mock the man that he used to be. He sighed and rolled up the sleeve on his navy-blue uniform, then threaded his right forearm into an open scanner sleeve beside the door. He waited for the prismatic sensor to slide over the skin above his wrist in search of his implanted identification tag. An automated ding signaled that the tag was accepted, and a retinal scanner slid open above the sleeve. After a quick wash over his eyes the door clattered open.

He was a bit surprised that the retinal scanner could read his eyes given how dry and sandpapered they felt, but it had worked and he could go on with his day. Inside the cluttered booth he could see down into the massive server vault below. There were thousands of spiraling rows of storage orbs, each capable of holding hundreds of zettabytes of data. The automated machinations were zipping around in a frenzy, even more so than usual. In fact the vault looked like a tornado of sleek organic metal.

The technician from the previous shift was still collecting his things as Ashford walked inside. He was also an older man, as most senior analysts were, but thin and frail. He was oblivious to his coworker's entry until Ashford hacked a wet cough that sounded a bit like a broken lawnmower.

"Hey, Ash, how's it going?" the thin man asked.

"Losing a lung here, Dyson," Ashford wheezed, thumping on his soft chest. "I've gotta give up smoking."

"I thought you quit already?"

"Didn't take," Ashford said, logging into the server near the door. "How's the grandkids?"

"They're good," Dyson said, beaming. "I've got my two days off after this, and my son is bringing them to spend the day with me tomorrow. Been looking forward to this for a while."

"Anything pending I need to know about?"

"A few background checks. But we're still getting a ton of requests about the whole Griffin thing."

"*Griffin thing*?" Ashford asked, puzzled.

"Yeah, that whole disaster going on with Commander Griffin. You haven't heard about that?"

Ashford felt the color drain from his face. What was it the Marshal had said about Commander Griffin? He remembered his name being mentioned in the briefing about the files he was to obtain, but his head was pounding and he couldn't recall. Was this somehow related?

"I've been off for the last thirty-six hours," Ashford said. "I haven't heard anything."

"How could you not have heard?" Dyson exclaimed. "It's been all over the wire for hours! Have you been sleeping in a cave for the last day and a half?"

"No, in a whiskey bottle," Ashford moaned. "Tell me what happened. And stop yelling, please."

"Apparently, he had a total meltdown, blew up an entire squadron on Vadara. Word is he's defected. Gone over to the savages. Crazy shit, eh?"

"Wait, you mean he's actually been turned?"

"That's what the intel is saying. Him and his whole unit. Oh, and his uncle. Some colonel over in the Emporia system. Farmer, Forrester, some shit like that."

"Foster," Ashford said. "Bryan Foster."

"Yeah, that's it." Dyson frowned. "How'd you know that?"

"So what are they going to do?" Ashford asked, ignoring the question. "They're going after them, yes?"

"They already have. They set a trap for him at his parents' home, killed his mother and everything. But apparently, he blew through that too. The guy is a fucking monster. I don't know how they're going to stop him."

"Whoa, whoa, he's still on the loose?" Ashford gasped.

"Yeah, what did you think I was telling you?"

Ashford thought he might vomit, but it wasn't the hangover. What the hell had Foster gotten him involved in? The Gentry would never stop until he got to the roots of this, and that would lead them to his doorstep. He let out a cough that turned into a fit of gagging that doubled him over.

"Shit, man, you all right?" Dyson asked.

"Ugh, I'm just hung over," Ashford grumbled, wiping the drool from his lip. "Forget about it."

"You sure you can handle an eighteen-hour shift? There's a lot of shit going on in here."

"I'll be fine, so long as you give me some space to work. I'll talk to you later."

"All right, all right," Dyson said. "Just trying to help."

Dyson signed out and then used the scanner sleeve on the inside of the door. The door slid open, but he stopped suddenly as there was a man standing in the threshold. Dyson was startled and stepped back, and the much thicker man stepped in with him. His heavy brow was wrinkled into a snarl, and he had a gun in his hand.

"Hey, man, you can't come in here—"

The man slammed his gun into Dyson's jaw, and the thin man crumpled to the floor. Ashford took half a step forward, but another handful of men swarmed in with guns raised.

"What is this?" Ashford demanded. "What do you want?"

Something hard crunched off the back of Ashford's head, and his vision went white for a moment. He slouched into the grasp of the intruders, the blow ringing in his ears. He felt something trickling down the back of his neck—blood from a throbbing gash in his scalp.

"Do you know who I am?" the first man asked.

"No," Ashford muttered.

"Hmpf, I'm disappointed that my reputation didn't precede me here. It makes things like this so much easier."

"I don't understand."

"Oh, you will," the man said, his tone lowering. "You will understand very soon."

"Who are you?" Ashford asked.

"Right, where are my manners? My name is Vaughn Donovan."

Ashford's head was swimming, but the name struck a chord. "Tact General Donovan?"

"Ah, you do know who I am after all," Vaughn said. "That's good. Because we certainly know who you are, Jonathan Ashford. We've come here just to talk with you."

"We haven't done anything!" Ashford exclaimed. "You can't just muscle in here—"

Vaughn raised his hand, and Ashford immediately went quiet.

"Watch your mouth, Colonel," Vaughn hissed. "We know that you've been feeding classified information to the Splinter. We know that you're in league with Bryan Foster. You are a *spy*. What is it you think we do to spies?"

"General, I swear I don't know what you're—"

Vaughn lashed out and struck Ashford just beneath the left eye, splitting the skin. Vaughn grabbed Ashford's chin and lifted his face with fingernails that dug into his fat cheeks like the bite of a raptor.

"I told you to watch your mouth," Vaughn said. "There is no mistake here. We have your registry as the sole analyst on duty when very sensitive files were stolen from this facility. Your communications history shows multiple contacts with Emporia. You own encoding software that is known to be used by Splinter cyber-thieves."

Vaughn pulled Ashford's face closer. Ashford tried to look away, but one of the other soldiers clutched his hair and forced his eyes forward. His heartbeat was rapidly accelerating.

"But even more than that, I can smell the traitor on you," Vaughn seethed. "You reek like the coward you are. Normally I would take great pleasure in purging that rotten stink from your hide, but I am in a hurry. So I am going to give you a choice: tell me where Colonel Foster has taken Griffin and his men, and your life will be ended quickly. Tell me one more lie, and I swear that the pain you will suffer will be enough for a thousand lifetimes."

Ashford swallowed hard. He had heard rumors of General Donovan's savagery in the past, and to be in his clutches was even more terrifying than it seemed. Every nightmare he ever had came rushing back to him, every intimate fear suddenly laid out at his feet. Thirty-three years of his life lived as a lie. He felt oddly proud of it.

"Even if I knew where they were, I would never tell you," he whispered.

"You're lying," Vaughn said.

"Why would they take the risk of telling me? We're not as stupid as you think."

"Your contacts. Where do you make your intel drops?"

"It's always a different location," Ashford said. "Always an anonymous contact. I can't help you find them. You might as well just kill me now."

Vaughn paused momentarily, then pulled his sidearm from its holster. He fondled the trigger deviously as he pondered his captive's last moments. Ashford's heart was racing painfully in his chest.

"Very well," Vaughn said. "If you won't talk for your own life, then perhaps you will for another's."

Vaughn grabbed Dyson by a handful of his graying hair, and he squealed like a wounded rat. His face was spattered with blood, and he had lost a pair of teeth already. He looked so frail and vulnerable that Ashford's pounding heart immediately climbed into his throat as he tried to shout.

"What are you doing?" Ashford asked.

"Providing some motivation," Vaughn said, pressing the muzzle of the gun against Dyson's temple.

"No, don't," Ashford pleaded. "I swear I don't know anything."

"I don't believe you," Vaughn snarled.

"Please, don't do this," Ashford begged. "I can't tell you anything!"

"You're lying!" Vaughn shouted, digging the gun into Dyson's skin. "Say goodbye!"

"No! No, no, stop please!" Ashford implored, his voice cracking in desperation. "I can't tell what I don't know. Do whatever you want to me. Just let him go, I'm begging you."

Vaughn's snarl never faltered as he squeezed the trigger. The opposite side of Dyson's head erupted, and a shower of blood and brains sprayed across the room. He never even had a chance to scream.

Ashford was terrified and enraged all at the same time, though his mesmerized disbelief outweighed them both. He stood without blinking or breathing, staring at Vaughn as if he was begging for him to take it back. Vaughn glared back as if to insist he would not recant even if he could.

"Don't ever forget who you're dealing with," Vaughn said. "We don't make deals with traitors. You *will* tell us everything you know, or I'll be forced to find more people like this to make examples of. Do we understand each other?"

Ashford nodded.

"Excellent," Vaughn said. "Captain Jones, have your men take Jonathan down to our transport. I want lists of every file he has ever handled. We'll see if we can find something that will jog our new friend's memory."

Vaughn handed his gun to the captain as he walked out, wiping his hands as though he had just completed some tedious chore. Jones gave a wry smile as he looked back at Ashford, whose eyes were flooded with tears.

"You heard the general," Jones said. "Just make sure that he makes it to the ship alive."

The remaining soldiers swarmed over Ashford, but this time he didn't resist. He didn't hear their taunts or feel their blows, but only saw the image of his friend tumbling lifelessly to the ground. Despite all his careful planning and stealth, from this point on his life belonged to them.

Chapter 16

Morning was quickly approaching the Splinter complex on the Aranow moon, though the bottom of the canyon was still black as night. The bitter cold had started to lift off the plains above the chasm, leaving a sparkling dew along the ground and a chilled mist just above the canyon walls. It was actually quite peaceful, with a void of black below and a sea of stars overhead.

Kyle was sitting on a narrow ledge just a few hundred feet below the crest of the canyon, staring out into the fading night. The red glow of Aranow's aura was breaking the horizon in front of him, though he had no interest in its celestial beauty at the moment. He had climbed up to this perch nearly eight hours ago after his spat with Angel, hoping that the crisp air and solitude would clear his head. In truth it had just given him more time within his thoughts, which was exactly where he did not want to be. But he knew that if he returned to the compound he would most likely fail to sleep, and even if he did, he feared his dreams. At least if he was awake he had a chance to control what ran through his mind.

And yet his thoughts were dark all night long. They bounced between memories of his mother, concern for his father, and fears for his future and his friends. But as the night wore on, he found himself focused more and more on the argument with Angel. He couldn't recall another time when the two of them were at odds, and how that rift had started he struggled to understand. Had he really been so absent? So oblivious that he had driven her away? He scoured his eidetic memory, looking for ways he could have made more time, but couldn't find anything else he could have done. It offended him to think that she asked for so much when he was stretched so thin to begin with, but then he remembered that he was supposed to be her friend. How long had it been since he had been there for her? He could count the days if he wanted, but the numbers just seemed so large.

And so it went for hours on end. One moment he felt unappreciated and the next he wanted to run and apologize. He had started gnawing on his fingernails, something he had never caught himself doing before.

The artificial daylights winked on beneath him, flooding the canyon floor with their glow. From his perch the lights seemed dim, even to his godlike eyes. No wonder the Dominion had never been able to find them here. Their fortress was nothing more than a speck on an insignificant moon floating through an abandoned sector of space. Kyle wondered for moment if the other Splinter cells were wallowing in similar situations.

The swirling winds whipped across the ledge, cutting through the poorly stitched fabric of the military jacket he was wearing. Its brown and gray camouflage blended smoothly with the surrounding rock, but it offered little protection against the moon's bitter gusts. It had been a long time since he had actually felt cold, so it was an unusual sensation to say the least. He realized that the feeling had finally distracted him, and he didn't want to get sucked back into the pits of his emotions. He stood up and looked over the ledge down to the awakening colony below. There was still much to be done, so he chose to lose himself in his work again. He took one last breath of the chilled air, then stepped off the edge.

Moments later he pushed open the door to the engineering bay and walked into the towering warehouse. It was still odd to have to open doors by hand, but then most maintenance docks in the Dominion were staffed with computerized machinations or nanotech repair systems. Here the work on their outdated fleet was done by human hands, and done so without the resources of a hundred thousand star systems. It was a wonder that any of their ships worked at all.

The *Gemini* was up on a lift near the gate, the damage from the exodus to the Aranow system on full display under the lights of the garage. Mac and Jay were already hard at work, with an audience of a dozen or more men watching as they toiled. Jay had removed the damaged cloaking panels, and Mac was swearing into an open access panel on the left thrusters.

"This thing is totally *fucked*," Mac hollered, banging a wrench against the side of the engine. "It's like a sieve in here with all these holes."

"It's not much better down here," Jay said. "This panel is shredded. I can't fix this."

Sensing the awed silence in response to Kyle's presence, Mac spun around but the grimace on his face didn't change. His sleeves were rolled up and he was sweating already, his reddish hair slicked back from his freckled face. He dropped down from the boom that had lifted him up to the engine casing with Jay following behind. Jay had stripped down to a tank top, showing the full sleeves of tattoos that adorned his arms.

"This doesn't sound like the good news I was hoping for," Kyle said.

"This is the wrong place to be looking for good news," Mac said. "We are action-packed with issues."

"All right, just run it down for me," Kyle said. "What are we looking at?"

"I don't even know where to start," Mac replied.

"Dammit, Mac, you're the engineer. What's wrong with it?"

"The biggest issue is with the thrusters," Mac started. "A half-dozen of the solenoid disks are trashed. Without them we can't produce the magnetic field that generates the propulsion. I'm not even sure this thing will get off the ground again."

"But the electric current?" Kyle asked. "The fusion generator?"

"Oh, it's fine, it's in the ship's hull," Mac said. "It wasn't touched. But we've got no way to focus the thrust. It's dead in the water."

"Why can't we just replace the solenoids?"

"We could, if they had any here. But they don't. None of their ships have electromagnetic propulsion."

"What about the cloaks?" Kyle asked, turning to Jay.

"They're not in good shape either," Jay said. "Five different panels are damaged, but I think I can fix four of them. But the last one, the prism mesh is ripped to pieces. We'll have to replace it."

"And let me guess, they don't have that here either," Kyle said.

"Most of these guys haven't even heard of it," Jay said. "They've been working on combustion engines that still require fossil fuels. This tech is totally alien to them."

"So what are our options?"

"I'm not sure we have any. We can't manufacture these components here. We could try to convert it to a combustion engine, but we'd lose a ton of power and maneuverability."

"That's not an option," Kyle said. "It's not worth fixing if we have to do that."

"Then we've gotta find a place where we can get these from," Mac said.

"That's pretty risky business," Jay said. "These are military technologies. They're not gonna be easy to get."

"Wait a minute," Mac said. "What about The Guy?"

"What guy?" Kyle asked.

"*The* Guy," Mac repeated.

"Yeah, Mac, I hear you," Kyle said. "What guy are you talking about?"

"It's not 'a guy,' it's '*The Guy*,'" Mac clarified. "That's what he goes by—The Guy. He's a smuggler we ran into a few years ago."

"He goes by 'The Guy?'" Kyle asked. "You're kidding, right?"

"What can I say?" Mac said. "He's a hallucinogen addict, so what do you expect?"

"Well, this definitely sounds promising," Jay said.

"Mac, we can't trust this to a guy who's chasing pretty colors all day," Kyle said.

"No, I'm serious," Mac said. "He's a total whack-job but he can get his hands on these types of materials."

"You're certain?" Kyle asked.

"Positive," Mac replied.

"I don't know, Mac," Kyle said, shaking his head. "This sounds a little too sketchy."

"It's safer than raiding a military installation just for parts," Mac said.

"He's got a point there," Jay said.

Kyle sighed. "Does this guy have an actual name?"

"I don't know, probably," Mac said. "He's not somebody I spend a lot of time with."

"All right," Kyle groaned hesitantly. "If you say he can get what we need, go ahead and make the call."

Mac's eyes shifted over Kyle's shoulder, and Kyle followed his gaze to a young corporal waiting patiently behind him. The corporal was lean and gangly, with a long neck and sloped shoulders. He had a long pointed nose and a narrow cleft chin. He was trying to stand at sharp attention, but had a slight lean to his right. Kyle looked down and noticed the thin profile of a cybernetic prosthesis through his pants. The Dominion Medical Research Division had long since abandoned prosthetics in favor of regenerative treatments, but in this place, this young man was lucky to have been given anything at all.

"Excuse me, Commander Griffin, sir, but Star Marshal Foster wishes to speak with you," the corporal reported. "He is in his office, whenever you have a moment."

"Thank you, Corporal," Kyle said. "I'll be there in a moment."

The corporal saluted and limped away. Kyle recognized his face from somewhere, but couldn't quite place it. He thought maybe it was the uniform, or perhaps the leg, that threw him off, but after a moment he decided it wasn't important. He had likely seen many of these people's faces in battle before, and if he took the time to remember them all, he wouldn't have time for much else. He turned back to his men.

"All right, I'm gonna go handle this," Kyle said. "Figure out what we need to get these parts from 'The Guy' - can't believe I'm actually calling him that. Then see if you can get the Dominion transport I boosted running. It'd be good to have another ship with a hyperdrive available."

"We're on it," Mac said.

Kyle left them to do their work and made his way to Bryan's office on the upper level. The halls were starting to fill with people beginning their day, and there seemed to be some newfound enthusiasm among them. Several people stopped to shake his hand, and he tried his best to acknowledge them with a few words. As he went by the entrance to the hospital wing, he briefly caught himself wondering whether Ellie was inside. He still felt bad about how he had acted the night before, but that thought brought Angel to mind, so he shook his head and hastened his pace.

He pushed open the door to his uncle's office, and the flood of light from the artificial morning had already washed inside. Bryan was sitting on the edge of his desk, with Brady not far away, as usual. Jackson was sitting on one of the ratty old couches, and Kyle was surprise to see Dr. Preston beside him.

"Good morning, Commander," Bryan said. "Did you get enough rest last night?"

"I'm managing," Kyle said, stopping in front of the desk. "What's going on?"

"Well, the good doctor came to see me last night," Bryan said. "Seems he's also been inspired by your efforts against the Infernal. He's going to help us train our men for insurgency."

"Is that right?" Kyle asked, pivoting toward the doctor. "Just like that?"

"Just like that, Commander," Preston said. "If you're willing to risk so much, then I should be as well." The doctor stood up and took a few steps toward his protégé. "Does that surprise you?"

"I've just never known you to be someone to change his mind very easily, sir," Kyle said. "But I'm certain we'll welcome the assistance."

"If we're gonna attempt the types of incursions you're considering, we'll need all the help we can get," Bryan said. "The major has done an admiral job training his men, but we just don't have the manpower trained in these tactics."

"Speaking of, Commander," Brady said. "Have you given any thought to potential targets?"

"Nothing concrete yet," Kyle said. "There's still several things that need to be taken care of here before we can start planning an operation."

"Such as?" Brady asked.

"Our ship has to be repaired. We'll need its capabilities available to us. I've got Mac and Jay working on that now."

"Any assistance we can give you there?" Bryan asked.

"I don't think so," Kyle said. "We need parts that we can't get here. But Mac seems to think he can get them from an underground source that'll be less of a risk."

"He knows this for certain?" Bryan asked.

"I trust my men to make those decisions."

"Very well," Bryan said. "Getting back to the training protocol, how many men do you believe you'll need?"

"As many as you can muster," Kyle replied. "Ideally we'll be able to run multiple missions in different sectors and still be able to maintain a standing guard here. Average size incursion units would run about twelve to fifteen men. Full-scale assaults would require at least two hundred."

"That sounds like a tall order," Bryan said. "Doctor?"

"We've never trained a group of more than ten at a time," Preston responded. "We may be able to handle fifteen, but more than that is pushing it."

"Major, can you select a dozen or so men to start the training regimen?" Bryan asked.

"I've already got a list prepared," Brady said.

"Good," Bryan said. "Now what kind of timeframe are we looking at, Doctor?"

"It will have to be an extremely truncated timetable," Preston said. "The Infinity Protocol that Kyle and his men went through takes years to complete. We'll have to cut it down significantly."

"I need these men familiar with our tactics," Kyle said. "They don't have to be leading the charge, but they need to do better than just keeping up."

"Our men will handle it," Brady said. "They've been waiting a long time to go on the offensive. They'll eat this up."

"We'll get things working right away," the doctor said. "I'll be able to give you a better idea of the timeframe after I spend some time with the men."

"If you don't mind, sir, I would like to have Captain Hilton sit in with you," Kyle said. "I want his opinion of how ready these men are before we take them into a combat situation."

The doctor paused for just a moment and looked over his protégé. Kyle's return gaze was steely and uncompromising. This was not a request.

"Well, Commander, if that's what you want, I'm not in a position to argue," Preston said.

"All right then, it sounds like we have enough to get started," Bryan said. "Major, gather your men. I'd like to have them meet with the doctor and Captain Hilton before the end of the day."

"Yes, sir," Brady said, filing out the door.

Kyle looked over to Jackson and Dr. Preston on the couch in front of him. "I have to go check in with Mac and Jay about the *Gemini*. But after that I'll come meet with you two to discuss more specifics about what we need from these men."

"You didn't want to talk about it in front of the major?" Bryan asked.

"We're finally able to stand in the same room together," Kyle said. "The last thing we need is any hard feelings if he doesn't agree with our breakdown."

"We'll arrange a room for you to meet in," Bryan said. "Take all the time you need."

Dr. Preston was quick to gather himself and head for the door. Kyle's stare followed him out for a moment before he decided to chase him into the hall. The sudden change of heart seemed too convenient, especially for a man as deliberate as David Preston. This was a calculated decision, not an emotional reaction, and Kyle had to know what was running through the doctor's mind.

"Doctor," Kyle hollered, but his mentor didn't stop. "David, give me one moment."

Preston stopped without turning around. "I don't think you've ever called me by my first name. You're really trying to take charge here, aren't you?"

"Apparently that's what's expected of me here," Kyle said. "But that's not so different. You, on the other hand, have gone from damning us all as traitors to suddenly trying to help us. Why the change of heart?"

"I told you that already," Preston said.

"Yeah, and I can smell bullshit from a thousand miles away," Kyle replied. "It's one of my lesser-known powers. What's the real reason you're doing this?"

"Commander, you wanted my help, and now you've got it. Does it really matter why?"

"Let's just say I'm a bit more cautious right now than I've been in the past. And I think you owe me an answer."

"What do you want me to tell you?" Preston asked, meeting Kyle's eyes for the first time. "That I felt blindsided by what's happened? That I'm angry that your choices have dragged my family into this dead end? Is that what you're looking for?"

"No, I'm looking for a reason to trust you."

"And what can I say that'll make you feel better, son? I think you've already made up your mind."

"If I have," Kyle said, "what makes you think I'll let you anywhere near our men?"

"You won't," Preston said. "And you shouldn't. But I don't think it's that simple. I realize now that if I went back to the Dominion that they'd torture and kill me just for having been here, regardless of what information I gave them. So you've really left me with no choice. Everyone I care about is here, and the only way I can help them is to help you."

Kyle stepped back without a reply. Jackson was standing behind him, and Kyle nearly tripped over him as he turned away. Kyle took a long breath in as he shared a gaze with his captain before looking back at the deflated man standing in the hall. The doctor had always been so stately, so in control. To see him this flustered and uncertain was a disconcerting sight.

"I'll see you shortly," Kyle said finally.

Preston barely acknowledged Kyle's acquiescence. He dropped his eyes again and walked away without a word. Kyle watched his mentor disappear down the hall and then turned back to his friend.

"I need you to stick real close to him, Jacks," Kyle said.

"You really think he's a risk?"

"Just let me know if anything seems out of whack," Kyle replied. "I've gotta go find Mac and Jay. I'll catch up with you later."

Kyle's mind felt clearer now, though it had taken the confrontation to focus him. The complex was a blur to him this time as he went back to the garage. He could still hear the doctor's words from a few days ago. *It's not safe here. We can tell them where their enemies are. She got what she deserved.* Before he knew it, his blood was boiling again.

"Kyle! Yo, Kyle! What are you doing, man?"

Kyle snapped out of his daze only to realize that he had walked right past his friends. Mac had both hands out to the sides, palms skyward.

"What's going on?" Mac asked, his forehead still glistening with beads of sweat. "You look like a zombie walking through here."

"Sorry, I'm a little distracted," Kyle said.

"What now?" Jay asked.

"Dr. Preston apparently wants in. First, he wants nothing to do with it, then he wants to turn us in, now he wants to help us. It's a total clusterfuck."

"So what, you think he's still gonna try to throw us to the wulps?" Mac asked.

"Mac, it's not 'wulps,' it's 'wolves,'" Jay said. "We've been over this already."

"You know what I mean," Mac said. "What difference does it make?"

"You sound ridiculous. That's the difference."

"All right, let's not go down this road again," Kyle said. "I've got Jackson keeping tabs on him. Where do we stand on getting these components?"

"I talked to The Guy and we're good to go," Mac said. "He's already got everything we need. We just need to go get it."

"Okay, so where do we go?" Kyle asked.

"Raefflesia," Mac replied.

Kyle grunted. "Mac, that's one of the most populated planets in the galaxy. The military Garrison there is heavier than at some outposts."

"Yeah, but we should be able to blend into the crowd some, and we don't have to engage the troops like we would going into an installation. I still think it's our best bet."

"What do you think, Jay?" Kyle asked.

"I think Mac's right. Anything we can do to avoid a confrontation right now is a good idea."

"You know, I don't think I've ever heard you say I'm right before," Mac said.

Jay chuckled and rubbed his beard. "Yeah, well, don't get too used to it."

"We'd better prep a transport then," Kyle said. "I need to get back before this afternoon."

"Why don't you let us handle it?" Mac suggested. "All we've gotta do is make the pickup and get outta there. Plus, you don't exactly blend in."

"I can blend in just fine."

"You think? It's one thing to stay out of sight, but it's totally different to not get noticed in a crowd. I feel like they'll be looking for you. Plus, this Guy's usually pretty skittish. Having you tower over him might freak him out."

"You're not making me feel any better about this," Kyle said. "And how are we supposed to pay for this anyway?"

"Looks like we had just enough Dominion credits stashed on board the *Gemini* to cover it," Jay said. "Otherwise we probably would have had to give him Mac."

"Oh, ha ha," Mac said.

"He does sound like the type to be into redheads," Kyle said. "Maybe we should save the credits for something else?"

"How about you both go fuck yourselves, eh?" Mac said.

"Oh come on, Mac," Jay said. "When was the last time you took one for the team?"

"I'll show you taking one for the team—"

"Okay, I'm not sure I like where this is going," Kyle interrupted. "Get yourselves a civilian transport and some street clothes. I want you back here by midday."

"Piece of cake," Mac said.

Chapter 17

Just under three hours later, Jay weaved a small shipping vessel through the busy skyways of Raefflesia. It was a clunky old starship retrofitted with a hyperdrive engine, and when the cloud cover split in front of the cockpit, the fatigued metal of the hull let out a loud moan. The heavy cargo bay in the belly of the ship made for a difficult navigation as the strong gravity of the massive planet took hold. Raefflesia was one of the largest known habitable worlds in the galaxy at nearly three times the size of Earth, and it also had several layers of manmade urban-scaping that rose nearly two miles above the surface of the planet. These were complete city blocks built like the tiers of a tree house elevating from the planetary surface. Nearly eighty-seven billion souls called this planet home, with millions more voyaging to its borders every day to partake in the swarming galactic marketplace.

Mac adjusted a tight-fitting billed cap across his hairline for the thirtieth time since they had left the orbit of the Aranow moon. Jay looked over at him with a frustrated glare, but a tremor in the controls quickly recaptured his attention. His own clothes weren't exactly the most comfortable thing he had ever worn—a pair of brown cardboard-stiff work pants and an itchy woolen sweatshirt with a ratty hood. Besides the cap, Mac had pulled together a set of black denim pants with frayed knees and a stained leather jacket. None of it was ideal, but it should serve their purpose once they land.

"Goddam hat!" Mac cursed. "Shoulda gotten a hood like you did."

"Why don't you just take the fucking thing off," Jay said. "You're making me anxious."

"If I leave it on, it'll stretch out some."

"Yeah, if you leave it on for a couple of days."

"Well, I gotta cover my face somehow," Mac said.

"Not while we're on the ship," Jay shouted. "I swear, you're like a toddler sometimes."

"Yada, yada, yada." Mac leaned forward and pointed out the cockpit window. "That's the building there."

Jay peered over the controls down to a circular, three-towered apartment complex jutting out of the bustling market on the tier below. Most of the windows were small and dim, with tracks of external piping running between the cramped units. The exterior was charred in several places where some of the flats had previously caught fire, and many of them had already lost their meager balconies to structural collapse. It was run down like it had been neglected for decades. However, the top three stories of the center tower seemed to merge into an oval-domed palace ringed with reflective windows and surrounded by a wraparound terrace. Its finishes belied the ragged floors beneath it, like a crown on the head of swine.

The structure disappeared into an ocean of street vendors and food carts some sixty stories down, but most of this borough was dominated by vagrants and small-time thieves that preyed on any tourists who ventured into this area from the more upscale resorts nearby. Properties such as these on the surface tiers were typically highly desirable, but this one had fallen on hard times.

"Let me guess, The Guy's place is that penthouse on top of the center spire?" Jay asked.

"What makes you say that?"

"Cuz it looks like it's loaded with security," Jay said, leaning into a bank around the building. "And that's just our luck."

"Well, you're not wrong," Mac said. "Look, there's a docking lot about two blocks down. We should set down there in case there's surveillance near the towers."

Jay gave Mac a cockeyed look. "So we're gonna have to walk through the market? This isn't exactly the best place to be wandering around in."

"We've been through worse."

"Yeah, with Kyle and Jackson and a whole brigade behind us."

"Well, what do you want to do?" Mac asked. "We can't be linked to this ship if there's video ports on the building. He's a known smuggler—they might be surveilling him."

"What the fuck? You didn't want to mention that before we got here?"

"It's still less security than we'd see at a Dominion installation."

"You keep saying that," Jay said. "I'm less convinced every time."

"Just set it down. We'll be fine. In and out."

Jay shrugged and angled the shipping vessel toward the rooftop docks. The spaces were mostly filled with residential vehicles, though many looked like they hadn't been moved in months. As the engines shut off, Jay followed Mac into the cargo bay beneath the cockpit and pulled a pair of sidearms from his duffel. Mac grabbed his wrist.

"Hang on," he said. "We can't bring these weapons in there with us."

"What are you talking about?"

"The Guy doesn't allow any firearms in his house."

Jay shook his head. "You're fucking kidding me."

"No, they'll search us when we come in," Mac said. "Those things will get us in deep shit."

"Mac, you're fucking killing me here," Jay said. "We can't go into this place unarmed."

"I didn't say we'd be unarmed. I said we can't bring those sidearms in. Here, put these on."

Mac pulled out a pair of metal gauntlets and handed them to his friend. Jay looked down at the smooth metal cylinders for a moment, then looked back Mac with raised eyebrows.

"What's this supposed to be? Jewelry?"

"I've showed you these before," Mac replied. "They're my assault gauntlets."

"Mac, these things look like women's bracelets."

"Maybe, but those wristbands hold a miniaturized automatic rifle with a 330-shot charge. Way more firepower than that handgun."

"These little things pack that much ammunition?"

"Damn right they do," Mac said. "They've also got a thousand meters of high-tension wire, a plasma explosive, and electrostatic grappling gloves. There's a neurotransmitter it'll implant in your wrist that allows them to react to your thoughts. They're the real deal."

"Implant in my wrist?"

"Means it'll never work for anyone but you."

"Fuck me, why haven't we been using these before?" Jay asked, examining the devices.

"Well, they're still just prototypes," Mac said. "I haven't actually had the chance to test them yet."

"I knew there had to be a catch."

"The design is solid," Mac insisted.

"'The design is *solid*?' That's the best you got?" Jay asked. "Dammit, just when you had me feeling better about this operation…"

"Dude, calm down, we probably won't even need them."

"We should have brought Kyle with us…"

"All right, you need some reassurance?" Mac asked. "Here, I'll show you."

Mac slapped on one of the gauntlets with a clack. There was a short hissing noise and Mac winced perceptively. He aimed his fist at a locker on the far side of the cargo bay and suddenly the metal of the device began to twist and slide, revealing the small barrel of the rifle hidden inside.

"What are you doing?" Jay demanded.

"Showing you this works," Mac answered.

"You can't fire that thing in here. It'll pierce the hull."

Suddenly the weapon fired with a flash. The locker buckled into a creased heap and toppled over. The crash echoed through the deep cargo bay, and Jay recoiled and ducked behind Mac, expecting a ricochet or worse. He smacked Mac across the back of his head.

"Are you fucking nuts?" Jay hollered. "You know we need to fly this thing later, right?"

"Relax, those lockers are made out of three quarter inch iron," Mac said. "These charges won't go through that."

"I swear to God, I should have made you do this by yourself," Jay said.

"What? You wanted to know if the gauntlets work, right?" Mac replied. "Well, what more proof do you need?"

"Whatever, man, let's just get this over with," Jay said. He clicked on the two gauntlets and felt a sudden piercing sting through the skin on his wrists. He yelped audibly and glared at Mac, who quickly gave him a shrug. Jay pumped his hands into fists and swung his wrists in circles. The gauntlets weren't heavy, but he could feel them all the way up his arms. The rifle opened with just a thought, and Jay couldn't hide a smile.

"See?" Mac smirked.

Jay shook his head. "I'm not patting you on the back yet."

They opened the airlock and stepped down onto the platform of the docking lot. It was muggy and warm on the rooftop, and the sweatshirt Jay was wearing didn't make it any more comfortable. The hot smell of spices and roasted meat clashed with the stink of human sweat and melting asphalt. The lift on the edge of the lot was broken, so they were forced to climb down a set of decaying concrete stairs to the crowded streets below.

Jay was still panting from the twenty-seven-story descent as they walked into the market. It had to be ten degrees hotter among the glut of people milling around the maze of street carts and vendors. Several people brushed against Jay's shoulders, and another stumbled right into his chest. Mac reached over the top of the crowd and tapped Jay on the shoulder, pointing down the street to their left. Jay shoved the man away from his chest and started pushing through the herd.

The two blocks on the street seemed like miles. Hands were all over them from every direction, pressing trinkets and bruised fruit in front of their faces. Jay pulled his hood over his head as he saw a group of six Garrison soldiers pass out of an alley in ahead of them.

As they walked up to the entrance to the towers, Jay saw the glint of security cameras above the doors. He was keeping his face hidden beneath the shadow of his hood, but the sound of a pair of patrol speeders dashing overhead made him look back over his shoulder. They darted down the street and banked around another building, rustling several of the vendors' tents in their wake.

Mac pressed the button for the penthouse. A holographic display appeared in front of him with the image of a wide-faced young man with narrow eyes and thin lips. He had a stenciled tattoo down the left side of his face that read "Live the Dream, Dream to Live" in stylized glyphs.

"What's your business?" he asked.

"Yeah, we're here to pick up a package," Mac said.

"Authorization?"

"Outlaw."

The image looked away for a moment, showing the ponytail on the back of his head. Then he nodded and turned his narrow eyes back to Mac.

"Enter the keycode you were given on the pad," he said. "Last lift in the lobby. Be prepared to be searched."

Mac pulled out a scrap of paper and punched in the numbers listed on it. The clunky bolts on the metal doors ratcheted open and they quickly stepped inside. The lobby smelled of boiled potatoes and mildew. There were three men standing in the open doorway to one of the ground-floor apartments dressed in tattered leather and gaudy jewelry. They peered over with curled-down mouths and squinted at the two strangers walking in. Jay saw the handle of a pistol in the waistband of one of them, though he assumed all three were armed. Mac nodded at them and lowered the brim of his hat, but never stopped walking. Jay could feel their suspicious stares following them down the hall toward the lifts, but there were no footsteps to accompany their gaze.

They climbed onto the larger lift in the back of the corridor, and Mac again dialed in the keycode from the piece of paper in his pocket. The doors glided closed and the lift smoothly started its ascent. Jay pulled off his hood and ran his hand through his hair. He let out a deep sigh, and Mac gave him a thump on his shoulder. The lift was moving quickly up the sixty-some stories toward the penthouse, and the doors slid open again before Jay truly had a chance to wrap his head around what they were about to do.

There were two armed men waiting as they stepped off the lift, including the narrow-eyed man with the tattoo on his face. Both men were huge, easily as tall as Kyle and nearly twice as wide around the waist, and they both had heavy-duty Dominion-issue firearms just like Jackson's lost sniper rifle nestled against their shoulders. The room was dark and enclosed, with neon pink lighting and glowing graffiti on the walls behind them. There was a haze hanging in the air that Jay swore smelled of pesticides and ammonia.

"Howdy fellas," Mac said. "Thanks for having us over."

A third guard stepped out from beside the door to the lift and snatched the hat off Mac's head. Another guard grabbed the back of Jay's shirt and yanked him against the wall. A huge hand pressed against his chest pinned him to the wall, and he had to curb the urge to push back. The brute in front of him must have been seven feet tall, with a toothless grin plastered on his frying-pan face. Mac hit the wall right next to him, his hands overhead in surrender.

"Whoa, whoa, guys!" Mac exclaimed. "I'm sure it gets lonely up here, but we're not into it."

"That's very funny," the tattooed man said. "I heard you had a nice mouth."

"Wow, you hear that, Mac?" Jay asked. "I think he likes you."

The toothless giant bounced Jay's head off the wall. Jay bit his tongue and tasted a flash of blood in his mouth. He grunted and gave the goon a tight-lipped sneer. The big man just smiled back.

"I think I like you more," the tattooed man said. "You've got a real nice bumpkin vibe to you. I used to know a guy like that. I've got my fingers crossed you like cock as much as he did."

"Yikes, I think we got off on the wrong foot," Mac said. "We're just here to pick up a package from The Guy.'"

"We know why you're here," the man said. "But maybe I want to deliver a package of my own before we take you back."

A nasally laugh cut through the tension. Everyone's eyes moved over to an open door in the corner of the foyer where a short rail-thin man was buckled over trying to stifle a hyena's cackle. He had a swath of greasy hair draped past his shoulders, and was wearing only a pink tank top and a pair of boxer shorts. He put up one hand, still fighting off a hilarity all his own.

"Damen … heh, heh … I told you to be nice to our guests," he said, his eyes wrinkling as laughter overwhelmed him. "They've got a hundred thousand Dominion credits for us. Isn't that right, Lieutenant McArthur?"

"Hey, Guy, how's it hanging?" Mac asked, still pancaked against the wall. "Helluva place you've got here."

The Guy chuckled again through his nose, the veins in his temples protruding like swollen hoses. "Well, thank you ... heh heh heh ... You'll have to forgive my associates. They don't get out very often."

"Think you can call off the bandit here and we can get down to business?" Mac asked.

"Yes ... heh heh ... we do need to get down to business," The Guy said. "But nobody comes into my house without being searched. Heh heh ... go ahead and get it done, ladies."

Damen pushed aside the giant with the frying pan face and smiled a toothless grin at Jay. His breath reeked of onions and tar. Jay rolled his eyes in frustration but lifted his hands over his head. The thug licked his lips and started patting him down, eventually kneeling down and running his hands up Jay's leg and into his crotch.

Jay jumped back into the wall. "What the fuck? Does your girlfriend here really think I'm hiding weapons in my junk?"

"Heh heh heh ... we could have him strip search you, if you prefer, honey?" The Guy said. "Now be a good little girl and let him finish ... heh heh."

"Let's just get this over with, Jay," Mac said.

Jay gritted his teeth. Damen smirked and reached around to Jay's backside. The goon grunted with satisfaction, and Jay leered over at his friend. Mac could only shrug.

"How does he feel, Damen?" another tall guard asked.

"Country strong," Damen replied. "He's a fine piece."

The tattooed man again reached into Jay's groin and grabbed him. This time, however, Jay's patience failed him. He snatched the man's hand by the thumb and twisted his arm away with a snap. Damen squealed and Jay plugged him right across the bridge of his nose. Two of the other guards darted forward and hit Jay first in the jaw and then in the gut. They pinned him against the wall while the others aimed their rifles.

"Whoa, whoa, whoa … heh heh heh … that's enough. Let him be," The Guy said. "Lieutenant McArthur probably wouldn't want to pay us if we killed his friend. Besides, it would be a pity to spoil such a nice hayseed."

"He's spunky," the giant with the frying pan face grunted. "I like him."

"I think he broke my nose!" Damen shouted.

"Heh heh heh … Oh Damen, stop being such a princess," The Guy said. "Finish checking them for weapons, then bring them inside."

The frying pan man completed frisking Jay while Damen continued to glare at him from a few feet away. Jay taunted him with a deep breath through his nose, but the satisfaction was short-lived. The seven-foot thug grabbed both Jay and Mac by the shirts and pushed them into the room beyond the foyer.

The light in the next room was nearly blinding after the dimness of the previous one. Everything was lined in white, which seemed to amplify the light pouring in from outside. The Guy was sitting on a huge circular couch in a sunken seating area in the middle of the room with a small injector in his mouth. He bit down on it and a puff of smoke threaded out of his nose. His eyelids fluttered open and shut and he shivered all the way from head to toe. When his eyes opened again and he saw the two of them, he stood up and pulled on a pink robe, gesturing for them to join him on the couch.

"Come sit with me, you two … heh heh," he said. His pupils were practically the size of quarters. "I thought for certain you would have brought your beefcake commander with you."

"Sorry to disappoint," Mac said.

The Guy batted his dilated eyes. "Well, at least you brought the farmer to make up for it…heh heh…and I can imagine that the commander is quite busy … heh heh … what with your very public mutiny and all."

"It's slightly more complicated than that," Jay said.

"Oh, it always is ... heh heh."

'The Guy' smirked. His thin cheeks were stretched tight across the bones of his face. His nose was tilted up like a skeleton. Jay couldn't help but wonder whether he ever put anything in his mouth other than drug paraphernalia.

"Listen, Guy, we're not long on time here," Mac said. "Do you have the components that we spoke about?"

"My, aren't we in a rush?" The Guy said, pressing his fingers to his bony chest. "I've barely gotten the chance to get to know our country boy here. Tell me, sweetie, what do you do for the team?"

Jay sighed. "I'm a pilot."

"Oh my! You just keep getting better and better," 'The Guy' gasped. "You know, Damen here is quite the pilot also. He he...You two would be a great couple."

"Not sure his nose could handle much more of me," Jay snarked.

Damen grunted standing behind them, now holding a rag over his bleeding nose.

"He's charmed by you. I can tell," 'The Guy' continued. "Have you ever heard of a Stratys starship?"

Jay nodded. "I have. They have the new helios engines. Supposedly the fastest commercially available starship on the market."

"Not supposedly, and not just commercially," The Guy said. "It's the fastest ship in the galaxy. I've recently purchased one. Even your lovely starship isn't on par with it."

"That's great," Jay said.

"You're not interested in defending your ship?" The Guy asked.

"Our ship is on the shelf right now. That's why we're here."

"Well, you two are certainly all business," The Guy said. "I suppose we'd better get you your parts. Before you manage to kill my buzz completely." He nodded to his henchmen. "Take them down to the vault."

The man with the frying pan face tapped his foot on the floor twice and one of the massive floor tiles slid open with a hiss. There was a metal staircase beneath the floor leading into a dark room. Jay hesitated as the goon motioned for him to go ahead. Then with a resigned sigh he started down the stairs.

The lights came on as he reached the landing. Jay was legitimately shocked by the breadth of the space, which spanned the whole width of the flat and stood two stories tall. There were rows upon rows of stacked shelves loaded with components and munitions, things even many divisions of the Dominion military were not privy to have. It was like a black-market paradise.

"Holy shit!" Mac exclaimed as he stepped off the stairs. "Look at this fucking place. Where do you get all this stuff?"

"The Guy prefers not to say," the seven-footer said. "We have your package just over here."

Around the right side of the stairs there was a table against the back wall with several pieces lying on it. Mac hurried over and picked up two of the dozen solenoids, closely looking them over. Jay followed and lifted the rolled sheet of prism mesh.

"These solenoids look good," Mac said. "You got a matching model number on that mesh?"

Jay nodded. "Yeah, it's compatible."

"Are we satisfied?" the giant asked from behind them.

"Yeah, we're happy," Mac said. "You guys are a weird group, but you really came through—"

There was a loud crack, and Mac went down to the floor in a heap. Jay spun around just in time to see the giant's heavy fist flying at him. He tried to duck the blow, but it glanced off the crown of his head before denting the wall behind him. His scalp started screaming and he stumbled backward. His shoulders hit the wall, and suddenly there was nowhere for him to go.

"Time to go down, country boy!" the giant shouted.

Jay got his left hand up to deflect a second blow, though it hit so hard it nearly broke his arm. In desperation he kicked hard with his right foot into the brute's knee, and it buckled. He hit it a second time, then a third. With the fourth kick the giant finally crumpled and fell into a kneel. Jay landed an overhead blow to the giant's nose with his right hand, but the man barely flinched. One of his huge mitts caught Jay high in the chest and lifted him off the ground.

"Stop playing with him!" Damen hollered from the stairs. "Put him down already!"

The giant reared back with his free hand. Jay panicked, begging for a weapon, and the gauntlet rifle snapped open and rattled off several rounds into the ceiling. Chunks of mortar and metal came raining down on both of them as the shots echoed through the warehouse. Jay felt himself pulled away from the wall and then slammed back against it. Again, another blow. And again.

Jay was reeling. His lungs were empty from the pounding. His vision started to go hazy. He swung the gauntlet around blindly, firing a few shots into the giant's ribs beneath his arm.

The hand slide off his throat as the henchman dropped to the ground in a bloody heap. Jay's head bounced off the edge of the table and the room started to wail like a siren. Through the fog in his vision he saw Damen's toothless grin approaching, kneeling next to his fallen associate. He shouted some expletives that sounded like screeching tires before standing up again. He swung his knee into the side of Jay's jaw and the room went black.

CHAPTER 18

Kyle still couldn't sleep. His eyelids were heavy and his mind was weary, but he couldn't find the rest he needed. He had started dwelling on it, and that just seemed to make things harder, almost like his own subconscious was taunting him. Like anything else, he looked at it as a physical task, letting his body recuperate—and like any other physical task, he felt he should be able to master it. But he couldn't. And that just made the insomnia even worse.

The restlessness seemed especially bad at the moment, and he knew exactly why. Mac and Jay had left the colony nearly nine hours ago to fetch the supplies they needed to repair the *Gemini*, and they had heard nothing from them since. Kyle hated letting them go on their own, and he allowed it against his better judgment. It wasn't because he didn't trust them, but he believed the danger should be his to endure. This whole thing was his doing, after all.

After a few hours he resorted to fidgeting with his powers, using his telekinesis to stack odds and ends in his room on top of each other. He hoped it would distract him, but it just served to highlight yet another problem: his powers appeared unstable.

He started with a pair of his boots, moved on to a canteen, then a set of collapsible eating utensils and the scope of his assault rifle. He lined them up vertically one after the other, placing each in a more perilous position than the last. It was a game, and one he'd played periodically since he was just a boy. But for some reason, he was struggling with it. The stack kept falling despite his undivided concentration. It started to make him angry, which was typically a solid trigger for his powers. But not today.

Eventually he moved on to larger items, trying to force his hand to be steadier. Currently he had three cinderblocks balanced on their corners, with the frame of his bed and the mirror from the wall in the bathroom teetering on top of them. And teetering was the right word. The objects wobbled clumsily about the room, looking oddly like Mac when he tried to dance. Kyle grit his teeth and commanded them to be still, but somewhere in the thought his concentration broke and it all came crashing down.

The cinderblocks cracked, the mirror shattered, and the creaky old bed frame warped. Kyle roared an angry curse. He didn't understand. It was such a simple game, one that he'd been able to do without a second thought since he was ten. Why was he suddenly struggling with control, especially as his powers seemed to have been vastly augmented when he needed them against Vaughn's squadron and when fighting the Infernal? It didn't make any sense.

Finally his frustration got the better of him, and he left his room to venture into the communications center. When he found it, he realized it was essentially just a pair of technicians monitoring their short list of contacts scattered throughout the galaxy. It was far from a comforting sight, especially considering that these were the men responsible for supervising his team's missions. However, Kyle couldn't say that he was overly surprised.

"Anything yet?" Kyle asked.

The first technician shook his head, his chubby cheeks jiggling with the motion. "Nothing yet, sir. We did manage to isolate the signature on their ship. It hasn't moved for more than eight hours."

Kyle frowned. "Do we have any other contacts in the sector?"

"No, sir," the technician said. "We don't have anything within a hyperjump of that planet."

"How long would it take for another transport to get there?"

"I don't know, sir. We don't have many warp capable ships."

"Just tell me how long," Kyle demanded.

"Too long," a voice answered from the doorway.

Kyle turned and saw the Major Brady loitering in the doorway. He was leaning against the doorjamb, his left shoulder drooped and all his weight resting on his right leg. It was an uncomfortable posture to be sure, one that Kyle could only assume was residual from old battle wounds. He wondered briefly how many of those had come from him.

"Are you stalking me now, Major?" Kyle asked.

"Stalking you?" the major repeated. "Not really my style."

"Shouldn't you be getting some sleep?"

"Sleep? You're kidding, right? No one sleeps here. Not anyone really plugged in to this, anyway."

"Is that what we are?" Kyle said. "'Plugged in?'"

"Well, whatever you want to call it," Brady said, shrugging away from the door and sauntering into the room. "Still keeps us up at night, doesn't it?"

Kyle sighed, frustrated. "What do you want, Major?"

"Nothing. I check in with communications every night around this time. But if my hearing is still good, it sounded like you were thinking of taking another ship and going after your friends. Did I catch that right?"

"Is that a problem?"

"Depends on how you're looking at it," Brady answered. "On one hand, I can see how you'd want to rush off and help your men if they're in trouble. As an officer, I'd want to do the same thing." The major's eyes looked tired, but they still seemed sharp. It was an odd duality, but one he could relate to. His own body was starting to fatigue rapidly with this incessant lack of sleep. Seemed to be something of an epidemic around the compound. "On the other hand, I know how few ships we have with warp capability, and I know that going to Raefflesia likely would only end in us losing both ships."

"Are you saying that's more important than the lives of my men?"

"No, that's not what I'm saying at all. Your men are good soldiers, and we need those even more than we do the ships. But I can't see the Marshal approving another launch to rescue them. I think you know that."

"And I think you understand that wouldn't stop me," Kyle replied.

Brady nodded. "Oh, I was sure of that. I just thought I'd pass it along."

"Listen, Major, this isn't just about me wanting to help my friends. If something did happen to them, and the Dominion is involved, we'll have to find out what they may know. Because whatever information they got from them, however little it may be, it could still potentially compromise this colony."

Kyle hadn't known the major long, but he knew that he'd struck a nerve. This colony—this cause—was what Brady lived for. Kyle could see the pulse of his artery thumping heavily against the scar on his neck. Finally, the major looked down at his watch.

"Give them another hour," Brady whispered. "If we haven't heard anything by then, I'll find us a ship to go after them."

Kyle grinned. "Thank you, Major."

Brady walked out without another word while Kyle lingered for just a moment. He'd have to find something to occupy his attention for the next hour, which was no easy task in this place. He considered briefing Jackson and Dan about their potential excursion, but eventually he decided that it would be better if they stayed behind. If something were to happen to him, one of them would have to step in as acting commander. He found it odd that he wasn't immediately sure which one it should be.

After a few moments, he decided to go check on his father. He'd been so distracted with the recruits' training, and the planning for their first assault, that he'd allowed himself to become too lax in visiting Marcus. In truth he didn't expect much to have changed, but at the very least, it would allow him some time with thoughts outside of the tactical part of his brain. And perhaps he needed that even more than sleep.

† † †

His father looked like a withered corpse lying in that damned hospital bed. If it weren't for the occasional rise and fall of his narrow chest, Kyle would swear that Marcus was already dead. There were agonizing pauses between every breath, and with each gasp those pauses seemed to grow longer. Each hiatus made Kyle feel like he was watching his father breathe his last. It was torturous beyond belief.

The minutes passed slowly as he stood there wondering whether his choices would eventually take his father's life too. It was a damning thought, but one that he couldn't deny. As much as he would love to lay the blame for all of this at the feet of the Gentry, or even of General Donovan, he knew where the real responsibility resided. And it was right there with him.

The lights dimmed, and Kyle barely heard the murmur of the shift change outside. The door to his father's room slid open, and Dr. Decker walked inside.

"Good evening, Doc," Kyle said, turning back to his father's bed.

"How are you, Commander?" she asked.

"I'm … managing. But please, I don't want to be the commander when I'm in here. Call me Kyle, would you please?"

Ellie gave him a smile. "Of course. I keep forgetting." She walked to the end of the bed and pulled Marcus's file from the footboard. She leafed through the pages before going over to the far side and checking his vitals by hand.

"Any change?" Kyle asked.

Ellie shook her head. "I'm afraid not."

Kyle sighed. "Is there anything I can do for him?"

"I wish I knew if there was. But I don't know how you managed to save him in the first place. To me it's a miracle that he's still with us at all."

"It's been two and a half months. Nothing has changed. I'm starting to feel like he's going to be stuck like this forever."

"Comas can be a tricky thing," Ellie said. "I've seen them last for years. I've seen them last for just a few hours. Nothing about it is predicable. Especially with the injury your father had."

Kyle paused, remembering the moment he saw his father outside his bedroom. At first glance he'd thought Marcus was doomed. Those wounds would have killed most any other man, but somehow Marcus survived long enough for Kyle to help him. That seemed to be the crux of his very subtle mutation. His body always did just enough to survive—and beyond that, it did very little else. Even now, it just seemed to be doing what was necessary to hold on despite the best efforts of everyone involved. And because of that, Kyle couldn't help but wonder: did he miss his chance to really save his father?

"Tell me something …," Kyle began. "If I had gotten there a few minutes earlier … if I could have healed him just a little faster … would he be awake right now?"

Ellie rumpled her brow. "I can't answer that. And you shouldn't do that to yourself. You did what you could. We just have to let it play out."

Kyle grunted, running his hand down his face. "I'm not very good when things are out of my hands," he admitted.

"I can see that. But even your hands are only so big."

Kyle nodded half-heartedly. He wasn't even sure where his reach ended anymore. It seemed as though his abilities had grown almost exponentially in some cases, but at the same time had become less predictable. Suddenly he could reach into the depths of this moon and pull a geyser of subterranean water through its bedrock, but he couldn't manage to balance a few simple items in his bedroom. His frustration must have been obvious, as the doctor seemed to notice it right away.

"Is everything all right?" she asked.

Kyle grunted audibly, making whatever answer he gave a moot point. "I…I…," he stuttered, realizing he couldn't even fabricate a lie about it anymore. "I don't know, Doc. I just don't know."

"Is it something I can help you with?"

"I wish it were," Kyle said, the answer coming before he could censor it.

"Well, why don't you tell me about it?"

Kyle paused, considering the question. Normally he would shake his head and turn into a piece of stone. But this issue with his powers was sapping his confidence, and with his fatigue building, he knew he couldn't sort through it on his own. With Mac gone, and Angel still unwilling to speak to him, he needed to talk to someone. Briefly, he looked over his shoulder through the door. Nobody was watching.

"My powers … there's something wrong with them."

"Wrong with them? How so?"

"That's part of the problem, I don't really know. They seem like they're stronger than ever, but my control…I feel like my control is slipping. It's like I'm just losing my hold on them. I haven't felt that way since I was seven years old."

"You think it's because you came here?" she asked.

"No, it started before I arrived here. At Angel's house, I practically broke the planet in half fighting off Vaughn's men."

Ellie's eyes went wide. "What then?"

"The Infernal," Kyle responded. "I did things to fight it that I never could have done before. And I don't know how. I just *did* them. No warning, no training, no grand epiphany … just … there it was. I can do all those unbelievable things, but then I can't even manipulate simple household objects in my room. How does that make any sense?"

"So you're afraid you're losing control of your powers?"

Kyle nodded. "I've always been afraid of that."

"Come with me," Ellie said, nodding toward the door. She led him into another examination room and Kyle reluctantly laid down on the bed. She proceeded to poke and prod in ways he'd never seen before. This antiquated hospital left her precious little in the way of examination, so she used her hands. She used her eyes. It was impressive, really. But after several minutes she was left shaking her head.

"Well, I don't see anything wrong with you. At least not physically."

"What does that mean?" Kyle asked.

Ellie tapped her temple. "Means it's probably in your head."

"Great. So what do I do?"

"Probably should start by getting some sleep," Ellie suggested.

Kyle gave her a wry look. Ellie shrugged.

"You're not sleeping much, right?" she asked.

"How do you know that?" Kyle asked back.

"Your skin is dry, very tight like it's lost some collagen. Pretty common occurrence when you're not sleeping well," Ellie answered. "Plus, I'm not an idiot."

"So that's it? Get some sleep, and everything will be okay?"

"'*Everything*' is never okay. But a lack of sleep can sap your focus, drag down your immune system, and screw with your emotions too. Aren't your powers at least a little affected by your mood?"

Kyle shrugged.

"Think of what you've been through the last three months," Ellie said. "You lost your mother, your home, basically your life as you knew it. Everything you were ever comfortable with was suddenly gone. Even here, with what's happening with your father. I'd think that would torture anyone emotionally."

A light flickered on in Kyle's head. In some ways it made perfect sense. Harnessing his emotions was how the Dominion trained him to use his powers in the first place. But they only focused on his rage. Ellie's thought seemed to have a much wider spectrum than that. It was something he'd never considered before. What if there was more to it than rage?

Kyle didn't even know where to start. He needed time to think. And he wouldn't find that here. He slid off the bed and started toward the door.

"Kyle, wait—"

"I'm sorry, Ellie. I have to go."

Ellie looked back up at him with a pair of penetrating eyes. "I really…I hope that I didn't embarrass you the other night."

"Embarrass me? Don't be ridiculous. I wasn't embarrassed."

"Really? Because you seemed pretty uncomfortable."

"It's got nothing to do with you," Kyle insisted. "It's all me. I'm just not usually so scatterbrained around people."

The young doctor blushed and looked away. Kyle felt a brief yet undeniable satisfaction in that. It had been some time since he'd stumbled over his words like a self-conscious schoolboy—probably since he was a teenager with Angel in fact, and the sensation was an oddly welcome relief. Anything that made him feel more human was an enviable experience.

"Well, thank you, Commander," Ellie replied as the red started to drain from her cheeks. "That's very nice of you to say."

Kyle nodded, giving her a warm smile. He looked her over for a moment, finally taking in what Dan had been telling him months ago. Her allure was certainly much different from Angel's, his old friend being a seductive, ravishing beauty that demanded to be noticed. But Ellie had a far more understated appeal to her. It seemed to be a characteristic that she didn't reveal to just anyone, and that made him even more pleased that she'd somehow let him in.

Her eyes rose again to meet his, and Kyle looked away.

"So, Commander … do you mind if I ask you something?"

Kyle nodded. "I suppose."

"Your powers … they come from the Gentry himself?"

"That's right."

"And your mutation," she paused, apparently reconsidering the word, "your *gift*...it's what allows you to survive it? To control it?"

Kyle nodded.

"That's...amazing," she said. "Unbelievable, really."

"Why do you say that?"

"Oh, it's just a fascinating thing," Ellie replied, suddenly looking very sheepish.

Kyle looked away for a moment, then came back to her sharply. "Fascinating?"

"Kyle, I'm not trying to objectify you. But you're just such a unique phenomenon," she said reluctantly. "Scientifically speaking, I mean. You're practically the perfect mix of raw mutant strength and Celestial power. The only mortal in the galaxy able to wield it all. I can't help but think just how rare you are."

Kyle didn't respond. He couldn't. There just wasn't much to be said to that. And if he were being honest, it confused him. When his gaze eventually found its way back to Ellie, her eyes were fixed on him, and it snapped his stupor. He wasn't seeing the same shy, abashed expression she had worn previously. These were piercing, purposeful eyes, ones that cut through his grizzled exterior and plunged themselves into whatever soft, human element laid underneath. The look was both invigorating and devastating at the same time, and it laid him to waste.

And then, just as quickly as it came, the feeling retreated. Kyle suddenly remembered his missing friends, and a wave of disgust and self-loathing washed over him. Mac and Jay were still out there, still in any unknown sort of danger, and here he was making puppy-dog eyes with his father's doctor. The realization hit him like a wrecking ball, digging a pit in his stomach that he couldn't find the bottom of. He felt grossly ashamed, and he knew that he couldn't live with himself if he let it continue.

His eyes closed, and his lips went taut. He breathed out a frustrated sigh, and shook his head.

"I'm sorry, Ellie," he said. "I have to go."

Kyle didn't even let her ask why. His nimble feet stepped around her, and just like that, he was gone.

CHAPTER 19

Jay's eyes cracked open, his ears still ringing. There was a shadow just a few feet in front of him, and it took him a moment to realize the shadow was his own. He was staring straight down at the floor while bent over a metal counter, and his hands and feet were bound with a set of shackles. He pulled at the restraints, but the swelling bruise across his left forearm screamed at him and he quickly relented. He craned his neck to search around the room. The walls were a sterile white with blotches of exposed concrete, but it was dim enough that his foggy eyes couldn't make out much. Finally he was able to focus and see Mac dangling by his arms in the corner to his right.

"Mac ..." he whimpered. "Mac ... can you hear me?"

Mac's head lazily swished side to side, like it was a chore to support its weight. His hands and feet were encased in a conjoined constraint, and each was tethered to a magnetic pole above and below him. He managed to lift his chin for a moment, but his head quickly dipped back between his extended arms and his whole body wobbled inside the magnetic field like a stick in the wind.

"Mac, are you all right? Get it together. We've got major problems."

Mac finally got control over his wobbly neck and made eye contact with his friend. He didn't even seem to recognize him.

"C'mon Mac, wake up," Jay said in a muted voice. "I need you to wake up."

Mac moaned. "Where are we?" he managed.

"I don't know. Somewhere in The Guy's place, I'm guessing. Can you see anything?"

"All I see is the door," Mac squinted like an old man to look around. "Fuck, my head hurts. What the hell happened?"

"Your boy turned on us," Jay said.

"Oh, man, this is bad," Mac groaned. "Can you get loose?"

"Of course, I was just waiting for you to wake up to do it," Jay quipped. "Can you get out of that thing?"

Mac pulled against the shackles, but they barely moved. "Fuck, I can't even budge it. They even pulled off my gauntlets."

"Mine are gone too," Jay said. "It's a real nice fucking situation you've gotten us into."

"*I* got us into? Why, because he hit me first?"

"This was your plan!" Jay said. "Who else's fault would it be?"

"Shh, stop yelling. My head is pounding."

"Yeah, my head fucking hurts too. Thanks a lot."

"No, jackass, they might hear you," Mac said. "You want them coming back while you're posed like you need your colon probed?"

The words were barely out of Mac's mouth before the door opened behind Jay and The Guy and Damen walked in. The lights switched on automatically as they entered, flushing the dungeon-like room with a yellowish glow. The Guy's pink robe was still undone and dragging on the floor behind him, and he was chomping on an apple like a cow chewing a cud. He smacked Jay on the backside as he walked by and hooted in exasperation. Jay tensed against the restraints again and tried to pull away, but The Guy thrust his face in front of him, a sinister grin filled with crushed apple meal spreading open. Jay could still smell the hallucinogen smoke emanating from his mouth, and it made him recoil with a snap.

"Heh, heh, heh … this is what I like to see when I walk into a room. It looks like a buffet."

"You let me out of here and I'll show you who the piece of meat is," Jay growled.

"Oooh, there's that spunk again," 'The Guy' said. "He he…you know we like you already, you don't have to ham it up."

"Guy, what the fuck is the deal?" Mac demanded. "Why did you do this?"

"It's simple, Lieutenant," The Guy replied. "Money. It's always about money in my business."

"*Money*? We were going to pay you!"

"A measly hundred thousand credits. The Dominion has a two million–credit reward for each of you. A ten million–credit reward for your commander. It's a shame he didn't come along."

"That would have been something to see," Jay said. "You realize he would've killed you all by now, right?"

"You think very highly of him, I can see," The Guy replied. "We have heavy doses of serosa chloride here to neutralize his powers. We would be prepared for him and his parlor tricks."

"It's cute that you think so," Jay said.

"All the same, I don't suppose you'd like to tell us where he is? It would really save us a lot of trouble."

"Fuck off, shitbag," Jay replied.

"I've warned you already today to watch your mouth," Damen said, stepping forward and squeezing Jay's cheeks together. "I'll still be happy to fill it up for you."

"Okay, okay, okay," Mac said. "Look, if it's just the money you want, we can do better. We can give you inside info on Dominion patrols, shipping routes, whatever you want. They'll never be able to touch you again."

"That's very generous of you. But we've already contacted the Garrison. Part of our deal with them is immunity in our dealings. There's nothing you can offer us that we don't already have … heh, heh."

"You've already called them?" Mac asked.

"That's right," The Guy said. "But we told them we were bringing you back from off-planet. They don't expect us for several hours. Gives us plenty of time to have some fun with you before we send you on your way."

"You fucking cowards," Jay hissed. "You can't even fight us like men."

"Actually…heh heh…you should consider yourselves lucky we got a hold of you," The Guy said. "I wouldn't want to get caught by the Gentry's new charmed army. Oooh, they sound dreadful."

Mac tilted his head. "Wait a minute," he said. "'*New army*?' What new army?"

"Whoops, there I go again, running my mouth off," The Guy said. "You weren't supposed to know about that…heh heh."

"What are you talking about?" Jay asked.

"Oh, no no no, bumpkin," The Guy insisted. "Sorry, those are state secrets…heh heh. I'm keeping that just for me."

"Typical," Jay puffed. "You're all mouth and no balls."

"This was your doing, hayseed," Damen said. "If you hadn't killed our Staub, we might have just turned you over. Now you're going to be our lady."

"Staub? The big freak with the flat face?" Jay asked.

"Actually that reminds me, I meant to ask you about these toys that you brought with you." The Guy lifted one of the gauntlets from a basket in the corner. "I'm quite certain you won't be able to use your jaw later, so we'd better talk now."

"What makes you think I'll tell you anything?" Mac said.

"A girl can dream, can't he?" The Guy answered. "Besides, I've still got your friend here to persuade you with. Unless, of course, you have some perverted desire to see Damen here fuck his brains out."

"You won't get shit out him on my behalf," Jay interrupted. "Mac, don't tell them anything."

Damen backhanded Jay across the right cheek, splitting the skin under his eye with a wide ring on one of his fingers.

"Do what you want, he won't tell you anything," Jay snarled.

"It's not worth it, Jay," Mac said. "What do you want to know?"

"Mac, what are you doing?" Jay demanded.

"Relax," Mac replied. "I'm trying to help you out."

"Don't be an idiot!" Jay exclaimed. "This isn't going to help us."

Mac turned to The Guy. "Think you can have your boy shut him up again?"

"Certainly," The Guy said, nodding to his tattooed associate.

Damen unloaded on Jay's jaw again. Jay's head dangled like a pendulum on his neck for a moment, a thin line of blood and drool trickling off his lip.

"Heh heh heh…Oh I just love it when they start to soften up. Now where were we, Lieutenant?" The Guy asked, tapping his lip with his forefinger. "Ah yes, you were going to tell me where you acquired these wonderful toys."

"I didn't acquire them, I designed them. They're the only ones that exist."

"Well, I think they'll make a nice addition to my personal arsenal," The Guy said, attaching the gauntlet to his forearm. Immediately the rifle whirred out of the metal, the barrel just barely kissing the back of his hand. The Guy looked it over thoughtfully, licking the front of his teeth like a horny teenager.

"How do I get it to shoot?"

"Let me show you," Mac replied.

Suddenly the smile drained from The Guy's face. He clenched his fist tight, but his whole hand was already shaking. The gauntlet started beeping, slowly at first but becoming more fast-paced.

"What the hell is this?" The Guy demanded.

"Shit, I forgot to tell you," Mac said. "Those come with neural implants that are coded to the original user. Unfortunately, that's not you."

The beeps kept getting faster. The vein on The Guy's temple seemed to hasten with its pace.

"You've just activated its self-destruct," Mac added.

The Guy started clawing at the gauntlet like it was burning through his arm. "Make it stop!"

"Sure," Mac replied. "Just let us out of here."

The Guy didn't respond. He turned to Damen and lifted the gauntlet toward him. Damen stepped forward and pulled at the weapon's edges, but to no avail.

"Turn it off!" Damen yelled.

"Not a chance, ass-bag," Mac said.

The metal twisted and turned, and the gun barrel appeared again. Damen barely had a chance to gasp before six rounds went through his chest. Each shot made the big man shiver like a leaf, and his eyes quickly went blank. He fell to the floor with a thud.

"Damen! My God, no!" The Guy shrieked. "What have you done?"

"He went quick," Mac said. "That's more than I can say will happen for you. The charge in that thing will blow your arm off, and you'll spend the next hour bleeding to death. Sounds pretty awful, doesn't it?" Mac tilted his head facetiously. "Bet you never knew that one of the side effects of hallucinogens is some serious blood-thinning."

The beeps became a steady screech. Time was very short.

"Release our shackles," Mac ordered. "Do it now, or you die."

"I won't do it. You killed my Damen."

"Suit yourself."

The Guy squeezed his eyes shut and bared his teeth, revealing his receding gum line. Jay's eyes were still hazy, but he knew he had never seen his friend so stone-faced.

"All right!" The Guy yelled. "All right, all right. I'll do it. Just shut off the bomb."

"You let us go!" Mac shouted. "Do it, the clock is ticking."

The Guy reached into the pocket of his robe and pulled out a small transmitter. He pressed a pair of buttons on the display and the restraints released Jay from his precarious pose, and dropped Mac from the magnetic field. The beeping abruptly stopped, and The Guy let out a relieved sigh.

However, it was quite short-lived. Jay's eyes saw red as he stomped around the counter and grabbed the gangly smuggler by the back of his robe. The transmitter clattered to the ground as Jay's beaten and grim face drew closer. The Guy winced, anticipating a blow.

Mac grabbed Jay by the shoulder. He held up the set of shackles that had him bound earlier, and Jay nodded with a sigh. He heaved The Guy headfirst into the apparatus that he had been strapped to a moment ago, and went over to the basket in the corner to collect his gauntlets. Mac pulled his gauntlet off The Guy's wrist and replaced it with the magnetic restraints.

"You all right?" Mac asked, placing the gauntlet back on his own wrist.

"Oh yeah, I'm fucking great," Jay said, wiping a streak of blood from the split beneath his right eye. "This has been a lot of fun, thanks."

"Well, how was I supposed to know this was gonna go like this?" Mac asked.

"You coulda listened to me for starters."

"Right, if I listened to you, we'd never go anywhere."

"What's that supposed to mean?"

"Nothing, forget it," Mac said, pulling on his other gauntlet. "You know what, how about a 'Thanks, Mac, for saving my ass.' Literally, I saved your *ass.*"

"That dude wasn't really gonna try to fuck me, was he?" Jay asked. "That was just some shit to try and scare us, right?"

"No, I'm pretty sure he was gonna fuck you," Mac replied. "Isn't that right, Guy?"

The Guy was still reeling from crashing into his own instruments of intimidation, but he did manage a meek nod. Jay shot Mac a furious look.

"I am gonna beat the shit out of you when we get out of here," Jay said.

"You know what, that's fine if it helps you focus. We've still gotta get what we came here for and get outta dodge before the Garrison gets here."

Jay stepped over and hoisted the gaunt man back to his feet. "You heard the man. Where's the package we came here for?"

"It's still in our inventory," The Guy said, the whirl of the hallucinogens seemingly gone from his demeanor.

"How many more men are in the house?" Mac demanded.

"Four or five."

Jay smacked him in the cheek with an open palm. "Is it four or is it five?"

"It's five, it's five!" The Guy wailed. "You *are* a brute!"

"That's nothing," Jay said. "Mac, do we have any reason to keep this piece of shit alive?"

"Not at this point," Mac said.

"You would kill me, just like that?" The Guy asked.

"Imagine that," Jay replied, grabbing the thin man by the collar of his pink robe.

Just then there was a faint rattle near the door. Jay looked at Mac, wondering if it was a figment of his imagination. Mac raised his eyebrows at his friend's hesitation, but then there was another muffled noise. Jay looked up and saw the security cameras perched in the corners of the room. They wouldn't have to go looking for the other five henchmen after all.

"Son of a bitch, we're falling asleep in here," Jay said. "What do you want to do?"

"I'll lob one of these plasma grenades over there," Mac said, pulling The Guy down behind the restraint apparatus. "You clean it up."

The gauntlet on Mac's right arm shifted and turned, revealing a larger barrel on the palm side of his wrist. Jay swept around to the wall adjacent the door, the rifle on both his gauntlets drawn and ready. A small burst from beneath Mac's wrist fired the explosive into the door. It erupted on impact, raining a shower of flaming plasma into the stairwell. A chorus of screams echoed behind the blast.

Jay didn't even wait for the smoke to clear. He spun into the stairwell, stepping over a pair of blackened bodies. A third man was lying on the bottom of the stairs, his entire front side charred like a burnt log, but he was still wailing through lips that had been peeled back from his teeth. Jay mercifully put a round through his temple and he went limp.

There was a clunk of footsteps above the smoke, and Jay quickly opened fire. The first few shots caught nothing but metal and mortar, but then the soft sound of flesh tearing took over. A fourth body rolled down the stairs to Jay's feet. He sidestepped it adeptly, but had to lunge against the railing to his left as a burst of gunfire followed the body through the haze. The wall spit chunks of debris from the shots, and another huge thug dove down on top of him. They tumbled back into the warehouse beneath the apartment, scattering components across the floor.

Jay landed on his back, and the goon came down on top of him, pinning his left arm down under his knee. Jay swung his right arm forward, but the thug caught his wrist and smashed the gauntlet down into the floor. Jay heard the rifle barrel crunch.

The goon reached behind him and pulled a sidearm out of his waistband with his free hand. Jay heaved, but the man sitting on his chest felt like he weighed a ton. Finally, he remembered the electrostatic grappling gloves, and instantly he heard the gauntlet shifting. As the gun nestled against his forehead, the pulse of the gauntlet hit the thug man like a bolt of lightning. His eyes went white and he rolled off him in a daze.

Jay tried to scramble to his feet, but his muscles were still dancing with electricity. He managed to roll onto his stomach, but his opponent was already on his feet. He stumbled a few steps forward and reached down for his gun. But before he got hold of it, three shots dotted him, twice in the chest and once in between the eyes. He crumbled into a heap, and Mac helped Jay back to his feet.

"You all right?" Mac asked.

Jay's arms were still shuddering from the shock as he wiped himself off. "I think so. Next time you get to take the stairs."

"As long as that means not having to bail you out again. Seems to be happening a lot today."

"You're such an asshole," Jay moaned, still half hunched over. He looked down at the tangled device on his right wrist. "How'd you get that thing to work without wearing it?"

"I told you, the neural transmitter only works for one person. Once it's implanted, it's there permanently. Someone else puts it on, it goes into self-destruct."

"Think you can fix this one?"

"Oh, you like this thing now, huh?"

"Comes in pretty handy. So what do you think?"

"Just looks a little dinged up," Mac said. "Few hours with a forge and it'll be good as new."

"What'd you do with our new friend?" Jay asked.

Mac walked back into the interrogation room and pulled The Guy through the hole in the wall. His skinny arms were dwarfed by the oversized shackles, and he stumbled over the fallen bodies as Mac yanked him around. He tripped and fell at Jay's feet.

"Show us where our package is," Jay said. "And while you're at it, how about showing us where you keep those fancy Dominion-issue sniper rifles your men were carrying earlier. I think I know someone who would be happy to have one."

"Whoa, one second," Mac said. "First tell us about this new army the Gentry is building."

The Guy just shook his head.

"You said he was building a new army. A charmed army," Mac said. "You tell us about it, now!"

"Oh no no no," The Guy huffed. "I can't tell you that. They'll kill me if they find out."

"Mother fucker, what do you think we'll do?" Jay snapped.

The Guy looked over at Mac, but Mac just nodded.

"Spill it," Mac said.

"All right…all right, if you're so demanding," the skinny man acquiesced. "My intelligence contacts informed me several years ago that the Gentry was working on creating a group of charmed super-soldiers. Vicars, he calls them."

"*Vicars*?" Jay asked. "What the hell are they supposed to be?"

"They are you," The Guy replied. "Infinity Protocol recruits, but enchanted with the Gentry's own Celestial powers. His own private army of divine warriors."

"How is that possible?" Mac asked. "How can he do that?"

"He's a god, he can do whatever he likes. And is it so hard to imagine? This was always just the next step in building an unbeatable army. First the Fury, then the Infinity Program … now this."

Mac and Jay exchanged concerned looks. "Take us to our package," Jay ordered.

The Guy nodded and allowed them to pilfer his precious inventory. They collected the parts they needed for the repairs to the *Gemini*, two portable plasma cutters, a pair of rifles matching the one that Jackson had lost in the chaos of their escape, a dozen carboranium weave battle suit underlayments, and a full case of earbud communicators. Jay wished that they could have returned with another transport to plunder the rest of the goods, but he knew with the Garrison en route they could only take whatever could fit into a pair of duffel bags. They gathered their loot at the top of the warehouse stairs, but Mac wanted one last thing before they left.

"Where are the credits we brought for this package?" he asked. "I'm sure you've got a cache of currency around here somewhere."

"If I give it all to you, will you let me go?" The Guy meekly asked.

Jay smacked him in the back of the head. "Can't hurt your chances. Now speak up."

"It's beneath the fireplace. The code is my first name."

Jay hit him in the back of the head again. "Well, spill it."

Just as The Guy opened his mouth, a loud ring shuddered through the apartment. Mac spun around, the rifles on his gauntlets drawn.

"What the hell was that?" Jay demanded.

"The buzzer from the lobby," The Guy said. "Someone is downstairs."

"You've got security cameras down there," Mac said. "Where are the monitors?"

"There's a keypad on the wall by the door. You can pull them up there."

Mac ran to the door leading into the foyer. He swiped at the keypad and the holographic display lit up with an image of the lobby.

"What is it?" Jay asked.

"Dominion troopers," Mac said. "Apparently they didn't care too much for his timeline."

"How many?" Jay asked.

"At least a dozen that I can see," Mac replied, peering out the floor-to-ceiling windows. "Probably a whole brigade waiting in the streets."

Jay rushed over to the windows on the other side of the flat. The angle was steep, but he could see people rushing away from the building in droves. There were soldiers filing onto the roofs across the way, and he saw a pair of hoverships floating past.

"Shit, they're everywhere," Jay said.

"We'll never get through all of that," Mac said.

Jay stormed across the flat and snatched up The Guy in a fury. He pulled the thin man's skeleton-face close to his, enough so that he could smell the tar-tinged smoke on his breath again.

"You're a sneaky little bastard. Do you have a backdoor out of here?"

"No, there's nothing."

Jay reared back and drove his fist right through The Guy's mouth, knocking out half a dozen of the rotting teeth. 'The Guy' spit a wad of blood and gums out into a splatter on the white floor, moaning like a wounded mule. Jay pulled The Guy's face up in front of his again.

"Try again. How do we get out of here?"

"There's only … the elevator. I swear."

"You're gonna start running out of teeth to lose in a minute," Jay snarled. "Then we'll have to start looking at other body parts to rip off."

Jay wound up again, and The Guy threw up his hands to protect his face. "I swear, there's no other way!" he slurred through his mangled gums. "We built it that way to make sure no one could get in here without our say so. There's no way for you to get out, not unless you want to jump out the window."

The words hit Jay as more of an idea than a threat. He glanced at Mac, who seemed to have the same revelation as he did. The high-tension cables in their gauntlets might be able to get them to an adjacent building or down to the street. At the very least it might give them some options beyond pulling weapons from the inventory and hunkering down for a last stand. Jay dropped The Guy without another thought.

"Can we reach any of the other roofs from here?" Jay asked.

"I think so," Mac noted. "Out this window there's an angled roof at about a hundred meters. If we can get there, we might have a few options."

"Our transport is on the opposite side of this building," Jay said. "We'll never make it back if we go out this way."

"Then maybe we should try taking his," Mac said, nodding at the groaning man on the floor behind them.

"Oh, now you're speaking my language," Jay said. He rolled The Guy onto his back. "Your ship, the one you told us about earlier. Where do you keep it?"

"It's in a garage in sublevel 6," The Guy said. "But you can't take it."

"You're not exactly in a position to stop us," Mac noted.

"No, you can't take it without me. The engines are DNA coded. They can't start unless the sensors read that I am on board."

"Well, then, stand up" Jay said. "How do we get there?"

The Guy reached into the pocket of his pink robe and pulled out a small starter key. "I'll show you."

The low ring of the lobby buzzer turned into the buzz of an alarm. The elevator had been overridden and was quickly rising toward the penthouse.

"We've gotta go now," Jay said. "Get the window."

Mac fired a handful of shots through one of the giant windows and it shattered with a crash. There was an immediate swirl of wind that swept through the apartment, and it made Jay's feet feel unsteady. Mac stepped to the opening and fired the piercing grappler across the alley. It sank through the aluminum roof and the line went taut. He anchored the other end into the apartment ceiling and grabbed the line with the electrostatic gloves. Then he dove into the air.

Jay watched him zip across the gap and drop onto the roof on the other side. It appeared steep and he needed the grip of the gloves to hold on. But he made it.

Jay unwound a length of his own cable and looped it over Mac's line. He had to be able to hold the wire and their passenger at the same time. If he could tone down the pulse of the grappling glove on one hand, he could fortify his grip without electrocuting him. Or at least he thought he could.

"All right, Guy, get your skinny ass over here," Jay said. "We're next."

The ding of the elevator stopped and Jay heard the clatter of boots storming through the foyer. A charge erupted through the second door. Jay was thrown to the floor and slid into the window next to the opening. He squeezed the wire tight in his right hand, but the wind was strong over his back. Beyond the smoke the footsteps grew louder, and the zing of gunfire started screaming past him. The Guy had been thrown into the couch in the middle of the room, but he was still alive.

"Hurry!" Jay shouted, firing several shots back at the troopers from his left gauntlet. "You can make it! C'mon!"

The Guy scampered to his feet, his hands still bound by the heavy shackles. He stumbled up the short stairs and rushed toward Jay, his dirty pink robe fluttering behind him. Jay reached out his hand, but The Guy never made it. A pair of shots ripped open his leg, and then a third exploded through his temple. He sprawled across the white floor several feet from Jay. Dead.

Jay cursed to himself and fired one of his plasma grenades toward the coming soldiers. The explosion brought a brief stop to the gunfire, and Jay didn't waste it. He slid across the floor and grabbed The Guy's bonds with his free hand. The grappler ignited and his hand clamped down like a vice. He scurried toward the window and leapt into the air.

The cable in his right hand screamed as it careened down the tension wire, but Jay could barely hear it over the roar of the breeze whipping past him. His eyes watered from the blast of air, and he couldn't even see the roof when he slammed into it. His back hit the metal first, forcing the breath from his lungs. He gasped but his scream came up hollow.

"Jay, this way!" Mac called.

Jay heard it coming from his left. He rolled over and let the grappler on his right gauntlet catch the roof for him. It was steeper than he had expected, and the weight of The Guy's body was pulling him down. His chest burned as his lungs reinflated with the hot, smoggy air. He stumbled and slipped, planting his face into the roof.

Mac jumped back onto the roof and clambered over to him. Together they dragged the corpse to a landing at the corner of the building and dropped it with a thud. Mac kicked in the door and they pulled the body inside.

"What the fuck happened?" Mac asked. "I leave you alone for ten seconds and you get his head blown off!"

"Yeah, I'm okay, thanks," Jay said, still wheezing.

"What are we gonna do? We've gotta have him to start the ship. We can't carry him all the way down there."

"We don't need all of him. Just a piece of him."

"What are you gonna do, pull his hair out?"

"Get me one of the plasma cutters out of that bag," Jay said.

Mac shivered and turned away. Jay shook his head and pulled out one of the cutters himself. The Guy's hands were still bound, so Jay moved down to his feet. They were still dirty from walking across the fallen walls and debris in his apartment. Jay caught himself wishing that Jackson was there. He could cut off a person's leg without batting an eye. But in the end, he fired up the cutter and blazed through the flesh and bone about halfway down his calf. The smell was not quite like sawdust and burning plastic, and it made Jay's throat burn.

He shoved the cauterized foot and ankle into Mac's hand and then spun to puke into the corner. He spit on the wall twice as he turned back to his friend, trying to get the bitter acid taste out of his mouth.

"Where do we go now?" he asked, wiping the spittle from his beard.

"We go down," Mac said, jamming the severed foot into the duffel.

"Right," Jay answered, searching around the small enclave and finding nothing but walls. "How do we do that?"

"I guess we start looking for a lift."

There was a narrow door behind him made of heavy alloy. Jay blew through the bolt with the plasma cutter, and the door opened into what looked like an attic beneath the crowned roof. It was hot under the metal sheathing, with little but a ring of scaffolding separating them from the level below. Mac pulled the starter key out of The Guy's robe pocket, then threw his duffel back over his shoulder and followed Jay across the catwalk.

On the far side of the room there was a staircase that led them down. There was a modest grumbling of gears and hydraulics, and Jay pointed out what appeared to be a set of lift mechanics off to their left. However, they couldn't access the shaft or the compartment from that floor. They would have to enter the stairwell.

The door to the stairs was already cracked open. It creaked audibly as Jay leaned through the opening, and it echoed down the winding staircase. The noise from the room seemed to drown out as he leaned inside, but it was replaced with another sound: footsteps.

Jay looked down the center of the spiraling staircase and could just make out a rush of men hurrying upward some dozen floors below. Jay waved at Mac to follow him, and they quickly started down. Their boots sounded heavy on the treads, but they didn't have time to censor them. They had to reach the next floor.

Four landings down they finally came to another door. It was locked, forcing Jay to burn through the bolt with the plasma cutter. Its sizzle sounded like a buzz saw in the hollow of the stairwell, and he still had to kick it open after the bolt severed. Mac pushed it closed, but with the bolt gone it immediately listed back open.

They darted away from the door as the footsteps drew closer. The building was some kind of factory, but they had stumbled onto some offices overlooking the plant floor. There were a handful of cubicles scattered around the room, but it looked as though the place had been evacuated. Some holographic screens still flickered, and several chairs had been overturned. Below them in the work area there were dozens of soldiers scouring the equipment. Their exits were filling up fast.

"I don't see another way out," Jay whispered. "Where the fuck are we going?"

Mac stopped suddenly and Jay stumbled into his back. Before Jay could start shouting at him, Mac turned down one of the aisles of cubicles and slid down onto the floor. There was a square access panel nestled against one of the partitions. It was small, barely a few feet wide, but they had few other options. They pried it open, though the tunnel inside was even smaller, built just to house a bundle of fiber optic cables and allow room for any necessary repairs. It would fit a grown man, but not by much.

"All right, squeeze your ass in there," Mac said.

"I think you're going first this time," Jay answered.

"No, I went out the damn window first. It's your turn."

The door to the stairwell burst open, and the argument became a moot point. Jay shoved his duffel into the duct and shimmied in behind it. He'd barely made it a few feet before the light went out as Mac closed the panel behind them. Jay's back was pressed against the roof of the tunnel like a sardine at the top of the can, and he could feel the thump of feet rattling over the top of him. He paused as the soldiers shouted through the office, waiting to see if they would clear out, but then he felt Mac prodding him on the bottom of his boot to get moving.

He couldn't see anything in front of him. He could barely even stretch his arms out far enough to pull himself forward, but he started crawling ahead anyway. After several moments he started to see a few strands of light peeking around the bag, and finally it ran into something at the end of the tunnel. He gave the duffel another push, and a grate burst open into the lift shaft.

Jay felt like he was being squeezed out of a tube of toothpaste. There wasn't much in the way of footing along the side of the shaft, especially with the weight of the duffel bag dangling off his shoulders. However, he was able to grab onto a girder and pull himself up as he crawled out of the narrow vent, using the grappling gloves to get a firm grip. Mac grunted as he climbed out behind him, and the noise reverberated down the shaft. The lift cabin was just a few floors above them, and dull utility lighting lined the walls below. Jay couldn't even see the bottom as he peered down.

"You think it goes all the way to the sublevels?" Jay asked.

"I don't know," Mac said. "I guess we'll have to find out."

"Do we even have enough cable to reach the lower tiers from here?"

"Probably not," Mac replied.

"Well, this should be fun then," Jay said.

Mac fired his remaining cable through the bottom of the lift, and Jay followed suit. They swung into the void, dangling for a moment before slowly starting to lower themselves down. After a long drop Jay felt the cord go tight and he was jerked to a halt. He bounced upward with a painful jolt, narrowly missing Mac a handful of times as they whipped past each other. There was still a long tunnel beneath them, with no end in sight.

"Now what do we do?" Jay asked, grasping his shoulder.

"We're gonna have to climb," Mac answered.

The walls were almost sheer at this level. The lift door just below them read "Sublevel 2," but each lower tier was likely ten stories deep. They had a long way to go counting on the grappling gloves to keep them from tumbling down the shaft. Jay heaved and threw his legs forward, swinging toward the wall. The glove on his free hand hit the surface like a glob of tar, making good purchase against the flat wall. He released the cable from the other gauntlet, and hung from the wall like a spider.

The climb down was grueling, burning his shoulders and scraping his knees with each pass. The walls became coated with moisture as their depth increased, causing the gauntlets to slide several feet at times. After nearly half an hour of inching downward, they came to a door labeled Sublevel 6. Jay was pouring sweat by then, soaking his sweatshirt and dripping into his eyes. He was able to kick open the release to the door and mercifully swing inside.

He dropped directly to his knees after landing on the pavement. His arms and legs all felt like lead, and he was gasping for breath. Mac hit the ground beside him and immediately rolled to his back, his red hair matted down with perspiration. Jay forced himself to raise his head and look around. The whole tier was some kind of starship garage, lit with spotlights shining down on the armada of vessels parked inside.

The buzz of a Garrison cruiser whipped past them. Jay grabbed Mac and pulled him behind the nearest ship. Once his gasps subsided, he could hear the shouts of other troops off in the distance. They were searching all the ships capable of going off-planet, and the net was tightening.

"You know what this thing is going to look like?" Mac asked.

"Yeah, if it is what he said it is. The bigger question is if we'll be able to get to it, and then get it past all the Garrison patrols."

"That's up to you. I've got faith."

"At least one of us does," Jay replied, peering down the lane beyond the transport in front of them. He could see a distinctive profile of a high-speed ship about a hundred meters away, and then saw a patrol move to the next aisle over. They had a window to make a move.

"C'mon, let's go," Jay said, sprinting ahead.

Mac chased after him through the garage, splashing through puddles scattered across the ground. For a moment they seemed home free. The ship was there, and it seemed launch ready. But as they turned the corner, a squad of troopers was waiting. Jay skidded to a halt, slipping in the water and falling onto his back. The soldiers spun toward them, reaching for their weapons. Mac thrust his gauntlet rifles over the top of his fallen friend and fired off a volley of shots. The first line of troopers dropped, but another three managed to scamper away.

Mac jumped over Jay in pursuit. He fired another barrage after the fleeing troopers, the shots echoing against the high ceilings. As Jay climbed to his feet, a nearby ship exploded with a roar, dislodging a row of wide metal pipes from the roof. The clang of pipes and boom of the explosion sounded like the end of the world in the covered garage. Jay ran to the Stratys and started working on its hatch.

"You had to go blow something up, didn't you?" Jay shouted.

"Shut up! Just get this thing running!" Mac hollered as they leapt into the starcraft.

Jay rushed Mac into the streamlined cockpit and dumped his duffel next to the entry. He held out his hand.

"You've got the starter key, and the foot's in your bag!" Jay shouted. "I can't start this thing without them."

Mac fumbled through his pocket and handed Jay the starter. Jay climbed into the pilot's seat and slid the key into its slot. The heads-up display asked for DNA verification and a circular scanner whirled open. Mac slapped the sole of the severed foot onto the lens, and the engines rumbled to life.

"All right, we're hot," Jay said. "Buckle up. This is gonna get a little nuts."

As another group of soldiers swarmed toward them, Jay hit the throttle and they were thrown back into their seats. The ship ripped over the other vessels like a missile, and even Jay's eyes widened at the force of the thrust. The controls were crisp and sharp, and he overcorrected several times as they shot through the enclosure.

"Holy shit! Get us the hell outta here!" Mac shouted.

"I'm trying!" Jay yelled back. "Find me the exit!"

Jay could make out the muffled sounds of gunfire outside. He clenched his teeth trying to bank through and above the rows of other starships without clipping the wings. Finally he saw the launch ramp in the far corner and made a beeline for the exit.

They hit the ramp and it immediately arced toward the right in a spiral as it rose toward the surface tiers. Jay barely slowed the ship even in the cramped exit, and Mac put his foot up against the instrument dashboard to steady himself. When he finally saw the light at the other end, Jay threw the throttle forward and the Stratys screamed into the open sky. They banked upward, but the skies weren't clear for long. The collision alarms started blaring and their path filled with Dominion cruisers.

"Whoa! Whoa! Whoa!" Mac hollered. "They're everywhere!"

Jay hit the rudders as hard as he could and the ship spun back between the buildings. Windows shattered in the surrounding skyscrapers as they rifled by, but by then their tracking system showed a cluster of Dominion Predators and patrol skiffs trailing behind them.

"We've got fighters on our tail," Mac said. "Where are the munitions controls?"

"There aren't any," Jay replied.

"What do you mean there *aren't* any?" Mac demanded.

"This is a civilian ship. What did you expect?"

"We've gotta do something. We've got a dozen ships chasing us!"

"Just hang on, I'm gonna lose 'em."

Jay leaned on the stick and pulled back on the throttle, whipping low along the streets. Mac moaned as the ship slalomed through the buildings, tossing him from side to side in his seat. They heard the boom of explosions behind them as a pair of their pursuers plowed into the surrounding structures.

"We've got two down," Mac said. "But there's more inbound. We've gotta get outta the atmosphere so we can hit hyperspace."

"Yeah, start setting the coordinates," Jay said. "I'll find us an alley out of here. And check the instruments for a homing device. We can't let them track us back to Aranow."

Mac spun his chair toward the hyperdrive controls. He dialed in a few instructions, but then stopped and pulled open the panel underneath. He yanked a tracking beacon off the hyperdrive's coordinates system, then finished completing the course that would take them back to Aranow.

"Coordinates are set," Mac announced, spinning back around. "Get us out of here!"

Jay didn't respond. He arced the ship above the buildings, swerving upside down and diving into a gap between the surface tiers. The light from above the clouds disappeared as they dipped into the sublevels again. They could see a shower of artillery splashing off the lower-tier buildings around them, but Jay was able to just avoid their aim. Mac started screaming.

"Two missiles away!" Mac shouted. "Closing fast!"

Jay dropped them another level down in the tiers, and the missiles erupted against the edge of the concrete platform. The blast forced the tail of the ship down, and it screeched across the ground of the level below. The controls shook in Jay's hands, but he managed to level them out and accelerate through the street. They pulled away from their pursuers, and at the next opening Jay lifted the streaking ship back into the skies above. He unleashed the throttle, and the Stratys boomed into ultrasonic speed.

Mac's head hit the back of his chair as the sky turned black. They flashed by the looming Dominion cruisers, and the grip of the planet's gravity relented. Jay could see a dozen more ships coming at them from outside Raefflesia's orbit.

"Hit the hyperdrive, now!" Jay shouted.

Mac hit the ignition, and instantly they felt themselves stretched across the expanse of space. The huge world disappeared behind them, their new home waiting on the other side.

CHAPTER 20

Kyle and Brady had already boarded a ship with the intent to go in search of their missing teammates when word came in about their harrowing escape. It was a relief, but not one that came without consequences. Bryan had caught wind of their unannounced endeavor, and he was not pleased. He resolved to make an example out of each of them and send them both to the stockade, but it never materialized. In Kyle's case, he simply rolled his eyes and told his uncle that he wasn't interested in his discipline. Brady seemed resigned to do his time, but in the end, Bryan decided to sweep the whole thing under the rug. It did him no good to punish one without the other. Bryan went back to fretting about the security of his colony, Brady returned to, well, whatever it was that Brady did, and Kyle was able to reconvene his surveillance of the new Infinity recruits.

The mid-afternoon light on the Aranow moon was surprisingly bright, and Kyle was once again struck by how warm it was during the day. He had initially thought that the reflected sunlight from the system's star would be relatively cool, but the heat of the planet's atmosphere was warm enough to affect the nearby moon. At times he thought it may just be an illusion of the stark cold present at night, but by then it didn't really matter. The daytime temperatures *felt* relatively comfortable, even in the depths of the canyon.

Kyle was standing on a rooftop overlooking the yard of the Splinter compound, gazing down on the day's training session for the Infinity Protocol recruits. He had been keeping tabs on their practices since they began several weeks ago, though most days it was from an inconspicuous vantage point. Today, however, he was out in the open. He had decided it was important for them to be aware of his presence from time to time to keep their focus.

The task for the day appeared to be hand-to-hand combat. Jackson was standing in the middle of the group with five recruits circling him. Two trainees darted at him from either side. One swung high, and the other kicked low, but the captain deftly ducked below the fist and lifted his leg over the sweep. He caught the wrist of the soldier to his left and flipped him over his shoulder onto the man on his right. As he spun around, he deflected a pair of quick jabs from a third assailant, and then landed a front kick into the man's chest. He arched backward, avoiding a whirling roundhouse from a fourth man, then pivoted to spin his own kick against the attacker's chin. The final soldier lunged forward with a high kick, but Jackson blocked it down with both hands. He dodged a couple of wild punches and raked his fist across the soldier's cheek.

Kyle shook his head in frustration. It had now been seventy-two days since the training had begun, and still Jackson was barely breaking a sweat. At this point any run-of-the-mill Dominion infantryman would eat most of these recruits alive. For them to be any use to him, they had to be better.

"No, no, no!" Doctor Preston boomed from the sideline. "Leverage! Leverage! Use your opponent's momentum, use *your* momentum! It makes you faster, it makes you stronger."

The doctor's voice echoed just like Kyle remembered. Even a dozen years later, the message was exactly the same.

"We'll keep doing this until you get it right," the doctor continued. "Split into your groups and go through it again."

Jackson stepped over a couple of the men without offering to help them up. Kyle snickered to himself as his friend walked up to the doctor and exchanged a few observations. It was just loud enough in the colony to drown out their conversation, even to Kyle's superhuman ears. After a moment Dr. Preston nodded over Jackson's shoulder, and the captain spun around to see Kyle peering down at them. He gave the doctor a few parting words before making his way across the courtyard. A few moments later he walked out onto the rooftop and came up alongside his commander.

"I see you're not taking it easy on them," Kyle said.

"Would it help us if I did?" Jackson asked.

"No, and that's why I asked you to do this and not Mac or Jay. Though I think you could probably pull your punches a little bit."

Jackson looked over the edge at one of the recruits being helped out of the courtyard by a couple of his comrades. He shrugged.

"He's got a glass jaw," Jackson said. "I didn't hit him that hard."

"If you say so. How are the rest of them doing?"

"Depends on who you ask about. Some days I wonder how some of them manage to get dressed without hurting themselves. Though there's a few that I'm reasonably encouraged about. The two guys from the old Infinity program, Mitchell and Logan, are both doing really well."

"They should be," Kyle said. "They've been through this before. What about the others? Are there any viable options among the Splinter soldiers?"

Jackson sighed and surveyed the men below them. "There's three or four that I'd take right now."

"Really? Are we looking at the same soldiers? I haven't seen anything that inspires much confidence."

"Well, you haven't seen them as much as I have. There are a few pretty good marksmen," Jackson insisted. "The twins and the woman … I'd let them cover my back any time."

"You're sure about that?" Kyle asked.

"Well, if there's one thing I know a little bit about, it's shooting," Jackson said. "And they can shoot."

"Anyone else?"

"No, those are the ones that I'd feel comfortable with right now."

Kyle grunted. "I'd hoped it would go faster."

"Well, what do you expect, Kyle?" Jackson said. "It's only been, what, like two months?"

"Seventy-two days."

"Whatever, it's still nothing," Jackson stated. "You realize that even we trained in this system for years before we were combat ready."

"Jacks, we don't have years," Kyle said.

"I don't know what to tell you, Kyle. The others just aren't ready," Jackson said. "They're learning, but they're not ready."

Kyle turned away and ran his hand through his thickening blonde hair, squeezing the skin on the back of his neck. "All right, I guess we just keep at it."

Jackson nodded and turned to head back to his class, but Kyle wasn't quite done.

"Whoa, hey, hang on a second," Kyle said, waiting for his captain to look back in his direction. "Tell me about how Dr. Preston has been."

"How he's *been*?" Jackson asked.

"You know what I mean, Jacks," Kyle said. "How's Preston handling himself?"

Jackson sighed. "Look, I know you're expecting me to tell you that he's brainwashing these guys to turn us in and all, but it's just not happening. He's putting in sixteen-hour days with the men, and at least four or five more afterward. And that's just what I know about. He's doing everything he can."

"He's a man that's very good at getting what he wants out of people." Kyle paused. "Especially when they don't even know that they're giving it to him."

"Well, I don't know what he's gotta do to get you to trust him again."

"You trust him?"

"I don't have any reason not to," Jackson said.

Kyle looked down at the doctor shouting instructions at his recruits. It was a familiar sight, one that should have eased Kyle's concerns about his mentor's allegiances. However, the doctor's words about his mother continued to resonate in his photographic memory, even more than two months later.

"Just stick with him, all right?" Kyle said.

Jackson nodded. "Yeah. Will do."

"I've gotta go check on Mac and Jay," Kyle shrugged. "They should be finishing the repairs on the *Gemini* today."

The two of them went their separate ways. Kyle's walk down to the garage was a blur. He still wasn't sleeping, and his nerves had started to fray. The nightmares had started to chew away at his sanity. But he couldn't help it. Every night it was the same thing. Every night he saw his mother die.

And now he had more problems to consider. The intel that Mac and Jay had brought back from Raefflesia was troubling. Bryan suspected that the Gentry's enchanted army was just Dominion propaganda, but Kyle didn't think they had the luxury of doubting its legitimacy. If there was a chance that it existed, then they would have to take it as a certainty, and an imminent one at that.

His hand hit the door to the maintenance bay, and he was pulled back out of his head. The *Gemini* was in its place at the end of the row, scaffolding surrounding its hull. It was finally starting to look like the vessel he remembered, sleek and glimmering like the day it had been commissioned. A crowd of Splinter mechanics had gathered to see it.

"Hey, there he is!" Mac exclaimed, climbing down the ladder. "Just in time to see us button up this baby of yours."

"She looks good," Kyle said.

"You know," Mac said, wiping sweat from his forehead, "I don't know why every ship needs to be a '*she*.' We should get a giant pair of testicles to hang off this thing's thrusters just to prove that it's a *man's* ship."

"If you can find a pair to put up there, I'm okay with it," Kyle said.

"Well, I've got the perfect mold, right here," Mac said, pointing into his crotch.

"I think you've been down here too long, Mac," Kyle said. "Jay, how you feeling?"

Jay's eyes were still a bit glassy from the trip to Raefflesia. The concussion he suffered during their mission hadn't surfaced until nearly three days after they returned, but it was severe enough for Kyle to attempt to heal it himself, though to no avail—another disconcerting sign that his powers were suddenly uncoordinated.

"Relieved," Jay said. "This thing has been a pain in the ass."

"Yeah, it must've been tough watching me work for the last couple days," Mac said.

"Fuck off, Mac," Jay replied. "You're the one that got me punched in the head a bunch of times."

Mac shrugged. "I guess I didn't think that through, did I?"

"Yeah, for a genius you're not all that bright, are ya?"

"Go ahead, light me up. I can take it."

"You did a great job," Kyle said. "But seriously, Jay, how's the head?"

"I'm good. Dr. Decker cleared me this morning," Jay replied. "Just in time to let him finish all this work."

"I think you slow-played me," Mac said.

"Oh, for fuck's sake, cut the shit and just fire the thing up," Kyle snapped. "I want to hear it."

Mac raised his eyebrows and ran into the *Gemini's* open hatch. A moment later the electromagnetic thrusters roared to life, rumbling off the high ceilings of the garage. Kyle nodded with satisfaction.

"Nice work," Kyle said.

"I know, right?" Mac responded. "It's got me chucking wood already."

"We all know it doesn't take much for that," Jay joked. "What do you say, Kyle?"

They both looked at their commander, but Kyle didn't answer. He just stared up at the ship blankly, his mind still a billion miles away.

"Kyle, where you at, buddy?" Mac asked finally. "I thought you'd be pumped to finally have the *Gemini* back up and running."

"I am, Mac," Kyle replied. "Just got a lot on my mind."

"Oh, c'mon, this is good news for us," Mac said. "Anything we're going to do, we gotta have this ship, right?"

"Yeah," Kyle muttered, trying to shake his apathy. "Why don't you two go get some rest. I'll come get you if anything comes up."

Mac quickly set his sights on a bottle of whiskey and a lounge chair. Jay decided he would stay and tune the engines a bit more since he had been on the sidelines for so long. The redhead tried to goad him into blowing it off, but in the end, the ship was as much his baby as it was Kyle's, and there was no convincing him otherwise. Mac shook his head and set off for the mess hall.

Kyle lingered there in a daze, his eyes still on his ship. It reminded him of a simpler time, when his life revolved around his orders, around the next mission in line. In a way he almost missed it. Things had become so convoluted since their arrival here. And now with a threat of a new, a somehow more powerful army looming over them, he felt like their time was running out.

Kyle rubbed his hand across his face. His head felt cloudy from lack of sleep. It was sapping his focus, just like Ellie said. He needed to talk to someone, or at least have someone listen while he ranted in hopes of something clicking. That's when he realized that his typical sounding board was walking out the door behind him. He spun around quickly and chased Mac down the corridor.

"Mac, hold on a second," Kyle said. "I need to talk to you for a minute."

"You gonna come have a few sips of the sacrament with me?" Mac asked.

Kyle's face remained stern. His lieutenant gave him a sideways look.

"This is gonna cut into my drinking time, isn't it?" he grumbled.

"It'll just take a minute. Come on."

Kyle took him out into an alcove in the courtyard, away from the garage and any curious ears. Mac looked around and turned his palms up.

"What's going on?" he asked. "Everything okay?"

"I just need to bounce a few things off you," Kyle replied. "I've been thinking about all these assault scenarios for weeks. And with this new intel you brought back, I'm afraid by the time I come up with an answer we'll be too late."

"Well, what are the options?"

"Honestly, Mac, nothing good. We don't have the resources to go to war with an army of Celestial soldiers. We just don't."

"There's gotta be a solution," Mac said. "What do we know?"

"Not enough," Kyle said. "We don't know where they are, we don't know how many there are. Hell, we don't even know if they exist yet."

"And we don't know what they'll be capable of," Mac mused.

"Right," Kyle continued. "Shit, why is this so hard…?"

"Maybe we do some recon."

Kyle shook his head. "Bryan's man in the Archives is dead."

"So we make some raids for better weaponry. Get some lightning suits or a few Sentinel armors…"

"We don't have the time to train the men here how to use them. We wouldn't be able to resupply them anyway."

"Well, fuck," Mac muttered. "Maybe there's a way we can stop the Gentry from making the Vicars in the first place?"

"That's what I've been trying to come up with. Everything I've thought of we either don't have the equipment or the personnel to realistically attempt. I'm starting to think we're in over our heads with all this."

"That's because we are."

"Wow, thanks," Kyle said. "You sure know how to build up a guy's confidence, you know that?"

"Is that why you wanted to talk to me? To boost your confidence?"

"What's wrong with that?"

"Kyle, you have *never* come to me looking for a shot of confidence," Mac replied. "If anything, I usually have to talk you out of something that's crazy."

Kyle huffed and raked his hand through his hair.

"What's really going on?" Mac asked.

Kyle glanced around, then back at his friend. "Look, I need to know if I'm reaching too far with this. I mean, am I looking at this from too far up? Can we really do this with what we have here?"

"You're starting to scare me, you know that, right?" Mac said.

"I'm serious, Mac," Kyle continued. "Am I asking too much of these people to go to war with us?"

"Maybe … or maybe not. I don't know."

"This isn't exactly the help I was looking for."

"Well, what do you want me to say?" Mac asked. "Can these people handle it? I don't know. We may not know until we get out there with them."

"I should have talked to Jackson. At least he would have lied to me."

"Let me finish. I can't tell you how they'll react in battle. I really can't. But what I can tell you is this: *this* is why they wanted you here. They want to do this. It gives them hope that they're not gonna be stuck in this god-forsaken canyon forever."

"That's what I needed to hear," Kyle said, the resolve returning to his voice.

"Seriously, I think you're just gonna have to be patient with them. I mean, it's not like we're gonna run out and try to kill the Gentry right now or anything."

Kyle's eyes widened. The words tumbled through his head. *Kill the Gentry*. It sounded so simple, so devious. The Dominion would never see it coming.

"Why can't we?" he asked.

"Why can't we what?" Mac asked back.

"Why can't we kill the Gentry?" Kyle replied.

Mac paused, his expression a mix of confusion and concern. "You're not really asking me that, are you?"

"Mac, you just said we could try to kill the Gentry," Kyle dreamed.

"No, I didn't," Mac refuted. "I said 'it's not like we're gonna *try* to kill the Gentry.' That's a pretty glaring difference."

At that point Kyle's ears were deaf. His mind was a million miles away, firing a billion thoughts a second.

"Mac, I think you're a genius," he said finally.

"Oh, no, no, no, you can't be thinking that's a good idea," Mac pleaded.

"It's not a good idea. It's an outstanding idea," Kyle said, his mind racing through the scenario. "I've gotta go."

Kyle got two steps away before Mac grabbed him by the shoulder.

"Whoa, buddy, I was just joking," Mac said. "This isn't something you should actually consider."

"Oh, I'm not considering it," Kyle replied. "This is what we're doing."

"Hold on a second," Mac said. "Five minutes ago you didn't even feel comfortable with a simple assault. Now you think it's a good idea to attempt an assassination on Aeron himself? How do you even turn around that quickly?"

"It's the best idea you've ever had," Kyle said. "Go get the others and meet me in Bryan's office."

"No way," Mac said. "Not until you start being reasonable."

"Fine, I'll go get them myself," Kyle said. He turned toward the exit.

"You're losing it, pal," Mac said. "This is crazy."

"Thanks for listening, Mac. It was a huge help," Kyle said. "I'll see you up there."

Mac opened his mouth to yell after him, but Kyle was already gone.

† † †

About ten minutes later Kyle pushed open the door to Bryan's office with Jay, Jackson, Mac, and Dan following him inside. Bryan and Brady were standing near a situation table on the left side of the room, and Dr. Preston was waiting near the window behind Bryan's desk.

"There he is," Bryan said, tapping Brady on the shoulder. "Commander, didn't think I'd hear from you today. What's so urgent?"

"I know what we can do to go after the Dominion," Kyle said.

"That's great news. What did you have in mind?"

Kyle grinned. "We're going to kill the Gentry."

The room went quiet. Mac rubbed his brow in frustration, shaking his head.

"I'm sorry, what?" Bryan asked.

"Aeron," Kyle repeated. "We're gonna kill him."

Bryan glanced at Brady and then at the others. "Commander, what the hell are you talking about?"

"The Gentry is our problem," Kyle said. "None of this changes unless we deal with him."

"Whoa, wait a minute. This is some kind of joke, right?" Brady asked. "You don't actually want to try and assassinate the most powerful being in the galaxy, do you?"

"I'm not going to *try* to do this," Kyle answered. "I'm *going* to do this."

"You're not kidding?" Brady asked again.

"No, Major, I'm not kidding," Kyle replied.

"Have you lost your fucking mind?" Brady demanded. "The Gentry is a god. We don't even know if he *can* be killed."

"I thought you didn't believe he was a god," Kyle said.

"Just because I don't worship him doesn't mean I don't think he's a god," Brady retorted.

"And just because the Dominion says he's invincible doesn't mean it's true," Kyle replied. "Jackson and I have seen him bleed."

"Yeah, actually that's true," Jackson said. "He cut himself on the metal that Kyle forged his sword out of. Bled like crazy too."

"What's your point, Commander?" Brady asked.

"The point is, if he can bleed, then we can kill him," Kyle said.

"Even if that's true, it's only one of our problems," Brady said. "We would still have to find a way to Dynasteria and get through the palace defenses just to have a shot at him."

"I honestly don't know what's going on in that head of yours. I really don't," Bryan said. "But you can't seriously expect us to try to assassinate the Gentry."

"I don't know why we're having such a hard time with this," Kyle said. "This was the line of shit they fed us for all those years, wasn't it? That the Council sent someone to try and kill him? That was it, correct? The gospel of his church. Well, all we're doing is making it real. Only this time, we're going to succeed."

"Kyle, I'm glad you're finding some enthusiasm, but we don't have time for these games," Bryan said. "We have to find a way to deal with this Vicar threat, and we have to do it in short order—"

"Don't you see? He can't create this army if he's dead. And we get to show everyone in the galaxy that he's not God." Kyle glared at Bryan, remembering their conversation outside the Infinity Compound. Bryan just rolled his eyes and looked away.

"God or not, you have to think about what you're asking of us right now," Brady said. "We barely have the resources to mount an offensive at all, let alone attempt an assault on the palace."

"You haven't even heard my plan yet…"

"They're assuming that you're making this more about your personal vendetta with the Gentry than about their cause," Preston interjected. "And I think they're right."

Kyle turned and scowled at his old mentor. "I'm not interested in what *you* think. I'm here to talk with them."

"Well, you had better get interested, because you're about to make a huge mistake," the doctor said.

"I've heard your objection," Kyle said. "Are you going to let me finish?"

"When are you going to stop being so stubborn?" Dr. Preston asked. "This is exactly what got you into this situation in the first place."

"What's worse, being stubborn or being a liar?"

"Liar?" Preston asked. "You're calling me a *liar*?"

"You heard me," Kyle sneered. "You were the Deputy Director of Intelligence. You were privy to every state secret on record. You knew about these Vicars, didn't you? You knew, and you didn't tell us."

Preston sighed. "It was for your own good. You're an amazing soldier, Kyle. But sometimes you have to see things from more than one angle."

"I think I'm seeing just fine now. And you know what, I don't remember asking for you to be here. I think maybe you should excuse yourself now."

The doctor pursed his lips. "Fine. Good luck, everyone. Try not to let his ego get you all killed."

Preston stormed out without another word, but he had said enough. Kyle had to pause for a moment to let the red wash from in front of his eyes. When it finally did, he looked up at a room of unconvinced expressions.

"I'm sorry," Kyle said. "I didn't want to go through that again."

"Kyle…," Bryan started cautiously, "he raises an important question. Are you just doing this out of a need for revenge?"

"Is that what you think?" Kyle asked.

"Right now I don't know what to think," Bryan replied.

"Do I want revenge for what they did to my family?" Kyle said. "You're damn right I do. But is that why I want to do this? No. No, I actually think we can do this. And I think it's exactly what we need to tip the scales in our favor."

"I don't know, Kyle, this is…this is way more than what I was expecting to take on," Bryan said.

"The hell with that," Brady said. "This is total lunacy."

"Major, that's enough," Bryan said. "Commander, you may have to give us some time to get our heads around this."

Kyle grit his teeth. "Fine. But I'm gonna tell you this: I'm not here asking for your permission. I'm going to do this with or without your help. So do yourselves a favor while you're thinking it over, and don't get in my way when I go."

Kyle stormed out, slamming the door open on his way. He was already halfway down the hallway by the time Jackson chased him down.

"Kyle, you've gotta give me a second here," Jackson pleaded. "C'mon, at least let me talk to you."

"You're not going to talk me out of this, Jacks," Kyle said.

"Yeah, well, I've known you long enough to have figured that out already," Jackson said. "But I've gotta tell you, this is way over the top, even for you."

"We can do this, Jacks," Kyle said. "I *know* we can do it."

"Kyle, even if I believed that, you gotta understand what this sounds like to Bryan and Brady. All they can hear is you wanting to rush off and attack the most fortified place in the galaxy."

"They don't want to hear anything," Kyle said. "All they want to do is stay here curled up in their shell."

"C'mon, you're not being fair."

"You can't tell me that," Kyle rumbled. "They brought us here to change things, and as soon as we try to do that, they want to stick their heads back in the sand."

"Well, look at what you're asking of them. This mission, what you're planning, it scares even me. These people have never done anything like this before. You've gotta cut them some slack."

"That's exactly what I've been doing," Kyle said. "We've been here for three months, and Mac and Jay are the only people that have even left the colony since we got here. They want to analyze and debate every option to no end. Well, I'm not waiting for them to sleep on it anymore."

"I think you're making a mistake," Jackson said. "Even if you're able to do this, you're still gonna need help."

"Commander, Captain, excuse me," Bryan said, hanging out the door to his office.

Kyle cleared his throat. "What is it, Bryan?"

"We'd like to talk to you," Bryan responded. "If you'll come back inside."

Kyle grumbled, but eventually nodded reluctantly and walked back into the office. Nobody had moved. Their faces still bore the same confusion and concern as when he walked out. But they were still there.

Bryan closed the door behind them and walked back to his desk. He shuffled a few things around aimlessly, then looked back at his nephew. Kyle could see that the burden of command was starting to wear on him. His eyes seemed heavier, his hair just a little more silver-streaked. For a moment Kyle almost pitied him, seeing the toll that this position was taking on his uncle. He finally considered the gravity that Bryan's decisions carried in this place. If he was swayed by emotion, or by the pleas of an overeager soldier, he could endanger every soul who called this colony home.

"Well, Commander," Bryan said, "I still think you're batshit crazy to even consider this, but if you've got a realistic plan, then we'll listen. I suppose we owe you at least that much, considering what you've already given up for us."

"Bryan, listen, we've been doing this together a long time," Kyle started, trying to be more reasonable, and more cordial. "You *know* me. I wouldn't suggest this unless I knew that we could make it happen."

Bryan nodded unconvincingly. "Tell us about your plan."

Kyle sighed and glanced around, then dove right in. "Getting to the capital will be just as difficult as once we're on it," he said. "They have a ring of orbiting defense stations around Dynasteria. Without clearance codes there's no way to get past them."

"And you have a solution for that?" Brady asked.

"Actually, the colony has the solution," Kyle replied. "The uranium reactor."

"The reactor?" Brady asked. "Commander, what are you talking about?"

"The same thing that got all those old ships decommissioned in the first place," Kyle said.

"You want to make it a bomb," Mac said.

Kyle nodded. "If we take a piece of the uranium core, we can weaponize it, and drop it right on one of those defense stations."

"Is that actually possible?" Bryan asked.

"Yeah, I think it would be," Mac said. "All we'd need is an explosive trigger. Some heavy hydrogen maybe, and we could probably find that in the subterranean water."

"What kind of yield are we talking about?" Bryan asked.

"It would be big," Mac said. "More than enough to take down one of those stations."

"And then we slip though during the panic," Kyle said.

"That could work," Jay added. "It would empty the palace yard and give us a chance to get inside."

"Hold on a second," Brady said. "Wouldn't they lock down the palace?"

"Yeah, they would," Kyle said. "Protocol is for nonessential personnel to clear out and aid in the fallout. They would count on the palace defense systems to secure the compound."

"So how the hell are we supposed to get by those?" Brady asked.

"Who do you think designed those systems, Major?" Kyle said, looking over at Mac.

"Yeah, I *did* design them," Mac said, shaking his head, "but I guarantee they've replaced those systems by now."

"The systems might have been replaced," Kyle noted, "but I doubt their power supply has been."

Mac's eyes lit up. "Oh! Now you're really thinking."

"Thinking what?" Brady asked. "What are we missing?"

"The palace defenses aren't powered by an onsite generator," Mac said. "They channel geothermal energy from about fifteen miles to the east. It's why the whole palace is surrounded by forest and not by priceless high-rises. If we can interrupt the power supply, the automated defenses would go dead."

"How many men would still be on site?" Bryan asked.

"Four, maybe five hundred," Kyle answered.

"Five hundred?" Brady exclaimed. "And that's with it cleared out?"

"I said it was doable," Kyle noted. "I never said it would be easy."

"No, this is fucking brilliant though," Mac exclaimed. "That power supply also runs to the communications systems. If we can set up another distraction on one side of the palace, we could slip right in the back without anyone even noticing."

"Lieutenant, you seemed less excited about this scenario ten minutes ago than any of us," Brady said. "You've changed your mind this quickly?"

"Yeah, well, as crazy as this sounds, this actually sounds like a legitimate plan," Mac said. "We can do this."

All eyes turned toward Bryan, whose expression was stoic. He stroked his graying beard and stared off beyond the group.

"You really think you can kill him, Kyle?" Bryan asked.

"He's not invincible, and I think he knows it," Kyle said. "Why else would he have tried so hard to kill us?"

"What else would you need?" Bryan asked.

"Sir?" Brady interrupted. "Are you actually considering this?"

"It doesn't hurt us to consider it, Major," Bryan said. "If it turns out not to be a plausible scenario, then we don't move forward."

"Sir, I want to caution you not to make this decision just to appease the commander," Brady said. He looked at Kyle. "I mean no disrespect to you, Commander Griffin, but this is exactly why we are so cautious with our decisions."

"Your objection is noted, Major," Bryan said. "But I'd like to explore this. It would be, like the commander said, just what we brought him here for." He turned back to his nephew. "What would you need to make this happen?"

"I need whatever guys you have working on the reactor to help Mac build this bomb," Kyle said. "We'll want the ship that Jay and Mac brought back from Raefflesia. It's unregistered and off the grid. We can retrofit it with a few armaments."

"What were you thinking for manpower?" Bryan asked.

"I'll need all my guys and maybe a half dozen of the strongest recruits from the doctor's program. Two six-man teams would be ideal. One to take out the power supply and set some charges for a distraction, and one to enter the palace."

"I would want the major to accompany you," Bryan said.

"Wouldn't dream of doing this without him," Kyle nodded.

"Sir, I want to make my concerns very clear," Brady said. "We have never done anything like this before. It could end very poorly for us."

"Just like with every mission," Kyle said. "But I think you know this is the opportunity you've always wanted. A chance to really hurt them."

Brady sighed. "You're certain you can do this?"

"Absolutely," Kyle said.

Brady swallowed hard, then nodded.

Chapter 21

Mac felt a line of sweat trickling down his forehead as he followed the reactor technicians inside the core vessel. It tickled maddeningly as it dribbled over the tip of his nose, and he found himself hitting his fingertips against the visor of the radiation suit he was wearing. He shook his head and puffed a breath out of his nostrils, spraying a ribbon of perspiration across the inside of his helmet. The heat of the reactor was even worse than he had expected.

The whole thing looked like it had crash-landed into the side of the canyon, with the metal of the reactor having melted into the iron ore surrounding it. There were three separate shielding doors along the tunnel from the military compound into the cavern where the reactor had been established. Mac had looked over the saturation numbers earlier, and even he, with his minimal experience with an ancient power source like nuclear energy, felt like the third door and the nearly mile and a half of winding tunnels was overkill to contain the yield of radiation. It made him think that there were no real calculations done in designing the unit, and that they simply threw the containment together and decided it would be enough. Suddenly, any comfort the suit had given him went up in smoke.

"The uranium is in the cylinders in the center," one of the techs said. "We've got a graphite moderator in some lead containers in the corner. How much did you figure to need?"

"At least two hundred pounds," Mac replied.

"Each one of the rods is about twenty-eight pounds. Can you work with a little overflow?"

"Yeah, I'll just have to make some recalculations. That'll be easier than altering the uranium pieces."

"We'll start pulling the rods out for you," the second tech said.

"I appreciate it," Mac said. "And the two engineers will have a work station set up for us?"

"Yes, sir," the first tech answered.

"Do you retain any of the depleted uranium?" Mac asked.

"Yes, sir, we have another storage vessel a little deeper into the mountain."

"I'll need an equal ratio of that material as well."

"We can do that, sir," the tech said.

The second technician started to work on the cylinders, but the other lingered near Mac for a moment. He was about Mac's height, but heavier, with a round face and pink cheeks. The two of them were the military liaisons to the reactor staff, both sergeants, and obviously a long time removed from active duty. They were supposedly the only two with a background in the management of hazardous materials, though Mac would later learn that their prior experience was with engine degreasers and other cleansers. However, they were also the only two soldiers who had volunteered for the detail.

"Pardon me for asking, sir, but what do you need this stuff for?" the technician asked. "We don't get a lot of requests to take this material out of the reactor."

"I'm afraid I can't tell you that, Sergeant," Mac said. "We've got that whole classified thing going on."

"Well, this is a pretty good chunk of our uranium reserves. This was supposed to last us for the next two years."

"Where do you mine this from anyway?"

"There's a deposit on Englestad a little closer to the system's interior," the tech said. "We've got a small mining station there, but it takes us a lot of time to refine this into usable fuel. We'll be short before we can replace this."

"Well, I apologize for that, Sergeant, but we've gotta have it," Mac replied. "They'll just have to manage."

There was a knock on the vessel's containment hatch. Mac saw one of the non-military technicians waving to him from the small window panel in the door. He excused himself and climbed out of the narrow opening, the heat of the radiation dropping drastically as they closed the hatch behind him. The middle-aged woman behind the shield was small, and the long sleeves of the oversized suit hung off her arms like curtains.

"Lieutenant McArthur, we just got a call from the major that you're needed upstairs," she said through the fog on her radiation suit. "Something about a briefing."

"Okay, thank you," Mac said. "Will you have your men notify me when everything is ready?"

"I'll let them know, Lieutenant," the tech said.

Mac nodded and followed the long winding tunnel back to the entrance of the military compound. He stepped into an airlock and shed the radiation suit, then was blasted with a deionizing vacuum. The process was loud and jarring, leaving his ears ringing and his red hair standing on end. He wiped the beading sweat from his neck and forehead, then made his way back to Bryan's office.

Kyle and Jackson were waiting outside. Both were in dark grey fatigues that barely fit over their shoulders, even though the waists were baggy above their hips. Jackson was giving Kyle a rundown of the chosen recruits from Doctor Preston's program as Mac joined them. Kyle's expression looked labored, though he seemed to be doing his best to hide it. It was difficult for Mac to see such physical exhaustion overwhelming his usually powerful commander. He wondered for a moment if that sympathy was for Kyle's benefit or his own.

"How we doing, boys?" Mac asked.

"Good so far," Kyle said. "Just getting one last scouting report on the new guys."

"And girl," Jackson added.

"*Girl*?" Mac asked. "Seriously?"

"Her name's Jenna, and she was one of the top candidates," Jackson insisted. "So yeah, she's coming with us."

"Easy, killer, I was just asking," Mac said. "You got a thing for her, or what?"

"Keep it down," Kyle said. "They're inside."

"Oh, sorry, didn't mean to give you away there, Jacks," Mac said in a half-whisper.

"How are things down in the reactor?" Kyle asked.

"They're going. We should have plenty to get this thing rolling."

"Good," Kyle said.

He motioned them inside. Jay and Dan were talking with Mitchell and Logan, the former Infinity recruits, on one side of the situation table. They were both relatively young, in their late twenties, but seemed older based on their firm expressions. Mitchell Hughes was dark-haired and top-heavy, while Logan Helm was thin and fair, with dimpled cheeks and a high hairline. Each of them wore sergeants' stripes, as well as the shaped spears that indicated their time in recon duty. Both were good soldiers as Mac remembered, but they never quite lived up to Dr. Preston's expectations. Of course, there were days when Mac wondered how anybody other than Kyle ever had.

The woman, Jenna Emerson, was standing along the wall with the other three Splinter soldiers. Mac could immediately see why Jackson had been so defensive. She was tall and exotic, with supple olive skin and jet-black hair that made her green eyes glow. Mac had to force his gaze back to the rest of the group as she caught his stare. He cleared his throat, trying to appear uninterested, but by then it was a bit late. He noticed an aviation badge as well as a snipers' insignia on her fatigues while he was looking, which was a surprise. Women rarely were admitted as pilots in the Dominion, but here they apparently didn't have the luxury of being so selective. But even despite that, he didn't know many soldiers that were versed in both marksmanship and piloting in *either* military. This woman wasn't just stunning, she was a bad ass as well.

He didn't recognize any of the others after spending most of the last two months in the garage with the *Gemini*. Physically, they were less than imposing—Jenna was the tallest by several inches. Mac went over to introduce himself. The first, Thomas Jamison, was easily into his mid-forties. He had a hardened jawline and shaved head, but his slumped shoulders and rounded back likely made him weak in the upper body and would make his aim drift low. The other two, Brett and Cullen Candless, were already veterans of their food raid team by their early twenties. The two of them were identical twins, though at some point Cullen had acquired a long scar across his scalp, making the two of them quite distinguishable. The injury happened when a blast door closed on him during a raid on an agricultural plant several years ago. Brett had lost the last three fingers on his left hand trying to pull him to safety.

Kyle pulled up a video mockup of the palace grounds that Dan had put together. "Now that you've all had a chance to meet, we've got plenty to go over," he said. "By now everyone's been informed of what the objective of this mission is. You've had time to think about it, so if there's anyone here that is uncertain of this operation or its objective, this is your last chance to step aside."

The room was quiet as Kyle paused. Mac kept an eye on the Splinter soldiers during the hush. They seemed calm despite Kyle's ominous tone.

"Very well, we'll go on then," Kyle said. "Our entry into Dynasteria's atmosphere is contingent upon an initial assault on one of these satellite defense stations." He pointed to the orbiting compounds. "Jay, have we isolated one as a target at this point?"

"Well, there's one almost directly over the palace, but we think we should target the one just to the east," Jay replied. "The Stratys that we're using doesn't have the same caliber heat shields that the *Gemini* does, so we'll have to take a more tapered angle of entry. If we take out this station, we can still come in above the forest surrounding the palace at an appropriate altitude."

"Good, we'll have you get those coordinates to Mac so he can use them for the targeting systems," Kyle said. "Mac, tell us about the bomb."

"Yeah, we're using an implosion-type device that should increase the efficiency of the uranium," Mac said. "We'll also use a depleted uranium tamper that should up the yield a little."

"What kind of power are we looking at here?" Jackson asked.

"It should be about four to five hundred kilotons," Mac replied. "I need to keep it under one megaton at the most."

"What's the point of that?" Brady asked.

"We want to cripple the station, not completely destroy it," Mac said. "If we blow it to smithereens, they'll have no reason to send troops from the palace or the surrounding boroughs. We need it to help empty the palace yard."

"So how do we deliver the package?" Jenna asked.

"The bomb will be mounted on a combustion rocket that we'll drop from the Stratys after coming out of hyperspace," Mac said. "We'll be retrofitting the ship to release the rocket from the base of the hull."

"Are we still planning on using a halo drop to reach the palace yard?" Brady asked.

"We are, but we don't want to come down in the yard," Kyle said. "We need time to disable the power to the defense armaments and their communication systems. Our target will be in the trees to the east of the compound."

"Once on the ground we're splitting up into two six-person teams," Jackson added. "Dan, Mac, Jenna, and the twins will come with me to handle the power supply. Jay, Thomas, Logan,

Mitchell, and the major will accompany Kyle to the west courtyards for entry into the palace."

"What kind of resistance can we expect once we're inside the perimeter?" Logan asked.

"There could be as many as a few hundred troops still on site even after the bomb is detonated," Kyle replied. "The west entrance is a multi-tiered courtyard mostly for tourists, so it should have the lowest concentration of men."

Kyle pointed to a spot to the left of the main entrance, away from the grandiose staircase and towering pillars. There was a small door tucked among the crevasses of the structure.

"This will be our target point of entry," Kyle said. "It leads into the utility catacombs underneath the primary structure. There may be more troops in the tunnels, but the narrow passages will bottleneck them. It'll even out those numbers pretty effectively."

"All right, so let's say we get onto the planet," Thomas said, his voice as gruff as his expression. "And we manage to kill the power to the defenses—"

"And their communications," Mac added.

"Right, the communications," Thomas conceded. "Say we do all that. And we get into the palace, and past the hundreds of guards waiting for us—"

"Without getting seen by any of the cameras," Jackson interrupted.

"Cameras?" Brady asked.

"Yeah, I forgot about those," Kyle said. "They're on a separate circuit with a different power supply."

"Yeah, of course they are," Thomas continued. "Forget any more surprises. Say we get through all of that shit. How in the hell are we supposed to actually kill the Gentry?"

"With these," Kyle said, pulling an eight-inch-long clip from a pocket in his pants. "These are projectile sabre rounds that Lieutenant McArthur developed a few years back. They're a carboranium alloy laced with the remnants of the same starmetal that my war sword was forged out of."

"And you're certain that these things can kill him?" Thomas asked.

"I'm confident that they can," Kyle said. "I think that's why the weapons secretary decommissioned them. The Dominion didn't want these out in the world."

"You'll each be issued a separate firearm for these clips," Jackson added. "We have barely enough of them for everyone, and there's only fifty rounds in each, so don't waste them. Only use them if you have a shot at Aeron."

"So, I've got a question," Dan started. "After we've done all this, what's our exit strategy? Or is this a suicide mission?"

"We'll have a secondary ship follow us through our hyperjump and touch down in this clearing in the northwest corner of the surrounding woods," Kyle said. He gestured to a small vacancy on the projected map nearly three miles from the perimeter of the palace yard. It was down a long slope and across a small ravine, but was the only opening in the surrounding trees for a transport to set down. "Our emergency option would be to requisition a vehicle from the tarmac on the north side of the palace and use it to make our way to a safe point for a hyperjump."

Mac scratched his scalp, knowing that neither of those choices were ideal. In fact they were downright damning. He glanced around at the rest of the group, half of whom were shaking their heads.

"That's it?" Thomas asked. "That's how we're getting home?"

"Those are our options, yeah," Kyle said.

"What are the odds we're able to get either of those to work without getting blown out of the sky?" Thomas demanded.

"Look, we are going into this mission, with the very real possibility that we will not make it home," Kyle said, his tone lowering. "Like I said earlier, if you have reservations about that, now is the time to back away. Because right now we have no time for doubt."

Kyle paused halfway through his thought, taking a deep breath as though he was trying to stifle another emotional outburst.

"I understand that this doesn't sound easy," Kyle started. "And I know that you'd be making a huge leap of faith following me into this. It's a scary thought that some of us may never see this place again. Maybe none of us will. I wish I could guarantee that we'll all come back, but I can't do that. What I can guarantee, whether we succeed or not, is that by the end of this mission the Dominion will know that we are still here."

Thomas nodded, his objections disappearing with the rest of the room. Mac looked up at his commander. He was so strong, even while hiding his fatigue, Mac suddenly remembered why he had so often charged into raging infernos with insurmountable odds with no regard for life or limb. He remembered that Kyle made it all seem possible.

"All right," Kyle said. "We leave in three days. You've each got your preflight assignments. We'll check in again tomorrow."

Mac gave a quick wink to Jenna as the room cleared out, unable to help himself. She leaned her shoulder into him when she went by, knocking him off balance. Mac chuckled as he stumbled backward, his boots squeaking against the tile floor. He watched her walk out, though she never turned to look back at him.

"She's out of your league," Kyle said.

"Yeah, I can see that," Mac responded. "At least she's not taller than me, though."

"What are you still doing here? You've got more to do than anybody."

"I just wanted to congratulate you on your speech. It was very 'rah, rah.' A good touch before we drag them off into oblivion."

"Fuck off, Mac," Kyle said. "What do you really want?"

"You're very keen, boss," Mac replied. "But I think you know that."

"Mac, either tell me what you want, or I'm outta here."

"You're not sleeping much, are you? You look like you're barely keeping yourself upright. Have you slept at all since we got here?"

"Is that what this is about?" Kyle asked. "You're worried about what I'm doing at night?"

"You know exactly what I'm worried about," Mac said. "You're running on fumes, buddy. How the hell do you expect to stack up against Aeron when you can barely keep your eyes open?"

"Mac, I'm fine."

"C'mon, Kyle, you and I both know that's not true," Mac said. "You're lying to yourself if that's what you believe."

"I don't need to be listening to this right now," Kyle said, trying to brush past his lieutenant.

Mac grabbed Kyle's elbow, his fingers barely making it halfway around his commander's hulking arm.

"I think you *do* need to listen to this," Mac said. "You asked me earlier if we could really go to war with these people. Now I didn't feel great about it then, but the only reason I had any hope at all was because *you* were on our side. But if you can't even stand up, that doesn't leave us with much hope now, does it?"

Kyle pulled his arm out of Mac's hand and walked to the door.

"Fine, leave!" Mac hollered. "But if you walk out that door, you're gonna be doing this without me. And without your bomb."

Kyle stopped in his tracks. He turned back into the room but didn't say a word. His shoulders slumped. Mac shook his head once, his mouth tightly squeezed shut. He braced himself for his commander's ire, knowing that Kyle's thirst for vengeance was scalding a hole in the back of his mind. He had seen people step between Kyle and his goal before. It never ended well. But after a moment Kyle took a deep breath, and his angst slowly dissipated.

"I'm being stubborn again, aren't I?" he said.

"You said it, not me," Mac said.

"To be honest, Mac, sleep scares me right now. Every time I fall asleep … all I can see is my mother dying. And I can't save her."

"This isn't about saving her anymore. This is about avenging her. And only *you* can do that."

Kyle nodded, Mac's words seeming to strike him right between the eyes. "Why don't you get back to work, Mac? I'm gonna try to get some rest."

"Hey, you're the one slowing me up," Mac said with a wry grin.

Kyle chuckled. "You're an asshole, you know that?"

"It's been mentioned once or twice. Go on. I'll let you know if we need you."

And then Kyle was gone. Mac lingered in the hall just long enough to watch him skulk away.

CHAPTER 22

The light valley breeze swept across Kyle's face as he sauntered down the gentle slope of the river basin near Marcus and Becca's home. The grass was cool and damp from the morning dew, and the sun was only an hour or so above the east horizon. The air was crisp and smelled of flowers and fresh herbs from the gardens below. From there he could see his parents' home just as he remembered it, tall and groomed among a sea of green and trees. It looked so calm, so pristine, like the day it was built.

As he walked along the basin floor, he could see his mother milling about her garden in the front lawn. An old straw hat shaded her slim face, and she was wearing the same ratty work gloves she had been using since he was little boy. She seemed so peaceful, it gave him a wave of goosebumps down his back. His pace quickened without a thought. She was so close. He wanted to grab her and drag her away, but he couldn't remember why. All he knew was that he needed to get there. And get there fast.

He broke into a sprint, but his legs felt heavy. With every step she seemed further away, no matter how hard he ran. He screamed for her with all the air in his lungs, but the sound barely made a whisper. Still she casually glanced in his direction, and waved with a glowing smile as he strained to move faster.

Suddenly the morning sky darkened behind her. The yellow sun disappeared behind a sweltering black and red cloud. It crackled and thundered with an elemental energy, but Becca seemed wholly unaware. Her eyes remained fixed her son, still smiling, and she reached out her hand. The crown of Aeron rose from the cloud, his red eyes searing the air. He towered some thirty feet over the top of the roof, each step of his armored boots shaking the ground like an earthquake. Becca still never saw him.

Kyle wailed hysterically, churning his mutant legs as hard as he could. The ground went soft and his feet sunk into a swamp of tar. He started sinking, the black ooze swallowing his legs and waist with each thrust of his body. He scratched and clawed at the swelling ground in front of him, but his arms were smothered by the melting world.

Aeron's eyes blazed, and a wave of fire swept over the landscape. Becca was still reaching for her son, still yearning for him to save her, when she was consumed by the rushing inferno. Kyle saw her turn to dust and heard the Gentry's deafening laugh ...

† † †

His eyes snapped open and he shot up in bed. The same freezing sweat coated his neck and chest as every other night. He choked down several ragged breaths, trying to calm his pounding heart. For the last week it had been the same dream that had tortured him. No matter how hard he struggled, no matter how desperately he screamed, he could never get close enough to save her. And every morning he had to beg his mother's forgiveness for his failure.

He looked over at the clock and realized that he had been asleep for nearly six hours. That was nearly twice as much as he'd gotten in the two previous weeks combined. His eyes seemed clearer, his ears sharper. He spun around and slipped his feet onto the floor, his legs finally feeling strong beneath him. With each breath he felt his former vigor return, fading the nightmare into the depths of his mind.

There was an urgent rapping on his door. It was Mac's voice outside, but it was so rushed that Kyle couldn't make out what he was saying. He stood up from the bed and pulled on a shirt before opening the door.

"Mac, what the hell?" Kyle said. "It's the middle of the night. You're gonna wake up everyone on the floor."

"Yeah, sorry, Kyle, I just couldn't wait. I had to talk to you right away."

"What is it?" Kyle demanded. "What's happened?"

"It's your dad," Mac said. "He's awake."

† † †

Just a few moments later Kyle hurried into the hospital wing. Ellie was just coming down the hall from Marcus's room, carrying a case of medications. She gave Kyle a relieved look as he stopped in front of her. She looked tired, as though she had already been there all night.

"How is he?" Kyle asked. "Has he said anything? Is he all right?"

"He's okay," Ellie said, her voice exhausted and dulled. "He woke up about an hour ago."

"An hour? Why didn't anyone come get me?"

"I'm sorry, Kyle, we wanted to send someone, but he had a very … unsettling reaction to the situation."

"What happened?" Kyle asked.

"He woke up and didn't know where he was. We had to restrain him for a moment, and I gave him a light sedative."

"You gave a man coming out of a coma a sedative?" Kyle demanded. "Couldn't that kill him?"

"If I didn't give it to him, it might have killed him," Ellie said. "His heart rate was through the roof. He's still so weak, he could have had a heart attack."

Kyle swallowed hard, looking down toward his father's room. "Is he still awake? Can I see him?"

"He's fine now, Kyle. The sedative did what I wanted it to. He's awake, but I've got to warn you before you go in there, he's very upset."

"Thank you, Ellie," Kyle said. "I'm sorry."

"It's fine. He's your father. Of course you'd be worried."

Kyle winced as Ellie walked away, still ashamed of how he had handled some of their previous encounters.

"Ellie, wait one second."

Her expression was solemn as she turned back. Kyle felt like she could see right through him, and it made him feel vulnerable. It was an awkward sensation, but one that wasn't entirely unwelcome.

"I want you to know that I really do appreciate everything you've done," he said. "I'll talk to you soon."

Her smooth lips curled into a slight grin. Kyle couldn't decide whether she was angry, disappointed, or simply exhausted.

The door to Marcus's room was cracked open just a bit. Kyle could see his father through the slim opening, his head arched backward over the pillow on the reclining bed. His chest shivered with each broken breath, a tortured scowl inscribed on his face.

Kyle felt a pit brewing in his stomach. It was not often that he was truly frightened, but he was terrified of what loomed. He didn't even know if his father realized that his wife was dead.

Kyle pushed the door open with a squeal of the aging hinges. The lights were on, but their pale glow was barely able to reach the floor from the ceiling. Despite that, Kyle could see the trails of dried tears stretching across his father's ashen face.

"Dad...," Kyle said meekly. *Get it together. This is your father. Be a man and talk to him.*

Marcus's head craned to his left. His eyes were veined with red, his cheeks thin from IV nutrition. He looked like a man whose whole life had been taken away.

"Kyle," Marcus moaned, his voice swimming through Ellie's sedative. "Where have you been?"

"I've been here, Dad," Kyle said, pulling a chair next to his father's bed. "I'm here now."

Marcus let out a labored sigh. "Son, I've been dreaming. Do you … do you still have dreams?"

"More than I care to remember."

"I was watching you play in the sand. Do you remember the trip we took to the Sierra system? Those beautiful white beaches. You couldn't have been more than seven years old."

"Yeah, I was six," Kyle said. "You and Mom rented that ridiculous skimmer that broke down like a mile out on the water."

Marcus chuckled. "That's right. How do you remember those things?"

"I don't know, Dad," Kyle answered. "It was a good trip. It's tough to forget."

"You cried for almost an hour. Nothing we did could calm you down."

"I didn't like sitting still. I guess I still don't."

"Your mother was so calm with you. I don't know how she did it. I was so … uncomfortable."

"You seemed to handle it pretty well to me, Dad," Kyle said.

"Well, it never mattered," Marcus noted. "Eventually you waved your hand at the engine, and it came back to life. Took us right back to shore. First time I ever saw you use your powers. It was amazing."

Marcus started coughing, softly at first and then more violently. He groaned after each fit, his eyes watering as he tried to catch his breath. Kyle poured him a glass of water, and Marcus was able to choke down the spasm after a few sips.

"You okay?" Kyle asked.

"I think so."

"What made you think about that, Dad?" Kyle asked.

"It was your mother," Marcus said. "I was thinking about her."

Kyle paused for a moment, considering his words carefully. "Dad, how much do you remember about what happened?"

Marcus didn't acknowledge his son's question. His mind was clearly someplace else.

"When I first met her, she seemed too good to be true," Marcus said. "Now I know that she was."

"Dad—"

"Don't try to defend her!" Marcus barked. "General Donovan told me what she did."

"He *told* you?" Kyle asked. "What did he say?"

"He told me that she was a Splinter spy. That she was a traitor."

"And you believed him? Just like that?"

"It's true, isn't it?"

"That's not the point, Dad. She was your wife, and Vaughn tried to kill you."

"He had no choice. But your mother…she used me," Marcus growled. "I thought she was the one person that didn't look at me like a pawn. But she was worse than anyone."

"What are you saying? You can't believe that."

"Everything she ever said to me was a lie. Nothing about her was real. She got what was coming to her."

Kyle was caught breathless. "You don't believe that."

Marcus fumed and crossed his arms but didn't respond. Kyle could barely believe what he had heard. His father had always been so calm, so rational. It was like hearing a different person speaking from inside his father's body.

"Dad, the whole reason we're here is because of what they did to her, what they tried to do to all of us. They almost killed you. How can you still be siding with them?"

"Son, listen to me. We cannot trust these people," Marcus said. "You have to get us out of here."

"Dad, no. I can't do that."

"Kyle, just us being here … it's treason."

"None of that matters anymore, Dad," Kyle replied. "I know this must be really hard, but just let me try and explain what happened—"

"It *does* matter. What you're doing here isn't just a crime, it's blasphemy."

"I don't think you understand what the Gentry has done. He's not what he's made himself out to be."

"I know about the Council," Marcus said. "I know about the miners. And I've known about a thousand others since then. I'm not as oblivious as you think I am."

Kyle's eyes narrowed.

"You knew?" he gasped. "What do you mean *you knew*? How could you have possibly known?"

"I was the Gentry's son. It was going to be my task to ensure his continued rule, by any means necessary. After me, it was going to fall to you. But I was never strong enough. And you, well, you were just too righteous. That's when the Gentry turned to Donovan."

"I don't believe this. All this time, you knew about what he had done. And you let it all happen?" Kyle's face grew hot, even in the cold of the room. "How do you live with yourself?"

"Because it was the Gentry's will!" Marcus shouted. "Only he knows what is right for his galaxy."

"My god, listen to yourself. You're as much to blame for all this as Mom was."

"Don't you do that," Marcus seethed. "Don't you do it. Don't try to compare me to that traitorous whore!"

Kyle erupted out of his seat. The chair toppled over, a loud crash ringing through the hospital. His hulking shoulders cast a shadow over his father like a mountain shading a valley. His fists were clenched white and his jaw clamped shut. Marcus looked as feeble as ever as he shirked from his powerful son's glare. For a moment Kyle felt his control slip, and he could almost see himself ripping his father to shreds.

Then the door creaked open.

"Kyle," Ellie's voice called from the doorway. "Is everything all right?"

Kyle's anger dulled. He took in a deep gulp of air, and let his hands relax.

"I can't listen to this anymore," he said. He turned and walked to the door. "Ellie, will you make sure some security is posted in this room? I believe that my father is a danger to himself right now."

Ellie nodded and Kyle stepped out into the hall. Behind him he could hear his father's wails, some of them discernible, others seeming to be only tattered screams.

"Don't you do this, Kyle! Don't you defy the Gentry! It will be the end of you! The *end*! Do you hear me?"

Kyle ignored the rants, the taunts as best he could. He started down the hall, and made it all the way to the elevator doors before Ellie caught up with him. She looked perplexed, but there was a real concern behind her curious stare.

"Kyle, what's going on?"

"I think he needs to be watched right now. That's all I can tell you."

The doors to the elevator opened, and Kyle stepped inside. He wanted to get out of there, to get far away from his father's screams, but the doors seemed to take forever to close. When they finally did, Ellie stuck her hand in and stopped them from taking him away.

"Kyle, hold on a second. I can hear what he's saying. Pretty soon somebody else will hear him too. Eventually they'll come and take him away."

"No, they won't, Ellie," Kyle shook his head.

"To them he'll just be another security risk," Ellie pressed. "I've seen it happen before."

Kyle paused. She was right, and he knew she was. As angry as Marcus had made him, he was still his father, and some of the only family he had left.

"Can you keep him sedated for me, Ellie?" he asked. "Keep him quiet?"

"I don't know, Kyle. Is he really dangerous? I could get in a lot of trouble ..."

"He's not dangerous. He's my father."

Ellie sighed. Her eyes were locked on him, searching for reassurance that she should help him. Then the elevator door tried to close again and seemed to break her trance. Kyle reached forward and held it open.

"Please, Ellie," he pleaded. "I can't let them take him."

Ellie's gaze softened. "All right. I'll do what I can."

"Thank you," Kyle said. "Thank you."

Ellie stepped aside and the elevator doors slid closed. He realized as they shut that he had no idea where he was going. His thoughts seemed cloudy, and he could still hear his father screaming even through the doors. Without thinking he hit the button for the roof, hoping the crisp canyon air would clear his head.

The gate slid open and he followed the short stairs up to the roof. The door to outside was already wedged open, and he realized that he apparently wasn't the only one who needed some time to himself. But he was surprised to see Angel. She turned to look at him, and her smile faded. She pulled a ribbon of hair away from her face and tucked it behind her ear, then gave Kyle a forced smile, one with no joy in it at all.

Kyle felt that awkward feeling creep back over him. However, he couldn't help but feel overwhelmed by how stunning she looked. She had curled her auburn hair, and was wearing a slim-fitting pair of pants with a short, rib-length jacket. It didn't hide her tapered waist in the least, instead highlighting her sensuous curves and taut stomach. He could smell some kind of floral perfume from the doorway, and her lips shimmered with a bright red gloss.

"Angel, what are you doing up here?" he asked.

"I'm…um…just getting a little air," she replied, again tucking her hair behind her ear. "Why, am I not allowed up here?"

"No, that's not it," Kyle backtracked. "I've just never seen you up here before. I wasn't expecting to see you."

"It gets pretty stuffy being inside all day long."

"Right …" Kyle trailed off, soaking in a long look at her. "You … you look fantastic. Were you…were you waiting for someone…?"

She laughed. "No…just looking for some fresh air. But I didn't realize it was so cold up here."

"Well, it's still early yet, but it can get pretty chilly once the light passes. In a few hours it'll be well below freezing."

Angel glanced back at the door behind him. "So, what are you doing up here?" she asked.

"I just come up here to get away from things for a bit," Kyle replied, glancing at the crest of the canyon. He knew he should go. He was still far too angry and nothing about their interactions lately had been cordial. But looking at her, he couldn't drag himself away. "Gives me a chance to…to clear my head."

"Sounds like you come up here a lot," Angel observed.

"I guess I do," Kyle said. "Most nights, actually. I haven't been sleeping well. Usually I'll climb up to the top of the canyon. Gives me a little bit more perspective."

"I can go, if you'd like to be alone," Angel offered. "I've been here a while already."

"No … no, it's okay," Kyle said. "To be honest, I think I'd rather have the company."

Angel gave him another half-smile and turned to look out over the cement railing. Kyle nestled up next to her, his elbow grazing hers. She flinched just enough for him to notice and moved her arm away. Kyle looked down for a moment at the sudden space between them, then shifted his eyes out to the lights of the colony beyond the compound walls.

"So what brings you out here tonight?" Angel asked. "Still can't sleep?"

"It's my father," Kyle answered. "He woke up this afternoon."

"Oh my God!" Angel exclaimed, her tone suddenly much more involved. "That's great news. How is he?"

Kyle shook his head. "He's not handling this very well. He does not want to be here."

"Well, it's gotta be hard on him. Having lost his wife, then waking up here without any idea about what happened. I can't even imagine."

Kyle sighed and wiped across his brow, his father's screams about the Gentry still echoing in his head.

"I'm sorry, Angel, I … I don't think I can talk about it too much," he muttered, looking for a way to change the subject. "How have you been?"

"I've been okay, I guess."

Kyle laughed. "That's all you've got?"

"Well, what did you want me to say?"

"I don't know, maybe something about how you're settling in, how you've been keeping busy. Maybe some of the people you've met?"

Angel glanced over at the door again. "I haven't really talked to many people."

"I find that hard to believe. Being social seems so easy for you."

"Not anymore," Angel replied. "Not for a while now."

Kyle cringed, realizing he had stumbled back onto a sore subject. "Angel, listen, I've got to apologize for everything that's happened. The last thing I wanted was to drag you into all of this—"

"Kyle, please, let's not do this again," Angel groaned. "Can't we just have a normal conversation?"

"That would be a nice change, I guess. Actually, you know what I did think of the other day? The time you broke my nose during that snowball fight when we were kids. Do you remember that?"

"Oh God, what made you think of that?" Angel asked.

"I don't know, it was just something that crossed my mind. We told my dad that I had slipped out of a tree because he didn't want us throwing snowballs."

"And he didn't believe that for a second. Definitely wasn't my proudest moment."

"I don't know, I had to laugh about it a little bit when I thought about it," Kyle said. "There's probably plenty of people who wish they could say they've broken my nose."

"I suppose if that's the worst thing you remember about me, that's not so bad."

"I never said that was the worst. I still remember the day you lost your father's officer's ring."

Angel was silent for a moment. "How do you know about that?"

"Oh, I'll never forget it," Kyle said. "It was the first day we met."

"I never told you about that. I never told *anyone* about that. How did you find out?"

"Well, I kinda saw the whole thing happen."

"*What*?" Angel exclaimed. "You better explain."

"It wasn't long after I was brought to the program. We were ten years old. I saw you running down the hall of the dormitories, wearing a bunch of your mom's clothes and jewelry. You were even clopping around in a pair of her shoes. I remember they were blue."

"How do you remember this stuff?"

Kyle shrugged. "Do you want to hear the rest of the story, or what?"

"Of course."

"So, anyway, you were dancing around in the hallway, just giggling to yourself. You had this huge ring on your right hand, and I could tell right away that it was an officer's ring. I didn't know where you got it from, but I was pretty sure it wasn't yours."

"You didn't have to be a prodigy to figure that out, did you?"

"No, that one wasn't too hard."

"So what happened next?" Angel asked, anxious.

"Well, eventually you went out into one of the courtyards, and started playing on those rocks right at the edge of the big gulley that was out the east doors," Kyle said. You slipped, and the ring slid right off your finger. And I'll tell you, I was still a long way away, but I could hear that thing clanking down the rocks so loud…"

"Wait a minute," Angel interrupted. "You were following me?"

"Yeah, I was curious."

"God, I can't believe you saw that. He was *so* mad about that, he wouldn't stop talking about it for weeks. I was so scared, I never even told him I was the one that lost it. At some point he just went and got a new one and it kinda blew over."

"Yeah, it wasn't a new one," Kyle said. "I found the original one."

"What?" she gasped. "How? I spent hours looking for that thing."

"I don't know, Angel. Back then I just *did* things, I never knew how."

"What even made you go look for it?"

"It was you," he said, his voice growing more serious. "I watched you frantically looking for this thing for the entire afternoon. You were so upset and crying, but you still looked … *beautiful.*"

Angel blushed. "Kyle … why didn't you say anything?"

"Well, I just … uh, this is embarrassing, but I thought if I had the ring that I'd have a reason to come talk to you." Kyle swallowed what felt like a chunk of cement, but he was already talking, so he just let the snowball drag him down the mountain. "But then your dad introduced us later that day, and after that I just felt weird that I had it. I didn't know what to do with it. So I held onto it for a couple of weeks, and kind of debated whether or not I should just throw the thing away."

"You were going to throw it away?"

"Well, think about it from my side for a second. "I had my commanding officer's ring, just so I could try and talk to his daughter. So yeah, I thought about throwing that thing away a lot. But I kinda noticed that your dad was really mad about it. So I picked the lock and snuck it back into his locker."

"I can't believe you did that," Angel sighed. "That's…that's unbelievable."

Kyle sighed and looked over at her. "Even back then, Angel, I would've done anything for you."

Angel looked up at him, her silken, sultry lips reflecting the lights of the buildings below. Kyle wondered what they might taste like. He felt a tremor of desire sweep down his back as he soaked in every detail of her face. The caramel skin, the radiant green eyes, and especially those lips. They made every thought in his head sound like gibberish, and all his worldly worries finally seem miles away. He leaned toward her, his mouth reaching for hers.

But then she pulled away. He was close enough to smell the oil in the gloss, and suddenly she had her hand against his chest, pushing him an arm's length back. His daydream shattered, and again he felt the cold of the canyon creep back into his bones.

"I'm sorry, I can't," Angel said, her green eyes turned down.

"You *can't*?" Kyle asked, stupefied.

"No, I can't," she repeated. "I never see you anymore, Kyle. You're barely even a part of my life."

Kyle blinked. "Well, that sounds fair."

"It's not?" Angel demanded, stepping back. "Kyle, we've known each other for more than twenty years, and *this* is the time that you decide you want this?"

"Angel, I…I don't know what you want me to say to that."

"You don't have to say anything," Angel huffed. "You've always been pretty good at that."

"Whoa, whoa, hold on a second," Kyle said, his shock turning to consternation. "We've known each other a long time, like you said. You can't possibly tell me you never saw this coming."

"But that's my point," Angel said. "There's always been something in the way. Another mission, another assignment. You can't just expect me to be waiting for you when it's convenient."

"Angel, what do you want me to do?" Kyle demanded. "I had a responsibility."

"If you really wanted it, Kyle, you would have made it work."

Kyle opened his mouth, ready to pour out all his frustrations. But just as the flood of words started to come, the door to the roof creaked open. Mac was standing in the entry, a quizzical look on his face.

"Uh, hey guys," he said. "Is this a bad time?"

"No, it's fine," Angel said, shooting an angry stare at Kyle. "I was leaving anyway."

She crossed her arms and stormed away. Kyle threw up his left hand and let it drop to his side, stymied. Angel brushed past Mac without a word. Mac watched her slam the door, and then turned back to his commander with raised eyebrows and wide eyes.

"What was that all about?" he asked.

"I don't even know, Mac," Kyle said, his voice dry and coarse. "Apparently I'll never know."

"You, uh, you want to talk about it?" Mac asked.

"I wouldn't even know where to start," Kyle said. "Were you supposed to meet her up here?"

"What? No, I came up here looking for you."

"I swear she was waiting for someone," Kyle muttered. "What did you want, Mac?"

"You sure you're okay?" Mac asked.

"Mac, seriously, I don't have it in me right now," Kyle said. "Why are you here?"

"Well, I just thought you'd want to know," Mac started, "the bomb is ready."

† † †

Angel tromped down the stairwell and then to the officer's wing of the dormitories. She cursed to herself the whole way. There was a time when she would have ached to have Kyle reach for her like that. She spent most of her young adulthood waiting for that moment. But now all she could see in him was a soldier yearning to hold on to his humanity, and she didn't want to be that kind of anchor.

She stopped in the middle of the hall for a moment, wondering if she was making a mistake. Coming here felt like a betrayal, like it was a forbidden place that tempted her just because it was forbidden. But she couldn't help it. This was where her heart was taking her.

She heard a door open behind her. Brady walked toward her with his usual limp, a thin black folio under one arm. He cracked a toothy grin, the squint lines around his eyes creasing above his cheeks.

"Funny seeing you here," he said. "I thought we were going to meet on the roof? Am I running that late?"

"No, I was early. And then I started to get cold," Angel said. "So I figured I'd just come meet you here."

"How'd you know where my room was?" Brady asked.

"I didn't," Angel replied. "Honestly, I was really just wandering around hoping I'd run into you."

"Are you all right? You seem a little … preoccupied."

"No, I'm fine. I'm …" Angel paused, squeezing her eyes shut. "Actually, I'm not. I'm not fine. I am preoccupied. I'm sorry."

"You want to tell me about it?" Brady asked.

"I don't know," she said. "It's stupid."

"I bet it'll make you feel better."

"All right, okay," Angel said. "I just got into another ridiculous fight with Kyle. Again. It's all we do anymore."

"What happened?"

"He tried to kiss me," Angel answered.

"Oh," Brady said, taken aback. "And what did you do?"

"I told him no," Angel said emphatically. "He's just…he's just trying to find something to hold on to, and I can't be the thing that holds him together."

"Wow. And how did he take that?"

"I don't know, I left right away," Angel said. "He can be very … temperamental at times."

"Yeah, I get that impression about him."

Angel looked into Brady's eyes. They were clear and concerned. He was intent on what she was saying, and not because he was searching for some kind of misguided connection, but because he wanted to be. She had almost forgotten what it felt like to have someone pay attention to her under normal circumstances.

"I'm sorry, I shouldn't be dropping this on you," Angel said. "We were supposed to be having fun."

"Actually, you'd be surprised how much more enjoyable this is than what I would normally be doing," Brady .

"That's sad," Angel noted. "What would you normally be doing?"

"This time of night?" he asked, ticking his eyes at the ceiling. "Probably would be in the surveillance center mapping out supply routes that we could exploit. Or planning a raid to look for food or medicine. Something like that."

"That does sound glamorous," Angel said, a hint of sarcasm lacing her voice.

"Somebody has to do it," Brady said, shifting the folio from one arm to the other.

"Is that what that thing is for?" Angel nodding at his folio. "Trying to squeeze a little work in with pleasure?"

Brady looked down at the black, leather-bound booklet in his hands like he just remembered he had it. "This? No, actually this is for you."

He handed the folio to her. She gave him a crooked look for a moment, running her fingers down the stitched leather cover.

"I know you like to draw, so I managed to piece together some decent paper and a few pieces of graphite," Brady said. "I hope you like it."

Angel's breath suddenly felt staggered. Her lips curled into a grin. She turned opened the cover and touched the crisp paper inside. The pages were a little boxed around the edges, but they were blank and waiting for the thick, grainy lead. She looked at Brady, her eyes welling up.

"I know it's not the greatest material in the world," Brady said, "but it was the best I could do."

"No, no, this is … this is beautiful."

Angel pulled the book into her chest and held it tight. Her lungs swallowed an emotional breath, half laugh and half sob, but every bit spellbound by the gesture. She lunged forward, her lips locking onto his. The heat of his mouth made her cheeks warm, and while foreign and new, she quickly surrendered to the passion of it. By the time she finally pulled away, her heart was fluttering like a leaf in the wind.

"Do you think we can go inside?" she asked, biting her lower lip.

Brady nodded and took her hand. He opened the door to his room and beckoned her to follow him. She paused for just the barest of instants, then tossed away her inhibitions, and stepped inside.

Chapter 23

The musk of the hospital wing seemed especially bad in the early hours of the morning. Maybe it was because they shut the vents at night to save power. Or maybe because there were fewer people moving around the keep the air circulating. Whatever the reason, it kept the corridors saturated with the stale smell of mildew and ammonia.

Kyle found himself wondering why he was always standing in these hallways at the equivalent to three o'clock in the morning. He was starting to feel very morbid about it, especially when the orderlies would wheel out a covered gurney and take it toward the morgue. It had already happened twice in the hours since he had climbed down from the top of the canyon. There had been an outbreak of a pulmonary infection brought back by some miners on one of the other Aranow moons recently, and it had claimed some eighty-six lives in the colony so far. He had initially been concerned about his father contracting the illness given his proximity to it, but at this point he was far more occupied with Marcus's state of mind than his physical well-being.

He was standing across the hall from Marcus's room, glaring through the plate-glass windows. Marcus was sedated, just like he had asked, but Kyle still didn't want to go inside. For some reason he felt like it would complicate things. For now he would just watch from a distance.

A tap on his left shoulder startled him. His muscles tensed and he stepped back. It took a conscious effort not to lash out, as would be his reflex. It was Ellie.

"I'm sorry, I didn't mean to sneak up on you," she said.

"It's all right," Kyle said. "I must be a little distracted."

"You *look* a little distracted. He's resting well," she added, following his gaze. "Though it took a lot to get him to calm down."

"Has anyone mentioned his rants?"

"No, not to me. I think we got him calmed down before anyone noticed."

"Thank you for that," Kyle said.

Kyle snuck a glance at Ellie's face. It seemed amazing what a few hours of sleep could do. Her skin appeared smoother and more hydrated, the color of her supple lips sharply defined against her creamy complexion. He was getting distracted again.

"I'm happy to help you," Ellie said, her eyes fixing onto his. "I think you know that I want to help you."

Kyle felt a brief flutter of butterflies in his stomach. Her eyes had him off balance again. And he couldn't have that right now.

"Ellie, I'm sorry, I don't mean to keep doing this to you, but I've got to go," he said. "I want to talk to you, I really do. I just can't right now."

"You're leaving, aren't you?" she observed. He realized he already had on the lower half of his combat suit.

"I really can't tell you anything," Kyle said. "All I can say is that I will be back. We can talk when I get back, if you still want to."

"I'm gonna hold you to that," she said, placing a hand on his arm. The hair on his skin stood up as if electrified. "Please be safe."

Kyle chuckled, wondering what could possibly be safe about what they were about to do.

"If you insist," he said finally.

† † †

The time for departure to Dynasteria was less than half an hour away as Kyle made his way into the preflight staging area. The gear that they had gathered for this mission had been laid out in organized fashion, from the earbud communicators and carboranium undergarments Jay and Mac had procured on Raefflesia, to the starmetal-laced firearms that they hoped would help them kill the Gentry. The rest of the mission team had already gathered.

"Kyle, where have you been?" Mac demanded. "We've been looking for you for the last sixteen hours."

"I was at the top of the canyon," Kyle said. "I just needed some time to think."

"You know that if Bryan knew you were fucking AWOL for the last day, they would scrap his whole crazy mission you've got us going on?"

"Knock it off, Mac," Kyle said. "I'm here now."

"Oh, you're fucking killing me here," Mac groaned, his hands waving like antennae. "I've been running around like an idiot."

"So what was so important, Mac?"

Mac paused. "I just … I just wanted to check on you. You seemed a little wound up, and I wanted to make sure you were all right."

"I appreciate the concern, but I'm fine."

"Are you sure? You missed our last strategy session, you missed preflight. We're lucky your dad woke up cuz I was able to use that as an excuse."

"Mac, please, just leave it alone."

"You haven't slept again," Mac noticed. "Kyle, I'm worried about you."

"You don't have to worry about me, Mac," Kyle insisted.

"Well, somebody has to," Mac continued. "You seem like you're pretty pissed off."

"So what if I am?" Kyle asked. "Is that a bad thing with what we're about to walk into?"

"It is if it makes you do something stupid," Mac said, turning his commander's shoulders away from the group. "Just listen to me for a second, please. And remember, I'm saying this as your friend. You cannot let an argument with Angel affect your focus on this mission. Because there is no way any of us get out of this one without your head being on straight."

Kyle shut his eyes. "Mac, believe me, she is the last thing I want to be thinking about right now."

"Then why are you still so angry?"

"Because I still want to have that anger when I'm standing in front of the Gentry," Kyle said.

"You better be careful with that temper, boss," Mac said. "One of these days we won't be able to get you pointed in the right direction."

Bryan walked up with a shuffle of his boots against the floor. "Are we all right over here, gentlemen?" he asked.

"Damn skippy, sir," Mac answered. "Ready to go kick some ass."

"Glad to hear it," Bryan said. "I was starting to wonder if you would make it, Commander. We missed you during pre-flight."

"Yeah, I'm sorry about that," Kyle said. "I had to be down in the hospital."

"It's all right, I understand," Bryan replied. "How's your father?"

"We had to sedate him. He was having a … difficult time with the transition."

"I can't say I blame him. He'll be all right though, yes?"

"I suppose we'll have to wait and see," Kyle said.

"Well, I'll make certain that they get him the best care we can give," Bryan said, patting his nephew on his immense shoulder. "We'll all be pulling for him."

"I'm sure you will."

Bryan gave Kyle a cockeyed look, his eyes suspicious. Mac seemed to notice it and stepped in between.

"So, Marshal, you think we're ready to light the fire on this thing, or what?" Mac asked.

Bryan nodded, his gaze finally drifting from his nephew. "These men are as ready as they're gonna get. Take that how you will."

"They're ready," Kyle insisted. "They'll be fine."

"I should let you know, Kyle, that Dr. Preston wanted me to send his regards," Bryan said. "He does wish you luck."

"Is that right?" Kyle asked. "He didn't want to be here to tell us that himself?"

"No, you know what? That's great, sir," Mac interrupted, stepping in as the voice of reason. "I think we'll take all the luck we can get right now."

"Very good, Lieutenant," Bryan said. "Commander, would you be opposed to me addressing the men before you ship out?"

"No, sir," Kyle said. "I think they'd be glad to hear from you."

Bryan walked back toward the gathered men near the boarding ramp of the Stratys. Several of them were pacing around like skittish felines, mostly the Splinter recruits who were about to venture into their first offensive. Others like Jackson and Brady were sitting and composed, though even an experienced soldier like Jay was anxiously gnawing through a wad of tobacco root. Kyle started forward to join them, but Mac grabbed his arm.

"Dude, I get the whole anger thing, but do me a favor and don't pick a fight with everyone before we even leave."

"Can't promise anything at this point, Mac," Kyle said. "Now shut up and follow me."

Mac chuckled briefly, but Kyle wasn't joking. He knew the savagery that he would have to embrace in order to win this fight, and he had no time for pleasantries now. He had found a place inside his own head even he didn't know was there, and he was intent on riding that rage all the way to the throne room.

He walked over to Dan and gave him thump on the shoulder. The young lieutenant was sitting off to the side by himself, drilling a hole into the dock floor with his stare. His head barely moved as he looked up at Kyle, and he managed a meager nod. Still, he was the last person Kyle was concerned about. Dan was a rare combat talent, and his training was more than adequate. He would be ready when the fight started.

Bryan whispered a few words to Brady, and the major called for everyone's attention. The room was quiet already, but it went silent at the major's request.

"I'm not going to keep you," Bryan said. "But I had to take a moment to let you to know that we're proud of what you're going to do today. This is the day that our cause has been waiting for for generations. And I have every faith that you are the right team to make this happen. Commander?"

"We've got a forty-five-minute warp jump to the drop point," Kyle started. "It's going to seem like a lot longer. Keep your minds focused. You can worry about your family and loved ones after we get back. Once we come out of hyperspace, Lieutenant McArthur will target the defense station. After detonation, we'll have a twenty-minute window to breach the atmosphere and get on the ground. Are we good so far?"

There were a few nods from the group, but no words.

Kyle paused. "There is one more thing I want to make very clear before we go," he said. "This is an act of war. We are not there to take prisoners, and we cannot afford to give any quarter. You will shoot to kill and then move on to the next target. Is that clear?"

A loud "Yes, sir!" rang out from the group. There was conviction in their voices. It made Kyle grin.

"Anything else, Marshal?" Kyle asked.

"We'll have some whiskey chilled and poured when you get back," Bryan said. "You're our dagger, men. Good luck." He gave Kyle a nod. It was time.

"You heard the man!" Kyle roared. "Load it up."

The team bounced to their feet and rushed up the loading ramp. Kyle took in each of their faces as they ran by. They were an amalgam of tense expressions and eager trigger fingers. He couldn't help but wonder how many of them would be on the flight home.

Kyle threw his rifle over the shoulder opposite his sword, his starmetal weapon already holstered on his right hip. He scooped up his utility vest, helmet, and communicator and marched up the ramp behind his men. The hatch whispered closed and the thrusters rumbled to life.

The passenger cabin of the Stratys wasn't exactly built for carrying military personnel, with its rows of leather-covered seats and high-end chrome accents, but it would certainly make do. Mac plunked down on a seat next to Major Brady while Kyle settled in across from them. The major's typical consternation was absent from his expression. In fact he looked almost happy.

"You look like you're in a good mood today, Major," Mac said. "You get your beak wet last night, or what?"

"I don't think that's any of your business, Lieutenant," Brady replied.

"Ah, so you did!" Mac exclaimed. "You dog, you! How was it? Did you have her speaking in tongues the whole time?"

"Not sure this is the best place to be talking about this, McArthur," Brady insisted.

"Are you kidding?" Mac asked. "We're flying into death's door here. This is the *perfect* place to be talking about this."

Brady sighed and flashed a look over at Kyle.

"Good for you, Major," Kyle said. "I'm sure there's more than a few of us that wish we could've spent last night in that situation."

Brady groaned, but Mac's stare was persistent. Kyle could only shrug.

"She got what she was looking for," Brady said finally.

"Oh, man!" Mac hollered. "That's so hot. You should give these kinds of details for a living."

"Some people like to say a gentleman should respect a lady's privacy," the major said.

Mac rolled his eyes. "Whoever said that obviously wasn't on a transport about to storm the capital—"

"All right, Mac, calm down," Kyle interrupted. "What did I just say about staying focused?"

"Okay, okay," Mac conceded. "I didn't want to think about him being naked anyway."

Brady about choked. Clearly Mac's sense of humor was lost on him. And that was apparently amusing to the others as several of them let out an audible laugh.

The ship's escape thrusters kicked in and rocketed them through the depths of the canyon and toward the reaches of space. The Stratys was truly a luxury vessel, transferring very little of the escape velocity to the cabin's occupants. What little tremor they did feel invigorated Kyle. He never wanted to admit just how addicted he had become to this particular theater. He craved it. He missed it over these last months. And now he was back to it. The thought had his blood churning. This would be the first time he had been off-planet since their arrival in the Aranow system. Thinking back, he realized it had been the longest stretch he had been on a single planet since he was a boy.

Suddenly he realized that he could never give this up. Perhaps Angel was right. Perhaps it would always be in the way.

Kyle looked around at his team. They were all scared. The bouncing knees, the white knuckles, the green faces … it all screamed of apprehension and uncertainty. And he couldn't blame them. Hell, he was apprehensive himself. *He* was scared. What they were doing was lunacy. But it was what they needed, regardless of his own personal vendetta. So live or die he would see it done.

Gravity lost its grip as they passed into the void, drawing Kyle's weight off his seat. They had elected not to turn on the artificial gravity generators as they would have made a ship more prominent on certain tracking systems. The added energy output gave off a higher heat signature, and that was attention they didn't need. It wasn't a concern on cloaked ships like the *Gemini*, but civilian transports weren't as neatly outfitted.

Kyle looked through the door at the two Splinter pilots behind the controls. They were both older, near the end of their service. In fact one had been retired for more than a year when he was coaxed back into duty for this mission. Both Brady and Bryan had insisted that they were the most qualified to pilot this ship under these circumstances, though Kyle had to wonder if either of them had even seen a ship of this caliber during their careers. As always, he would have preferred to have Jay running the controls and Mac working the navigation, but they had to be prepared for the halo jump and obviously wouldn't be able to pilot the ship afterward.

His gaze shifted past the pilots toward the expanse. There weren't many stars visible from this sector, but one of the few marked the capital system. The vacuum stretched out beneath them as the hyperdrive ignited, whirling the two ends of space together. Through all that emptiness he would drag every ounce of anger he had ever felt, in hopes that it would fuel a coup that he had spent his life trying to prevent. One way or another, it ended tonight.

CHAPTER 24

The screaming path through hyperspace was said to be different for everyone. Some see searing streaks of light. Some see a melted vision of the ship in front of them. Others seem to go blind. For Kyle, however, the picture was always clear. Stars and worlds whipped past him, but he saw it all. This journey was no different, except the target at the end of the wormhole. Today he barreled toward the only truly cosmic force in the galaxy. A colossus. A *god.* Would he still have the strength to put him down? He would find out soon enough.

The Stratys dropped out of hyperspace. Kyle looked out the cockpit windows as the hyperdrive disengaged. To the right was the city-sized defense station orbiting the planet. To the left was the sparkling metropolis of the capital. The system's star was on the other side of the planet, leaving the city lights to glisten like a prism in the dark. It was serene, peaceful. And about to be blown to hell.

Kyle swung his head over to Mac. "Arm the rocket."

Mac pulled up a holographic display from a palm-sized transmitter in his vest. A few swipes and codes gave him an "armed" return. He struck the "execute" command, and seconds later the device sailed past the cockpit, a subtle orange glow trailing behind. Its path was visible through the front windows as the ship listed toward the stratosphere. The rocket shrunk quickly against the cold metal backdrop and then disappeared into a web of pipes and bulkheads. A moment passed, and then the belly of the structure buckled and heaved. An avalanche of oxygen-starved explosions burst through the seams just as the planet's gravity took hold of the ship. Kyle felt himself sink back into his seat, but his eyes stayed on the station. The fusion reaction vaporized the upper quadrosphere of the satellite complex, the flash blinding even Kyle's mutant eyes.

The nose of the Stratys dipped quickly. The drag of the rapidly thickening atmosphere sent a tremor through the hull. Then, like an oncoming train, the pulse of the nuclear blast pounded the roof of the ship. Kyle's head snapped back against the rear of his seat, and the cabin lights went red with an alarm.

"Mac?" Kyle hollered over the wail of the siren. "What the fuck was that?"

Mac clasped the arm of his seat like it was the only thing holding him down. "I don't know! We got hit by the blast radius! We were supposed to be totally clear of it!"

The Stratys trembled and lurched again, then started to veer toward its left. The panicked screams from the cockpit came immediately.

"Commander, we've lost one of the engines!" the elder shouted roared. "We're going into a spin! We can't hold it for long, we're gonna go down!"

Kyle's head turned toward the rear of the plane, and he popped the latch on his harness. "Jay, blow the hatch! We've gotta go now."

"What?" Brady hollered from across the aisle. "Commander, we're too high! The jet wash will tear us apart!"

Kyle rose from his seat, steadying himself against the wall of the cockpit. "If we go into a spin we'll never clear the ship. We've got no choice. It's now or never."

Jay stumbled from his seat and threw the lever for the hatch. A shrill whistle of wind swept through the cabin, the dark night sky screaming past them as the ship began to plummet.

"Griffin, we'll never make it!" Brady shouted.

"If you want to stay here, Major, be my guest," Kyle said, starting down the aisle. "Get those chutes ready, boys! We're going now."

The other crewmembers did as they were told. The parachutes were packed into their combat vests, but from this height they would need supplemented oxygen. They had mouthpiece-sized atmospheric accelerators that would draw raw oxygen from the air and concentrate it. It would buy them time until the air thickened.

A huge crash rattled the cabin, throwing the occupants off their feet. The ship had started to spiral to the left.

"Jacks, take 'em down!" Kyle screamed.

Jackson buckled his helmet and chomped down on his respirator. He stepped off the edge and tumbled away into the night sky. The others slowly followed behind. Kyle glanced back at the pilots.

"I'm sorry," he said.

"Good luck, Commander!" the elder pilot said, his weight leaning against the stick to slow their spin.

As Kyle pivoted back toward the ramp Brady was still hesitating near his seat, but Kyle wasn't waiting for him to make up his mind. He grabbed the major by the collar of his vest and carried him down the aisle. Apparently it made his point because Brady bit down on his respirator and shut the visor on his helmet.

Another explosion rang out as the other engine failed. Kyle pushed Brady off the precipice, then dove into the sky behind him. His body half-turned over as he felt the rush of wind sweep over him, the angle and weight of his shoulders drawing him headfirst toward the ground. At first the roar of the air deafened him. The spin of the Stratys whipped past like a tornado, sending him head over heels as the planet's gravity and the ship's momentum pulled him in opposite directions. He arched his back as sharply as he could to steady himself, the dizzying swirl of ground and sky scrambling his senses.

His summersault halted just in time for him to see the first parachutes bloom over the forest. He let himself sail downward before pulling his own chute. A sudden yank hit him beneath the arms, and he floated down like a leaf in the wind. There was a strong downdraft from the orbital explosion pushing him deep into the northern woods, nearly a mile from his expected drop zone. The first branches snapped against the bottom of his boots, and then the tops of the trees swallowed him whole. The ropes on the parachute tangled in the branches of the canopy, and his tumble screeched to a halt.

He dangled there for a moment, tracking the path of the falling Stratys through the leaves. The ship came apart like a ball of twine, disappearing over the horizon and then slamming into the ground with a boom. Overhead the night sky was still awash with the flash of the nuclear explosion, and shards of the searing debris had started to pierce the atmosphere.

Kyle pulled a blade from his boot and cut through the ropes tethering him to the tree. He dropped through the web of branches, a chorus of snaps and cracks following him down. His feet hit the ground with a thud.

Beneath the canopy it was dark. Only a few slivers of light weaved through the branches. In the shadows Kyle noticed the warmth of his blood trickling from a tear in the left sleeve of his suit. He slid his hand inside and winced as his fingers ran over a gaping cut just below his shoulder. Instinctively he let his powers flow and stitch the wound back together. The brief flash of light illuminated the grimace on his face before disappearing back into his skin. The brief burst of Celestial power was smooth, it was controlled, and it did what he asked.

Finally, Kyle thought.

He checked his communicator but found only static on the line. He then turned to the digital tracker, but the holographic image on his wrist display was scrambled as well. He knew little about nuclear explosions, but he had to guess that the signal had been fractured by the pulse of the blast. And that meant he was on his own for now.

He decided his best option was to head for the rally point at the northwest corner of the palace yard. If anyone was still on task, they would meet him there. He checked his rifle and the starmetal firearm, then started through the forest.

The terrain on the north side of the palace was grueling, with deep ravines and crashing waterfalls pouring down from the mountains in the distance. Kyle was able to bound across the chasms and clear the rapids easily enough, though the woods thickened considerably as he approached the palace wall. The lights of the Palace spires started to creep through the trees, and finally the walls came into sight. Two figures waited along the edge of the wall, crouched among the shadows. Kyle came up on them quickly and quietly, staying hidden until he was certain who he was seeing. Eventually he could make out Jay and Mitchell's faces, a look of panic plastered across both.

"You two look lost," Kyle said.

Mitchell tried to swing his rifle around, but Jay caught the barrel in his left hand. Kyle tucked himself into the shadows with them, patting Mitchell on the shoulder.

"This has gone to shit pretty quickly," Jay said.

"Every plan has got some bumps," Kyle replied.

"Bumps?" Jay huffed. "That's what you're calling this? A bump?"

"Jay, shut up, all right?" Kyle ordered. "Have you two seen any of the others?"

Jay sighed. "Yeah, we found Thomas. He's dead."

Kyle winced. "How?"

"He must have lost his respirator during the drop," Jay said. "He suffocated."

"Goddammit," Kyle grunted. "Are either of your communicators working?"

"No, just static. It's like the whole thing is fried."

"No, if it was fried, it'd be dead. There's still static on the line. It's gotta be recalibrating after the explosion."

"That sounds like wishful thinking to me," Jay said.

The sound of transport thrusters swept through the courtyard. Nearly two dozen ships rose overhead and climbed into the sky, hurrying toward the still-smoldering station above. However, Kyle's attention was stolen back by the sound of Jackson's voice coming across the communicators.

" … come in … does anybody copy?" Jackson called. "Come back …"

"Jacks, this is Kyle, I copy. What's your position?"

"I'm at my rally point on the east side," Jackson answered. "I have Dan and Jenna on site."

"Good. I've got Jay and Mitchell at our rally point at the northwest corner," Kyle said. "We're a man down, I repeat, Thomas is down. I need everyone else to sound off."

One by one the others rang in. Cullen and Brett, Logan then Brady, and finally Mac. Kyle glanced at the tracker on his wrist. It was back online as well. "Everybody get to your rally point," he said, "and double time it. Jackson, I need the power down in no more than twenty minutes."

"We're on it," Jackson said.

† † †

Dan's hand was sweating against the metal stock of his rifle. He had thought he was prepared for this, but the rock resting in his queasy stomach made him think differently. The woods around the palace were spooky in ways he couldn't describe. There were few lights and no wildlife, a testament to the dominance of the human influence in this area. But worse yet, there was always the sensation of a watchful eye stalking your every move. It was like walking in a fishbowl.

Cullen was the last to join them at the rally point. He had twisted his ankle coming down from the canopy. Mac shot it full of a numbing agent and splinted it with extra layers of the carboranium-weaved undergarment. He was still slowed, but at least it would help him keep up.

They made their way across the tree line, tiptoeing over long-forgotten booby traps and avoiding the vast array of surveillance cameras buried within the landscape. If not for Jackson and Mac's intimate knowledge of the systems, they would have blindly walked into at least a dozen of them. As it was it took them the full fifteen minutes to locate the maintenance shed and identify the automated defense systems protecting it.

"Alpha team, we have located the maintenance shed," Jackson said through his communicator. "Looks like we've got some security. Stand by."

Jackson knelt down next to Mac, who was scouring the surroundings for further traps. The entrance to the shed was barely six meters square, and was buried against the base of a large boulder. It blended seamlessly into the natural landscape, so much so that Dan would never have seen it without being able to follow the gazes of Mac and Jackson.

"What do we got, Mac?" Jackson asked.

"I make out three separate turrets," Mac muttered. "One to the upper left of the door. Two more in the elm to the right."

"And one in the hedges on the far left," Dan interjected.

Jackson peered over to the left, then nodded. "And that one. What's our play?"

"They're motion activated, with an infrared backup," Mac said. "Think you can hit their sensors from here?"

"As long as I have a clear line of sight," Jackson answered.

"Well, dial up that fancy scope of yours."

Jackson squeezed his left eye into the lens of his sniper's scope. He paused briefly, calming his breath. Then a pair of muffled shots stung the two turrets to the right, a third popped the sensor above the door, and finally a fourth burst near the turret in the shrubbery to their left. It was quick and easy, but between shots a noise caught Dan's ear. He looked to the right beyond the trees, and saw a light swiftly approaching.

Dan grabbed Jackson's arm before he could leave the cover of the brush. A Dominion speeder swept around the boulder into the clearing. A trio of soldiers stepped off the vehicle, each carrying heavy assault rifles.

Jackson gave Mac a hand signal to stay put, then motioned to Dan to follow him. If those soldiers saw the blown-out sensors, the forest would be swarming with Dominion troopers and Fury foot soldiers within minutes. They had to deal with them quickly.

Dan's nerves melted away as they skulked through the trees to flank behind their opposition. They were silent even on the imperfect terrain, and came upon the troopers without a sound. Jackson came out of the brush first, blade drawn. He felled the nearest soldier with a plunging blow to back of his neck, but a shot echoed from the soldier's weapon before he hit the ground. The other two turned sharply.

Dan burst out of the trees like a tidal wave. He caught the rifle barrel of the first man with his right hand, and sliced through his neck with the left. Another shot fired into the ground in front of him. He spun to his right, whipping the butt end of the stolen rifle across the second soldier's temple. The soldier dropped to his knees, and Dan sank his blade into the flesh beneath the man's eye.

It was over in less than a second. But the clap of the shots had already boomed into the night air. It wouldn't go unnoticed in the courtyard.

† † †

Brady and Logan had finally made their way to the rally point on the northwest corner just as Jackson informed them that the Echo team had reached the maintenance shed.

"What the fuck was that?" Kyle demanded after the first gunshot echoed across the palace grounds. "Jay, get them on the radio, now!"

Jay's hand darted up to his ear. "Echo team, this is Jay. We're hearing gunfire at our position. What the hell is going on?"

"We ran into a handful of armed guards out here," Jackson replied. "We handled it, but they got a couple of shots off."

"Any casualties?" Jay asked.

"No, they were strays."

"All right," Kyle cut in, "Echo team, you've got three minutes to cut the power and get those defenses down. We hit the ground on the other side of this wall two seconds after that."

"Mac's already on it," Jackson responded. "Give me ninety seconds."

The line went quiet. Kyle glared up at the twenty-foot wall in front of him. If the clock was ticking when they arrived, it was leapfrogging away now.

Brady grabbed Kyle by the shoulder. "Commander, those shots are going to draw attention. Maybe we should consider pulling out."

Kyle shook his head. "Our second transport won't be on site for at least another half hour. We can't just sit here until then. Our only option is to go forward."

Brady grit his teeth and looked up at the wall in front of them. "We're in this to the last man now, eh?" he asked.

"We always were," Kyle replied.

† † †

Mac dispatched with the pleasantries of trying to pick the lock on the access hatch, instead slapping a plastic charge on the hinges. With another loud bang the door went tumbling into the clearing. They could hear the wail of the palace alarms ringing in the distance as Mac ducked through the smoke and squeezed into the narrow opening. Their task here was a simple one: disrupt the steam piping before it reached the turbines down the line, and blow out the fiber-optic cables carrying the electricity produced at the harvest site. Mac secured another set of charges against the utility lines and climbed back out of the shed.

"Everyone take cover!" he shouted.

The shed imploded with a muffled crackle. Dan shielded his eyes as he was hit with a wash of dust and rock. By the time the shower of debris had settled, the cry of the alarms had gone silent.

"Alpha team, this is Echo," Jackson said. "We are good to go. Repeat you are clear to enter the courtyard."

"Copy, Echo," Jay responded. "Proceed to your entry point and set up for support. Be prepared to encounter hostiles. You are cleared to disable with extreme prejudice."

"Roger that, Alpha," Jackson said. "We'll be on site in eight minutes."

† † †

Kyle sprung to his feet the moment the alarms went silent. He checked the charge on his rifle as Jackson confirmed that the defenses were down, then turned his eyes to the wall.

"Safeties off," he said. "We're going over."

His coiled legs burst him upward, vaulting over the wall with a tap of his left hand. He landed softly among a patch of manicured trees. In front of him was a half-mile of stacked garden terraces and fountains. It was all heavy stone blocks and carefully stylized plant life, a path with plenty of cover and few impasses. Beyond it all he could see the door that led into the utility tunnels beneath the palace halls.

Jay hit the ground next to him and tucked his rifle against the crease of his shoulder. Brady, Mitchell, and Logan followed shortly behind, but Kyle had already started up the tiers. His eyes darted from side to side, his ears perked to any approaching noise. The others swarmed across the landscape, creeping over the grounds like a crack spreading across a pane of glass.

Within just a few moments Kyle reached the edge of the main courtyard, a wide-open field of silken grass just outside the palace's foundation. The others panted as they tried to keep up. Kyle was finding himself very anxious and thus having a difficult time moderating his pace. He could feel the Eye inside the palace walls like a loose stitch scratching at his neck. The sheer magnitude of its looming power came down on him hard. It made him dizzy.

Jay grabbed his commander's arm, and it seemed to break Kyle from the Celestial trance.

"You good?" he asked.

Kyle nodded, feeling the weight of the Eye retreat. He looked back at the palace walls. The door was just a few dozen meters away. Nothing stood between it and them.

That's when Kyle heard it. The scrape of boots against pavement. The clatter of weapons against body armor. Then the burst of gunfire.

The snap and whistle of several shots rattled off the surrounding stones, spraying chunks of rock across the face of Kyle's helmet. His left ear started ringing as he slid behind the edge of the stone wall. Logan was hit in the side of the head, gouging out a slab of his helmet and a shard of his skull. The blood splattered across Brady's face as Logan collapsed.

"Son of a bitch!" Brady bellowed. "Son of a bitch!"

"Stay down! Stay down!" Kyle yelled, pulling Mitchell onto the ground.

Logan was dead. His mouth gaped open aimlessly, a puddle of blood seeping into the lush grass. Kyle's eyes creased in anger.

"Where did it come from?" Jay demanded.

"They're coming from the west!" Kyle said, stealing a glance above the rocks. "The upper gate. Twenty, maybe twenty-five of them."

"What do we do?" Brady shouted. "We're gonna get pinned!"

"Just stay down," Kyle said. "When you see me move, give me some cover fire. I'll buy us some time."

"Whatever you're gonna do, do it fast!" Brady said.

"Just be ready. I'm gonna go quick."

Kyle threw his automatic rifle over his shoulder, then pulled a pair of handguns off the back of his belt. He checked their charges and released the safety catches. The others turned in their crouches to face the onslaught, waiting for their commander to make his move. Kyle loaded his weight on his right leg, then sprung into the air as though shot out of a cannon.

He rocketed nearly three stories up, the rush of air squealing inside his helmet. His weapons flew forward, rattling off two dozen shots before the oncoming soldiers saw him coming. The shots came so quickly nearly half of them dropped in an instant. Kyle came down among the survivors like a landslide, his left boot striking the chest of a man near their center. His ribs crunched as he was sent sailing backward, toppling several of his companions like a set of dominoes.

Kyle hit the ground smoothly, his weapons still firing like a turret. Four more bodies fell in front of him. He dropped the gun in his right hand to the turf and planted the free hand on the ground. His legs arched over his head as he dodged the disjointed fire of the remaining troops. He pounded his fist into the sternum of another soldier as his feet hit the ground again, then whipped back to his right and crushed the cheek of a third man with the heel of his boot.

The Dominion squadron bumbled into each other, their gunfire staggered and erratic. By then the covering fire of Jay and the others had drawn some of their attention, and several of the troopers turned away from him.

He ducked beneath a slashing blade, grabbing the knife from his boot again. He blocked another blow with his left forearm, and then plunged the tip in between a pair of the man's ribs. The action blurred in front of him as the soldier hit the ground, his knife tearing into the neck of the next in line. Most of the guns went silent as his team swarmed into the fray, turning the battle into a brawl. The fight shifted in their favor, and Kyle began to turn his attention back to the palace.

But then he saw him. Vaughn Donovan, the general himself, skulking across the border of the skirmish. Their eyes met through the dust of the battle, and suddenly the palace and the Gentry were light-years away. Kyle marched forward, ignoring the carnage that surrounded him.

"I have to admit, this is the last place I thought I'd see you," Vaughn said. "I never thought you'd have the gall to come here."

"And I never thought I'd get lucky enough to come across you," Kyle snarled. "I figured you'd tuck tail and run the moment you saw me coming."

"How could I miss this?" Vaughn asked. He had a gun in his right hand. "Now I've got the chance to finish off your whole traitorous family once we kill you and those parasitic friends of yours. You've done me a favor."

Vaughn put his hand to his ear, and a perplexed look spread across his face.

"Trying to radio for help?" Kyle asked. "You didn't think we'd be prepared?"

"No matter," Vaughn said, raising his weapon toward Kyle. "I'll just have to handle you myself."

Kyle reached out with a telekinetic hand and ripped the gun from the general's grasp. He caught it between his hands, and with a quick twitch of his dense mutant muscle the chamber snapped off the hilt. The color drained from the Vaughn's cheeks, and for a moment Kyle thought he might run. He *should* have run. But he didn't. Maybe he knew he couldn't outrace

Kyle. Or maybe he didn't want to die with his back turned. Whatever it was, instead of fleeing like the coward Kyle always took him for, he swallowed hard and steadied himself, the type of assuasive gesture a man makes when he knows he has no choice but to fight.

Kyle's eyes started burning as his powers surged to the surface, begging to be released. It would be so easy just to let it happen, to scorch Vaughn into ashes like a flame charring dry grass. But he didn't. He forced himself to fight the impulse in favor of finding a satisfaction he could only achieve by breaking his enemy with his own two hands. He grit his teeth and tossed away his knife, then started forward.

Vaughn came at him quickly, throwing two reckless punches that caught nothing but air. Kyle toyed with him for a moment, evading half a dozen fruitless attacks before finally catching Vaughn's right wrist with his left hand. He clenched it so fiercely he could feel the bones begin the crumble against his fingertips. Vaughn's knees started to buckle beneath him, and Kyle jerked him forward, pounding his heavy fist into the general's chest like a jackhammer. The blow was so ferocious it nearly crushed his internal organs, and he heard the sickening sound of Vaughn's sternum fracturing as he tumbled backward. The general's head snapped back and cracked against the ground, his eyes immediately going crossed.

"Get up, General," Kyle taunted, his mind searing red. "Get up!"

Vaughn wheezed and rolled onto his side, hoisting himself up to one knee as he struggled for breath. His neck looked like a wilted stem as it tried to hold his head over his shoulders. Kyle soaked it in. Vaughn grunted and threw a weary punch in Kyle's direction, the motion itself clearly painful. Kyle ducked away, then landed another blow to Vaughn's midsection. The loud crack of his ribs was followed by the sound of Kyle's fist crunching against Vaughn's jaw. The general went sprawling across the courtyard, shredding the skin off his arm as he slid across the ground.

"You … you fucking … traitor," Vaughn gasped through tight teeth, his jaw clearly broken. "This won't … change anything … The Gentry … will still … make you bleed."

"Not in your lifetime," Kyle growled.

Vaughn had landed only a few feet from where Kyle had tossed his knife. In his desperation he picked it up with a trembling hand, then lashed out like a madman. Kyle caught the general's forearm with his left hand. The fury of his grip could have crushed a diamond, overpowering any strength that Vaughn had left. Pure malice oozed from Vaughn's eyes even with so little authority left, and at that moment Kyle's patience escaped him. The muscles in his wrist flexed, and the bones in Vaughn's forearm snapped like a piece of wicker. His hand dangled beneath Kyle's fist like it was being held together only by skin, though the shock was so great he failed to even scream.

Kyle's right hand shot forward and grabbed hold of Vaughn's throat. His right foot came down on the front of the general's left knee, and the joint violently folded backward. Vaughn wailed, but his cry was quickly garbled by the blood building in his throat. By then it didn't matter. Kyle couldn't hear a sound. The rage scalding through his mind had turned him deaf. All he desired was more blood, and there was nothing to stop him from taking it.

He swung the knife around and buried it into Vaughn's belly. The abrupt intrusion spurted blood across the front of Kyle's combat suit, and robbed Vaughn of any breath left in his lungs. There was a brief look of helplessness in the general's eyes before they glossed over, and Kyle dropped the twitching body to the ground.

Kyle looked away from the body, frightened by the unbridled gratification that the sight gave him. He took three deep breaths as he raised his eyes toward the night sky. Finally he turned back toward the palace. His team had dispatched the remaining Dominion soldiers, but the spectacle of his raw fury had them transfixed like a line of statues.

Kyle felt as though he was snorting fire. The madness didn't disperse with Vaughn's last breaths. He wanted more. He wanted to bleed every drop from the rest of the palace, as though that would somehow bring his mother back to life.

Finally, Jay broke the silence. "Kyle, we have to go. There will be more coming."

"Right," Kyle answered, his scowl never changing. "We're on the door."

† † †

Dan flung his legs over the top of the wall and came down on hard pavement. Jackson and Mac were already on the ground in front of him, moving away from the perimeter wall. The east side of the palace grounds housed a drove of satellite towers spread across several hundred square meters, and to the south was the main palace entrance. The river from the northern mountains crossed the courtyard just in front of them, roaring through a manmade channel that plunged beneath the landscape. It made for an undulating network of bridges and canals between them and the east face of the palace.

The twins and Jenna dropped from the top of the wall as Dan started across the yard. He pointed them to flanking positions on either side of him, then followed Jackson and Mac across the first bridge to the base of one of the satellite towers. There was gunfire in the distance, followed by faint panicked screams.

Mac's hand shot up to his ear. "Alpha team, this is Echo, we are hearing gunfire. Do you need assistance, over?"

Nothing.

"Alpha team, this is Echo, please acknowledge," Mac repeated.

Again, nothing.

"Kyle, Jay … anybody … do you copy?"

Mac shook his head. The gunfire continued. Dan looked to the west, but he couldn't see more than a few hundred meters in that direction. The tarmac was also on the northeast edge of the grounds just around the corner, and the clusters of parked shipping vessels and transports obscured their view.

"I've got nothing, Jacks," Mac said finally. "They're not responding."

"So what's the move?" Dan asked. "Do we head to their position?"

"No, we stay on task," Jackson said. "We can't risk getting bunched together, and we've only got maybe another fifteen, twenty minutes before they find a way to get their communications running. After that this place will be swarming with soldiers. That firefight might actually give us a window to get inside. We better use it."

"Doesn't feel right leaving them like this," Dan said.

"Kyle's orders," Jackson replied. "Stay on target, no matter what."

"All right, so what's the plan?" Dan asked. "Looks like we've got some movement to the south."

Jackson followed Dan's eyes, then peered farther with the scope of his sniper rifle. "Yeah, and that's a big platoon. I'm counting forty … check that, forty-two men. We've got to get inside before they start sweeping this area."

"We'd better hurry because they're coming this way," Dan said.

"Our entry point is just to our left," Jackson noted, pointing to a service entrance about sixty meters away. "I want to get someone at the base of the satellite tower about twenty meters south of that to give the rest of us some cover fire if we need it."

"I'll do it," Dan said.

"All right, Danny, you're hired," Jackson said. "Keep your head down. And if anybody gets too close, let 'em have it."

"Piece of cake," Dan said. He shouldered his rifle and scampered across the closest bridge. It arched up and over the river channel before spilling out onto a large stone patio on the other side. The team of Dominion troopers was moving closer, so he tucked his head as low as it could get without dropping the barrel of his gun or slowing him down. After just a few seconds he slid behind the corner of the second satellite tower, and quickly took aim toward the oncoming platoon.

The others started toward the bridge once Dan was in position, but before they were even halfway across Dan heard an uncomfortably familiar noise. He looked up just as a Dominion Predator came swooping over the tree line toward the tarmac to the west. The gust of wind forced Jackson and the others to clamber to the bridge railings as it passed overhead. The ship's searchlights seemed to miss them, but Dan kept his rifle trained on the engine housing as it roared across the courtyard. Finally it moved beyond the huddled group, leaving them behind without a shot fired.

Dan breathed a sigh of relief. He spun back toward the squadron. They had paused as the battle vessel passed but were now back on the move. Dan hazarded a glance back at Jackson and the others. They were stumbling to their feet after the disruption when a whistling in the distance caught Dan's ears. It rapidly started getting louder, and Dan's eyes quickly shot back toward the sky.

A plasma shell exploded against the nearest edge of the bridge. A geyser of stone and mortar erupted into the air, and Dan was thrown backward into the base of the satellite tower. His back slammed into the hard metal construct, sending a pang of pain across his torso. A shower of rock and dust pummeled down on him as he was strewn across the pavement.

Dan's ears wailed from the percussion of the blast. His ribs stung as he pressed up onto all fours. He tasted dirt and blood in his mouth. The ground appeared to shake back and forth as he fumbled to regain a grip on his rifle, and he staggered back against the satellite. He struggled to get a visual on the rest of his team through the haze of debris, but finally caught a glimpse of Mac and Jenna dragging Jackson back toward the perimeter wall. Jackson was on his feet but hobbling on one leg, each arm draped around Mac and Jenna's necks. Cullen and Brett stumbled along behind them, a spray of gunfire chasing as they ran.

Dan wiped the dirt from his eyes, then spun his rifle toward the oncoming squadron. He fired a volley of shots and felled three men before they turned their barrage in his direction. The ping and rattle of shots bouncing off the satellite forced him back under cover. As the buzz in his ears faded he started to make out Mac's voice through their comms.

" … repeat, we are cut off!" Mac yelled. "Dan, do you copy?"

"I'm here, Mac!" Dan answered, firing another salvo. "I'm all right. What's your status?"

"We've got two wounded, but nothing fatal," Mac said. There was a din of panicked screams behind his voice. "The bridge is gone. I don't think we can't reach you!"

"You've gotta fall back!" Dan said. "That platoon's closing fast. Find some shelter, I'll buy you some time."

"Dan, can you see the door?" Mac asked.

Dan glanced behind him. "Yes."

"You've gotta get to that door. Kyle and his team are already inside, but they're getting some resistance. They're gonna need your help if they make it to the throne room."

"No, I can't just leave you here!" Dan roared.

"Dammit, Dan, just do it!" The uncharacteristic harshness in Mac's voice stung Dan's ears. "We've only got one shot at this! They need you more than we do."

"Mac—"

"That's an order, Lieutenant!"

Dan pulled back the barrel of his rifle. The door was only a few paces away. He had a small charge in his vest that could give him the window he needed to get there. He hated everything about leaving them here, but he also knew that Mac was right. It would all be for nothing if they didn't succeed.

"Don't make me regret this," Dan said.

"We'll try not to," Mac said. "Get going."

Dan lobbed the charge into the oncoming mob. It exploded with a flash, scattering the unit like a flock of birds. He fired another short volley into the swarm, then bolted for the door.

The service entrances were often electrified to reinforce the bolt, but with the defense systems down, the charge would be deactivated. Dan fired half a dozen rounds through the lock, then kicked it open with a bang. He fell inside and pushed the door closed.

The hallway was dark. It took several moments for Dan's eyes to adjust as he climbed back to a knee. He checked the charge on his rifle. Still had a little more than sixty percent available, probably about two hundred rounds. The corridor was long, but empty. He started to think that he was lucky.

Then he tried to stand up. His side started screaming immediately, and he realized that he was bleeding. A tattered gouge in his suit was sticky with blood. He pulled it open, trying to examine the wound in the dark. His fingers ran across the jagged end of a shard of stone buried in the skin just above his left hip. He pulled it out and let it drop to the floor, wincing as he did so. The gash wasn't deep, maybe an inch or so, probably because the blow was slowed by his armored undergarment. He pulled a chemical cauterizing agent from his utility vest and smeared it across the exposed skin. It seared him like a branding iron, and a yelp escaped from his throat.

The burning lasted for several moments, and his head felt like it was swimming after the pain subsided. When his wits finally returned, it seemed like he had been crouched there forever. It wouldn't take long before the squadron outside found this door, even if the others managed to keep them occupied. He had to keep moving. He struggled to his feet and started down the hall.

† † †

Kyle's second handgun clicked empty and he dropped it without a thought. The security team had gotten too close for firearms anyway. He ducked and dodged several wild assaults, the swarm growing around him. Each blow he landed started to sting his knuckles, but by then he was moving so fast he barely had a chance to see his target before he hit them.

A blade caught his left shoulder, spinning him in that direction. Something swept out his right foot and he dropped to a knee. An arm wrapped around his neck as one of the soldiers jumped on his back, followed by another, and another. His left arm was heavy from the wound, his hips off balance from the men piling on. He let his powers roar to life, and a bolt of Celestial lightning scorched through the hallway in front of him. The men on his back crumbled like dead sticks, and he regained his footing.

Jay and the others were behind him near the last fork in the corridors. The brow above Jay's right eye was split wide open, and he was wiping at another streak of blood from beneath his nose. Brady was limping even more than usual, his leg clearly laboring. Mitchell was bent over at the waist, a pair of gunshot marks smoldering against his armored undergarment. They all looked ragged, but they were still on their feet.

"Maybe next time you need to lead with that, Kyle," Jay said, choking down a ball of bloody snot.

"Yeah, next time," Kyle gasped. "Still takes a lot out of me."

"I'd rather not have a next time," Mitchell moaned. "What's next?"

Kyle pointed past the pile of dead and stunned Dominion soldiers. "About a hundred meters down this passage there's an access panel that leads into a utility tunnel. Should drop us right in front of the throne room."

"What are we waiting for then?" Brady asked.

A set of booming footsteps was followed by a massive mutant storming around the corner on all fours, its chunky teeth snarling between tattered lips.

"Get down!" Kyle shouted. He was in full sprint after one stride. He leapt into the air, seeming to hang suspended there as the beast closed. His left knee struck the mutant in the jaw, and it went tumbling backward as its feet flew out from under it. Kyle hit the ground on his left hip, skidding across the floor in a heap.

The mutant wriggled back to its feet like a turtle climbing off its shell and turned to face Kyle again. It was a truly hideous abomination. The entire right side of its body was rebuilt with organic cybernetics, hiding much of its grotesque features behind a weave of artificial hinges and piping. An embedded hunk of metal took the place of the right side of its skull, and a hollow black eye rested unevenly in the center. It looked over Kyle cautiously, having lost several of its craggy teeth from Kyle's first blow.

Kyle drew his sword from its sheath. The beast roared and lumbered forward.

Kyle sidestepped an overhead blow, and its metal fist slammed into the floor. The floor buckled from the impact, and Kyle was nearly thrown off his feet from the tremor. An erratic backhand swing sailed over his head, and its arm smashed through the wall. Kyle hacked at its exposed torso with the blade of his sword, but there was even more metal buried beneath its skin. A spray of sparks and lubricant forced him to turn his head, and in that instant the mutant's hand snared him around the neck and shoulders. His feet kicked for the floor as he was lifted away from the ground.

His arms were pinned to his side. He couldn't budge them even with all his strength. The mutant thumped him against the wall, then drew back its metal limb. The cybernetic arm shifted and morphed, revealing the gaping barrel of a gun underneath. Kyle landed two kicks against the beast's jaw, but it barely flinched. The gun barrel yawned toward him.

A volley of laser fire from the right rattled off its armored prosthesis. The mutant paused and looked away. Jay and the others had opened fire, buying Kyle precious seconds. He shot another stream of Celestial magic from his eyes, burying it into the crux of the beast's throat. The elemental power blew the mutant backward like a tumbleweed, and it crashed into the opposite wall as Kyle hit the ground. A pulse of gunfire from its cyborg arm flailed down the hall, and another, more human wail followed it.

Kyle's eyes darted toward his men, and his heart sank. A shot had hit Jay near the chest. He was sprawled across the floor on his back, a puddle of blood starting to seep out from beneath him.

Kyle screamed. His face filled with the heat of his own blood. He could heal him, he thought. Get to him quick. Stop the bleeding. Repair the wound. He would be all right. *Dammit, get your legs moving,* he demanded.

But then there was a grunt and a crackle from across the hall. The mutant was climbing back to its feet. Kyle thundered across the hall and pounded the heel of his boot into the beast's chest, pinning it to the floor. He hoisted his war sword over his head, its deadly tip staring at the struggling monster, and then plunged it through the remaining flesh of its neck. He twisted the blade with a crunch and then ripped it free, and a mixed stream of hydraulic fluid and blood spilled out across its chest.

The trail of blood chased Kyle all the way to Jay's side. He dropped his sword and slid on his knees next to his fallen friend, his pants soaking up a swath of Jay's oozing blood. Jay's skin had gone so cold he was shaking. The shot had hit him just above the left collarbone, above the top of his armor. Kyle put his hand over the wound, the blood seeping up through his fingers like a muffled geyser.

"Oh God, Jay, hang on," Kyle said. "I've got you. It'll be all right. Just hang on ..."

Jay coughed, trickling two thin lines of blood out of each corner of his mouth. Kyle's powers poured through his hand and into Jay's severed neck, and Jay's muscles went rigid. He grabbed hold of Kyle's hand and squeezed his eyes shut. Finally Kyle's spell subsided and the wound was healed, but Jay's eyes never reopened.

"Is he …?" Mitchell began.

"No," Kyle insisted. "No, he's still breathing. He's still alive."

"What do we do?" Brady asked. "We can't just leave him here."

Kyle's eyes were welled with tears. "You two get him out of here," he said. "Go find the others. Get to a transport and get the hell out of here."

"And what are you going to do?" Brady asked.

"I'm gonna go finish this."

"No way," Brady said. "If we go, we *all* go. We can't just leave you here alone."

"We're not debating this. Go. Keep him safe."

The conviction in Kyle's voice wasn't to be argued with. Brady handed over his starmetal weapon, then helped Mitchell lift up their fallen comrade. He watched them as they moved down the hall, a tinge of anxiety sweeping over him. Would this be the last time he saw any of his friends? If it was, could he make all their sacrifices count? He resolved to find out.

He steeled himself with a deep breath, then gathered his sword and hurried down the corridor. With the others gone he no longer had a reason to pace himself. Each stride was five times that of an average human's, and he reached the access panel for the utility shaft in just a few seconds. He pulled it open and glanced back down the hall. There were more footsteps coming. More big ones. Only this time they weren't alone.

While he would relish the opportunity to deliver some punishment to the approaching foot soldiers, his vengeance was reserved for another. And right now there was nothing left to stand between them.

The climb to the throne room was cramped, but swift. He kicked open another access panel and dropped into a wide foyer. The security lights had reactivated, and he could hear the perimeter alarms blaring outside. The defense systems had come back online.

Kyle pulled his starmetal weapon from its holster on his hip. He started around the bend toward the gates to the Gentry's chambers. There were voices in front of him, a squad guarding the gates. He fired two shots and dropped the first two soldiers to oppose him. The kick from the gun was rough, but his shots were still on target.

As the first two fell, another thirty gathered behind them. Kyle lowered his weapon as they raised theirs, suddenly lacking the patience to deal with them conventionally. Another web of his elemental power sparked from his left hand and electrified the entire corridor. The whole unit was scorched by the cascading energy, their screams muted by the speed of the attack. They hit the ground amid a chorus of thumps and thuds, a haze of smoke rising into the air.

Kyle felt a wave of vertigo billow through his head. The floor danced in circles around him, and he had to swallow a mouthful of drool after it faded. It took a moment for him to catch his breath, his arms feeling a bit heavy. He looked up and saw the doors waiting in front of him, and he realized he had come too far to let fatigue overwhelm him now.

Suddenly there was a sound. What was it? Was it a breath? How long had he been distracted?

Kyle spun around with his gun aimed recklessly, only to have it caught in Dan's hand. Kyle pulled free, frustrated he had been caught so unaware. Was it that or was his young friend just that good?

"Fuck, Dan, how did you get here?" Kyle asked.

"I walked," Dan answered.

"That's not what I meant."

"I know what you meant. I got separated from the others."

"How?" Kyle asked.

"There were patrols sweeping the east courtyard," Dan answered. "We were caught in an explosion. I couldn't get back to them."

"Are they all right?" Kyle asked.

"Last I saw."

"Where are they now?" Kyle inquired.

"I don't know," Dan said. "My tracers went dead when the defense systems came back online."

"Well, you've gotta go find them. They'll need your help to get out of here."

"And what about you?" Dan asked, eyeing the huge metal portcullis in front of them. "You don't need my help?"

"I can't ask you to come in there with me, Dan."

"Why, is something different now?" Dan demanded.

"Danny, I'm just not sure that I'll be coming back from this," Kyle stated. His voice was grave.

Dan huffed and shook his head. "Well…maybe if we both go in we can both make it home."

Kyle sighed. "You're not going to let this go, are you?"

"Not unless you want to take the time to make me leave," Dan confirmed.

Kyle looked back at the gates. They were huge, armored barriers that were likely re-electrified by this point. Behind them he could feel the raging cosmic power of the Gentry waiting. He knew that he had been a stubborn bastard most of his life. If these were going to be his last moments, he decided he could use the company.

"Do you remember how to use the starmetal gun?" Kyle asked.

"Yeah, nothing to it," Dan replied.

"Well, it's got a helluva kick, so aim a little low," Kyle said.

"Yeah, okay," Dan said, lifting his gun from its holster. "Thanks."

Kyle handed Dan the spare weapon that Brady had left him and pulled his sword from its sheath. The thick carboranium doors were an intimidating barricade, with heavily reinforced paneling and the electrified shielding protecting the entrance. They had no chance of prying open the bolts or short-circuiting the shields, but his sword was as good as any key. Its enchanted edge wouldn't be denied by layers of armor or electricity.

Dan seemed to suddenly take stock of where they were as he looked up at the doors, guns in hand. "You think he's really in there?"

"I know he is. He doesn't think we can hurt him."

"Can we?" Dan asked, his eyes drifting toward is commander.

Kyle kinked his head to the side. "I guess we'll find out."

He sank his sword into the thick metal of the door, its charmed edges tearing through the carboranium paneling until its tip pierced the other side. He raked the sword down toward the floor, first to the left and then to the right, the heavy doors resisting every inch of his effort. After a moment he pulled the blade from the door and sheathed it, then lowered the heel of his right boot into the severed piece with a boom.

They squeezed inside and were greeted with more lingering darkness. The Gentry typically kept his throne room bathed in light, but tonight it was as black as the Aranow canyon. Those first steps inside felt like they were walking into a crypt. The air was cold. The darkness was suffocating. It was like every soul had been chased away, leaving only the damned behind. What that made them, well, they would soon find out.

The sound of the alarms outside were magnified from the gaping balcony ahead of them, but the light of the stars above seemed drowned out by the time it reached the floor. Even Kyle's superhuman eyes couldn't see the end of the corridor where the Gentry's throne rested.

He waved Dan to the left side of the room, then slid toward the marble columns lining the right. Their strides were soft in spite of the echoing height of the ceiling, aided by the commotion continuing outside. The dark seemed to push against them as they moved forward, like walking through fields of tar. The cold air grew heavier with each step. Aeron was close.

Kyle heard a breath, a low rumbling growl that made his skin crawl. He came to an abrupt stop, and across the room Dan did the same. They slowly stepped toward the center of the chamber, their weapons forward. And that's when Kyle saw the glowing eyes behind the mask of the Gentry.

"I knew you'd be waiting," Kyle said.

Aeron's eyes flashed even brighter as he tilted his masked brow forward. The throne room lights slowly crackled to life as the intensity of the Gentry's stare increased. Finally they were able to see the full gargantuan form of their enemy sitting before them. His armored regalia and mountainous shoulders dwarfed them from high on his pedestal. The sheer size of the centuries-old monarch seemed as imposing as entire battalions of the Dominion army.

"**And I knew someday you would return to me, Commander.**"

"Then you should have thought to run," Kyle said.

A devious laugh emanated from behind the Gentry's cowl. "**You'll never lose that arrogance, will you, boy? It will prove to be your undoing.**"

"I've heard that a thousand times before. And I'm still here."

The Gentry shook his head and looked up at the crystal ceiling.

"**Oh Commander, how did it come to this?**" he asked finally. "**None of this would have been necessary if you had just done your job.**"

"And what? Trade one life for another?" Kyle demanded. "For a thousand other lives you would have forced me to take? No...not anymore. That ended the day you took my family from me."

"You think I owe you for the life of your mother? But you conveniently forget that *bitch* was both a liar and a traitor." He paused, letting that barb sink itself in deep. "**She corrupted my house in ways that will find her a special place in damnation.**"

"And what about your sins? Did you really think I'd never find out what you've done?"

"I didn't think anything, Kyle. I simply didn't care."

"And that's where you made your mistake. I won't stand for this anymore. I can't. Your time of living without consequence has come to an end."

"**Don't try to lecture me, boy!**" Aeron roared. "**The merits of what I do are not open for debate!**"

"And that's exactly why we're here," Kyle said. "Your actions are not beyond reproach, Gentry. It's time you answered for the lives you've taken."

"They are human lives, Kyle. They come and go in a heartbeat. Their existence is nothing to me."

"Right, the all-powerful Aeron," Kyle said. "Lord of the Galaxy. And yet you forget, it's us mortals who make up your empire. If it weren't for humans, what would be left for you to rule? Without us, you'd just be master of an empty kingdom."

"You speak as though you are one of them, Kyle. But we both know that's not true. You're not one of them. You are a *mutant*. You are as different from them as I am."

"This isn't about me anymore. This is about you and what you've done."

Aeron hissed like a viper. **"I have heard your thoughts, Kyle, and I can see your mind. You are afraid."**

"Fear is a human emotion, Grandfather," Kyle said. "And like you said, I'm not human."

"I think he's the one that's afraid, Kyle," Dan said. "He doesn't want to fight us."

"**You insect!**" Aeron bellowed. "**How dare you try to saddle me with your petty mortal emotions?**"

"That's it then, isn't it?" Kyle asked, seeing his chance to pile on. "Does your own flesh and blood terrify you, Gentry?"

"**You little bastard!**" Aeron roared, shooting out of his throne. "**I'm going to tear you limb from limb!**"

"Danny, let him have it!" Kyle said, raising his starmetal weapon.

Their guns erupted with a burst of their specialized ammunition. The Gentry's armor splintered and cracked with each shot, and he wailed as the starmetal shells punctured the flesh underneath. He shrieked like a wounded animal, high-pitched and shrill. It was a beautiful sound. He stumbled clumsily over the edge of the throne, dropping onto his elbow before the gunfire finally went silent.

Blood dripped from the chinks in Aeron's armor. Kyle couldn't believe how red it was. But what was more unbelievable was that he was still standing. And he was angry.

"Empty 'em, Danny!" Kyle shouted.

Their guns reignited. Aeron writhed with each shot that found its mark. A spray of his blood coated the golden pedestal behind him, and the mighty behemoth dropped to his knees.

Their clips snapped empty, but Aeron wasn't dead. He rose back to his feet, those glowing eyes boiling over with his elemental energy. Kyle pushed Dan to the side as the power behind the Gentry's eyes surged forward like a geyser. The floor exploded between them, and Kyle tumbled through the air. He slammed into one of the marble pillars, jamming his sword's scabbard into his ribs. He hit the ground in a heap with a pile of debris showering over him.

His eyes were swirling as he pushed up to his knees. He looked across the room and made out Dan among the haze. His young lieutenant was also struggling to his feet near the far wall. The Gentry swept along the edge of the room toward his friend.

Kyle erupted out of his crouch, his powerful mutant legs driving him forward. He came upon his grandfather so quickly that not even the all-powerful Lord of the Galaxy was able to avoid him. Kyle's shoulder pounded into Aeron's side, lifting him off his feet and crushing him into the wall. Stone shattered under the impact, and the two of them went tumbling into the night air. They hit the roof of the adjacent tower, and it tore asunder as their collective weight came crashing down upon it. Kyle felt his shoulder hit the ground hard amid a wash of debris. The blow sent a shock of pain across his back and into his neck, but he was able to force himself back to his feet. The rubble slid off his shoulders as he steadied his legs beneath him.

"Kyle!" Dan called from above. "Kyle, are you okay?"

"I'm all right," Kyle answered. "Go find the others. I'll handle this."

"Kyle ..."

The rubble in front of him rumbled. Kyle turned to face it, knowing that Aeron would quickly rise from underneath.

"Go, Danny," Kyle ordered. "I'll be at the ship."

The pile of debris split open, and the Gentry ascended to his feet. His once-shimmering metallic armor was covered in dust and powder, with webs of cracks sprawling out from the bullet holes across his chest. Kyle was dwarfed by Aeron's monumental stature, which blotted out the light of the hallway behind his colossal shoulders.

Kyle drew his sword as the Gentry raised his arm over his head. He swung his fist down like a hammer, but Kyle deflected the blow with the broad edge of the enchanted blade. Aeron's fist slammed into the already weakened floor and again it began to crumble beneath them. The beams buckled and the ground started to slant downward. In a sudden wave the floor gave way, swallowing both of them in a pitch of rubble.

The fall was much longer this time. It forced Kyle's stomach into his chest until his back and legs smashed into some utility piping. He tore right through them, each one spewing either steam or liquid onto his plummeting body before he finally crashed onto a hard cement floor. Metal and plaster landed on top of him, a shard of metal shearing a chunk of flesh off the side of his right thigh. The shock of the wound was dizzying, but he dragged himself back to his knees, and then braced himself against his sword to get to his feet. They had fallen all the way into the substructure of the palace, landing in the engineering room that stretched nearly the entire length of the complex. A heavy fog filled the room from the severed steam pipes, leaving him struggling to see what had become of the Gentry.

Rows upon rows of massive turbines and generators surrounded him, and for a moment he felt grateful that he had not landed on one of them. However, that gratitude was short-lived with the first step on his wounded leg. The gash was not terribly deep or threatening, but it burned with every ounce of weight levied on it. His first thought was to heal it, but a rumbling from his left forced him into motion. He stumbled to the edge of the generators where the aisles met and peered through the haze. At first there was nothing, but then the dark silhouette of the Gentry appeared.

Kyle hugged the side of the generator next to him, using it and the thickening fog to remain out of sight. Above him he noticed a series of catwalks, and just across the aisle there was a large rack of insulated piping, each very heavy and lined with lead. He clanged the hilt of his sword against the generator and then dashed across the walkway to the other side of the rack. Aeron's gaze swirled in Kyle's direction, and he started lumbering toward him.

Kyle faded back into the shadows between two of the pipe racks. The Gentry's steps were heavy, lending no disguise to his imminent approach. Kyle held his breath so as not to disturb the smoke-filled air around him, and his heartbeat slowed to keep its rhythm away from Aeron's ears.

The Gentry's blazing eyes cut through the mist like spotlights as he approached. The giant slowed with each step, lingering for several moments just in front of Kyle's niche. The mask swung from side to side, expressionless and unseeing. After several tense moments the Gentry turned away.

The haze parted quickly as Kyle sliced through the back of Aeron's leg. A deafening wail leapt from the Gentry's mouth as his flesh was severed, showering a stream of blood across the walkway. He stumbled around in a circle, clutching at the back of his leg. Before Kyle could strike again the Gentry's blood retreated back into the wound like it had somehow hit rewind. Kyle took a step back, the satisfaction of the blow swiftly fading as its effects were so easily negated. He chopped through the nearest support to the piping racks, then dove away as tons of concrete and lead barreled down on top of the giant.

Kyle's wounded leg wailed as he scrambled away from the pile of rubble. He had barely gotten clear in time with the pain sapping the strength from his leg, forcing him to sprawl across the floor to avoid being crushed himself. As he hobbled back to his feet the room had a sudden hush to it. The debris was still…if only for a moment.

The heap began to shift and heave, and Kyle tightened his grip on the hilt of his sword. The Gentry burst through the pile, shrugging away huge slabs of rock. But it wasn't his rise that caught Kyle off guard. More than half of his crown had been shattered by the crushing weight, revealing the face hidden behind the mask. It was neither gallant nor regal, demonic nor divine. It was the face of a *man*—a caved-in, withered, mortal husk that had been shrouded by his royal adornments for all those years. His cheeks and eyes had collapsed and receded with great age, shrinking around the bones beneath the ever-thinning skin. It was a face whose humanity had been stripped away by centuries of surrendering to the power of the Eye, with nothing but rage and frustration in its stare.

The hollow eyes poured out another stream of magic as Kyle paused, but he was able to raise his sword and weave an elemental shield around himself as the assault slammed against him. The sheer force behind the blast drove him backward even as he locked his legs in resistance. His heels skidded across the floor, burning through the bottom of his boots. He could see nothing through the blaze of color and fire searing against his invisible armor, and with each second the torrent of power that beat down upon him became stronger. The air leaked from his lungs as he strained to stave off the unrelenting onslaught, and inevitably he felt his shield begin to waver. In desperation he turned his sword to the left, deflecting the blast into the palace foundation. The wall erupted as though it had been hit by a missile, battering Kyle mercilessly backward and pounding him into the floor.

His ears were ringing as he sat up against the wall at the end of the room, but that was the least of his concerns. His left arm had gone completely limp from a long iron spike that had pierced his shoulder just below his collarbone. The other end had blown out through his back, splattering his blood across the wall. His vision had been rattled and he could hear practically nothing, but the ground was shaking beneath him. Aeron was coming.

He finally saw the glint of his sword a few feet away and tried feebly to drag himself over to it. However, he suddenly felt the Gentry take hold of the rail through his chest and jerk him into the air.

Kyle screamed as his feet went kicking for the ground, but there was none to be had. His head began swimming as the pain overwhelmed him, and every time he struggled it felt as though his arm was being torn from his body. Through the blur Kyle saw Aeron's wretched, skeleton-like teeth grinning at him from behind his decrepit old lips. It was a hideous smirk, but it gave Kyle something to focus on to steady his rolling eyes. He heaved his fist into Aeron's face, then cracked his knee against the bottom of Aeron's jaw. The Gentry's head snapped backward as he lost his grip.

Kyle landed on his feet and staggered back against the wall. He threw his right hand forward and hit his grandfather with a burst of telekinetic power that sent him sailing into a turbine. The entire construct collapsed as the Gentry went tumbling through it, setting off a series of small explosions as several pistons punctured the shell of one of the generators.

Kyle pulled at the spike jutting out of his chest, feeling every inch of it grinding over the shredded fibers of his body. Finally he felt a massive release in pressure, and the rail went clattering to the floor with a rope of blood trailing behind. Again, he dropped to a knee.

He shook his head, trying to clear his mind, but by then the rumbling from across the room was no longer caused by explosions. Aeron was coming for him again, and this time he had no choice but to run.

He grabbed his sword from among the shrapnel on the ground, then hobbled up a staircase to the catwalks above him. His legs could barely withstand his weight, forcing him to lean on the guardrails to keep his balance. The catwalk shook beneath him as his pursuer started up the stairs, and his feet slid out from beneath him. He landed flat on his stomach and spat up a wad of phlegm and blood. The taste of it suddenly made him nauseous. He felt like he was swimming in molasses as he climbed back to his knees, the wounds seeming to sap every ounce of strength from his body. He grabbed the railing and slowly pulled himself to his feet just as the Gentry stepped onto the catwalk.

Aeron's hips barely fit between the guardrails as he lurked at the top of the stairs. His sunken eyes looked like black holes against his pale, rotting skin, but the glow of the flames below seemed to give his whole face a hell-red spark. Kyle glanced over his shoulder and saw a ladder just around the corner that would lead back to the main level. It was a chance—perhaps his only chance—to get back to his friends and escape. To save himself.

But…if he did, Aeron would surely follow him. In trying to save himself, he would surely bring this furious titan down on the others. And then his friends wouldn't stand a chance either. Kyle looked down at the thick tide of blood oozing from his chest, at the blood already crusting on his pants, and he realized that his rapidly fatiguing powers couldn't heal him. His fate was already sealed. He wouldn't seal theirs as well. So he tightened his grip on his sword as best he could, and used what strength he had left to raise it between himself and the Gentry.

"**You're beaten, my boy,**" Aeron said, his voice an octave higher and more mortal without the echo of his mask. "**I've already broken your body. Don't make me destroy the rest of you as well.**"

"I've … come this far," Kyle groaned, leaning against the railing for support. "I won't give in now."

"**Kyle, look at yourself,**" Aeron seethed. "**You can barely stand. Not even your powers can save you now. But *I* can. If you come back to me now, I can heal you. I can make you stronger than before. Then you and I could finally crush the Splinter rebellion. They would have no way to stop us.**"

"No," Kyle wheezed, his lungs emptying with each syllable. "No, I won't do that."

"**Think about it, Kyle,**" Aeron said, a wry smile peeling back his thinning lips. "**You know where they are now, you know everything about them. With your help, we can finally have the peace you have always fought for.**"

His voice dripped honey and battery acid all at the same time, but Kyle knew there was no substance to any of it. He would always be a threat to the power of the Gentry now, a threat that Aeron would never allow to survive.

"*Damn* you," Kyle snarled. "Damn you and your lies. Nothing you've ever told me has been true."

Kyle had to pause, gasping for breath as pressure built in his chest. His lung was collapsing, filling his ribcage with air. It made his heart pound like it was going to burst. It hurt like hell; it hurt like *death*. He knew he didn't have long.

"I'd rather die … than ever come back and serve you."

It would be prophetic. Aeron would kill him. He failed. Dammit, he just wasn't strong enough.

"**Very well,**" Aeron said. "**If that is the choice you've made, then you leave me no choice but to see it through.**"

The Gentry started forward, and Kyle didn't move. It wasn't courage, he just couldn't do it. The catwalk trembled with every step, and all Kyle could do was raise his sword for one last effort. He swung it down as hard as he could, but Aeron effortlessly snatched his hand. Kyle struggled, forcing every ounce of his energy against the Gentry's grip, but it was not enough. Aeron kicked Kyle in the chest and sent him screeching across the catwalk. He rolled onto his back, his already-wounded chest feeling like it had caved in. Aeron hovered over him, holding the enchanted sword in his hands.

"**I remember when I gave you the metal to make this sword,**" the Gentry said, admiring the workmanship of the blade. "**You were so proud the day you finished it. How old were you then? Seventeen? Eighteen? I'm sure it seems like a long time ago.**"

"There will be … others," Kyle said. "Others … like me that will … that will still fight you."

"**Oh, I'm afraid not,**" Aeron snickered. "**You were the best of them, my boy. You know that. Without you…the others stand no chance. You were their only hope, and yet you still managed to fail.**"

Aeron stooped closer, his fearsome, rotting face curling into an angry snarl.

"**Remember, Kyle…I made you what you are,**" he said, "**and I want you to go to your grave knowing that I will soon destroy everything that you old dear. And there is nothing you can do to stop me.**"

The Gentry hoisted the sword high over his head. The tip of the blade stared down at Kyle, and even as his mind screamed for him to move, his body simply could not respond. The sword plunged downward, burying the blade up to the hilt in the right side of Kyle's ribcage. He felt it peel through both flesh and bone, and then tear out his back and into the iron catwalk on which he laid. It forced a gasp as his other lung deflated, and almost instantly the taste of precious blood rose into his mouth.

This was it, Kyle thought. This was how he ended. Lying on his back with his own divine weapon stapled through his chest. It was less dramatic than he hoped, and far more disappointing. Dammit, why couldn't he get his powers to work?

Suddenly, a volley of gunfire struck Aeron in the shoulders and chest. Kyle watched the Gentry slowly stumble backward as each shot dotted his torso, until finally a small grenade round exploded in front of him and he went tumbling over the railing down to the floor below. Before the echo of the grenade faded, Dan's face appeared over his fallen commander.

"Oh my God … Kyle …" Dan muttered. "Hold on, I'll get you out of here."

Dan pulled the sword out of Kyle's chest, a thick ribbon of blood trailing behind. Kyle's torso seized, and a burst of color and light danced in front of his eyes. Dan slipped under his arm, and pulled him back to his feet.

"I've got you," Dan said with a grunt. "I've got you. We're getting out. C'mon, we're getting out."

Kyle still grasped his sword even as Dan dragged him toward the ladder. He had no strength remaining in his legs, but he refused to let his sacred weapon go. Dan moved quickly, but just as they reached the base of the ladder, the catwalk began shaking as Aeron ascended the stairs once again.

"Danny … you have to go," Kyle stammered, his face flushed white. "You have to … go now."

"Sorry, Kyle, not this time," Dan replied. "You're coming with me."

Dan pulled a thermal charge from his vest, set a short delay, and tagged it against the base of the catwalk. He looked back to see Aeron step onto the scaffolding, then hoisted Kyle over his shoulder and started up the ladder.

A loud explosion boomed from below, sending a rush of fire up the ladder behind them. The flames clawed at Dan's heels as he reached the top, throwing Kyle onto the main floor like a sack of grain. Kyle struggled to his knees, his arms trembling like grass in the wind. Dan took a moment to peer down the ladder, but the catwalk was gone and a thick veil of smoke had taken its place.

"Echo, this is Preston," Dan said into his comm. "I have Kyle. What is your location?"

"Northwest airfield," Jackson replied. "We have a transport. How far out are you?"

"We can be there in three minutes."

"We'll hold our position as long as we can."

Dan lifted Kyle up again and began following the twisted corridors toward the west entrance of the palace. Just the touch of Dan's hand against his beaten body made Kyle's wounds howl with pain, and suddenly their exodus through the hallways became a blur. Before he knew it, they were back outside among a field of sculptures not far from where Kyle's team had entered the courtyard. The airfield would be just around the bend. It was so close.

Kyle's eyes were getting heavy. He felt dried out, his heart jackhammering to pump what little blood he had left. The colors of grass and stone and sky in front of him started to melt together.

Suddenly, one of the towering sculptures erupted beside them in a burst of magical fire. The frame buckled, then started arching down toward them. Dan leapt forward, shielding Kyle beneath him.

The boom of Aeron's footsteps returned. Dan scrambled to his feet, but the Gentry was on top of him too quickly. He swatted the lieutenant away like a bothersome gnat, sending him sailing aside. Then his rage turned back toward Kyle.

Aeron grabbed hold of his grandson's neck, yanking him off the ground. His stone-heavy hand wrapped around Kyle's throat and pulled him so close that Kyle could smell the rot on his breath.

"I won't let you go, Kyle. Don't you understand that this is my galaxy, and that everything in it happens because *I* allow it? I have survived for thousands of years...did you really think that I would fall to someone like you?"

There were no words left in Kyle's throat. Aeron's grip squeezed like a python, and Kyle's head felt as though it was floating off his shoulders. His vision started fading to black, and he mercifully started accepting these moments as his last.

Then ...

Then he caught a glimpse of the Eye, the glistening amulet resting in the Gentry's chest piece. His gaze drifted back to the skeletal face glaring at him. Suddenly, he knew ... the Gentry was *mortal.* It was the Eye that was invincible. The power wasn't his own. Not like the kind that poured through Kyle's veins. He was human, he was mutant, and he was *god.* Only he could be the best of each. Finally, he knew what he was meant to be.

He dug into the depths of his mind, bypassing all the rage, anger, frustration, sadness, and despair his life had endured. Beyond it all he searched for a calm he'd never felt, a tranquility he'd never embraced. It was there, he knew it, hiding behind a lifetime of fury and wrath. He begged himself for it. Finally his mind's eye opened, spurred not by hate and hysteria, but by serenity. His memory opened like a book, and every moment of his life rushed back to him. His powers suddenly flickered to life, pulling him back from the brink of the abyss. His eyes flushed clear, and he saw the sheen of his sword lying just a few feet away.

He reached out beyond his body with a magical hand, and the sword slowly started sliding toward him. His eyes clamped shut, and at that moment it was as though his hand was already around the hilt. The enchanted weapon leapt into his grasp, the feel of the handle electrifying his arm. Aeron's growl quickly went silent as the sword appeared out of nowhere, but by then it was too late. Kyle sank the blade deep into the Gentry's chest, splitting open both armor and flesh in an explosion of Celestial blood.

The Gentry bellowed as the enchanted starmetal splayed his ribs apart. The ghastly wail pitched across the courtyard, seeming to strike every surface with its shrill horror. Through the flailing limbs and gyrations Kyle grabbed the shining amulet on Aeron's chest, then kicked himself free of his grandfather's grasp. He ripped both the sword and the Eye away with him as he tumbled toward the ground, slamming against the turf with a thud. The Eye popped from his hand on impact, skipping along the yard several times before settling into the silken grass. Its glow lingered for just a moment, then faded against the gathering dew.

Kyle's body went limp when he hit the ground, the surge of consciousness suddenly escaping him. He was able to see Aeron clutching at the wound in a mad frenzy, a look of very mortal terror swiftly overwhelming his aged face. The gash sprayed his blood across the landscape, but this time there was no divine salvation to rescue him. The mighty Lord of the Galaxy stumbled in an awkward, clumsy circle, his desperate blood-soaked cries for help going unheard. Then finally, mercifully, he fell to his end.

Kyle let his eyes close over, hoping that the good he had done in his life outweighed the bad. That comfort was all that he wished for.

A familiar voice called out to him, forcing his eyes to open once more. Dan's face was hovering above him, though his voice seemed to be coming from miles away. His lieutenant's head swiveled as if something caught his attention, and flashes of gunfire began lighting up the sky. Dan reached down and scooped up his injured commander again, and started lugging him toward the airfield.

Jackson and Mitchell were standing just outside an idling Dominion transport near the edge of the tarmac, laying down cover fire as Dan carried Kyle toward them. Brady came sprinting down the boarding ramp and helped pull Kyle on board. The ramp started lifting even before they reached the top, and the thrusters quickly ignited.

Dan and Brady laid Kyle down in the cargo bay next to another bloodied body. It appeared to be Brett, but he was so badly burned that there was no way to truly tell. Jackson stormed to the front of the ship, shouting orders to Mac and Jenna in the cockpit. Cullen was to the right of the cabin, looking over a still-unconscious Jay. The transport lurched into the air, the sound of gunfire rattling off the shields outside the ship's hull.

Kyle could still hear his men's panicked cries as they rushed about the cabin, though the sounds were fading quickly. Brady and Dan were both tending his wounds, shouting for him to be strong and hang on, but by then he had nothing left to give. Their voices faded and his eyes went dark, and finally he tumbled hopelessly away into the swirling blackness.

Epilogue

The stolen Dominion transport arched swiftly into the night sky, a barrage of scattered gunfire from the palace defense systems trailing behind. The rounds hit nothing as they sprayed across the sky, the targeting program still recalibrating following the power failure. The ship sank into the darkness, then bolted away in a flash of light as the warp of hyperspace swallowed it whole.

The courtyard below was awash with gathering soldiers. Dozens of wounded and dead littered the grounds, and the palace had been gutted by the battle between Commander Griffin and Lord Aeron. A team of Dominion Intelligence agents arrived promptly to commandeer the body of the Gentry. They swept through quickly and efficiently, and then were gone.

The system's star had started to rise on the horizon. The surrounding city had awakened to a war zone at its heart. Plumes of smoke gathered over the palace spires, and the heat of several lingering fires seared the crisp early morning air. The wail of the Palace alarms still echoed in the distance.

The smooth, manicured grass of the northwest courtyard had gathered a cool morning dew. A blood-soaked hand gripped the turf, dragging a wounded, dying body behind it. He could see it, lying there in the grass. The agents had missed it in their whirlwind to collect Aeron's remains. *The Eye.* Inching closer, the hand had gone numb. But it reached out, trembling with the effort, and finally the fingers closed around the divine amulet, squeezing it tight ...

And the war has just begun ...

Made in the USA
Columbia, SC
11 May 2020